ALI'S DREAM

ALI'S DREAM

JOHN S. HATCHER

Bahá'í
PUBLISHING
Wilmette, Illinois

Bahá'í Publishing
401 Greenleaf Avenue, Wilmette, Illinois 60091-2844

Printed in the United States of America on acid-free paper ∞

17 16 15 14 4 3 2 1

Library of Congress Cataloging-in-Publication Data

Hatcher, John, Dr.
Ali's dream : the story of Bahá'u'lláh / by John Hatcher. — Third edition.
pages cm
Originally published in Oxford by G. Ronald in 1980.
Summary: As he searches for the meaning of an unusual dream, eleven-year-old Ali, living with his family in the ancient city of Akka in 1912, gains a deeper understanding of his Bahai heritage and of his spiritual destiny.
ISBN 978-1-61851-068-6 (alk. paper)
1. Bahá'u'lláh, 1817–1892—Juvenile fiction. [1. Bahá'u'lláh, 1817–1892—Fiction. 2. Bahai Faith—History—Fiction.] I. Title.
PZ7.H28175Al 2014
[Fic]—dc23

2013045450

Cover design by Anis Mojgani
Book design by Patrick Falso

For

Cora Oliver (1907–1997)
Marion Hofman (1910–1995)
Roger White (1929–1993)
Lois Gobel (1930–1992)

in appreciation for the love and encouragement

Contents

Publisher's Preface

Have you ever had a dream, a special dream that you still remember, a dream that you will never forget? Most dreams vanish like fog in the morning, no more substantive than evaporating dew on your shoes. But every once in a while, a dream will sit and stay and linger. It is those lingering dreams that have power. Sometimes that power can whip you out of bed for an exciting adventure. Sometimes that power can make you laugh until tears stream down your face. And every once in a while, that powerful dream can be so peculiar that it remains in your mind much, much longer. In 1912, Alí-Riḍáy-i-Mas̲h̲hadí in 'Akká, Palestine had a dream that would not only claim his thoughts and attention but would also inspire him to answer a question that he didn't even know he was asking. It would help him answer what it meant to him to be a Bahá'í.

Ali's Dream has delighted readers for more than thirty years as they, hand in hand with Ali, have learned about the history of the Bahá'í Faith from Ali's family members and friends. The Bahá'í Faith is an independent world religion that began in 1844 in Persia (present-day 'Írán) and has spread now to 235 nations and territories and been accepted by more than five million people worldwide. This story colorfully weaves the fictional life of Ali and his intriguing dream with the real events of the early days of the Bahá'í Faith. Inspired by his dream, Ali sets out on a journey of study and discovery and learns of the repeated banishments of the Prophet-Founder, Bahá'u'lláh, and the dramatic events associated with His life. In this book, Ali not only learns the history of the Faith, but also hears stories that confirm many Bahá'í beliefs including the understanding that all the major religions of the world stem from the same omnipotent Source, that men and women share an equal place in this day and age, and that all of mankind is essentially part of one human family.

Ali's Dream was first published in 1980 and has as much value today as it did when it was first published. It contains a story that is resonant with anyone who has asked about his/her place in the world. It is hoped that readers enjoy the journey with Ali and his friends and personally find answers to, as author John S. Hatcher puts it, "the sincere questions and heartfelt longing that all of us in time encounter," by dreaming of and living "in the hearts and minds of these imaginary young Bahá'ís."

A Note to the Reader

The story of Ali and his family and friends is fictional. The accounts of the events in the life of Bahá'u'lláh and in Bahá'í history and the descriptions of the places in and around 'Akká are not; great care has been taken to ensure their historical accuracy.

The standard method of transliteration used in Bahá'í books to represent Persian words in the English alphabet has been used, except for the names of fictional characters—Ali, Neda, Ahmad, Bijan, Moayyed, Husayn, Nahid, Uncle Ibrahim, and Abdu'l Muhammad. However, Ali's full name, 'Alí-Riḍáy-i-Mas͟hhadí, *is* transliterated in the few places where it occurs.

A glossary at the back of the book gives notes on the main historical characters mentioned in the story and explains many of the Persian words and Bahá'í terms used.

A note on sources at the back of the book identifies those pages where exact quotations appear. Other related conversations and described events are based on authentic sources.

For more information on the transliteration and correct pronunciation of Persian, see Marzieh Gail's *Bahá'í Glossary,* Wilmette, Illinois, Bahá'í Publishing Trust, 1955.

1

The Dream

Some called it the "white city," because from a distance the stuccoed buildings and high walls seemed bright and clean in the Mediterranean sun. To the crusader soldiers hundreds of years before, the small town had been a great fortress. To Napoleon, only one hundred years before, the walled village had been a "grain of sand" that had stopped his mighty conquest by withstanding his assault. But in the year 1912, as 'Alí-Riḍáy-i-Ma<u>sh</u>hadí sat outside the town walls on the hill where Napoleon had placed his cannon, the hill called Tell al-Fa<u>khkh</u>ár, the young boy thought of 'Akká simply as his home, the place of his birth, the abode of his memories.

Ali was an eleven-year-old boy of average size. A shock of black hair hung over his forehead beneath his cap, and his olive complexion was beginning to show the tan of the spring sun. He had large, deep, lively eyes that seemed to pierce whatever they looked on, and they looked on everything. To Ali, this ancient town was important because he knew its secrets, its mysterious old dwellings and passageways, and because it was here that his friends and family lived.

'Akká was not at all what it seemed from a few kilometers away. From this distance one could not see the dirt of the streets, the old dogs that roamed through the open market, the dark doorways, the poor people who got along as best they could. Perched on the hill, Ali could see the dome of the Mosque of Jazzár Pá<u>sh</u>á, and the several towers from which the muezzin would call the Muslims to prayer—these thin spires rose above the other common dwellings that were bunched awkwardly together.

From the hill Ali could see the rough mountains to the right, which seemed like a high wall guarding the way north to Beirut. To the left, there was another long mountain range, but it was different in appearance, smooth and even as it jutted toward the sea before abruptly sloping down to the Mediterranean waters. At the bottom of the mountain of Carmel, Ali could make out the houses of the growing city of Haifa nine miles away. Halfway up the mountain, he thought he could see the building to which the remains of the Báb had been transferred only three years before.

Straight out in front of him spread the blue water of the mighty Mediterranean, forming a half-moon bay between 'Akká and Haifa, outlined by a white beach on which carriages traveled between the two towns. A steady breeze was blowing in from the sea, and several fishermen were casting their nets in the afternoon sun. "Soon my boat will be ready," thought Ali as he noticed a few sails on the horizon, no doubt much bigger than his own homemade craft.

He loved this spot, especially when no one else was there. It was quiet and serene. It made the world seem calm. Weeks before, he had come up the hill with his father in the early evening. He had lain down and watched the myriad of bright stars. Some had seemed clear and distinct. Others were bunched in clusters of sparkling light. That was not the first time Ali had been on the hill at night or had noticed how remarkable the night sky could be, but it was the beginning of a special time for him, a time when the troubled thoughts he had known for almost a year suddenly began to make sense.

That was the night when the Bahá'ís had gathered to say prayers for the Master, 'Abdu'l-Bahá 'Abbás, Whom they had learned was about to set sail from Egypt for a visit to America after His stay in England and Paris. 'Abdu'l-Bahá—the son of Bahá'u'lláh, Prophet-Founder of the Bahá'í Faith—was now the central figure for Bahá'ís since the passing of Bahá'u'lláh and was called "Master" by those in the Bahá'í community. The Bahá'ís in 'Akká had greatly missed the presence of 'Abdu'l-Bahá, Who, two years before, had quietly left Haifa on the beginning of His lengthy travels. The friends had sat around discussing how important the journey was, as the Master shared with Bahá'ís in other lands the love which the walls of 'Akká could not contain.

That evening after the Bahá'ís had left, Ali and his father had walked to the hill, and Ali had felt strangely sad and troubled. He had noticed these feelings over the previous year, but on that evening they had come together somehow, like tiny balls of mercury melting together in the palm of a hand. It was like trying to remember the name of a long ago playmate; he was sure if he thought long enough and hard enough, he would understand why hearing the Bahá'ís talk about 'Abdu'l-Bahá's journey had made him sad. But the evening passed, and Ali still did not completely understand. In fact, he had felt guilty because everyone else seemed so pleased and excited, especially his mother and father; so he did not dare tell them what he was thinking.

Now as he sat on the same hill, with the afternoon smell of the grass mingling with the scent of spring wildflowers, Ali once again thought about his secret. He thought about the first time he really became aware of these new thoughts. It had been at his uncle's, as he listened with other children to the stories of the early Bahá'ís, how they had given up everything, even their lives, because of their beliefs. It was then that he had begun to understand that these were not merely stories; these adventures had really happened, some of them to people he knew and had talked to.

On the way home from his uncle's, he had watched more carefully the faces of the children in 'Akká who were not Bahá'ís. Some were Jewish, most were Muslim, a few were Christian. They did not know about Bahá'u'lláh, or if they did, they didn't think He was particularly important. A couple of times the children had teased Ali, calling him a "Bahá'í" as if it were an insult, something to be ashamed of. A boy had even thrown a rock at Ali as he walked home from the market one afternoon.

But it was not fear that Ali felt. As he sat there with the afternoon sun on his face, he felt brave enough. "If only I could have been with Mullá Ḥusayn," he thought, and for a while he imagined that Tell al-Fakhkhár was a fort under attack and that he was defending himself against the armies of Náṣri'd-Dín Sháh—the former ruler of Persia.

Then he stopped, flopped back against the soft grass, and watched a gull tracing circles against the sky. "I would have been a good soldier," he said aloud. "I could have taken the letter to the Sh͟áh as Badí' did. But there are no battles to fight now, no kings to see." No, for Ali there seemed to be only routine days in 'Akká and the young lad doubted if there would ever be any great things for him to do.

He had prayed about it often. Sometimes he would chant the words of prayers he had memorized—the words of Bahá'u'lláh, 'Abdu'l-Bahá, or the Báb—but other times when he thought about the brave deeds he might do, he would just talk with God, as he might share his deepest secrets with a close friend.

The night before, he had asked God, "What is left for me to do? Now that 'Abdu'l-Bahá is traveling all over the world to tell everyone that You have sent a Prophet, what will be left for me?" He had continued, almost in tears as he complained that all the battles had been fought, all the heroic deeds had been done. Then he pleaded with God that he, 'Alí-Riḍáy might do something so brave, so memorable that one day a mother or father might tell children a story about him.

Now Ali sat up. He touched the engraved letters on the beautifully bound leather book he had brought with him. In his mind he knew he was too young to know his destiny, to discover exactly what he might do with his life, but he was growing tired of waiting. "The early believers didn't sit and wait," he thought. "They searched! They traveled until they found what they were looking for!"

Ali took a few deep breaths, stretched, and picked up the book, a handwritten copy of *The Seven Valleys*, which his grandmother had given him before she died. It was a hard book to understand, even though it was not long, and until now Ali had never been able to read very much of it. His uncle had told him that each of the seven parts described one of the steps that lead man closer to God, and Ali could understand some of the first few pages, but after that he began to get confused.

He had brought the book to the hill because he wanted to read one particular page from the first part, from the Valley of Search. There were other valleys he had read about in the book: the Valley of Love, the Valley of Knowledge, the Valley of Contentment, but Ali felt sure the Valley of Search held something important. He knew that Bahá'u'lláh was talking about how people should search for the new Prophet from God, just as the Wise Men had searched for the Christ-child or as Mullá Ḥusayn had searched for the Báb. But one particular phrase from the book kept going through his mind, perhaps because it seemed to fit what he was feeling: "The first is the Valley of Search. The steed of this Valley is patience; without patience the wayfarer on this journey will reach nowhere and attain no goal."

At first Ali remembered these verses without really knowing why, like those songs he would sing with the other children as they played their street games, tunes he would find himself humming during the day without thinking. But this morning before he had left for the hill, he had picked up the book quite purposefully because he too was searching, not for a Prophet of God, perhaps, but searching all the same. And as he carried the book, which until now had been only a reminder of his lovely grandmother, he felt as if it were magic, as if on some page he might suddenly discover his answer, a message telling him exactly what path he should follow or what heroic deed of service he might do so that someday Bahá'ís would remember him.

He knew it would not be so easy to find his answer as opening the pages of a book, but he thought that if he were very sincere, Bahá'u'lláh's own book might help him discover his special destiny. He rubbed his fingertips across the engraved leather cover. He tried to clear his mind of all other thoughts, to concentrate very hard. "Bahá'u'lláh," he whispered, "show me what I can do."

Then he did something strange. He held the book to his face, so close that he was aware of the sweet smell of the leather binding and the pleasant mustiness of old paper. *"Alláh-u-Abhá,"* he said. "God is Most Glorious." Then he opened the book, and without looking, placed his finger on a page. He looked expectantly at the passage his finger was touching: "One must judge of search by the standard of the Majnún of Love. It is related that one day they came upon Majnún sifting the dust, and his tears flowing down. They said, 'What doest thou?' He said, 'I seek for Laylí.' They cried, 'Alas for thee! Laylí is of pure spirit, and thou seekest her in the dust!' He said, 'I seek her everywhere; haply somewhere I shall find her.'" Ali read on: "Yea, although to the wise it be shameful to seek the Lord of Lords in the dust, yet this betokeneth intense ardor in searching. 'Whoso seeketh out a thing with zeal shall find it.'"

A smile brushed Ali's face. Had Bahá'u'lláh guided him to this verse? Was this Ali's special instruction? He was not quite sure, but he read the passage several times until he thought he knew what the words meant. He must have patience, it seemed to say, and yet he must continue to search if he would discover the special charge that God had reserved for him.

He looked up from the book, not much more sure of what he should do than before. Then he put it down on the grass and lay back beside it to look up at the clouds coasting silently toward the mountains. He picked up a green weed and began to chew it, but it tasted bitter so he flicked it away. He shifted himself so that his back felt better against the ground then he breathed a few long sighs. He yawned once or twice and stretched his arms over his head. A few minutes later he was fast asleep.

The raspy voice whispering in his ear came from a short man, a little man with a wrinkled face, a round man who wore a huge turban. "Speak, little boy!" he said. "Hurry before everyone goes away! They've all come just to hear you speak!"

The man chuckled as Ali looked at the crowd of restless citizens gathered in front of the mosque of Jazzár Pá<u>sh</u>á. Ali had something important to tell them. It was about Bahá'u'lláh! He wanted to tell them good news, that a new Prophet had been sent by God, but for some reason he could not think of how to explain it. He was sure the news would make them happy, but they would not be quiet, and they were mumbling to one another so loudly that Ali was sure he would not be heard.

"*Make* them be quiet, little boy!" whispered the little strange man as he smiled mockingly.

Ali felt angered by the taunts of the man, and he tried to shout, but only a whisper came from his mouth: "Listen, O people of 'Akká!" he tried to say, but no one could hear him.

The people stirred and became more restless. "Speak up!" said one. "Yes, why have you brought us here?" shouted another. "If you have something to say, then just say it! We have business to tend to!" Then they began to chant rhythmically louder and louder, "Speak! Speak! Speak!"

The more they shouted, the more frustrated Ali became. At last he raised his arms as a sign that they should be still. He tried to look serious and powerful so they would pay attention. Little by little the curious crowd calmed down. The murmur began to cease. Ali cleared his throat. "My dear friends," he tried to say, "I have joyous news to share with all of you . . ." He stopped. Each word became fainter and softer than the last until his voice disappeared completely. His throat felt tight and parched, as if he had run for miles in the heat of summer.

"What did he say?" murmured a few. "Speak! Speak!" shouted others, until the crowd was making as much noise as before. A few of the people in the back began wandering away. "Let's go! He's had his chance!"

"No! No! You mustn't go!" Ali tried to shout. But no one heard. The crowd began to trickle away down the dark, narrow streets that led away from the mosque to the other parts of 'Akká. Even the strange little man turned to walk away, but looked back as he departed, still smiling his wretched, mocking smile.

Ali was now alone and discouraged. He sat down in front of the mosque as tears flooded his eyes and his chest began to heave with giant sobs. He had lost his chance.

Suddenly, he was startled from his sorrow by the loud neighing of a horse. He sprang to his feet and turned to see a magnificent, beautiful black steed. It had a short-cropped mane, a polished black leather saddle with silver studs, and silver-linked reins. He had never seen such a splendid horse, not even in pictures. Then, as if on command, the horse walked up to Ali and rubbed its nose against his arm. The horse then knelt down as if it were signaling for Ali to mount.

Ali looked around in amazement to see if the owner were nearby so he could ask permission to ride, but there was no one. The city streets were completely deserted.

Cautiously, Ali straddled the horse, and immediately the steed stood up straight and began walking at an even pace down one of the streets as if it knew exactly where it was going. Strangely, the horse's hooves made no sound on the hard stones. Ali was not the least afraid, even though he had no idea where it was taking him. There was something oddly comforting in the horse's stride and manner, like the familiar presence of a cherished friend.

The street became narrower, darker, and deeper. It descended until gradually it became almost a tunnel, and soon there was no light at all. Now Ali was beginning to feel afraid when he saw directly in front of him a dim light.

As he approached the light, he could see that he was in a large, ancient stone hall. It looked like the inside of an ancient fortress, though it was not damp or cold or forbidding. At the far end of the great hall Ali could see a raised platform on which was seated an aged man who was simply but elegantly dressed in a dark red 'abá and a simple white turban.

The aged one sat cross-legged and motionless. His hazel eyes were clear, powerful, and loving. An eerie glow seemed to shine about him, as if light emanated from his body. The horse came up directly in front of the platform and stopped.

Ali's eyes were on the same level as those of the man, who raised his hand slowly, looked knowingly at the horse, and said in a firm yet gentle voice, "Well done, my patient one." Then, looking at the boy, the man said, "And you must be Ali, the young seeker."

"Yes, sir . . . I am," said Ali in a halting voice.

"I am Shaykh Aḥmad-i-Aḥsá'í," said the old man. "Like you, I was a seeker in my lifetime." Ali remembered the stories of Shaykh Aḥmad's search for the Promised One, how for forty years this venerated spiritual leader had prepared many people for the coming of the Báb.

"You were the teacher of Siyyid Káẓim, the teacher of Mullá Ḥusayn!" said Ali excitedly.

"Yes, Ali. And now I will help you in your search, but first you must tell me something. Tell me what it is you desire."

"I . . . I was trying to tell the townspeople about Bahá'u'lláh, but I could not speak. My voice . . ."

"There was nothing wrong with your voice, Ali. The ears of the townspeople were closed to you. You must leave this walled city. You must find people who will listen."

"But where? Where should I go, and how shall I get there?"

"Do not worry, my son," said the old man in a voice that resonated throughout the hall. "Once outside these walls, my steed will take you where you need to go. And when you get there, you will know what to do."

"But how will I get past the walls?" asked Ali. "They are so high and so thick!"

"You may go through the land gate, but only if you find the golden key."

"Golden key?" asked Ali. "What are you talking about?"

The old man reached beside him and picked up a large book marvelously bound in dark leather. On the cover etched in gold letters were the words *The Story of Bahá'u'lláh*. He handed the book to Ali, and as he did so he said, "The key is here, in this book, at the very end." Ali reached out to grasp the large volume. To his surprise it was not at all heavy.

As Ali looked at the gold lettering, the horse slowly backed a few paces away then turned. "Read and study so that you may possess the key," said the old man as the horse walked toward an arched doorway that led into another chamber. The room itself was not very large. It was dimly lit, except for one corner in which there were a large cushion and a pale blue lantern that made the walls of the chamber glow with blue light. The cool air was scented with rosewater.

The horse slowly knelt and Ali dismounted. He took the book and sat on the cushion, which was covered with soft satin cloth. He put the huge volume in his lap and turned the first few pages. The print was very small and hard to read. The sentences were long and confusing.

Several times Ali tried to read, but he could not concentrate and he quickly became discouraged. Finally, he gave up and flipped through all the pages at once until he was at the end of the volume. But there was no key there!

The horse whinnied loudly and reared up menacingly. Ali quickly turned back to the beginning of the book. Again he struggled with the words. He read until his eyes became sore and the print seemed to blur. Sleep, he wanted to sleep, to lie down on the soft, smooth cushion, just for a moment or two. But each time he felt himself nodding off, he jerked himself awake and forced himself to go on.

Gradually, the pages became easier to read, and Ali no longer felt sleepy at all. Before he knew it, it was done! He had finished the entire book, and when he turned the last page, there, just as the old man had promised, was a large, gleaming gold key about the size of Ali's hand.

"The key!" he exclaimed. "The key to the land gate!" Carefully he picked up the shiny key, and as soon as he did, the horse knelt down for him to mount. "I must show Shaykh Aḥmad," Ali thought, but when the horse went back through the door, the large hall had disappeared. Instead, Ali found himself outside in the streets of 'Akká!

The horse pranced through the streets toward the land gate as Ali held the key before him with both hands. He could see the townspeople only dimly through the thick haze, but he could see the amazement on their faces when they saw the young lad atop the magnificent horse and the bright gold key glistening in his hands.

When Ali arrived at the gate, a guard reached out for the key.

Ali had barely handed it to him when the gate doors crashed open and the horse rushed through like a gust of wind. Grasping the reins tightly in both hands, Ali tried to scream in his fright, but he could not. Everything was happening too fast!

The horse was speeding upwards through the air as Ali strained to hold on. Ali dared to look down and he saw the spires of the mosque disappear below him. Higher and higher Ali ascended, and as he did, 'Akká and Haifa became smaller and smaller.

"Mother! Father!" he gasped, but his voice was lost in the wind. Then, just as quickly, the upward movement slowed then ceased altogether just as a ball thrown high in the air might pause at the peak of a toss.

Ali grabbed the reins even tighter, ready for the fall . . . but there was none! He was completely weightless and seemed to float. Ali suddenly felt totally calm, as if no fears, no loneliness, no trouble of any sort could ever reach him.

When Ali looked down, 'Akká and Haifa seemed merely dots. And as he looked, he noticed pulsing halos of light emanating from these two points. As the rings of light spread out, shimmering like ripples on a rock-shattered pond, the villages and towns they passed over remained aglow. And when the next ring of light passed over, each point of light would become a little brighter.

Ali watched with hypnotic fascination the continual pulsing of light and the ever more brightly shining specks that were the cities and towns touched by that light. To Ali it seemed as though 'Akká and Haifa produced a vast heartbeat sending out vital energy to the rest of the planet. This thought filled him with delight and a peace of mind such as he had never felt before.

Then he began to move again, as if a huge magnet were now drawing him back to earth, except the steed had vanished from beneath him! First he was floating, then he was gliding by himself, his arms extended like wings. Suddenly he was hurtling headlong through space toward earth, toward one of the distant specks of light.

But he was strangely calm, fearless, content, strong and sure as he descended through space, aware from deep within that he had a special mission. He felt that he was part of something wonderful, as if he were singing in a vast and universal unseen choir intoning melodies of such splendid beauty that the whole earth was charmed by this rapturous sound. As he plummeted through space toward the glowing point that he now could make out to be a city, he tried to see if he could recognize any buildings or the patterns of streets. Had he seen this place before? He couldn't be sure.

Then something began to slow him down. The city became fainter and more hazy. He heard a familiar voice calling him from afar. "Ali! Ali!" it called. His flight slowed, then ceased, and Ali began to shake. "Ali!" the voice called again, but louder and clearer. "Ali, wake up, you lazy boy!"

The deep voice seemed to peel away the layers of sleep. Ali opened his eyes, and there, smiling at him, was his own father. Behind his father's head an early evening star glittered in the almost darkened sky. "Are you all right, my boy?" his father asked.

Without a word, Ali reached up, hugged his father's neck and held tightly.

"So this is where you have been! Your mother and I were terribly worried!" His father's voice was now somewhat stern.

Ali could only think of the dream. "It seemed so real, Father, so very real!"

"What did? What are you talking about?"

"The dream, father! I fell asleep and had the most marvelous dream I have ever had!" Ali tried to explain every detail of the dream—the little man, the crowd, the steed, Shaykh Aḥmad, the book, the key, the flight through space. And as they walked back to 'Akká, Husayn could scold Ali only a little. The boy was so happy, so excited, so unlike the somber lad of the past months that Husayn was grateful for whatever had cast such a lovely spell over his son.

Later as the two sat down with Ali's mother Nahid at the table for their now cold dinner, Husayn said, "You know, Ali, 'Abdu'l-Bahá tells us that we should pay attention to our dreams."

"Indeed," said Nahid, who, like Husayn, seemed genuinely interested in Ali's dream. "I only wish your grandmother were still alive. She could always interpret dreams so well."

"You mean she actually knew what they meant?" asked Ali.

"I think so," said Nahid. "I remember that my dreams always seemed to make sense after she explained them to me."

"Maybe she just told you what you wanted to hear," said Husayn with a smile.

"No, no," said Nahid seriously. "I could always tell if what she said didn't feel right, and I would tell her, and she'd try again."

"Could you tell me what my dream means?" asked Ali. "Could you at least try?"

Nahid reached over and placed her cool hand on Ali's. "Why don't you tell me what it means?"

"But how? How can I?"

"Just tell me the parts you understand, and we'll try to work out the parts you don't."

"All right," said Ali, placing his spoon on the plate.

"First you must eat something," said Nahid.

Ali ate his dinner much too quickly. When he was finished, he tried to wait while his mother poured tea for the three of them, but it was very hard for Ali to be very patient.

Finally, the dishes were gone, the tea was ready, and Ali began with his mother and father to discuss his dream. He talked about the strange little man, about the magnificent beauty of the horse. He described in animated detail how it felt to fly through space and float in the air. Most of all he tried to explain the wondrous vision of the rings of light that set aglow each town and village he passed over.

After a lengthy discussion, the three decided that the rings of light had something to do with the influence of Bahá'u'lláh and the spread of the Bahá'í Faith. They also agreed that Ali received the reward of his mission because he had studied the large book about Bahá'u'lláh. Then they talked some more about how the town seem to get brighter and brighter with each successive halo of light.

"But the town I was going to was not very bright at all," said Ali.

"Perhaps that's why you were headed there," said Husayn.

"What do you mean?"

"Since the townspeople wouldn't listen to you in 'Akká, perhaps you were being sent to some place where the people would pay attention. Perhaps the dream means that someday you will teach people about the Bahá'í Faith in another place, perhaps a city many miles from here."

"But where?" said Ali.

"Learn from your dream," said Nahid. "Remember that before you were worthy to receive the key, you had to study patiently."

"Yes, I had to read the huge book," said Ali. He paused, then said excitedly, "The horse! I know what the horse was!"

"What?" said Nahid.

"Before I fell asleep on the hill, I was reading in the book Grandmother gave me, *The Seven Valleys.* The horse was the steed of patience!"

"Yes, but unlike Majnún, you did not look for Laylí in the sand," said Husayn. "You searched in the book that Shaykh Aḥmad gave you. That's where the key was."

Ali paused. That much made sense, but then he wondered again about sailing through the air. "What did that mean?" he asked. "It felt so wonderful. I felt so excited and so happy."

Nahid puzzled, then looked up. "Perhaps it is the next valley, the Valley of Love. You were drawn upward, you said, as if a magnet were pulling you, and when you looked down, you saw that the center of the world, the source of light for all the other cities, is right here in 'Akká and Haifa."

"That's right!" said Ali jumping to his feet. "When I looked down, I remember thinking that it was all so clear, that I understood everything."

"The Valley of Knowledge," said Husayn, "the third of the seven valleys."

"But what about when I fell? Does that mean I stopped understanding?"

"Did it feel unpleasant?" asked his mother.

"Oh, no!" said Ali. "It wasn't like falling at all. It was a wonderful feeling, as if I were a part of everything and knew just what I was supposed to do."

Husayn laughed. "Amazing!" he said. "Really amazing!"

"What do you mean?" said Ali.

"Your father is laughing because the fourth valley is the Valley of Unity, Ali, and that's what you just said you were feeling."

"But I haven't read that far. How could I dream about something I haven't even read yet?"

"There are many unanswered questions about your dream, Ali," said his father. "For example, where is that beautiful large book Shaykh Aḥmad gave you?"

"Oh," said Ali, perplexed, "that's right."

"And why did the dream make you feel so happy?" said Nahid.

"I know the answer to that," said Ali. "Because I knew exactly what I was supposed to do, and it felt very important."

"Well, perhaps you should do what the dream says. You should read that book."

"But there is no such book, is there?"

"Do you think when you leave 'Akká you will fly through the air on a horse?"

"No," admitted Ali. "I suppose not. I guess that was just a symbol of something."

"Then perhaps the book was also a symbol," said Nahid.

"Of what?"

"Of learning about Bahá'u'lláh," said Husayn. "Learning about His teachings, about why He came and what the early Bahá'ís endured to make this Faith secure for you."

"But remember," added Nahid. "When you rushed through the book, the key was not there, was it?"

"No."

"I think that means you must learn more than names and dates and stories," she said. "I think it means you must begin to understand Bahá'u'lláh, not because there is a gold key waiting for you, but because you love what you are learning. Perhaps in that way the key will be there when you finish."

The three continued to talk awhile longer about Ali's dream and what it meant, about dreams that had come true, about the mysterious ways God speaks to us, even at times in our sleep. And the more they talked, the more Ali became sure that the dream was truly important, that he should think about it more, and that he should try to follow the guidance the dream seemed to reveal.

When they had finished their conversations and had chanted some evening prayers, Ali got ready for bed, though he did not feel at all tired. He tossed and stretched and called his mother into his room one more time. "Mother," he asked, "When can I start my search?"

Nahid bent over to kiss his brow. "Right now you must sleep, my child," and she blew out the lamp on his bedside table. Then she turned as she was about to leave the room. "But I think tomorrow might be a proper day to begin, don't you?"

2

The Secret Letter

Ali had hoped that his grandfather would be able to come along because the boy loved to hear the interesting stories that Moayyed would always tell. Of course, what Ali really wanted was to tell his grandfather about the dream.

Husayn and Nahid walked at a leisurely pace beside their son along the road to Bahjí on this brilliant spring day, but they were beginning to wonder about Ali's silence as he lagged a few steps behind.

"Whoops!" said Nahid when Ali suddenly tripped on the hard-packed gravel.

"Did a rock jump out in front of you?" said Husayn, helping the boy up and dusting him off. Ali bent over to rub his foot, then he glanced up to see his mother's knowing look. She was smiling, shaking her head, and in spite of the sore toe, Ali could not help smiling back. "You shouldn't try to do so many things at once," his father said. "Walking and meditating at the same time can be dangerous."

"Were you thinking about your dream again?" asked Nahid as she helped brush the dust from Ali's frock-coat.

"Yes," he replied. After a pause he added, "You really do think it means something, don't you?"

"Yes, I really do," said Nahid as the three resumed walking.

"And you think it means I should find out more about the life of Bahá'u'lláh?"

"I think it means more than that," said Husayn. "You see, to understand the life of a Prophet, you have to learn more than just facts—the things

He did, the places He went, or what He said. You have to understand *why* things happened and what He meant by the things He said and did."

"Of course, we can never know all there is to know," said Nahid. "But just as the morning sun gradually burns away the morning mist, your study, if it is sincere, will lead you to your life's path little by little."

Ali did not respond at first. "But if there is no book, how do I study the life of Bahá'u'lláh? You and Father and Grandfather have already taught me much about Bahá'u'lláh, so what do I do now? How should I begin?"

Nahid looked at Husayn to see if he would answer.

Finally, Husayn spoke. "I suppose you could begin your search by finding out more about Bahá'u'lláh's life, how He was brought up, and how He later became a Bábí."

"A Bábí?" said Ali. "I didn't know that Bahá'u'lláh was a follower of the Báb."

Nahid looked at Husayn. The two parents were surprised that Ali did not know this, and they wondered how much else they simply assumed Ali knew. "Oh, yes," said Nahid. "Bahá'u'lláh played an important part in helping the Báb. In fact, as soon as Bahá'u'lláh heard about the Báb, He became a Bábí and He began to teach about this new religion to anyone who would listen. But that's another story altogether."

"Well," said Ali with the curious smile he always got when he wanted his parents to do something for him, "could you help me begin my search now? Could you tell me something about those early years in the life of Bahá'u'lláh?"

"Of course we can," said Husayn. "After all, what better way to begin your study than with a visit to the Shrine of Bahá'u'lláh?"

Ali was surprised that his parents understood how important the dream was to him, and he felt grateful to them because they paid attention to his questions and because they always seemed to enjoy teaching him. "Tell me how Bahá'u'lláh grew up, how He became a Bábí."

"Certainly," said Nahid as she placed her arm around Ali's shoulder and gave him a firm squeeze. She looked at Husayn. "Why don't you tell him about the early years, and on the walk home this afternoon I can tell him how Bahá'u'lláh became a Bábí."

"Very well," said Husayn. "But first let me ask you some questions to see how much you already know. Let's see . . . do you know where Bahá'u'lláh was born?"

"In Ṭihrán, the capital city of Persia," said Ali.

"Yes, that's correct. Now, did you know that His father was well-respected, a man of importance, a nobleman and a vizier?"

"Not really," said Ali.

"Then let me start with something more simple. Do you know when Bahá'u'lláh was born?"

"November 12th, 1817," answered Ali quickly.

"Very good," said Husayn, becoming a bit more serious in his tone. "Bahá'u'lláh was the son of Mírzá Buzurg of Núr, which is an area in the province of Mázindarán in the northern part of Persia. They were a wealthy family. They even had several homes. They had a house in the mountains, for example, in the village of Tákur. But their main home was a lovely mansion in Ṭihrán. Of course, Bahá'u'lláh's name then was Mírzá Ḥusayn-'Alí—He took the title 'Bahá'u'lláh' years later.

"Well, Bahá'u'lláh's father had an important position in the court of the Sháh, so the young boy was able to talk with all sorts of scholars and learned men, even with important government officials and religious leaders."

"While he was still young, as young as I am?" asked Ali.

"Yes, as young as you. In fact, because he was so brilliant, those who met Him began to sense that this young one had special powers. They could tell He had a knowledge far beyond the kind of wisdom and learning you could expect from someone of His age, especially since Bahá'u'lláh never had any formal training.

"You see, Ali, a Manifestation of God is not an ordinary human being like you or me. A Prophet has innate knowledge, a wisdom that is His from the beginning. It is not the sort of learning that one can get from schools or teachers or study."

"You mean He knows things from the time He is born?"

"Perhaps even before," said Nahid. "You see, our soul, our consciousness begins when our physical bodies begin, but the soul of the Manifestation exists in the spiritual world before He is born."

"You mean He knows that He is a Prophet even before He tells anyone?"

"Most certainly," said Husayn, gesturing with his hands.

"I remember Grandfather telling me a story about Christ," said Ali, "about when Christ was twelve. I don't remember the whole story, but I do remember that He was twelve years old, just a year older than I am, and He was in the Temple conversing with the Jewish scholars. And I remember that when His parents were surprised to find Him there, He said, 'Did you not know that I must be about my Father's business?'"

"Precisely so," said Husayn, "and it's the same with every Manifestation. Indeed, there are many such stories about the Báb and Bahá'u'lláh when They were young. Of course, perhaps people were not completely surprised that Bahá'u'lláh would have such learning and such a noble character since He was the son of Mírzá Buzurg. You see, Mírzá Buzurg had a reputation throughout Ṭihrán as a man of noble character, a man of charm and great knowledge. He was also known for his humility and for his marvelous kindness to other people.

"Nevertheless, Ḥusayn-'Alí seemed to have qualities that could not be explained, and so in time it became clear to many that this young one had a most important destiny."

"How could they tell?" asked Ali, wondering what special role he too might play, studying his parents to discover if they saw in him qualities that might portend a bright future.

"You would be surprised how much grown-ups can tell about young people," said Husayn with a smile. Ali knew that his father understood what he was thinking. "When Bahá'u'lláh was only thirteen or fourteen years old, for example, He could talk on any subject and solve any problem."

"And, speaking of special dreams," said Nahid, "Mírzá Buzurg had a most mysterious dream about his son. He dreamed that Ḥusayn-'Alí was swimming in a vast ocean, and as He floated on the waters, His body seemed to shine, illuminate the entire sea, and His long black hair spread out from His head in all directions above the waves. Then fish began to gather around Him. Each one grabbed a strand of His hair and held onto the end with its mouth.

"These fish were fascinated by His face, and they followed Him wherever He swam. But they didn't hurt Him and they did not let His hair loose. Nor did they stop Him from moving about in the water.

"When Bahá'u'lláh's father thought about his dream," Husayn continued, "he was sure it had an important meaning. He summoned to the house a learned soothsayer, a man wise in such matters, and asked him to explain the dream. The soothsayer listened intently to the story. Afterwards he told Mírzá Buzurg what he thought the dream meant."

"What was that?" asked Ali eagerly.

"He said that in the dream the ocean represented the world and the dream signified that Mírzá Ḥusayn-'Alí by Himself would conquer the world. The soothsayer went on to say that Mírzá Ḥusayn-'Alí would also stir up turmoil among the peoples of the world. But even though many would follow Him and cling to Him, they would not harm Him.

"From that day on, Mírzá Buzurg was completely devoted to the young son whom he already loved so very much, for now he was convinced that his son possessed a great destiny." Ali was thrilled when he heard his father mention the word *destiny,* especially when speaking of Mírzá Buzurg's dream, because it reminded him about his own dream and his destiny.

"As Mírzá Ḥusayn-'Alí grew up, He became widely respected by all those who knew of Mírzá Buzurg's family. Most people assumed that Mírzá Ḥusayn-'Alí would become a government official like His father. But the boy was interested in other things, even at an early age."

"Like what?" asked Ali.

"Well, for one thing, He dearly loved nature, flowers, birds, and walks in the countryside. He especially cherished hiking through the fields and mountains of Mázindarán."

"Is that part of Persia pretty like here?" asked Ali.

"It is very beautiful," said Nahid. "But it is quite different from 'Akká. The mountains are higher than those around here. They are covered with beautiful trees, and small villages nestle in the valleys."

"These hills and villages," continued Husayn, "were Bahá'u'lláh's favorite places to go. You see, He not only loved the simple life of the countryside; He also loved the country folk who were so much more simple and honest than so many of the wealthy ones who came to the court of the Sháh.

"As He grew up, Bahá'u'lláh became loved and respected by people at every level of society because of His pleasant manner, His kindness and wisdom. He also became renowned for His skill as a calligrapher."

"What's that?" asked Ali.

"A calligrapher? That is one who has learned the art of exquisite handwriting."

"Someone like Uncle Mihdí?"

"Well, not exactly. What Uncle Mihdí does is to decorate a page of calligraphy with beautifully colored design, what is called 'illumination.' He does that by making beautifully colored designs around the lettering. But you see, in Persia, especially years ago, fine penmanship by itself was a sign of a person's education and class, because only the very well educated could write so exquisitely.

"So it was expected that Bahá'u'lláh, with His reputation and wisdom, with His many skills and fine upbringing, would surely go into politics or become a government official. But Bahá'u'lláh was very much like His father in this respect. You see, Mírzá Buzurg was always interested in helping others. In fact, he believed that the most important thing in life was being of service, even when things did not go well for him personally.

"For example, Mírzá Buzurg owned a great deal of land, and one year a great flood destroyed much of his property. But he did not become bitter or angry. He accepted these problems with serenity and calm and still cared for those who were less fortunate than himself. Even when some of the other members of the Sháh's court became jealous of his reputation for courtesy and humility and began to talk against him, Mírzá Buzurg never responded in anger, but treated everyone kindly.

"And so it was with Bahá'u'lláh as well. His main interest was always in helping the poor ones, the less fortunate ones. That is how He used His wealth and position. He would visit the sick or those who had been treated badly or who did not have enough to eat or decent clothes to wear. In time, Bahá'u'lláh became known throughout that area as a friend to the needy and as a helper to the poor."

"Just like 'Abdu'l-Bahá here in 'Akká," observed Ali.

"Yes, exactly so, just like 'Abdu'l-Bahá," said Husayn. "In fact, interestingly enough, it was Bahá'u'lláh's reputation for kindliness and generosity that played an important part in the story of how Bahá'u'lláh found out about the Báb."

"What do you mean?" asked Ali.

"It was like this," said Husayn, placing a strong hand on his son's shoulder as they walked. "Bahá'u'lláh grew up to be a responsible and brilliant young man. When He was nearly eighteen, he married Ásíyih Khánum, a beautiful young lady of noble birth, a delicate woman whose fine character was later shown by the three noble children she raised and by the brave way she withstood the incredible hardships during the years that followed. Just four years after Bahá'u'lláh's marriage, Mírzá Buzurg died, and in his will he left the management of his estate in the hands of Bahá'u'lláh, so naturally everyone assumed that Bahá'u'lláh would take His father's place at court, but He refused."

"You mean He could have been a part of the same government that later tried to kill Him?"

"That's right, Ali. You will discover as you study about Bahá'u'lláh that He could have avoided all the difficulties that came to Him in His life, but He did not choose that path. Instead, He chose to do what He knew would in due time render service to all the peoples of the world."

"Because he knew what was His destiny," volunteered Ali with a smile.

Husayn looked at Nahid with a smile. "I suppose so," he said. "Naturally, many of His friends did not understand why He should refuse the position. Most people would have cherished such an honor. But there were others who knew Bahá'u'lláh and understood that He had more important things to do than to become an official in the government of one country. Even the grand vizier told friends at court, 'Leave him to himself. Such a position is unworthy of him. He has some higher aim in view. I cannot understand him, but I am convinced that he is destined for some lofty career. His thoughts are not like ours. Let him alone.'"

"Do you think the grand vizier knew that Bahá'u'lláh was a Manifestation of God?" asked Ali.

"I don't know," replied Husayn. "But he knew that Bahá'u'lláh was a very wise and spiritual person, and I am sure he could tell that Bahá'u'lláh had a knowledge and a power that other people did not have.

"And the grand vizier was not the only person who recognized these qualities in Bahá'u'lláh. For example, one day while Bahá'u'lláh was walking with some of His friends, they happened to pass by a group of students who were listening to a famous Muslim teacher, a mujtahid who was very learned in the laws of Muḥammad. Over two hundred students sat listening respectfully to every word the teacher spoke. As Bahá'u'lláh and His companions passed by, the venerated mujtahid was asking his followers to explain a very difficult verse from the Qur'án. But none of those gathered around this teacher could interpret the passage. Finally, Bahá'u'lláh spoke up and explained what the verse meant, not to show how brilliant He was, but because He knew His answer would help them gain a clearer understanding of their own religion.

"Naturally, the teacher was amazed that this young man who had received no formal education could answer this question when his own highly trained students could not. And yet the teacher was not angry with Bahá'u'lláh. He sensed in Bahá'u'lláh's brilliant explanation that this young man had a divine power. So when Bahá'u'lláh had left, the mujtahid told his students two dreams he had had about the learned youth. He said that in one of his dreams Bahá'u'lláh was talking with the Qá'im Himself, the long-awaited Promised One of Islám. And in another dream the mujtahid was in a room where there were many small boxes, all of them belonging to Bahá'u'lláh. When he reached out and opened them, each box contained books, and every word and every letter in these books was set in beauteous and exquisite jewels."

"Then perhaps he knew Bahá'u'lláh was a Manifestation, a Messenger from God," said Ali excitedly. "At least he knew that Bahá'u'lláh was going to write many wonderful books."

"I suppose that's something we shall never know for certain," said Husayn, "but this learned mujtahid was not the only scholar who knew about Bahá'u'lláh's great knowledge and wisdom. In fact, it was because of Bahá'u'lláh's reputation as a wise and noble young man that Mullá Ḥusayn discovered Bahá'u'lláh."

"How did that happen?" asked Ali.

"Several years later, when Bahá'u'lláh was about twenty-seven years old, the Báb was preparing to make His long pilgrimage to the city of Mecca, the most holy place of the religion of Islám. Before the Báb departed, He summoned Mullá Ḥusayn, His first disciple, and told him that Quddús, His eighteenth disciple, would go with Him to Mecca while Mullá Ḥusayn went on a special mission."

"Was Mullá Ḥusayn sad that he could not go with the Báb?" asked Ali.

"Perhaps he would have liked to go, but he also knew that what the Báb wanted him to do was extremely important."

"What was his mission?"

"The Báb gave him a special letter, a very important letter, and told him to proceed toward the city of Ṭihrán. He told Mullá Ḥusayn that in Ṭihrán he would find a hidden secret which would turn the whole earth into a paradise when it was revealed."

"What did He mean by that?" asked Ali. "What was the secret?"

"Well, we now know that the 'secret' was Bahá'u'lláh, but, of course, Mullá Ḥusayn did not know this at the time. The Báb simply told him to find a special person worthy of receiving a letter from the Manifestation of God."

"But how would Mullá Ḥusayn know what that was?" the boy persisted. "What signs would there be?"

"The Báb promised Mullá Ḥusayn that if he had faith and followed the instructions he would know when he had met the right person, and naturally Mullá Ḥusayn had complete faith in the Báb's promise.

"And so it was that when the Báb and Quddús left by boat for Mecca, Mullá Ḥusayn began his journey toward Ṭihrán, excited by his mysterious search and wondering when he would meet this special person. As he traveled through the towns along the way, he taught people about the Báb, telling them that there was a new revelation from God. He traveled through Iṣfahán, then Káshán, and at long last he arrived in Ṭihrán.

"At this time Bahá'u'lláh was still known by the name Mírzá Ḥusayn-'Alí, and He lived in the beautiful family home with His young wife Ásíyih Khánum and their infant son, 'Abbás, Who had been born on the same day that the Báb had declared Himself to Mullá Ḥusayn—May 23, 1844.

"In Ṭihrán Mullá Ḥusayn talked with some of the religious leaders and learned scholars of the town. Since he knew it was in Ṭihrán that he would discover the special person to whom he was to give the letter, he spent a great deal of time talking with the learned students and scholars, discussing the various traditions of Islám as he had learned about them first from his teacher Siyyid Káẓim, and then from the Báb Himself.

"One night, as Mullá Ḥusayn was talking with one of these scholars, a student in the next room overheard the conversation and immediately sensed that Mullá Ḥusayn was speaking the truth. Later, when he could talk with Mullá Ḥusayn privately, the student, whose name was Mullá Muḥammad, became even more certain that Mullá Ḥusayn's words were true.

"During their conversation, when the young student mentioned that he was from Mázindarán, Mullá Ḥusayn happened to remember the exalted reputation of Mírzá Buzurg, who had lived in that same province.

"'Tell me,' asked Mullá Ḥusayn, 'is there today among the family of the late Mírzá Buzurg, who was so renowned for his character, his charm, and artistic and intellectual attainments, anyone who has proved himself capable of maintaining the high traditions of that illustrious house?' The student did not know why Mullá Ḥusayn asked, but he did indeed know of such a one. 'Yes,' he replied. 'Among his sons is one who has distinguished Himself by the very traits which characterized His father. By His virtuous life, His high attainments, His loving-kindness and liberality, He has proved Himself a noble descendant of a noble father.'

"As the young man spoke, Mullá Ḥusayn's face beamed with delight. 'What is His occupation?' asked Mullá Ḥusayn. 'Occupation?' asked Mullá Muḥammad with a knowing smile. 'His occupation is in cheering the sad, in feeding the hungry.' Mullá Ḥusayn became more excited with each reply. 'And what of His rank?' asked Mullá Ḥusayn. 'He has none,' said the student, 'besides being a friend to the poor and to the stranger.'

"Now Mullá Ḥusayn could barely contain himself. 'What is His name?' he asked. 'Mírzá Ḥusayn-'Alí,' the student replied, a bit perplexed at Mullá Ḥusayn's interest in Bahá'u'lláh. 'And how does this young man spend His time, besides helping the poor people?' 'Well, He loves the outdoors,' answered Mullá Muḥammad. 'He roams the woods and loves the beauty of the countryside.' 'How old is He?' 'Twenty-seven,' replied the student, still somewhat confused, for with each question and each answer, Mullá Ḥusayn's face became brighter and his expression ever more intense.

"'Do you ever visit Him?' asked Mullá Ḥusayn. 'Yes,' replied the student. Smiling broadly, Mullá Ḥusayn reached inside his robe and pulled out a curious scroll wrapped in a piece of cloth. He was now satisfied that Mírzá Ḥusayn-'Alí was the One Who was to receive the Báb's special letter.

"'Will you deliver this message to Him from me? Hand it to Mírzá Ḥusayn-'Alí tomorrow at the hour of dawn?' The student reached out and took the scroll, realizing that it must be a very special document to be wrapped so carefully. He agreed to do as Mullá Ḥusayn requested. 'And one more thing,' said Mullá Ḥusayn; 'If by chance He has a reply, some response to the message, would you please convey it to me?'

"Mullá Muḥammad agreed, took the scroll back to his own room, and guarded it carefully that whole night. Then promptly at dawn the next day, he went to the house of Mírzá Ḥusayn-'Alí.

"As he neared the house, Mullá Muḥammad saw Mírzá Músá, the faithful brother of Bahá'u'lláh, standing at the gate. The youth approached cautiously and told Mírzá Músá as best he could why he had come. Mírzá

Músá listened to the story about how the young student obtained the letter. He then went into the house to inform Bahá'u'lláh about the visitor and his strange gift.

"When Mírzá Músá returned, he told Mullá Muḥammad to enter the house, and the student nervously followed Mírzá Músá into the room where Bahá'u'lláh was sitting. When he observed Bahá'u'lláh's gracious manner and heard the gentle voice, he felt a sense of awe and peace. He immediately handed the scroll to Bahá' u'lláh and said, 'This is a message I was asked to give you by a young mullá whom I met yesterday.'

"Bahá'u'lláh asked Mullá Muḥammad to be seated and began to peruse the letter. Mullá Muḥammad waited anxiously to see what reaction Bahá'u'lláh would have. Bahá'u'lláh then began to read aloud some of the passages the Báb had written. After reading but a single page, He turned to Mírzá Músá and said, 'Músá, what have you to say? Verily I say, whoso believes in the Qur'án and recognizes its divine origin, and yet hesitates, though it be for a moment, to admit that these soul-stirring words are endowed with the same regenerating power, has most assuredly erred in his judgment and has strayed far from the path of justice.'"

Ali interrupted his father's story. The words of Bahá'u'lláh were beautiful to him, but they were hard to understand. "What did He mean, Father—that the letter of the Báb was as beautiful as the words of Muḥammad?"

"More than that," answered Husayn. "Bahá' u'lláh was telling His brother that the Person Who had written the letter was a Prophet, a Manifestation of God—that the words of the letter had the same spiritual power, the same importance as the words of Muḥammad in the Qu'rán."

"You mean without even seeing the Báb, Bahá'u'lláh knew Who He was?"

"Exactly," said Husayn, smiling at his son. Then he continued. "Before Bahá'u'lláh dismissed the young student from His presence, He asked him to take several gifts to Mullá Ḥusayn, gifts that would serve as a sign of His response."

"What were they, Father?"

"First He asked the student to give Mullá Ḥusayn His appreciation and love, then He handed Mullá Muḥammad a loaf of Russian sugar and a package of tea."

"Was this the answer that Mullá Ḥusayn was waiting for?"

"Yes, these were symbols to Mullá Ḥusayn that Bahá'u'lláh understood what the letter meant and that He understood Who the Báb was. Of course, the young student did not understand everything that was happening, but he was quite aware of the importance of this event. He arose immediately. He hurriedly left the house of Bahá'u'lláh, and he hastened to the dwelling where Mullá Ḥusayn eagerly awaited Bahá'u'lláh's response to the secret letter.

"Well, you can imagine the joy and amazement Mullá Ḥusayn felt when he heard about the meeting. He took into his hands the simple but precious gifts that were the tokens of Bahá'u'lláh's answer. He gazed at these gifts a moment, then reverently kissed them. After that he did something quite remarkable—he looked into the eyes of the faithful young student, embraced the lad and kissed both his eyes. He then said, 'My dearly beloved friend! I pray that even as you have rejoiced my heart, God may grant you eternal felicity and fill your heart with imperishable gladness.'"

"I guess Mullá Ḥusayn was happy because Bahá'u'lláh was now a Bábí?" asked Ali.

"More than that," said Husayn. "You see, Mullá Ḥusayn knew that the One Who was to receive the letter was a very important person. Perhaps he even knew that Bahá'u'lláh was 'Him Whom God shall make manifest,' the One Whose advent the Báb had come to announce."

"Then why didn't Mullá Ḥusayn tell everyone?" asked Ali.

"Because if Mullá Ḥusayn knew Who Bahá'u'lláh was, he also knew that the time had not yet come to let this information be shared with others."

"Perhaps that's one reason why Mullá Ḥusayn did not take the letter himself?"

"That very well may be so," said Husayn to his bright young son. "He also may have been trying to protect Bahá'u'lláh. You see, the Báb had told

Mullá Ḥusayn that this hidden secret, the identity of the person to Whom He had addressed this letter, would change the entire world. Therefore, before the young student left, Mullá Ḥusayn told him not to tell anyone else what had happened. 'Breathe not to anyone what you have heard and witnessed,' he said. 'Let this be a secret hidden within your heart. Divulge not His name, for they who envy His position will arise to harm Him. In your moments of meditation, pray that the Almighty may protect Him, that, through Him, He may exalt the downtrodden, enrich the poor, and redeem the fallen.'"

"He went on to tell the young man, 'The secret of things is concealed from our eyes. Ours is the duty to raise the call of the New Day and to proclaim this Divine Message unto all people. Many a soul will, in this city, shed his blood in this path. That blood will water the Tree of God, will cause it to flourish, and to overshadow all mankind.'"

"So Mullá Ḥusayn knew that problems would come and that Bahá'u'lláh would play an important part in it all?"

"Yes, he most certainly did."

"Then, Mírzá Buzurg's dream was beginning to come true?"

"Indeed it was," said Husayn.

"And did Bahá'u'lláh go to meet the Báb so They could plan what to do?"

"No, He didn't. In fact, They never even met each other in person, at least not in this world," said Husayn with a smile at Nahid.

Ali thought for a moment, then said, "Perhaps they didn't need to see each other. Maybe each knew what the other was thinking without having to be in the same room or even in the same town."

"I think you are absolutely correct, Ali. After all, unlike us, the Prophets begin Their lives in the spiritual kingdom before They are born, so possibly They are aware of each other there. Perhaps They even make plans there about how They will carry out Their missions on earth.

"In any case, Bahá'u'lláh was a now a Bábí, and, like most of the Bábís at that time, He began to teach others about this new religion. He began traveling throughout the province, teaching others about God's new Revelation. And later the next year, after the Báb was put in prison in Máh-Kú, Bahá'u'lláh would help lead the Bábís."

Ali and his parents had walked quite a distance as they talked, and Bahjí was now only a few hundred yards away. Already Ali was beginning to focus his attention on the small brown stone building that was set apart from the mansion. How very far Bahá'u'lláh had come from the time He had received that letter in 1844 in Ṭihrán until now in 1912, thought Ali. The story seemed to be about something so long ago and so far off, and yet there was the Qiblih, the point of adoration, the place to which Bahá'ís all over the world now turned in prayer every day less than seventy years later. How much spiritual energy must surround this precious point, thought Ali, and he wondered if when he came here, he might himself be affected by that unseen force.

True, Ali had visited the Shrine of Bahá'u'lláh many times before, but on this special morning after his dream this sacred place seemed quite different to him, as if for the first time he truly understood its significance. Suddenly, Ali found it incredibly exciting to think that the simple building before him contained the earthly remains of the very same Bahá'u'lláh Who had received that letter from the Báb, the same Bahá'u'lláh Who then went on to reveal His own teachings and start a religion which in time would transform the world, just as the Báb had promised, just as Mírzá Buzurg's dream had foretold.

3

The Trumpet Blast

Whenever Ali approached the shrine in which Bahá'u'lláh was buried, he became a little nervous. Sometimes he was not really sure that he wanted to pass through the doorway and enter the white garden room that had been constructed to shelter the believers as they prayed at the threshold of the burial chamber. Sometimes Ali felt unworthy to be in such a holy place, though he always felt more comfortable with himself after he went inside.

But on this beautiful spring morning only a few days after his strange and marvelous dream, he felt excited about entering the shrine, as if he had never really entered it before. It had always seemed to be a peaceful place, but now that his dream seemed to say that his own personal destiny was somehow linked to studying the life of Bahá'u'lláh, this place seemed particularly special.

As Ali removed his shoes at the covered portico in front of the entrance, he did not watch the others as he usually did, wondering if he were doing everything exactly as he was supposed to. Instead, he tried to concentrate on the person that was Bahá'u'lláh, this figure Who in Ali's mind had always seemed larger than life, almost mythical. He thought to himself that however wise and powerful, however miraculous Bahá'u'lláh was, He did inhabit a physical body. He ate and slept, walked and talked within these very same buildings that stood so majestically beside the shrine.

It was a simple thought, obvious perhaps, but it had never fully dawned on Ali, this human dimension of the Prophet's life. He had always considered Bahá'u'lláh quite beyond human concerns, quite untouched by the joys and sorrows, the anguish and pain that are all too often the lot of ordinary human beings.

As Ali reverently entered through the garden room door, he was still deep in thought about these things. Who was Bahá'u'lláh? What sort of personality did He have? What might it have been like to speak with Him or be in His presence? Did all those who attained that precious bounty recognize the power, the lofty station of this Messenger of God?

"A Manifestation," Ali thought. "Bahá'u'lláh was a Messenger from God!" Ali said this several times to himself and thought about the fact that the body of a Messenger from God was actually buried in the next room. He had always known this. Why did it suddenly seem so astounding?

Ali, Nahid, and Husayn walked silently into the sunlit room. Ali remained behind them and watched his mother, father, and three other believers take their places in different areas of the room until each could, one at a time, approach the sacred threshold of the door that led into the burial chamber. Ali became intensely aware of the fragrance of the rose petals gardeners had placed around the threshold.

Occasionally on previous visits Ali would walk in, turn to the threshold, kneel down, chant a prayer to himself, and then leave. But today he sat down at a distance from the threshold, his back against the wall as each adult stepped forward, kneeled, and prayed.

The sun was just coming in through the skylight which bordered the ceiling in the white outer room. Ali let the warm rays bathe his face as he looked up toward the sun, closing his eyes. He concentrated to see if he could feel the energy pouring in from all the prayers aimed at this holy spot from around the world. He imagined the warm rays of sunlight were that energy and that these rays were filling him with profound and abiding powers that would help him fulfill the destiny his dream had foretold. He stayed like that for a while, his eyes shut and face basking in the warm sun. Then, when everyone else had prayed and departed, he got up and walked slowly to the threshold. The beautiful Persian carpets felt soft beneath his feet, and he knelt down. He looked over the threshold into the dimly lit room, staring at the stone slab marking the spot where Bahá'u'lláh was buried.

He tried to imagine what Bahá'u'lláh had looked like from what he remembered about how the older Bahá'ís had described Him, but no clear picture came to mind. Then he placed his forehead on the fresh white linen that had been laid across the threshold. It felt cool and clean, and the sweet smell of roses was like an elixir.

As he began his prayers, he felt something he could not recall ever having felt before. It was almost a physical sensation, a sense of a presence in the room, though no one was there. It was Bahá'u'lláh's presence he felt, that and the waves of ecstatic comfort he had sensed in his dream on the hill, only this was no dream.

Ali remained kneeling for some time. He would begin intoning a prayer, but he could not stop his mind from wandering, so he stopped trying to force himself to say the words. Instead, he simply listened to his own thoughts.

Outside, Husayn was about to go back into the room to see what had happened to his son, but Nahid assured him that nothing could be the matter. Then Ali emerged from the shrine, his face beaming and a wry smile on his lips. Husayn wondered if he should question him about why he had stayed so long, but he decided against it because he knew his son would share with them what had happened if he wished to.

That afternoon, after a light lunch beneath tall, shady trees near the mansion, the three began the walk back toward 'Akká. In the distance they could see the blue Mediterranean and a few of the taller buildings in 'Akká rising up beyond the distant trees. The afternoon sun made the many colors of the landscape seem brighter the way a master painter might portray such a setting. Finally, Husayn could restrain his curiosity no longer. As gently as he could he said, "You stayed a long time in the shrine." Nahid instantly gave her husband a look with her eyes that told Husayn he should be quiet, that he should not ask such questions, but in the midst of this silent communication, Ali happily responded, and Husayn felt relieved.

"Yes." Ali smiled. "It was wonderful. I guess it had something to do with my dream, or maybe it was because of the story you told me this morning, but for some reason I felt really close to Bahá'u'lláh."

"That's wonderful," said Nahid.

"But I don't mean just spiritually," Ali continued. "I suppose I have never really thought that much about Bahá'u'lláh as a living, breathing person. I certainly never thought about Him as being a boy like me. Anyhow, when I was in the garden room, I felt that He was there with me, that He really understood what I was thinking and feeling, almost like a close friend."

"I think I know what you mean," said Nahid.

"And there's something else," Ali said. "I knew that Bahá'u'lláh was a follower of the Báb before He started the Bahá'í Faith, but I didn't know that He was so important from the beginning."

"What do you mean?" asked Husayn. "You thought that at some point He suddenly became changed, that He was a normal human being Who suddenly became completely different?"

"Yes," said Ali. "That's exactly what I mean. I guess I never really understood what I thought about Him. I think I was confused about it. I knew that what Bahá'u'lláh wrote was important because God told Him what to say, but I never really thought about what He was like, what feelings He had or what He knew. I guess I thought that His teachings were important, but His job was simply to tell us what God wanted us to know."

"He may wait until He lets other people know exactly Who He is, what His purpose is, or what power He has," said Nahid, "but a Manifestation of God is always aware, always teaching us with everything He does or says, even when He is a child, even before He begins to tell us the message God has told Him to give us."

"Then I have a question," said Ali as he walked between his mother and father. "It's something I've always wondered. Why didn't Bahá'u'lláh do something like the Báb's first eighteen disciples did, the Letters of the Living? Why didn't He join them at Fort Shaykh Ṭabarsí or at Zanján? Why wasn't He a Letter of the Living? After all, He was one of the first followers of the Báb."

Nahid smiled. "Oh my, Bahá'u'lláh did a *great* deal to help the Bábís, as much as the Letters of the Living did and more. In fact, it was often Bahá'u'lláh Who directed their plans and gave them advice."

"I didn't know that. Tell me some of the things Bahá'u'lláh did."

"All right," said Nahid. "I'll begin where your father left off this morning, because, you see, as your father told you, as soon as Bahá'u'lláh received the letter from the Báb, He began His work as a Bábí. First He visited the towns and villages in the province of Mázindarán where He lived, teaching everyone who would listen that the promised Qá'im had appeared.

"As your father also told you this morning, Bahá'u'lláh was a young man of twenty-eight at the time. Because of His position and wealth, He could have had anything He desired. But Bahá'u'lláh didn't care for money, lands, or power, only about carrying out His mission to serve the Will of God.

"Of course, very few people had heard about the Báb and the Bábí Faith, so when they heard that a young Persian merchant from Shíráz was claiming to be the Promised Qá'im, they told their religious teachers, the 'ulamá, and these teachers responded that the Bábís were troublemakers who were trying to destroy the religion of Islám.

"But Bahá'u'lláh never worried about what people might think. Besides, He was so greatly loved and respected by the people who knew Him that many of the villagers in Mázindarán listened to Him. In fact, many believed Him and became followers of the Báb, even though some of Bahá'u'lláh's own companions and relatives thought He was foolish to follow this strange new religion.

"People in villages like Tákur were always glad to see this young nobleman visiting the countryside from the great city of Ṭihrán. They would gather around Him in the fields or in their small homes and ask questions about the Sháh and the court, about the great buildings, the beautiful clothing, and the grand feasts—things these country people had only heard about and had never seen. But Bahá'u'lláh would not talk to them about these things. As soon as they would listen, He began to speak of the Promised One of Islám, the Qá'im, and He would tell them that the Báb was this Prophet Who had come to lead them to new truth, to a new understanding of God and His guidance for this day.

"At first, many were surprised that a young man of the court would even be concerned with religious matters, subjects that were usually discussed and taught only by older men—shaykhs, mujtahids, or 'ulamá. But as they heard Him explain so clearly and logically how the Báb fulfilled the prophecies and traditions of their religion, many found themselves eager to believe His words.

"Soon, people throughout the district knew about Bahá'u'lláh and the Bábí religion. When the leading mujtahid of Núr heard from the uncle of Bahá'u'lláh that his young nephew was teaching strange ideas to the people, he did not pay much attention at first. But as more people became Bábís, it seemed to the mujtahid as if Bahá'u'lláh were using some kind of magic to cast a spell over the people. He thought perhaps people were entranced by the beauty of Bahá'u'lláh as He spoke, by His dark eyes and flowing hair, His clear, strong face, His gentle and loving manner. And all who heard about the Báb from Bahá'u'lláh would talk to others until even the students of the mujtahid himself wanted to know about this new religion. So they pleaded with him to visit Bahá'u'lláh that he might talk with Bahá'u'lláh about the Bábí Faith.

"The teacher considered it, but something worried him about such a visit. Perhaps he feared it might be true and that he, too, might have to change his own beliefs. Or perhaps he was afraid that someone as young as Bahá'u'lláh might be wiser than he.

"But the students continued to plead with him, so, instead of going himself, he sent two of his best students to question Bahá'u'lláh, two young men so wise and learned that the mujtahid knew they would not be easy in their examination of Bahá'u'lláh's claims about the Báb. In fact, the teacher, whose name was Mullá Muḥammad, was so confident that his representatives would be able to refute Bahá'u'lláh's claims that he announced he would agree with whatever his students decided about Bahá'u'lláh and the religion He followed."

"Did the students go?" asked Ali with anticipation. "Did they meet Bahá'u'lláh?"

"The students did indeed set out toward the village of Tákur where Bahá'u'lláh was staying. Of course, they were tremendously excited that they were going to talk with Bahá'u'lláh, but in their hearts they were fairly confident that they could think of questions about the Qá'im that Bahá'u'lláh would not be able to answer.

"When they arrived at Tákur, they found that Bahá'u'lláh had left for His winter home. They were disappointed but decided they would seek Him out there. When they arrived, they found Him at work writing a commentary on the Qur'án, the most holy book of their own religion of Islám. The two students dared not interrupt as Bahá'u'lláh dictated this work. Instead, the young men sat down reverently and listened.

"What they heard shocked them. The exquisite beauty of Bahá'u'lláh's words and thoughts, the magnificent eloquence of His melodious voice captivated and enthralled the two young men. They had heard many teachers before, some of the wisest scholars in all of Persia, but never had they heard their own religion explained so clearly.

"Within but a few minutes one of the two students, whose name was 'Abbás, became so overwhelmed by Bahá'u'lláh's words and wisdom that he suddenly stood up. Bahá'u'lláh stopped dictating, and everyone in the room looked at the student, thinking perhaps he had been insulted. Instead, he turned, looked into the eyes of his fellow student, and announced confidently, 'You are free either to proceed with your inquiry or to return alone to our teacher and inform him of the state in which I find myself. Tell him from me that 'Abbás can no longer forsake this threshold.'"

"And did the other student tell the mujtahid what had happened?" asked Ali. "No, I am afraid he did not," said Nahid with a grin. "You see, he had also become so inspired by Bahá'u'lláh's verses that he, too, could no longer follow Mullá Muḥammad, but vowed to dedicate the rest of his life to the service of Bahá'u'lláh.

"Well, as you can imagine, the story of these two students spread quickly throughout Mázindarán. More and more people began flocking to the home of Bahá'u'lláh. There were villagers, religious leaders, even government officials. Some came thinking He had magical powers. Others believed He Himself was the head of this new religion. But after they visited Bahá'u'lláh, most were never the same again, and none had any doubts about His purpose. To everyone who came He gave the same message, that the Báb was the Promised Qá'im of Islám Who had come to give them new teachings for a new age."

"And what happened to Mullá Muḥammad?" asked Ali. "Did he also become a Bábí?"

"Well, that's an interesting story. You see, when the mujtahid did not come to Bahá'u'lláh, Bahá'u'lláh went to him. Naturally Mullá Muḥammad was quite astonished and a little embarrassed to see Him. After all, he had sent his own students to investigate and test Bahá'u'lláh. Nevertheless, he invited Bahá'u'lláh into his house.

"After they were seated, Bahá'u'lláh told Mullá Muḥammad the news that God had sent a new Prophet, that the Promised Qá'im had come at last, and that the Qá'im was called the Báb."

"What did the mujtahid say to Him?" asked Ali.

"At first, Mullá Muḥammad said nothing, so Bahá'u'lláh told him, 'Tell Me whatsoever perplexes your mind, or hinders you from recognizing the Truth,' for Bahá'u'lláh knew He could answer any question the Mullá had, no matter how difficult it might be. Finally, Mullá Muḥammad had an idea. He said to Bahá'u'lláh that he would take the Qur'án and, without looking, open the book and place his finger on the first page he came to in order to determine the truth of Bahá'u'lláh's words."

"Just as I did with *The Seven Valleys!*" said Ali.

"That's right," said Nahid. "So Bahá'u'lláh watched as the mujtahid took the Qur'án in both hands, opened the book, and placed his finger on a passage. Bahá'u'lláh remained silent as Mullá Muḥammad's eyes focused on the words. But as the Mullá read to himself, his eyes grew larger and his face became deathly pale. The mujtahid quickly shut the book without letting Bahá'u'lláh see what the passage said."

"And what *did* it say?" asked Ali.

"I don't know," answered Nahid, "but whatever it was, you can be sure it indicated to the Mullá that Bahá'u'lláh was telling the truth."

"What did Bahá'u'lláh do then?"

"Do? There was nothing for Him to do. Bahá'u'lláh was a wise teacher, the very wisest. He knew that a teacher cannot force a student to learn. Remember how it was in your dream when you tried to teach the people of 'Akká? So Bahá'u'lláh excused Himself and cordially left the house to avoid embarrassing the teacher.

"But there were other people who understood and weren't frightened by the truth. Some were wealthy. Some were poor. There were young people; others were elderly. There was no way of predicting who would recognize the truth and who would not.

"For example, one day Bahá'u'lláh was traveling along a road and came upon a young dervish. The young man was named Muṣṭafá, and he lived by himself in the country. He was a poor man who owned nothing but his begging bowl. Every day the dervish would sit beside the road and beg passersby for food and money.

"Bahá'u'lláh walked over to the dervish as the poor one was cooking a simple meal on a brazier. 'What is it that you are doing?' Bahá'u'lláh asked. The dervish replied, 'I am engaged in eating God. I am cooking God and am burning Him.'"

"What in the world did he mean?" asked Ali.

"Well, I'm not exactly sure, but possibly he meant that he did not really understand the nature of God, or maybe he was saying that God is a part of everything. At any rate, Bahá'u'lláh seemed to find the humor and the honesty of the young man refreshing, and He sat down beside him. Then, with tenderness and understanding, Bahá'u'lláh talked to the dervish about the nature of God and about how we can learn about God through His Prophets. When He then told him that the Báb was the most recent of these special Teachers from God, the dervish was delighted because he sensed that Bahá'u'lláh was a man of wisdom and honesty.

"Immediately he determined to leave behind his life as a dervish. In fact, he was so happy to hear Bahá'u'lláh's explanation of God and how God teaches us that he set aside his brazier, put down his begging bowl, and followed on foot behind Bahá'u'lláh's horse. And as Muṣṭafá walked along, he made up verses of praise to Bahá'u'lláh and he sang them as he walked."

"Do you know the song he sang?" asked Ali.

"A little," Nahid replied. She cleared her throat, and in a soft, melodious voice she sang the simple verses:

Thou art the Daystar of guidance,
Thou art the Light of Truth.
Unveil Thyself to men,
O Revealer of the Truth.

Ali watched his father as Nahid sang, the proud look on his face. For Ali that look on his father's face was like a window into his father's heart, and Ali would recall it many times in years to come because it would remind him how deeply his mother and father loved one another.

"So Bahá'u'lláh taught the new religion in Mázindarán," said Nahid, continuing her story, "just as the eighteen Letters of the Living were teaching in other parts of Persia and 'Iráq for the next several years. In the eastern part of the country, in Mas͟hhad, where we come from, Mullá Ḥusayn and Quddús gathered hundreds of followers. In fact, in Mas͟hhad there was a house they called 'the Bábíyyih' because its doors were always open to those who wished to meet Mullá Ḥusayn and learn about the Báb.

"In 'Iráq and in the western part of Persia, the beautiful Ṭáhirih was teaching people about the Bábí Faith, and all throughout the rest of the country this message was spreading like wildfire. However, in the meanwhile the Báb had been arrested after His return from pilgrimage. What is more, He was removed from the followers and was placed in prison in Máh-Kú among the remote and lonely mountains of the far north."

"But if He was in prison, how did He teach the Bábís, and how did He lead them?" asked Ali.

"Through Bahá'u'lláh. You see, the Báb and Bahá'u'lláh were in continual correspondence, even though They never met in person."

"You mean They wrote letters to each other, or do you mean They communicated spiritually?"

"I'm not sure," admitted Nahid, "but I suspect that at least part of Their communication was spiritual. After all, Manifestations can do things that you and I cannot fully understand."

"What do you think they talked about?" asked Ali.

"Well, one of the most important things They decided was that the Bábís should have a special conference."

"A conference about what?" asked Ali.

"A conference to make an important announcement. You see, many followers of the Báb knew that He was a special person, a holy man. Some even believed He was a Prophet, but many, perhaps most, did not fully understand exactly what was the Báb's mission. Most still thought of themselves as Muslims, and they still practiced their old religion. They didn't yet understand that the Bábí Faith was not a plan to change Islám and make it better—the Báb had brought a completely new revelation from God.

"Somehow, the members of this new religion needed to hear this message, but they needed to hear it in some way that would make clear to the believers what being a Bábí meant."

"Why was this so important?" asked Ali.

"Because soon the leaders of Islám would begin to persecute them, and they would be forced to make terribly difficult choices."

"Whether or not to deny their beliefs?" said Ali. "Exactly," said Nahid. "Many would lose their jobs and homes. Some would even lose their lives because of following the Báb. They would be given a simple choice—to believe and suffer, or to recant their faith. So, before they faced such tests, the Báb knew it was important for them to know exactly Who He was and what He was teaching."

"They had to understand that He had brought a religion," offered Ali.

"Exactly," said Nahid. "But, of course, since the Báb was in prison, He could not arrange for such a meeting, so Bahá'u'lláh had to direct the conference Himself. But before Bahá'u'lláh could make plans for the conference, He had to complete a most secret mission."

"What sort of mission?" asked Ali.

"About this time in 1848 Ṭáhirih had been arrested for teaching others about the Báb. She was then kept as a prisoner in her hometown of Qazvín, a place not far from Ṭihrán. What was worse, she was in grave danger of being executed. Bahá'u'lláh quickly learned about her plight, and He worked out a plan to free her.

"Bahá'u'lláh sent one of the faithful believers to Qazvín with a message that explained the plan. First, the wife of this believer disguised herself as a beggar. She then secretly traveled to the house where Ṭáhirih was being kept and delivered to her the message from Bahá'u'lláh explaining the plans. That night Ṭáhirih joined the woman, who led her to where her husband was waiting, and the three of them carefully made their way that same night through the city and past the gates of Qazvín. Bahá'u'lláh had arranged for another servant to wait with horses outside the gates. The rest of that night they rode over secret paths and roadways until at last at daybreak they reached the city of Ṭihrán. Before long, they had arrived safely at the home of Bahá'u'lláh.

"For several days Ṭáhirih stayed there in safety and comfort, cherishing the presence of Bahá'u'lláh."

"Did she already suspect Bahá'u'lláh was also a Manifestation?" asked Ali.

"I feel certain she did," responded Nahid. "In fact, while she was there, a most interesting thing happened that seems to indicate she knew Who He was."

"Can you tell me about it?" asked Ali.

"One day Vaḥíd, the learned Letter of the Living, had come to Bahá'u'lláh's home to converse with some of the many believers who came in a constant stream to that sacred household. As was the custom for women then, Ṭáhirih sat behind a curtain while the men discussed matters of beliefs and theology. As she listened, she held on her lap Bahá'u'lláh's firstborn son, 'Abdu'l-Bahá, Who was only three or four at the time. She sat patiently as Vaḥíd spoke with his usual eloquence about the many signs which clearly indicated that this was the time for God to send another Prophet.

"Finally, Ṭáhirih could restrain herself no longer. With great emotion she interrupted the discourse and said from behind the veil, 'O Yaḥyá! Let deeds, not words, testify to thy faith, if thou art a man of true learning. Cease idly repeating the traditions of the past, for the day of service, of steadfast action, is come. Now is the time to show forth the true signs of God, to rend asunder the veils of idle fancy, to promote the Word of God, and to sacrifice ourselves in His path. Let deeds, not words, be our adorning!'"

Ali shook his head in amazement as he considered Ṭáhirih's wisdom and courage.

"Oh, she was a fearless woman, I can tell you," Nahid continued. "When she saw the truth, she followed it, and when she knew the answer, she spoke it. And, of course, we know how right she was, because before too long both she and Vaḥíd had to choose between giving up their lives or denying their beliefs. In fact, it is my opinion that these very qualities of fearlessness and forthrightness helped make her the one Bahá'u'lláh chose to play a central role at the conference."

"How did He do that?" asked Ali?

"First, Bahá'u'lláh sent Ṭáhirih ahead to the site of the meeting in the village of Badas͟ht, which is east of Ṭihrán on the border of Mázindarán. He Himself followed a few days later. Meanwhile, Bahá'u'lláh had sent word to Quddús that he, too, should proceed from Mas͟hhad to the meeting-place in Badas͟ht.

"It was summertime, and eighty-one Bábís were all the guests of Bahá'u'lláh as they gathered in this village where Bahá'u'lláh had rented three gardens."

"Why three?" asked Ali.

"Well, that was part of His special plan, you see. He had one for Himself, one for Ṭáhirih, and another for Quddús. But before I tell you why these three gardens were important, let me tell you something about the conference itself. The meeting lasted several weeks—twenty-two days, to be exact. And during this time the Bábís were told, little by little, what the meeting was all about. Each day Bahá'u'lláh would reveal a tablet, which one of the assembled believers would chant before the others. Then to every Bábí Bahá'u'lláh gave a new name, a name which honored each one because the name would usually be a title that symbolized some spiritual virtue or quality.

"In fact, it was at this meeting that Ṭáhirih, who until this time had been called Qurratu'l-'Ayn, or 'Solace of the Eyes,' received the name Ṭáhirih, which means 'the Pure One.'"

"Did Bahá'u'lláh also receive a new name?" asked Ali.

"Yes, He did. Instead of Mírzá Ḥusayn-'Alí, He was addressed as Jináb-i-Bahá. Later on He became known as Bahá'u'lláh. But in addition to the new names, other important things happened. Each day another law or tradition of their former religion, Islám, was broken or changed, because now they would have new laws which the Báb would reveal.

"Naturally this shocked many of the Bábís, who had all their lives faithfully abided by the laws and traditions of Islám. Indeed, most of them still thought of themselves as Muslims because only a few had come to realize the importance of the Báb and the new religion He had founded.

"For some of these people, the changes were too painful to bear, and they left the gathering. And even for those who remained, Bahá'u'lláh had planned a special event that would explain to them what it meant to be a Bábí. But this event would also test even the strongest followers among them."

Ali became excited as he wondered what sort of test Bahá'u'lláh might have devised.

"With Ṭáhirih and Quddús to assist Him, Bahá'u'lláh devised a sort of play, except that the other Bábís did not know it was going to be a play. For several days Ṭáhirih and Quddús pretended they were arguing."

"But why would they argue?" asked Ali, somewhat disturbed that two of the Letters of the Living should quarrel with one another. "What would they find to disagree on?"

"They only pretended to argue," explained Nahid. "You see, the believers were divided about what path they should take and about what they were really doing as Bábís. Some believed that the Báb was not starting a new religion, that He was simply trying to purify Islám. And so Quddús took their side, arguing that they should all be faithful to the laws of Muḥammad and not try to start a new religion."

"What did Ṭáhirih say to that?" asked Ali.

Nahid smiled. "Well, Ṭáhirih argued that this was a new Day with a new Prophet from God, a new Revelation which would have its own laws."

"So what did the other believers think when they heard these two Letters of the Living arguing with each other?" said Ali, pondering how he himself might have felt in such a situation.

"As the other Bábís listened, most took one side or the other, depending on which way they felt. So, as you can imagine, the discussions became more and more heated as the conference continued. But that is exactly what Bahá'u'lláh had planned."

"But what was the rest of the plan?" asked Ali.

"One morning Bahá'u'lláh sent word that He was feeling ill, and He remained in bed in the tent located in His garden. When Quddús heard this, he went to visit Bahá'u'lláh. He was taken into the tent, and he sat down at the right side of Bahá'u'lláh. Some other Bábís were also admitted, and they gathered around. As they talked, a messenger from Ṭáhirih appeared at the door of the tent and told Quddús that Ṭáhirih wanted him to come join her in her garden. Quddús looked sternly at the messenger and remained seated: 'I have severed myself entirely from her. I refuse to meet with her.'

"The believers who heard this became quite nervous. They became even more disturbed a few minutes later when her messenger returned and said to Quddús, 'She insists on your visit. If you persist in your refusal, she herself will come to you.'"

"Did Quddús go?" asked Ali.

"Quddús refused, and when he did, the messenger took out his sword and put it at the feet of Quddús. 'I refuse to go without you,' the messenger said. 'Either choose to accompany me to the presence of Ṭáhirih or cut off my head with this sword.'

"The Bábís could not believe what was happening before them. They stood frozen with fear and dismay, and Quddús seemed to appear sterner and more severe than ever. He looked at the messenger who was seated in front of him and then at the sword. 'I am willing to comply with the alternative which you have chosen to put before me,' said the messenger, and with that the messenger stretched forth his neck and Quddús reached for the sword.

"Suddenly, at that exact moment, the believers saw something that was so startling that it was as if a bolt of lightning had struck at their feet. Ṭáhirih herself appeared in the doorway, and she was unveiled, something totally unacceptable for a Persian woman of her position at that time. The violation of this basic law of Islám by someone they deemed to be the epitome of virtue horrified and stunned the Bábís. Even to gaze at the shadow of this most respected of all Bábí women was deemed improper—to see her unveiled was unthinkable!

"Some stood silent and gaped. Others became angry at this violation of such a fundamental tradition of Islám. One Bábí was so shocked that he took a knife, cut his own throat, and ran screaming from the tent. Several others turned away from her, then left the conference, and no longer considered themselves Bábís.

"Amid all this confusion, Ṭáhirih stepped forward toward Quddús and seated herself beside him. She was calm, even serene before Quddús, who still had the sword in his hand. The face of Quddús seemed filled with rage, and he made a motion as if he would strike her with the sword.

"In a moment she rose to her feet, and as she did, all the assembled believers became completely quiet. Her face shone with joy and resolve, and she spoke to the assembled Bábís. She said that this was a new Day and a new religion with new laws. She said that this was the very moment foretold in their own holy book, the Qur'án, when a bugle blast would signal the dawn of a new Day. She said emphatically that she was that bugle: 'I am the Word which the Qá'im is to utter,' she said, 'the Word which shall put to flight the chiefs and nobles of the earth!' She told the speechless Bábís to embrace each other in joy. She said they should one and all celebrate the beginning of this new era.

"Some were too shocked to do anything, but others were filled with great excitement because they now understood precisely how important their new religion was. But regardless of how each one responded to this announcement, none was ever the same again."

"But why?" asked Ali.

"Because," said Nahid, "like Ṭáhirih, the religion of the Báb had now removed its veil to all those who called themselves followers of the Báb. It was clear to each of them from that day forward that what God required of them was no less than to abandon everything they had come to accept, and to place their fortunes and their very lives in the hands of the Báb and His teachings.

"Then Quddús and Ṭáhirih weren't really fighting?"

"No," said Nahid. "They loved and respected each other completely, but guided by Bahá'u'lláh, they had helped the believers examine what it meant to accept this new religion.

"Of course, it was still a very tense situation with a great deal of confusion, because the play was not over. You see, the harsh exchange of words between them didn't end immediately, and these discussions caused a kind of division in the opinion of the believers. Some welcomed the drastic changes in the manner of their worship and in other habits associated with their former lives as Muslims. These believers saw Ṭáhirih as the representative for this view. Others thought that Quddús was the sole representative of the Báb and denounced Ṭáhirih's behavior as a radical violation of Islámic precepts.

"For a few days this kind of tension among the believers continued until, at last, Bahá'u'lláh stepped in and settled the matter once and for all. In the masterful way He did everything, He brought tranquility to the assembled believers and explained to them how they could best direct their efforts."

"I think it must have been very difficult for some of them to give up being Muslim," said Ali.

"You can be sure it was," said Nahid. "Perhaps that was the main purpose for which Bahá'u'lláh arranged the conference in the first place, to let them talk about these feelings, to let them express their concerns to one another, to help them face this radical change in their lives, and to show them that they could continue to love Muḥammad and the truth He had brought, but that they now had a new identity, a new name, and a new set of laws and teachings to follow."

"Is that why there were three gardens?" asked Ali.

"What do you mean?" asked Nahid, not quite sure what Ali was asking.

"Well, one garden, the garden of Quddús, represented the past and the religion of Islám. Ṭáhirih's garden represented the new religion, the Bábí Faith. The third garden, the garden where their questions were finally answered, that was Bahá'u'lláh's garden, the Bahá'í Faith."

Nahid looked at her husband with no small amount of astonishment. What a lovely idea her son had expressed, and it was an understanding of these events that had never occurred to her before. She now appreciated as never before what a special child she had and what a beautiful mind he possessed, something she would tell Husayn that evening after Ali was asleep.

"What a lovely thought," said Husayn to Ali. "In fact, what you say reminds me of a certain passage in *The Hidden Words* where Bahá'u'lláh says, 'Proclaim unto the children of assurance that within the realms of holiness, nigh unto the celestial paradise, a new garden hath appeared. . . .'"

"You're right!" said Nahid. "It makes perfect sense. Because when the believers did not understand what had happened, Bahá'u'lláh explained it to them afterwards."

"Is that the end of the story?" asked Ali.

"Almost," said Nahid. "When the confusion at last subsided, Bahá'u'lláh called for a copy of the Qur'án to be brought to Him. He directed one of the believers to read from the fifty-sixth Súrih."

"What does it say?" asked Ali.

"It is a passage that tells what will happen as the trumpet sounds on the day of judgment. The verses say that some will understand but others will not. It states that for those who understand and follow the trumpet call, there will be great glory!"

Nahid paused. Without even realizing it, the three had nearly arrived at 'Akká, and they could see before them the dome of the Mosque of Jazzár Páshá in the middle of the town.

"Then Bahá'u'lláh really was a leader of the Bábí religion as well as the leader of the Bahá'í Faith," said Ali.

"That is true, but you see both religions are really two parts of one religion," said Husayn. "That is why we say that the Bahá'í Faith began in 1844 when the Báb declared to Mullá Ḥusayn that He was the Qá'im. It is very important that we understand how these two Prophets lived on earth at the same time and worked together to change the course of human history. That is why Bahá'u'lláh worked to teach the cause of the Báb, even after the Báb had been killed and even after Bahá'u'lláh had begun to receive His own revelation."

"Isn't it strange," said Ali, almost to himself, as he looked out across the many houses of 'Akká and the Mosque of Jazzár Páshá, "so many people still have not heard the call of that trumpet."

As they walked the remaining distance, he thought again about his dream. He remembered vividly his feelings of frustration as he stood in front of the noisy crowd, trying so hard to tell them what each of them would surely want dearly to understand. "There must be a way," he thought to himself, "and I will find it."

4

The Road to Shaykh Ṭabarsí

There was sometimes a sadness in the faces of the older Bahá'ís, or so it seemed to Ali. As a child he had always assumed that all older people had such a look in their eyes. But in the last year or so, Ali had noticed that many of the old men of 'Akká who weren't Bahá'ís had no such look. In their eyes he could see many things—pain, grief, sometimes kindliness, but it was not the same, not at all the same.

His grandmother had told him the year before she died that a person's eyes are windows to the soul. Then Ali would blush when she would say that Ali must have a beautiful soul because he had such large, clear, lovely eyes.

Several days after the trip to the Shrine of Bahá'u'lláh, Ali sat on the seawall one afternoon, watching the fishermen prepare their nets. He thought again about his dream—it was rarely far from his thoughts. He wondered if the mysterious look he saw in the eyes of the elderly Bahá'ís had something to do with understanding the life of Bahá'u'lláh. Perhaps if he could understand the depth and sadness in those aged eyes, he might also begin to understand what made the life of Bahá'u'lláh so special.

On the way back from the visit to the shrine, when his mother had told him about the conference of Badasht, Ali had begun to understand how hard it was for the early Bábís to change from their inherited religion of Islám to a completely new religion, the Bábí Faith. Perhaps that difficult change was somehow responsible for the look he saw.

But Ali also remembered nights when he was supposed to be asleep, and his mother and father and grandfather were talking in the next room about the difficulties of the Bahá'ís who lived in Persia. Ali had never really understood exactly what these problems were, and for some reason he was afraid to ask, as if these were matters that only the adults should discuss. But now he decided he must ask.

That evening at dinner as Ali sat in front of the simple pilau his mother had prepared, he stared blankly ahead instead of attacking his food, as was his custom. The mixture of steamed rice, raisins, meat, and spices was usually his favorite dish, and his mother immediately knew that something was wrong with her son.

"Are you feeling ill?" she asked.

Ali was embarrassed by her question. "No, no," he said. "I'm fine." And he quickly began to eat. Then he stopped again, put down his spoon, looked up, and began to tell his mother and father as best he could what he had noticed about the look in the eyes of the older Bahá'ís.

"I look into their eyes, into Grandfather's eyes, for example, and it's as if there is something they know that no one else knows, perhaps something they have seen or felt. It's like a missing piece of a puzzle to me, but I don't really know why."

"You think this missing piece will help you understand the life of Bahá'u'lláh? Is that part of the reason for your interest?" asked Husayn.

"I don't know, Father. Do you think it would?"

Husayn looked across the table at Nahid. They both sensed what Ali meant about the eyes of the older friends, but they did not know exactly how to respond to his question. Finally, Husayn spoke. "Ali, you have learned much about the history of the Bahá'í Faith from us and from your other Bahá'í teachers. As you know, the early believers suffered a great deal because of their beliefs."

"I still remember the first time you told me about the battle at Fort Shaykh Ṭabarsí," said Ali.

"Well, you were very young then. Possibly you thought these were just interesting stories, things that happened many, many years ago. But perhaps it's time you understood a little more about that time. You see, the people who were at Ṭabarsí and at the other places where the Bahá'ís were attacked were real people. And the sons and daughters and grandchildren of those heroic souls, even some of those early believers themselves, are among the Bahá'ís living here in 'Akká now."

Husayn stopped himself. "But this isn't the best time to talk about such things. I'll tell you what; in a few days I think I can help you understand. Is that all right with you?"

"Oh, yes!" said Ali, eagerly anticipating a special day with his father. Ali finished his pilau, and the conversation then changed to how Husayn's shop was doing and what news there was of 'Abdu'l-Bahá's journey to Europe and America.

Three days later, Ali began to worry that his father might have forgotten his promise, but that same evening, a few hours before bedtime, Husayn came quietly into the room where Ali was playing sticks. It was a simple game that Ali had made up himself. He would stack a handful of twigs on the floor. Then he would try to move each stick, one by one, without disturbing the others until only three or four sticks remained standing.

For a few moments Husayn watched Ali without saying a word. He marveled at how rapidly his young son was growing up, how his little boy was quickly becoming a young man. And though there was something sad about watching the child in Ali disappear, the fine and noble qualities that had developed were also beginning to show, and that made Husayn excited about what lay ahead for the lad.

Startled by his father's presence, Ali turned around, knocking over the stick pile and springing to his feet.

"So, what are you doing tomorrow, my young man?" said Husayn.

"Nothing in particular."

"You remember your question the other night at dinner—about the look in the eyes of the elderly believers?"

"Yes."

"How would you feel about going with me at dawn to the beach and we'll talk about your questions?"

"Oh, yes!" said Ali anxiously.

"Fine. Then let's get to bed early tonight so you won't grumble when I wake you in the morning. We shall have dawn prayers by the beach, and then we will spend as much time as you like talking."

Ali thanked his father several time, then quickly got ready for bed, even though it was an hour earlier than his usual bedtime.

That night he slept soundly in spite of his excitement, and he dreamed about the beach. He dreamed that he and his father were fishing in the surf with nets. In the dream, he watched his father toss the net with expert skill so that it opened into a large circle before it hit the water and sank beneath the calm surface of the water. Then he helped his father pull the net to the shore to see what they had caught. There were three small fish and one large fish with eyes that were big and brown like those of a human being. The fish looked at Ali, and its mouth seemed to curl at the corners as if it were smiling. Ali at once dropped the net, more amazed than frightened. "Don't let go!" his father shouted. "That's the very fish we've been looking for!"

But before Ali could discover more about the fish, he became aware that his father was gently shaking him awake. "It's time," he whispered.

As soon as Ali realized that this was the morning he would spend with his father, he jumped out of bed, washed his face, and put on some fresh clothes. He quickly sipped a cup of tea which his father had prepared, and both ate some bread and cheese.

It was still dark when the two passed through the land gate and walked by the wharves toward the beach. The city itself was mostly quiet, except for an occasional dog barking, or across the fields a distant rooster heralding the morning. A gentle mist hung over the ancient town and the fishermen were already setting out to sea.

The father and son spoke little as they walked. Husayn liked to have a quiet time in the morning before his prayers, and Ali was still not completely awake. Soon they were far from the city along the half-moon-shaped beach which curved around toward Haifa and Mount Carmel. They could see 'Akká silhouetted against the morning sky, and the city sounds were now faint and distant.

Husayn found a smooth plot of ground several yards away from the beach, and there he unfolded an old bedspread, which they used as a ground cloth. Ali placed the basket of food for their lunch on one side, then both of them removed their shoes and knelt on the cloth in the direction of Bahjí. Husayn chanted a long prayer, then Ali chanted a shorter one that his grandfather had taught him.

After a few moments of silence, Ali stretched out on his side to make himself comfortable, and Husayn turned to him, his legs still crossed and his face serious but not stern. Husayn looked at his bright young son and wondered how he could help Ali understand the sacrifices, the pain, and the suffering of the early believers, and also help him appreciate the ultimate beauty of these noble deeds and the strangely joyous spirit with which so many believers had faced terrifying circumstances and even death itself.

"Tell me, Ali," he began, "would you say that look in the eyes of the older believers is a sad look or a happy one?"

Ali thought for a moment, but he could not decide. "It's neither, really. Or it's both, somehow."

"Yes, I suppose it is both. You see, the early period of our religion was a time of indescribable joy and eagerness, but that spiritual energy and that wonderment of discovery was often blended with sadness and untold hardship. You already know a little about the battle at Fort Shaykh Ṭabarsí."

"I know that many were killed there."

"Well, Ali, the story of Ṭabarsí is really only one example of the heroism and the persecution that occurred during that time. And though some of the stories you have heard may seem as if they happened in some distant land long, long ago, these things really happened, and they happened to the families and friends of many Bahá'ís you know or have met." Husayn uncrossed his legs and looked out across the bay toward Mount Carmel, as if he were seeking some sort of inspiration or divine assistance.

"Let me see if I can explain it more clearly. You remember that we were talking the other day about the conference at Badasht."

"Yes," said Ali.

"Well, immediately after the conference at Badas͟ht in the summer of 1848, there seemed to arise throughout Persia a fire of hatred against the Bábís."

"But why?" asked Ali. "What did the Bábís do to cause such feelings?"

"The hatred resulted from the anger and jealousy people feel whenever a new Manifestation appears. You see, just as many of the believers assembled at Badas͟ht were troubled by the idea of giving up their old ways and beliefs, so the people in villages where the faith spread saw the rapid growth of the new religion as a threat to their own beliefs. And the more rapidly the religion spread, the more it threatened those who did not believe. Soon that fire of hatred raged and spread throughout the land of Persia. That fire was meant to consume the young Faith of the Báb, but you and I know that in the end it served only to ignite the hearts of the Bábís. And instead of destroying the young religion, that same fire tested the believers, made them strong, and cleansed away the bramble of superstitions and worn-out traditions in the hearts of the Bábís. Because of this fire, they became ready to face whatever obstacles were before them."

Husayn paused, took a deep breath, and sighed as if he were gathering the strength to face some ordeal himself. "Ali, I could never tell you all that happened during that time, all the people who suffered. Some of it is too painful for you to bear right now, and I don't know all the stories myself. But I can tell you enough. I can tell you some of the things that happened. You need to know something about those times, enough at least to understand that look you observe on the faces of the older believers. Also, it is important for you to know about the heroes of this religion, because, you see, these early heroes laid the foundations for our Faith. They made it possible for Bahá'ís here in 'Akká and throughout the world to know about Bahá'u'lláh and to become changed through His teachings."

"How did it all get started?" asked Ali.

"As soon as large numbers of people from several different villages and towns became Bábís, the Muslim leaders of those places became extremely angry. And in the town of Sárí, Quddús was placed under arrest for teaching others about the Báb. Well, when the Báb heard of this, He sent word to Mullá Ḥusayn telling him to go rescue Quddús. But that was not all the message said. The Báb sent His very own green turban."

"Why was the Báb's turban green?" asked Ali.

"A green turban is worn by those who are siyyids, those who are descended from Muḥammad. It is a symbol of great honor. In the message, the Báb told Mullá Ḥusayn, 'Adorn your head with My green turban, the emblem of My lineage, and, with the Black Standard unfurled before you, hasten to the Verdant Isle, and lend your assistance to My beloved Quddús.'"

"Why a *black* banner, Father?"

"Because the Prophet Muḥammad had said, 'Should your eyes behold the Black Standards proceeding from Khurásán, hasten ye toward them, even though ye should have to crawl over the snow, inasmuch as they proclaim the advent of the Promised Mihdí, the Vicegerent of God.' So, you see, this was the fulfillment of a prophecy, a sign to the Muslims that the new Manifestation had come."

"Did anybody follow them?"

"Yes, indeed they did!" said Husayn. "Many followed Mullá Ḥusayn and his men. In the autumn of 1848, a month after the conference of Badasht, Mullá Ḥusayn left with 202 men, and as they went westward toward the town of Sárí, many others joined them in the villages they passed through along the way.

"Then they came to a crossroads where Mullá Ḥusayn said they must camp and wait."

"But why?" asked Ali. "What was he waiting for?"

"Mullá Ḥusayn was waiting for a sign from God to tell him when they should begin the rest of their journey. 'We stand at the parting of the ways,' he told his men. 'We shall await His decree as to which direction we should take.'"

"In a few days, a great storm arose. Suddenly a fierce wind tore a large branch from a nearby tree. Mullá Ḥusayn saw the limb fall, and he told them this was the sign. 'The tree of the sovereignty of Muḥammad Sháh has, by the will of God, been uprooted and hurled to the ground,' Mullá Ḥusayn told them."

"What did he mean by that?" asked Ali.

"No one was exactly sure until three days later when a messenger brought news that the Sháh had died.

"On the following day, Mullá Ḥusayn gathered his men and told them, 'This is the way that leads to our martyrdom. Whoever is unprepared, let him return home now. I, together with seventy-two of my companions, shall suffer death for the sake of the Báb. Whosoever is unable to renounce the world, let him at this very moment depart, for later on he will be unable to escape.'

"He warned them several more times because he wanted to make sure they understood that death was almost certain for all those who went with him."

"Did any leave?" asked Ali, wondering if he would have had the courage to follow Mullá Ḥusayn.

"Twenty men chose to return."

"Do you think they were cowards?" asked Ali.

Husayn smiled at his son and placed his hand on the boy's knee. "Were you wondering if you would have stayed?"

"Yes."

"I wonder the same thing myself. I guess none of us knows what courage is until the moment when it is tested. So let us not try to judge those who left. Instead, let us consider those who stayed, the ones who went with Mullá Ḥusayn. Those we can judge more easily, I suspect."

"They were very brave," said Ali.

"They had faith, conviction," said Husayn. "They knew they would be assisted by the hosts of heaven and emboldened by the Holy Spirit. So they picked up the few belongings they had with them, broke camp, and set out for the town of Sárí to free Quddús.

"On the way, they reached the town of Bárfurúsh, a place where the religious leaders were already full of anger and hatred for the Bábís."

"Why?" asked Ali.

"Because Quddús had already been through the town and had taught the people about the Báb. As many as three hundred people in the village had become Bábís in one week, so the religious leader of Bárfurúsh called the people of the town together for a meeting. With angry gestures and harsh words he told the people they should attack Mullá Ḥusayn and his men at dawn and kill them.

"The townspeople listened intently, and the more he spoke, the angrier they became. Finally, they agreed with him because he had convinced them the Bábís were enemies of the religion of Islám."

"But they weren't, were they?" asked Ali.

"Certainly not. The Báb and Bahá'u'lláh both had great love and praise for the Prophet Muḥammad, but the townspeople did not know that. In fact, they believed, as many Muslims still do, that to attack the Bábís would be a sign of their devotion to God.

"The next morning, Mullá Ḥusayn told his men to cast away all their belongings except for their swords and horses. Mullá Ḥusayn thought that by doing this he could convince the townspeople that the Bábís had no desire for property or possessions and that the people of Bárfurúsh would not quarrel with them or start a fight.

"But as the Bábís marched toward Bárfurúsh, Mullá Ḥusayn and his men were stopped by the angry citizens. As the townspeople approached, some of the Bábís took out their swords to defend themselves, but Mullá Ḥusayn quickly made the Bábís sheathe their swords. He told them not to fight unless they were sure there was no other choice, unless they had to defend their lives."

"But were the people coming to hurt them?" asked Ali.

"Mullá Ḥusayn wanted the townspeople to have every chance to see that the Bábís wanted no trouble, that the Bábís were people of peace and students of religion, not soldiers. He wanted them to see that all the Bábís desired was to pass by peacefully on the road to Sárí."

"Then why did the Bábís have swords?" asked Ali.

"In that time it was customary for men to carry swords—it did not mean that they intended to hurt anyone. So the townspeople continued to move toward the Bábís. Then without warning the citizens shouldered their muskets and opened fire on the unsuspecting Bábís. Six Bábís immediately fell dead."

"Did the Bábís fight then?" asked Ali.

"No," said Husayn. "They obeyed Mullá Ḥusayn. They did not reach for their swords, but looked anxiously at Mullá Ḥusayn to see what they should do. Mullá Ḥusayn did not move. He sat patiently, almost motionless on his steed."

"Is that when Riḍá was killed?"

"Yes, Ali. Mullá Ḥusayn's dearest friend, Siyyid Riḍá, was struck in the chest as he stood beside Mullá Ḥusayn. Now the Bábí leader could restrain himself no longer. He shouted, 'Behold, O God, my God, the plight of Thy chosen companions, and witness the welcome which these people have accorded Thy loved ones. Thou knowest that we cherish no other desire than to guide them to the way of Truth!' Then he drew his sword, spurred his horse into full gallop, and led his men in an attack on those who were firing at them.

"As he charged forward, Mullá Ḥusayn spied the man who had shot Riḍá. The wretched villain was hiding behind a tree, holding his musket before him as protection. Mullá Ḥusayn quickly guided the horse toward the coward, raising his sword up high as he approached. Then, with one mighty stroke, he sliced through the tree, the musket, and even the man himself!

"The villagers were shocked and amazed! Never had they seen such power! Never had they even heard of such a feat! In an instant they became terrified and immediately fled from the battle, crying, 'Peace! Peace!'

"But Mullá Ḥusayn did not stop. He dashed away from his companions and rode toward the town of Bárfurú<u>sh</u>. Within minutes he was in front of the house of the religious leader who had told the people to attack. Mullá Ḥusayn demanded in a powerful voice that the man come out of the house, but the frightened leader would not. Moments later, Mullá Ḥusayn's men came riding into the town, and as they entered, they shouted out the battle cry, *'Yá Ṣáḥibu'z-Zamán!'*—'Oh Thou, the Lord of the Age!'. This tumultuous cry struck terror into the hearts of the townspeople. But when the Bábís saw that their leader was unharmed, they halted their steeds.

"Mullá Ḥusayn rode before the gathering of townspeople. He looked sternly at the bewildered mob, then asked, 'Why have you risen against us?

Why deem the shedding of our blood an act meritorious in the sight of God? Did we ever repudiate the truth of your Faith? Is this the hospitality which the Apostle of God has enjoined His followers to accord to both the faithful and the infidel?'"

"What did the people say?" asked Ali.

"The people said nothing. No doubt some sensed these words were true, but they were still determined to do what their leader told them. So, when the people would neither respond to the questions nor try to understand what Mullá Ḥusayn was saying, the band of Bábís left the village and proceeded to a caravansary to spend the night."

"But why didn't Mullá Ḥusayn and his men take over the town or make prisoners of the people?" asked Ali. "Wouldn't that have stopped any more trouble?"

"That is against the laws of the Báb, Ali. It is against our own law. You cannot stop evil by becoming evil, and it would be wrong to attack these people, just as it was wrong for the people to attack the Bábís. After all, the Bábís were trying to show the people that they were not soldiers, that they intended no harm to these confused citizens.

"But, of course, the religious leader of the town would not let things be. That evening he once again plotted how he might get rid of the Bábís. However, Mullá Ḥusayn discovered his intentions, and so when the time came for the call to evening prayer, he told his followers that whoever climbed the roof to make the call would be giving up his life for his beliefs.

"Without any hesitation, one brave young Bábí climbed to the roof and began the chant. Before he could finish, a bullet struck him and killed him instantly. At once the Bábís looked to Mullá Ḥusayn for guidance. He asked for another Bábí to sound the call to prayer. A second Bábí eagerly volunteered. He climbed to the roof, began the call, but managed only a few words before he, too, was shot and killed.

"The Bábís were now enraged at the senseless slaughter of their companions. But Mullá Ḥusayn told them they must give the townspeople one last chance. He asked for yet another youth to ascend the roof, but almost instantly this faithful believer was also shot and killed.

"Mullá Ḥusayn immediately threw open the doors of the caravansary. With his men beside him he shouted, 'Mount your steeds, O heroes of God!' The young followers immediately did as he commanded, and together they rushed toward the people from Bárfurú<u>sh</u> who had come to kill them. With their swords drawn the Bábís shouted their battle cry, 'O Thou, the Lord of the Age!'

"Spurred on by the sorrow and anger they felt at having watched their three young companions be slaughtered for merely trying to say a prayer, the Bábís fought more fiercely than before.

"Within a few short minutes the townspeople were screaming and running among the trees for safety. They could not comprehend the incredible ferocity and valor of these young students. Yet again the townspeople were forced to withdraw to the town and hide themselves for the night.

"Mullá Ḥusayn now knew that the townspeople would not leave them alone and that the Bábís must find a place where they could defend themselves."

"But what could they do?" asked Ali.

"The next morning at daybreak they set out on horseback, though the townspeople from Bárfurú<u>sh</u> stayed behind them and harassed them as they traveled. When they had gone about fourteen miles from Bárfurú<u>sh</u>, they stopped beside a Muslim holy shrine, the Shrine of <u>Sh</u>ay<u>kh</u> Ṭabarsí. Mullá Ḥusayn knew they could go no further without defending themselves, that they must make a stand.

"When he saw the small building of the shrine in the midst of a grassy field, he decided that this holy shrine would be as good a place as any to build a temporary fort.

"He told his men to dismount, and he went to greet the caretaker of the building. When the caretaker saw Mullá Ḥusayn, he was unable to believe his eyes! He had seen that very same face in a dream only the night before!"

As soon as Ali heard his father mention the dream, he immediately became excited. "What was the dream, Father? Can you tell me?"

"Indeed I can. In fact, the caretaker immediately began to tell the dream to Mullá Ḥusayn. In his dream he had seen a band of seventy-two men fight heroic battles. Then, one night during those battles, the Prophet of God had Himself arrived to join the company.

"When the caretaker had finished describing his dream, Mullá Ḥusayn smiled and told him, 'All that you have witnessed will come to pass.' Then Mullá Ḥusayn immediately set his men to work preparing the area around the shrine so that the Bábís could defend themselves.

"That was on the twelfth day of October, 1848. Mullá Ḥusayn divided the 313 Bábís into groups, and he gave each group a special task to carry out. For example, Mírzá Muḥammad Báqir planned how the fort would be built. He decided it should be from sixty to eighty paces wide, a sort of circular wall surrounding the building of the shrine. One group worked on building that massive wall. Another group dug the wells to supply them with the water they would need. Every single Bábí had a job to do while there was still time.

"Because of all this unusual activity, many villagers soon came to see what was going on. Each day the fortress became larger and more elaborate. From time to time a few of the villagers would attack them to try to prevent them from constructing the fort, but the Bábís would always mount their horses and chase them off.

"Well, about the time that the fort was finished, a messenger brought the news to Mullá Ḥusayn that Bahá'u'lláh would join them that very night, so Mullá Ḥusayn ordered his men to make the fort ready for this noble visitor. When Bahá'u'lláh arrived that evening, Mullá Ḥusayn welcomed Him with the utmost love, respect, and adoration.

"Naturally he told Bahá'u'lláh everything that had happened to them and what they had accomplished at the fort."

"Did Bahá'u'lláh stay with them?" asked Ali.

"Not for long. He inspected the fort and congratulated the Bábís on the fine job they had done. Then He told Mullá Ḥusayn that they had one thing left to do before they would be ready for what was going to happen. 'The one thing this fort and company require,' He told him, 'is the presence of Quddús. His association with this company would render it complete and perfect.' He went on to tell Mullá Ḥusayn to send seven men to Sárí to demand the release of Quddús.

"Mullá Husayn assured Bahá'u'lláh he would do exactly as Bahá'u'lláh had suggested. Then, before He left, Bahá'u'lláh gathered the entire company of Bábís together. He told them He would try His best to get back to the fort to be with them. 'If it be His will,' He said, 'We shall once again visit you at this same spot, and shall lend you Our assistance. You have been chosen of God to be the vanguard of His host and the establishers of His Faith. His host verily will conquer. Whatever may befall, victory is yours, a victory which is complete and certain.'

"After Bahá'u'lláh had encouraged them, He set out for His home in Ṭihrán, and things proceeded as planned. Mullá Ḥusayn sent men to Sárí to free Quddús. This was important because Quddús was their leader."

"But I thought Mullá Ḥusayn was the leader," said Ali.

"Mullá Ḥusayn led them in battle, but the Báb had indicated that Quddús was special—that's why he was chosen to go on pilgrimage with the Báb."

"Does that mean Quddús was a Prophet?" asked Ali.

"Bahá'u'lláh later indicated that Quddús had a lofty spiritual station, that he was second only to the Báb Himself, and Mullá Ḥusayn and the others were well aware of Quddús's lofty position. Consequently, when the Bábís returned with Quddús to the fort, he was welcomed with utmost respect.

"Quddús was very impressed with what had been done. The fort had walls ten meters high, made mostly of stone, with great logs on top. Wells had been dug to provide fresh water. Even a storehouse for food had been built. After he had inspected every part of the fort, he praised his companions for all that they had accomplished." Husayn stopped his story for a moment and sketched a circle in the sand to show Ali how the walls of the fort were arranged and how the main building, the shrine, was in the middle.

"Didn't the people in Bárfurúsh try to stop them from building the fort?" asked Ali.

"Oh yes," said Husayn. "The religious leader of the village even wrote to the king himself, Náṣiri'd-Dín Sháh, who had just replaced his father on the throne. In this message the jealous leader described the fort in detail and said that the Bábís were a threat to the whole country of Persia.

"When the Sháh learned of this he immediately sent word to his military officers in Mázindarán to stop the Bábís. He told them to kill the Bábís if necessary. Of course, the officers knew that the followers of the Báb were mostly frail students, not trained soldiers like themselves, so they were not really worried. They were sure they could defeat that insignificant band of students in an hour or so.

"Before too long the military leader 'Abdu'lláh Khán prepared his army of 12,000 to assault the fort. Before attacking, however, they managed to stop the daily supply of food from being taken to the fort. The Bábís soon became worried—not only was their food getting scarce, the wells had dried up, and their water was almost gone.

"Quddús tried to keep their spirits up. In the morning and afternoon he would summon Mullá Ḥusayn and the others together, and they would chant the writings of the Báb. When the water became quite scarce, Quddús told the men not to worry, that a rainstorm would come that very night and bring them all the water they needed."

"And was he right? Did it rain?" asked Ali.

"Yes," said Husayn, smiling. "It rained so hard that much of the ammunition of the Sháh's army was ruined. Then the next night it snowed. In fact, it snowed so hard the huge army outside the fort was quite cold and miserable.

"The following night Quddús told the Bábís to make ready for the attack the next morning so they could take advantage of what the weather had done to the encamped army. And sure enough, early the next morning at two hours after sunrise, Mullá Ḥusayn, Quddús, and the other Bábís charged out of the fort shouting, 'O Thou, the Lord of the Age!'

"Well, as you might imagine, the surprised army of 'Abdu'lláh Khán was absolutely terrified, and within only forty-five minutes the Bábís had scattered the large army into the surrounding woods. In fact, that small band of Bábís had killed 430 soldiers as well as 'Abdu'llah Khán himself before Quddús gave the command for the battle to cease and ordered the Bábís to return to the fort. 'We need not carry further the punishment,' he said. 'Our purpose is to protect ourselves, that we may be able to continue our labors for the regeneration of men.'"

"Did the army go away then?" asked Ali.

"No, not at all. They were extremely embarrassed and quite angry. So during the next days they began to reassemble the forces and repair their equipment."

"And what about the Bábís? What did they do?"

"They busied themselves digging a great trench around the entire fort. Day and night they worked for nineteen days until it was finished. In the meantime Quddús sent word to Prince Míhdí-Qulí Mírzá that the Bábís wished to harm no one, that they only wanted to tell people about the Promised Qá'im. He said the Bábís could prove that the Qá'im had come at last.

"But the prince did not care to listen to such claims. Instead, three days later he assembled his army, a much larger one than before. With three regiments of infantry and several regiments of cavalry he marched to the fort. When he got there, his troops began to open fire in hopes of frightening the Bábís so that he could attack them in force the next day. But Quddús had planned a surprise for the government soldiers.

"Just before daybreak the next day, Quddús ordered the Bábís to open the gates to the fort. Then he and Mullá Ḥusayn, together with two hundred other Bábís, sallied out swiftly in the morning darkness toward where the unsuspecting army was camped. The Bábís paid no heed to the mud and snow along the roads, nor did they seem concerned that they were running toward great numbers of well-trained soldiers.

"As they charged the sleeping soldiers, they once again shouted at the top of their voices, 'O Thou, the Lord of the Age!'

"You can imagine how the soldiers were completely startled and amazed at the courage and daring of these ill-equipped, vastly outnumbered Bábís. Some managed to fire their rifles, but nothing slowed the ferocious charge of the Bábís, and the army was so confused by the attack that it quickly retreated.

"Even the prince himself managed to escape only by climbing barefoot through a back window of the building that served as his headquarters."

"Was that the end of the troubles for the Bábís?" asked Ali, smiling contentedly at such a happy ending.

"I'm afraid not," said his father with a serious look. "The army scattered, but soon it began to reassemble and a number of soldiers on horseback began to charge. To his horror, Mullá Ḥusayn saw a host of enemy cavalry heading for Quddús. Mullá Ḥusayn tried to rescue Quddús, but the soldiers opened fire, and Quddús fell when one of the bullets struck him in the mouth."

"Did it kill him?" asked Ali anxiously.

"No, but when Mullá Ḥusayn rushed to his leader's side and saw the injury to Quddús, he became so angry that he took Quddús's sword in one hand and the sword he had taken from the fleeing prince in the other. Single-handed, Mullá Ḥusayn rushed toward the surrounding soldiers and so terrified the startled troops that they once again scattered in terror.

"The other Bábís were so heartened by Mullá Ḥusayn's bold actions that they rallied around him, and within about half an hour the entire army fled. Once more the small band of Bábís had defeated a multitude of trained soldiers."

"But what about Bahá'u'lláh?" asked Ali. "Did He return to the fort as He said He would?"

"As a matter of fact, it was about this same time in early December that Bahá'u'lláh set off from Ṭihrán and traveled toward the fort to join His fellow Bábís. He took with Him His younger half-brother Mírzá Yaḥyá and several others, and they traveled over the rough mountain path from the area of Núr in Mázindarán toward the fort, hoping to reach it that very night. Bahá'u'lláh knew that in the daylight they would be arrested by the soldiers who were trying to prevent help from any other Bábís from reaching the surrounded fort.

"But it was a most difficult journey, and Bahá'u'lláh knew that the small group could not afford to rest along the way because it would be too dangerous. Any minute they might encounter a suspicious official who would try to stop them. But toward the end of the day, Bahá'u'lláh's companions became quite tired, and they begged Him to stop so that they could rest.

"Finally, when they persisted in asking for a few hours of rest, Bahá'u'lláh agreed to halt at a lonely roadhouse. There they ate a brief meal, and everyone slept, except Bahá'u'lláh. He was well aware of the danger around them, and He chose to remain on watch.

"Sure enough, one of the local villagers warned some nearby guards that a group of Bábís was passing through. Soon after the others had fallen asleep, these same soldiers came to arrest them. 'We have received strict orders,' they told Bahá'u'lláh, 'to arrest every person we chance to meet in this vicinity, and are commanded to conduct him, without any previous investigation, to Ámul and deliver him into the hands of its governor.'

"Bahá'u'lláh calmly agreed to the officer's command, but then He said something that the solider thought quite strange. He gave him a warning, saying, 'I would advise you to act in a manner that will cause you eventually no regret.'

"Bahá'u'lláh and His companions then mounted their horses and followed the soldiers to the village of Ámul. As they traveled, Bahá'u'lláh secretly told the others to cast into the river whatever writings of the Báb they had in their possession. By daybreak they had arrived in Ámul and were met there by the acting governor. A messenger had already told him that Bábí prisoners were arriving. But when he saw Bahá'u'lláh, Whom he knew and respected, he was quite shocked and decided he would try to set Him free.

"A meeting was called with the local 'ulamás, who wanted to question the Bábís. With quiet dignity, Bahá'u'lláh warned the leaders to be careful in their treatment of Him and His companions. The governor, out of respect for Bahá'u'lláh, tried to calm the angry 'ulamás, but they were very jealous of the Bábís. When they discovered a manuscript on a companion of Bahá'u'lláh, the chief of the religious leaders looked at the writing and said that this must be one of the ignorantly written tablets of the Báb.

"To the utter dismay and embarrassment of this same figure, Bahá'u'lláh calmly told him that the tablet was not written by the Báb but was a passage from the writings of the Imám 'Alí, Muḥammad's chosen successor. When the religious leader realized his foolish mistake, he became furious and decided to punish Bahá'u'lláh and His companions with the bastinado."

"What is that?" asked Ali.

"A form of torture, Ali. The prisoner's shoes are removed, and iron rods are used to beat the soles of his feet. It is terribly painful and does a great deal of damage, so much so that if it is done more than a few times, the prisoner will never walk again."

"And they did this to Bahá'u'lláh and His companions?"

"Only to Bahá'u'lláh. You see, Bahá'u'lláh persuaded the acting governor not to punish His companions and offered Himself as their victim instead. And *so,* like the Báb five months before in Tabríz, Bahá'u'lláh was interrogated and beaten.

"When they were finished with the bastinado, Bahá'u'lláh was threatened by an angry mob of townspeople who had gathered to see the punishment of this One Whom they believed to be an enemy of their religion. But the acting governor stepped in to prevent them and personally conducted Bahá'u'lláh to his own house. He apologized profusely to this noble guest for the behavior of the religious leaders and the ignorant townspeople of Ámul. 'I am far from regarding you a prisoner in my home,' he told Bahá'u'lláh. 'This house, I believe, was built for the very purpose of affording you a shelter from the designs of your foes."

"For several days he kept Bahá'u'lláh safe in his home, until one night the governor himself returned. When he learned what had happened, he bitterly denounced the people of Ámul. You see, he had just returned from Fort Ṭabarsí, where he had personally witnessed the bravery and courage of the Bábís, so his opinion of them had completely changed. Humbly the governor went to Bahá'u'lláh, begged for His pardon, and praised the valor of Mullá Ḥusayn and the other defenders of the fort. A few days later, the governor arranged for the safe departure of Bahá'u'lláh and His companions for Ṭihrán."

"So Bahá'u'lláh wasn't able to get to the fort?"

"No, Ali. Perhaps God was protecting Him so that He could render an even greater service later on. Bahá'u'lláh's life was spared then and several other times as well.

"Of course, Bahá'u'lláh Himself was never worried about His personal safety. He knew that nothing would interfere with the plan of God. He even told His followers that if He were killed, they should not worry, because God would send someone else to do His work."

Ali looked up at his father, then out toward the sea. Husayn reached over and cupped his hand around Ali's neck affectionately. "After lunch, my son, you can learn about the rest of the battle at Fort Shaykh Ṭabarsí. For now, let us stretch our legs, breathe in the salt air, and eat some of the bread and cheese Mother purchased from your uncle's shop."

5

The Cleansing Fire

When Ali had finished eating the fresh bread and several pieces of cheese, he was so thirsty that the cool water in the leather container seemed wonderfully refreshing. His father continued to eat for awhile, so Ali walked toward the beach to skim some flat shells across the incoming surf. Husayn soon finished and went for a brief stroll up the beach.

When Husayn returned from his walk, Ali was chasing some gulls that made a raucous noise as if the young boy had no right to be on their beach. Husayn smiled to see Ali so carefree, so cheerful, so full of life. Husayn loved his son very much, and he felt grateful for special days they had together like this.

For a moment Husayn pondered what conversations might have taken place between Bahá'u'lláh and His eldest son, 'Abdu'l-Bahá. He considered how fortunate They both had been to share each other's company throughout all the difficulties They faced. Husayn recalled one of the tablets Bahá'u'lláh had written in honor of 'Abdu'l-Bahá. As he watched Ali and considered the purity of his young son's heart and mind, Husayn felt he was beginning to understand how mighty that bond was between the Prophet of God, pursuing that loneliest task of trying to change human hearts, and the one soul on earth Who understood Him completely, His faithful son and companion, 'Abdu'l-Bahá.

Husayn sat down on the cloth and watched the gulls swoop down around Ali, making patterns above the water as they weaved and circled. The wind was coming from the sea now. It felt cool, steady, comforting. Husayn looked toward 'Akká. The memories of his native city of Mashhad were still vivid in his mind, but 'Akká must be his home now. There could be no going back, not for him. For though 'Akká was not a pretty town, it was, for Husayn, the sacred center of the universe, and he was glad Ali was at long last ready to understand that fact.

"Father?"

Husayn was a little startled by Ali's voice and turned to see the boy standing in front of him.

"Now can we continue the story?"

Husayn smiled and patted the ground beside him as a signal that Ali should sit down. "Most certainly," said Husayn. "First, I will tell you about the rest of the battle at Ṭabarsí, and if we have time, I will also tell you a little about some of the other places where the Bábís demonstrated immense courage in the face of unbelievable odds."

"You mean like Nayríz and Zanján?"

"Exactly," said Husayn. "You see, the pattern was the same in almost every case. Always the Bábís were outnumbered, but if the truth be told, never were they truly defeated."

"But I thought that most of the Bábís at Ṭabarsí, Nayríz, and Zanján were killed," said Ali. "That is true. Many were killed," said Husayn, "but not because they were defeated."

"You mean they still completed their mission of preparing the people for the coming of Bahá'u'lláh?"

"They did indeed do that. But that is not what I mean. The Bábís were never really beaten at Ṭabarsí. Let me see if I can explain it to you.

"I told you the part Bahá'u'lláh played—how He tried to reach the fort. I also told you about how the Bábís built the fort and fought in those first battles when they were attacked by the government troops, but that was only the beginning, Ali. The attacks against the fort continued over and over again. And the more courageously the Bábís defended themselves, the more determined the soldiers became.

"For weeks and weeks the followers of the Báb resisted. They would attack only when they absolutely had to. Mullá Ḥusayn would shout, 'Mount your steeds, O heroes of God!' and the Bábís would charge out from the gates of the fort, yelling their battle cry, 'O Thou, the Lord of the Age!'

"These attacks went on for several months, until about the time Bahá'u'lláh was arrested and taken to Ámul. It was then that the prince reassembled his army and began to attack the fort more fiercely, both day and night. He ordered several regiments of his infantry and cavalry to camp around the fort. Then he commanded his army to build seven barricades so that the Bábís could not attack them. This way they could bombard the fort with cannon shells without having to worry about Mullá Ḥusayn and his men being able to do anything about it.

"Before too long the situation became truly wretched for the Bábís, and their makeshift fort began to seem more like a prison than a place of refuge. Their food was gone, and they needed water badly. Finally, on the first day of February in 1849, Mullá Ḥusayn gathered his men together and told them they would attack and get all the water they needed. The men sensed something strange in Mullá Ḥusayn's voice, but of course they trusted their leader completely, so they began to prepare their equipment for attack.

"Later that afternoon Mullá Ḥusayn clothed himself in fresh garments. He put on the green turban which the Báb had given him, and he went to talk privately with Quddús. That evening after midnight, when the morning star had risen, Mullá Ḥusayn assembled his men, and they charged out of the fort, shouting, 'O Thou, the Lord of the Age!'

"This attack caught the enemy soldiers completely by surprise, and the Bábís charged so swiftly that they managed to break through each of the seven barricades the prince had built. But as they were attacking the enemy camp, Mullá Ḥusayn's horse suddenly became tangled in some tent ropes. He struggled desperately to get free, but an enemy soldier who was hiding in a nearby tree to escape the Bábís saw Mullá Ḥusayn's dilemma. The soldier carefully raised his rifle and aimed at the Bábí leader. He fired his rifle, and Mullá Ḥusayn fell.

"Two of Mullá Ḥusayn's men rushed to his side as quickly as they could amidst the confusion of the battle. He was still alive. Together they picked up Mullá Ḥusayn and hurriedly carried him back to the fort. It was clear that their brave battle leader was mortally wounded, and so Quddús told the men to leave him alone with his cherished friend and fellow Letter of the Living. As Mullá Ḥusayn lay dying, Quddús said to him, 'Please God, I will ere long join you and taste the sweetness of heaven's ineffable delights.' No doubt it pleased the dying Bábí to know that he would soon be eternally with his beloved friend in the spiritual world. He looked up at Quddús, a faint smile upon his lips, and said to his friend and leader, 'May my life be a ransom for you. Are you well pleased with me?'"

"So Mullá Ḥusayn thought of Quddús as his leader?" said Ali.

"It would seem *so,*" said Husayn. "After all, it was Quddús whom the Báb took with Him on pilgrimage. In fact, when Mullá Ḥusayn was shocked that Quddús recognized the Báb before speaking with Him or even being told who He was, the Báb later told Mullá Ḥusayn, 'Marvel not at his strange behavior. We have in the world of the spirit been communing with that youth. We know him already. We indeed awaited his coming.'"

"That's amazing," said Ali. "So Quddús was *very* important!"

"Ali, every single one of these early Bábís was very important because each recognized the Prophet when almost no one knew that the Prophet had come. But you are right—Quddús was particularly special."

"So did Quddús also get killed at the fort?" asked Ali.

"Not right away. As you can imagine, Ali, the Bábís were very sad. They buried Mullá Ḥusayn in a secret spot within the shrine itself so that the enemy troops would not discover his body. Then they buried the thirty-six other Bábís who had also been killed that day in the fighting. Meanwhile, the enemy soldiers began trying to rebuild the camp which the Bábís had completely demolished in their attack.

"By this time, the Bábís had been holding out for 116 days. During that time seventy-two men had died in the fighting, and there is no telling how many soldiers had been killed. For the next forty-five days, the prince tried to reorganize his forces so that he could kill the remaining Bábís who still resided in the makeshift fort. Of course, he was greatly encouraged when he found out that Mullá Ḥusayn had been killed.

"At the head of two regiments of infantry and cavalry the confident prince once more surrounded the fort and ordered his men to begin fighting. Quddús realized that the prince now thought he could easily defeat these untrained students. So Quddús assembled the men and told them they must prove themselves worthy soldiers, even without the aid of Mullá Ḥusayn. They must go out and show the soldiers that the fierceness and power of the Bábís had not come from the leadership of Mullá Ḥusayn alone, but from Almighty God.

"Once again, a squad of nineteen Bábís charged out on their steeds shouting 'O Thou, the Lord of the Age!' As before, within minutes they chased away the confused soldiers, who thought surely a great mass of Bábís was about to pursue them.

"But while the victory was encouraging, it was brief. Within a few days their situation once again became perilous. The prince ordered that towers be built around the walls of the fort, and from those towers his men began to fire cannonballs into the fort. The Bábís had to tunnel underground to escape the bombardment.

"But soon another problem became apparent. It was now spring, and the moist earth began to rot their clothes and kept them damp and cold every day. Many soon became ill. What is worse, their food was now completely gone. At last they had to eat the few horses they still possessed."

Ali was shocked by the story his father told. Little by little, the envy he felt for the heroic Bábís in the fort faded. He began to realize that being a hero was not always a matter of one or two moments of glory with swords flashing and horses charging. He now understood that courage is sometimes measured minute by agonizing minute.

"Finally, when nothing else was left," Husayn continued, "they lived on what little grass they could find. They even ate their own shoe leather—anything that might keep them alive. For many days they existed in these wretched conditions. Only occasionally would they dash out of the fort to scare the enemy soldiers.

"Finally, after months of trying to overcome this small band of obstinate Bábís, the prince decided that if he could not defeat the Bábís or make them surrender, he would use trickery and lies to stop their resistance."

"How could he trick them?" asked Ali.

"He pretended to arrange for a truce, and as a token of his honest intentions, he sent to Quddús a copy of the Qur'án and swore an oath that if Quddús and his men would come out of the fort, not one of them would be harmed."

"Did Quddús believe him?" asked Ali, obviously worried.

"I am sure he knew exactly what the prince had in mind, but he also knew that he could best serve the Cause of the Báb by acting in good faith, by showing his trust in the government official."

"And did the Bábís come out from the fort?"

"Yes, they did. After seven long months they walked through the fort gates on the ninth day of May in 1849. And after they emerged from the fort, the prince's real intentions became apparent to them. As soon as they had passed through the gates of the fort amid the jeers and laughter of the well-fed army troops, most of the Bábís were killed."

"How?" asked Ali somberly. "How were they killed?"

"Some were killed with spears, others with swords, and some survived only to be sold as slaves. Nine of the original eighteen Letters of the Living were killed there. The fort itself was immediately destroyed and cleared away, as if the government troops thought they could wipe away the memory of this historic event by obliterating the physical remains of the small fort."

"But we know about it, Father."

"Yes, Ali, we do, and in time this event will be remembered by people all the world over."

"But what about Quddús? Was he also killed?"

"Quddús was taken to Bárfurúsh, the city of his birth. There he was put in chains and paraded through the streets. Then he was stripped of his clothes and pushed and dragged while townspeople attacked him furiously. In a frenzy of anger and passion they tore his body to pieces."

Husayn stopped. He could not go on, and he looked down to see the tears trickling down Ali's cheeks. "It is worthy of our tears, my son. It is hard to hear how these early believers were treated. And there is much more, things so horrible I cannot tell you now. But I must tell you enough so that you can understand the devotion, the courage, the sacrifices that cleansed the land of Persia, the faithful love that laid the foundation for this beloved Cause of God. If you remember nothing else, just remember this, Ali: Without the devotion that sustained those early believers, there would be no Bahá'í Faith today."

"But was it necessary for all that to happen?" said Ali tearfully. "Did it have to happen that way?"

"It is never necessary for people to turn away from the truth, Ali. But it seems that every time a Prophet appears, He and His first followers are treated this way. So the answer is that it does not have to happen like this. People are free to choose between right and wrong. Too often, I am afraid, they have made the wrong choices."

"But that doesn't mean they always will, does it?"

"No, it does not." And with that, Husayn comforted his son until Ali's tears stopped.

"And these things happened all over Persia?" Ali asked after a few minutes.

"For the next several years Persia was a horrible place for the Bábís. As you know, it is still extremely dangerous for the Bahá'ís living there. Of course, we may never know how many Bábís were killed during that time—how much suffering they endured rather than renounce their belief. I suppose that's why it's so important that we not forget the names of the believers whom we do know about and the places where they struggled, because they represent so many others whose names we may never know, at least, not in this life."

Ali smiled at his father. He understood for the first time that the stories he was hearing were one important way that the history of his religion would never be forgotten, but would be passed down from parents to children from generation to generation. "Then I suppose I should learn about some of the other things that happened," Ali said to his father. "After all, I will have children of my own someday, and I will want to be able to tell them these same stories."

Husayn placed his hand gently on his son's cheek. It was not a usual sort of gesture for Husayn, but Ali understood what it meant. Then he withdrew his hand and said, "As you wish, Ali, but it is not a happy story." Husayn took a deep breath, almost a sigh, and he continued. "Early that same summer, the summer of 1849, about a month or so after the battle, the Báb learned about the tragedy of Ṭabarsí. He was in a prison cell in Chihríq at the time, and a messenger told Him that nine of His Letters of the Living, including His beloved Mullá Ḥusayn and Quddús, had been slaughtered.

"The grief He felt is impossible to describe. These intimate friends and devoted followers had given their lives for the truth He had brought. For nine days He would see no one. He found it almost impossible to eat or drink. Tears flowed from His eyes without ceasing. For five whole months He was so sorrowful that He could not even write.

"At long last, when He was able to write once again, He revealed beautiful tablets in memory of these beloved martyrs. Then He sent a messenger to the site where the fort had stood to say prayers and to pay tribute to those who had fought there.

"On the way back from his journey the messenger stopped at the home of Bahá'u'lláh in Ṭihrán and learned that persecutions were continuing. Throughout the city of Ṭihrán officials were trying to discover which people were Bábís. The prime minister, Mírzá Táqí Khán, had fourteen prominent citizens suspected of being Bábís arrested. He told them that if they did not divulge the names of other Bábís, they would be put to death, but they refused. He then told them that unless they renounced their beliefs and recanted their Faith, they would be killed."

"You mean all they had to do was to say they were not Bábís?" asked Ali.

"That's right. You see, according to the beliefs of Islám, it is all right for one to recant his Faith if his life is in danger. It is called taqíyyih. But the Báb said that this was no longer allowed for the Bábís."

"And did any of them recant?"

"Seven of them did, but the other seven did not, including the uncle who had raised the Báb. These seven were taken one at a time and questioned and tortured for long hours. And when they still would not renounce their beliefs, they were executed."

"How were they killed?" asked Ali, not really sure he wanted to know.

Husayn paused, then looked Ali in the eyes. "They were beheaded, Ali. For three days their bodies remained in the streets for the citizens to kick at and spit on. Of course, their bodies were also intended to warn the other Bábís that they, too, might be killed if they continued to follow the Báb.

"But that wasn't the end of the persecution of the followers of the Báb. This hatred and fear of the Bábís spread like an infectious disease throughout the land. Only two months or so after the death of these seven respected citizens in Ṭihrán, a similar tragedy occurred in the south in a town called Nayríz.

"About a year before, during the latter part of the battle at Ṭabarsí, Vaḥíd, one of the most learned of the Báb's followers, had tried to join his companions at the fort. Like Bahá'u'lláh, Vaḥíd could not get through to the fort, and so for a while after that, he stayed at the home of Bahá'u'lláh. But after the Bábís had been tricked and slaughtered at the fort, and following the killing of the seven Bábís in Ṭihrán, Vaḥíd set out from Ṭihrán determined to follow the example of his fellow believers.

"He decided that he would spend whatever time remained in his life teaching others about the Báb with all the energy he had, regardless of what might happen to him. Day and night, in every city he passed through, Vaḥíd told all who would listen about the wondrous news that the Qá'im had come to fulfill the promise of Islám.

"Gradually, his teaching journey led him southwards from the city of Qazvín to Qum, then to Káshán, to Ardistán, and to Iṣfahán. Finally, by spring he had reached Yazd. There he had a beautiful house in which lived his wife and young children. In Yazd, as in the other cities he visited, Vaḥíd began telling the citizens about the Báb.

"Because he was such a respected scholar, many listened enthusiastically and decided to become Bábís. But others, particularly the Muslim religious leaders, were angered by these teachings. The Muslim clergy were concerned that if this religion became popular, their own position in the community might be threatened. Consequently, they met together and decided that the only solution to the growing popularity of these teachings was to kill Vaḥíd.

"It was not long before Vaḥíd discovered their plans, but he did not care. Like the other Bábís who had already given their lives, Vaḥíd determined that he would teach others as long as he was able. And so for the next forty days he continued to answer the questions of seekers, to show others how they could teach their friends. Very soon Vaḥíd's own home became the center for all this activity.

"As the interest in the religion began to spread, the local governor called a meeting of the townspeople."

"Just as the town leaders in Bárfurúsh had done," observed Ali.

"That's right," said Husayn. "And just as in Bárfurúsh, many of the citizens were convinced that they should attack Vaḥíd's home. Fortunately, some of Vaḥíd's friends heard about the plan and warned Vaḥíd so that the Bábís could escape before the attack began.

"However, some were captured. Among these was Vaḥíd's own faithful servant, Ḥasan, who was tortured and killed.

"Now Vaḥíd knew the time for his own martyrdom was near. He told his wife to leave their home in Yazd, to take their children and go to her father's house. Vaḥíd collected what writings of the Báb he had and kissed his wife and children good-bye, knowing full well he would probably never see them again.

"Then he headed south for the town of Nayríz, where he had another house and many faithful friends. All along the route from Yazd to Nayríz, Vaḥíd taught people about the Báb, and when he reached Nayríz, he boldly announced in public that the Promised One of Islám at long last had come.

"Many gathered to hear him because they knew of Vaḥíd's learning and respected what he had to say. Vaḥíd warned these eager souls that the governor of Nayríz would try to kill whoever followed Vaḥíd, but they still begged him to stay for a few days. In the meantime the governor was gathering an army and had managed to recruit a thousand cavalry and infantrymen.

"When Vaḥíd and his followers heard that these soldiers were coming to kill them, the Bábís, seventy-two in all, went to the nearby fort of Khájih. It was an old building, a shambles really, so Vaḥíd organized the Bábís to make the walls as sturdy as possible. As they worked on the fort, other citizens of the town came to the fort and asked if they, too, could join with them.

"Before long the troops arrived, and Vaḥíd saw immediately that these soldiers were intent on killing the Bábís. Vaḥíd then reasoned that since it was going to be impossible to discuss matters with the governor in order to prevent the fighting, he would use the same tactics the Bábís had used in battle at Fort Ṭabarsí."

"You mean they charged out of the fort like Mullá Ḥusayn and his men did?" asked Ali.

"Correct, and with the same results. Whenever the Bábís would charge out from the fort in their small bands, the governor's troops would scatter in fear. They would desert their positions and run for cover.

"Day after day this kind of fighting continued. It soon became clear that even with great numbers of government troops, the governor's forces could not defeat the small band of Bábís. Consequently, the governor decided to bring in even more soldiers. He ordered that trenches be dug around the fort so that the army could fire at the Bábís. But Vaḥíd responded by sending a small band of fourteen Bábís charging fiercely out from the fort on horseback crying, *'Alláh-u-Akbar!'*—'God is Most Great!' Yet again the government soldiers were completely shocked by the sudden attack, and once more they scattered in fright.

"Finally it became clear to the governor that he could not defeat the Bábís, so he decided to use the same sort of trickery that had been used against the Bábís at Ṭabarsí. He swore an oath on the Qur'án that none of the Bábís would be harmed if only Vaḥíd would talk with him and show him proofs that the Báb was indeed the Promised Qá'im.

"Like Quddús, Vaḥíd knew that the offer was false, but he also knew he could best show the honesty and trustworthiness of the Bábís and the new religion by acting in good faith. He emerged from the fort with five attendants, and for the next three days he talked with the governor and his men about the Báb. They asked the most difficult questions they could think of, and they appeared to listen to Vaḥíd's answers, but all the while they were actually trying to devise a plan to get the other Bábís out of the fort so that they could kill them.

"The governor decided to send a false message to the followers in the fort, telling them that Vaḥíd had convinced the whole army that the Báb was indeed the Qá'im. Naturally, the Bábís were happy to hear such news. They immediately put down their weapons and emerged from the fort. As they did, the government troops seized them, brutally tortured them, and then killed them.

"I will not tell you all the horrors that occurred then, Ali, but I will tell you that on June 29th, 1850, Vaḥíd was tortured and dragged through the town. Then . . ." Husayn paused and swallowed hard.

"Tell me, Father. I need to know. You said so yourself."

Husayn looked into Ali's eyes. The boy was right. Ali wanted to know what secrets were hidden behind the eyes of the Bahá'ís, and there was no other way to explain it.

"Very well, then, I will tell you. They severed Vaḥíd's head, Ali. They cut it off, removed the skin, and stuffed it with straw." Husayn paused again and swallowed hard. "Then the governor sent the head of the man who had been one of the most respected scholars in all of Persia as a trophy to the prince in Shíráz. This same hideous desecration was committed with many other Bábís in Nayríz by the five thousand soldiers who had been hired to torture them."

"But why?" exclaimed Ali in disbelief. "How could anyone do such things to other human beings?"

"The truth is, my son, I am not really sure. Perhaps to understand the heart of such people, you would have to be as perverse as they, and God forbid that such a thing should ever happen. I will tell you this much. Each one of us can become as wise and kind and good as an angel. But each one of us can also destroy that divine spark within us and become as wretched as a wild beast, even worse than a scavenger wolf, because a beast kills for a reason, for food or to protect its brood, but human beings who turn away from the light of truth and follow corrupt desires or evil leaders, they slaughter without reason.

"So I guess we must leave it to God to judge such behavior. All I can tell you is that this merciless evil was not an isolated event. It was not merely at Fort Ṭabarsí or at Nayríz that the Bábís were treated so abominably. Probably before the Báb heard news of what took place in Nayríz, He Himself was taken from His prison in Chihríq to the city of Tabríz, where He was questioned by the authorities."

"Is that when He sent His pen to Bahá'u'lláh?" asked Ali.

"Yes," said Husayn. "The Báb knew that the time for His own martyrdom was at hand, and He ordered His secretary, Mírzá Aḥmad, to take His seals, rings, and His pen-case, together with a beautiful scroll, to Bahá'u'lláh."

"What was on the scroll?" asked Ali.

"The Báb had written on the scroll three hundred verses, all containing various forms of the word *Bahá*."

"Was that how He showed the Bábís that Bahá'u'llah was the Promised Manifestation of God the Báb had talked about in His writings?"

"Yes, that was one of the signs," said Husayn. "Because almost immediately after that the Báb was brought to Tabríz, where He was placed in a carefully guarded cell in the barracks of the town square. You see, it was the plan of the prime minister, Mírzá Táqí Khán, to put an end to the Bábí Faith once and for all by killing the Báb Himself. However, the governor of Tabríz had great respect for the Báb and refused to obey the order to execute the Báb. So the job was given to the prime minister's brother.

"But a strange and marvelous thing happened as the Báb was being taken with His secretary, Siyyid Ḥusayn, to the barracks prison. First, the soldiers took the Báb's turban and sash, the signs of His rank as a siyyid. Then, as they approached the courtyard, a devout young Bábí, Mírzá Muḥammad-'Alí, flung himself at the feet of the Báb, grabbed the hem of His garment, and pleaded, 'Send me not from Thee, O Master. Wherever Thou goest, suffer me to follow Thee.' Of course, the youth knew that the Báb was soon to be executed, but he did not care, so the Báb assured him that he would be allowed to stay with Him, and the youth was placed in the cell with the Báb and Siyyid Ḥusayn.

"'That evening another mysterious thing happened. His face aglow with happiness, the Báb told His companions gathered there, 'Tomorrow will be the day of My martyrdom. Would that one of you might now arise and, with his own hands, end My life. I prefer to be slain by the hand of a friend rather than by that of the enemy.'"

"Did any of them agree to do such a thing?" asked Ali.

Husayn smiled, knowing that his son was wondering what his own response would have been.

"Yes," said Husayn. "All remained silent except for that very same faithful youth, Mírzá Muḥammad-'Alí, who suddenly jumped to his feet and said he would do whatever the Báb wished. The Báb said to the others that because the youth had risen to comply with the Báb's wish, that same boy would be given the honor of sharing the crown of martyrdom with the Báb."

"To be killed?" asked Ali. "That was his reward for being faithful?"

"Where is that youth today?" Husayn asked his son.

"Why, he's dead, I suppose."

"Yes, he now abides in the world of the spirit, but we sit here telling his story, do we not? And his body, his earthly remains, where are they?"

"I don't know," said Ali.

Husayn lifted his left hand and pointed toward Mount Carmel.

"There," said Husayn. "There in the tomb of the Báb, his dust commingled eternally with the sacred remains of the Prophet of God, and all because of that noble act. And there his remains will stay eternally as prayers of grateful believers bless that sacred dust every single day.

"But that's not the end of the story," Husayn continued, lowering his hand and adjusting his body. The next day when the soldiers came to the prison to take the Báb and the youth to be executed, the Báb told the soldiers that He had not yet finished dictating His last instructions to His secretary, Ḥusayn. He told them that no power on earth could prevent Him from completing this task. Nevertheless the guards took the Báb and the youth to the courtyard, and a firing squad was prepared to execute them. Sám Khán, the colonel in charge of the Armenian regiment that had been ordered to carry out the execution, was a Christian who greatly respected the Báb, and he begged not to be given this duty, but the Báb assured him that everything would be all right. He told him to follow the orders he had been given and that, if he were sincere, God would assist him.

"So it was that the Báb and the eighteen-year-old youth Mírzá Muḥammad-'Alí were led to the barracks courtyard. A spike was then driven into the barracks wall as thousands of townspeople looked on from windows, from rooftops, and from doorways. Many wondered who the Báb really was, the young siyyid Who claimed to be the Qá'im. They watched intently and waited to see if this One Who claimed to be a Manifestation of God would prove to be weak or cowardly as He faced death.

"The Báb and Mírzá Muḥammad-'Alí were securely tied and suspended from the spike. The firing squad consisted of three rows of riflemen, 750 men in all. The voices of the townspeople fell silent. Sám Khán gave the command, and a massive crash of bullets cleft the air, leaving a swift cloud of smoke.

"When the smoke cleared, there were cries of amazement from the crowd. There before them stood the youth unharmed, and the Báb Himself was gone. A great clamor arose among the astonished people. Sám Khán, who was now assured in himself that God's hand was in this, ordered his men to leave at once, and he refused to have anything more to do with harming the Báb.

"A search immediately ensued until soldiers found the Báb back in His barracks room, dictating final instructions to Ḥusayn. When He was finished, another regiment of soldiers was brought in, and once more the Báb and the youth were tied and suspended from the spike in the barracks wall. The soldiers once more took aim as the townspeople looked on. Amid the stark silence, the Báb's voice called out to them, 'Had you believed in Me, O wayward generation, everyone of you would have followed the example of this youth, who stood in rank above most of you, and willingly would have sacrificed himself in My path. The day will come when you will have recognized Me; that day I shall have ceased to be with you.'

"The rifles clicked on that ninth day of July 1850, and exploding bullets riddled the bodies of the Báb and the youth, blending them together, but leaving their faces almost untouched."

"That was a Miracle, wasn't it, Father?" asked Ali.

"What, after all, is a Miracle, Ali, but the will of God operating in ways we may not always understand?"

"Do you understand how God made this happen?" asked Ali.

"No," said Husayn forthrightly.

"Then I shall call it a Miracle."

"Call it what you wish," said Husayn with a chuckle, "for that period was filled with mysterious and wondrous events, all of which were brought about by the amazing courage and sacrifice of these early believers. For instead of quenching the faith that had been ignited in the hearts of Bábís throughout Persia, these deaths served only to win more people to the Báb's religion. For when the Persians saw the courage of the Bábís, they surmised that it must have some sort of truth—for what other reason would souls so eagerly make the ultimate sacrifice?

"And the killing hardly stopped with the execution of the Báb. Of course, there were not many Bábí leaders left: Ṭáhirih, Bahá'u'lláh, and a few others. But most had been killed. And yet there were always some souls among the new followers who became ennobled by the heroic challenges that this early period in the beginning of our religion demanded. For example, in the town of Zanján another battle was already taking place, and in some ways it was the most bitter struggle of all. It lasted longer and caused more deaths than any other single encounter between the Bábís and the government soldiers.

"The trouble in Zanján began when Ḥujjat, a young religious leader of the town, became a Bábí. Even before Ḥujjat become a follower of the Báb, the other religious leaders in Zanján were jealous of the popularity of this learned young man. They had even written to the Sh͟áh to complain about him.

"As a result of the letter, Muḥammad Sh͟áh had invited Ḥujjat to Ṭihrán to talk with him. Instead of finding fault with him, however, the Sh͟áh considered Ḥujjat a most noble and learned youth, and the Sháh refused to do anything. But when Ḥujjat became a Bábí, the anger of the ‘ulamás increased. Once more the Sháh ordered Ḥujjat to come to Tihrán to discuss the problem. There in Tihrán Ḥujjat was questioned by all the learned ‘ulamás, but his answers were so clear, so logical and forceful, that the Sháh once again was satisfied that he was not a troublemaker but a deserving and knowledgeable young man.

“Nevertheless, to keep peace in Zanján, Ḥujjat agreed to remain in Ṭihrán, even though he was treated like a prisoner. He could not go beyond the city gates or talk freely with his friends. When Muḥammad Sháh died in September of 1848, Ḥujjat learned that the new grand vizier wanted to have him killed, so he left Ṭihrán and went back to Zanján, where he was eagerly welcomed by his followers.

“During the next two years the ‘ulamás of Zanján became more and more jealous of Ḥujjat’s popularity. In particular they worried about the number of people who, like Ḥujjat, were becoming followers of the Báb. So they met together and decided on a plan to get rid of Ḥujjat. First they tortured and killed one of his closest companions in May of 1850. Then they persuaded the governor of the town to order everyone in Zanján to decide whether they would side with Ḥujjat and risk losing wives, children, property, and even their lives, or seek the protection of the town officials and the government. And so the town was cruelly divided, sometimes family against family and brother against brother. The whole city was in confusion and chaos.

“Ḥujjat did not know what to do. He wanted his religion to be a source of peace and comfort to the people, not a cause of division and bloodshed. So he called his followers together and told them that if they valued their lives and did not wish to die for the Cause of the Báb, they should immediately leave that part of Zanján, because Ḥujjat knew that the officials would not be satisfied until they had killed him and all who followed him.

“But only a few abandoned Ḥujjat. Instead, as the troops gathered from the neighboring villages, the Bábís and their families moved to the old fort of ‘Alí-Mardán Khán, which was in the part of town near where Ḥujjat lived.

"As at Ṭabarsí and Nayríz, the Bábís prepared to be attacked by government troops. But instead of a few hundred Bábís, there were three thousand in the fortress. As a result of the greater numbers, the Bábís at Zanján were able to withstand attack after attack and regiment after regiment for almost nine months.

"I can't begin to describe for you all the battles and the heroes, the victories and tragedies of those long months. Ḥujjat did not want to fight, nor did he want others to join him. It was their decision to go with him to the fort, and even then he warned them repeatedly: 'We are commanded not to wage holy war under any circumstances against the unbelievers, whatever be their attitude toward us.' And the Bábís were faithful to this teaching as they had been at Ṭabarsí and Nayríz. It was only when they were attacked that they defended themselves by fighting.

"As before, the Bábís were far outnumbered. They were simple townspeople fighting against professional soldiers. They had inadequate supplies of food, water, and other necessities. But they never became discouraged. When the governor's troops tried to attack the fort, Ḥujjat would order a few of the believers to sally out on horseback, and the fierce Bábís would shout out their battle cry, 'O Thou, the Lord of the Age!'—a sound that struck terror into the hearts of the soldiers and scattered them in fear.

"Then the grand vizier ordered two regiments of the Imperial Army to go to Zanján. He informed the general that he could do whatever he wanted so long as he killed the people in the fort. The general combined his troops with the thousands of soldiers that the governor had organized, and they attacked fiercely for three days and three nights, using many cannon to bombard the fort.

"In response, Ḥujjat again sent out the small bands of Bábís who once again frightened away the enemy with their quickness and undaunted courage. Even the forces of the Imperial Army soon became discouraged. And after much hard fighting, the Bábís actually defeated the troops of the general!"

"You mean the battle ended that way?" asked Ali.

"I'm afraid not," said Husayn. "The story of Zanján doesn't end there. You see, many Bábís were killed in these battles, and the people in the fort also ran out of supplies so that most were very hungry. Also, the fort had to be repaired almost all the time, and the Bábís had to make the repairs with their own hands. But when a messenger from the governor would come offering gifts of money or noble rank to anyone who would leave the fort, the believers would only shout together their refusals to recant their faith.

"And that is what confused the army troops. Why were these people so willing to give up their lives, and when things got worse for them, why did these people become stronger and fiercer?

"At times even the Bábí women joined in the fighting beside the men. For example, fairly early in the nine-month siege, a young maiden named Zaynab secretly dressed herself as a man and carried a sword into battle and fought as courageously as any other Bábí. Month after month she terrified the enemy with her shrill cry and flashing sword."

Ali smiled as he listened with fascination—never had he heard of a woman soldier like this.

"She could always be found in the thick of the fighting," Husayn continued. "What is more, not one enemy soldier suspected she was a woman.

"Then one day during a battle she tried to rescue some Bábís who were surrounded by enemy soldiers. Zaynab ran to the barricades that the enemy had erected. She chased off the soldiers who guarded the first three of these, but at the fourth, she was suddenly struck by several bullets and fell dead.

"It was this kind of spirit and courage, Ali, that caused the enemy soldiers gradually to have more and more respect for the Bábís as the days of fighting continued and the soldiers were still unable to overcome the followers of the Báb.

"Ḥujjat tried to send a message to the Sh̲áh to tell him that the Bábís in the fort wished him and his government no harm, but the messenger was taken prisoner by the government troops and killed immediately.

"Then news reached the fort that the Báb had been executed. When the soldiers learned this, they thought surely the Bábís would give up. They told the Bábís they now had nothing to fight for, but the Bábís seemed more determined than ever. Thcy would not leave the fort, nor would they recant their beliefs.

"Finally, five whole regiments were brought in with more ammunition and more guns. Now the soldiers had seventeen regiments of cavalry and infantry and fourteen cannon, and they were training five more regiments.

"The cannon began bombarding the fort without stopping. Many Bábís were killed by the constant rain of gunfire. But the Bábís would not surrender, and the troops still could not defeat them. As a last resort, the grand vizier gave orders that if the troops and townspeople could not defeat the Bábís, the whole city would be destroyed.

"Now the enemy soldiers had reason to fight even more fiercely than ever. Day after day, more of Ḥujjat's best soldiers were killed. In fact, no fewer than three hundred Bábís were killed on one day of fighting alone. Nevertheless, in each major battle the Bábís outfought the soldiers and won the victory.

"When it became clear that no power on earth could make the Bábís give up, the commander, the Amír-Túmán, sent a message to the Bábís saying that if they would leave the fort, they would not be harmed. To prove he was telling the truth, he placed his seal on a copy of the Qur'án."

"Did Ḥujjat leave the fort as Quddús and Vaḥid had done?" asked Ali, concerned that these brave ones would also become victims of this treachery.

Husayn smiled. "No, he did not. Instead, he sent a group of Bábís to investigate further the claims of the Amír-Túmán. Only, he did not send soldiers. He sent nine children who were ten years old or younger and several old men over eighty years of age. When this strange group arrived at the tent of the Amír-Túmán, he questioned them and became so angry that he ordered his men to tear out the beard of the spokesman. The other Bábís in the group immediately dashed back toward the fort, though some were captured.

"So this time the trick did not work, and the fighting began once more. It continued until near the end of December, when fortunes changed. While Ḥujjat was in prayer one day, he was struck in the arm by an enemy bullet. When the men in the fort rushed to his aid, they left the entrances unguarded, and enemy soldiers captured a hundred women and children.

"Those who remained managed to abandon the fort with the wounded Ḥujjat. They divided themselves into five companies, each consisting of 361 companions. Each of these groups hid in various houses in the neighborhood. Then, one at a time, nineteen men from each group would rush out, attack the enemy, and disappear again.

"But in the midst of this shrewd plan, Ḥujjat's wound gradually became worse until, on January 8th, 1851, nineteen days after he was shot, the noble Bábí leader died.

"Only 200 Bábís were now left to fight, and within several days they, too, were captured and tortured, then killed. Even Ḥujjat's young seven-year-old son was cut to pieces. The body of Ḥujjat was dragged through the streets to the sound of drums."

Husayn paused for a moment. "No one can say how many died at Zanján—1,800 or more. And we may never know all the horrible ways they died. But you can be sure of one thing, Ali—and remember this if you remember nothing else I have told you today—without the noble deeds and flawless courage of these early believers, without a devotion that could withstand every affliction, every hideous torture, we would not be sitting here now talking about our precious Bahá'í Faith, because it would not exist. These battles, these courageous people whose names we know, and the many others whose names and lives we know nothing about, they all made it possible for you and Neda and Ahmad, all of us all over the world, to be Bahá'ís."

Husayn looked into Ali's eyes with a piercing stare, a look such as Ali had never seen before. The face was calm, stern, almost unfamiliar. Then Husayn made a gesture that was not common for him. He took his son's hand in his own and, almost in a whisper, said, "This, Ali, is the gift that Bábís and Bahá'ís have given to you and me, this beloved Faith, not divided into pieces or tarnished, but a beautiful gem polished with their heroic deeds. This is the reason for the strange look you see in the eyes of the older Bahá'ís in 'Akká. They, too, know these stories because most of them have lived these stories, have seen these things happen. This is the reason that you and all the other Bahá'ís of your generation must work just as hard to pass this Faith on to others, polished ever more brightly with your own shining deeds and courageous acts."

Ali had no questions. His father's words hung there between them, and Ali sat motionless, unaware of himself. He saw only his father's face and eyes so like the eyes of the older believers. And it was not sadness he saw. Perhaps it was wisdom tempered by pain, a dauntless determination, a purity of heart refined by the cruelty of heartless ones. But also within this visage and reflected in these eyes was not sadness, not something to be pitied. There was in these eyes a certitude and a quiet courage that Ali now knew he himself longed to attain.

6

The Vision

The little boat was old and weatherbeaten. It had not been built to be a sailboat in the first place. Ali had been given the aging and discolored rowboat by one of the several fishermen he had befriended. Then, with the help of his grandfather and his friend Ahmad, Ali had attached a mast, a keel, and a sail made from pieces of canvas. But when, after months of hard work, Ali had finished his craft and his father had determined that the small boat was seaworthy, Ali was as proud of this dinghy as any captain would have been of a great schooner.

It was a Saturday morning, Ali's favorite day of the week, and for the first time his grandfather was letting him sail beyond the seawall. Ali had learned much about sailing from days and weeks of practicing on the calm water inside the long jetty that ran parallel to the beach. So on this bright calm morning, as the boat ventured into the open sea beyond the jetty, Ali turned the rudder to head his boat toward the old fortress walls surrounding the city, and he felt more grown-up than he had ever felt in his life. He could not see his friends, but he felt their eyes on him, as if he were on parade. Still, he was glad that his grandfather was there with him.

Moayyed pointed where Ali should go, and when it was necessary, he would caution the boy about the dangers of getting too close to the sharp rocks that jutted far out from the walls. "It's much rougher up close than it seems from here," he said, recalling in his own mind the time as a youth when he had almost drowned in a sudden squall that overtook him as he sailed a much larger boat in the Persian Gulf out from the seaport of Bú<u>sh</u>ihr. "That's good, that's good," Moayyed said confidentally as Ali brought the bow around."

It had been almost a week since Ali and his father had spent the day at the beach talking about the early heroes of the Faith. Now as the patched sail fluffed out full in the slight morning breeze and Ali nervously guided his craft through the blue swells, he was glad that his grandfather could share in this, his moment of victory. But the wind picked up the farther out they got, and the boat tilted more than usual. Ali let out the sail-rope and moved the rudder slightly to head more into the wind so that the boat evened out. He looked at his grandfather to see if the old man was afraid or worried. Moayyed appeared calm and smiled reassuringly at Ali, and the boy felt his stomach muscles relax a little.

"You know your boat well, Ali," said Moayyed.

"I have practiced with it a long time, Grandfather, but the water is rougher out here, and the change in the wind surprised me." He lifted his face a little to let the sun and wind caress his face.

"We should not go out too far this first time," Moayyed cautioned. "Let us go closer to the city walls, and I will show you something special."

The wind shifted and came from a southwesterly direction now, and Ali began to let out more sail to steer the boat closer to the city walls, though always keeping a safe distance from the jagged rocks that split the crashing waves. Ever since Ali could remember, his grandfather had thought up surprises, "adventures," Ali would call them. Always these special treats were exciting. Sometimes they were downright mysterious.

The boat began to make its way alongside the ancient city, in view of the old prison, which was taller than most of the other buildings. Ali held the rudder firmly with his right hand, the sailrope with his left. "When do I find out what you're going to show me?" he asked.

Moayyed looked toward the huge walls and put his hand over his brow to shade his view. His face was more serious now. Finally, he pointed toward the old prison.

"Do you see the part of the prison that sticks up a little higher than the rest?"

"Yes."

"Well, behind the two windows on the right side of the building is the cell where Bahá'u'lláh was kept when He was brought here to 'Akká as a prisoner."

Ali looked above the wall at the haggard stone fortress, a building he had seen all his life, but never before from this angle, and certainly not from a boat.

"Someday soon I will take you to the old prison," said Moayyed. "For now I have another treat for you. Lower your sail and I'll drop the anchor."

Ali untied the sail-rope and carefully lowered the sail while Moayyed, a man in his late sixties, but still very agile and strong, threw overboard the makeshift anchor, which was really nothing more than a piece of concrete with a short iron bar tied to a long rope.

"I am going to tell you something you may already know about, but I will tell you in a special way."

"What do you mean?" asked Ali as he let the sail-rope slide from his hand and released the rudder.

"It has to do with your dream, the part about Shaykh Aḥmad."

Ali recalled vividly the image of Shaykh Aḥmad bathed in the strange light in the darkened underground room.

"Do you think my dream was strange?" asked Ali.

"No, certainly not," said Moayyed. "Some dreams are strange, but mean nothing at all, but some dreams are full of meaning, like a cask of sparkling jewels waiting to be opened." Then Moayyed sat back against the side of the old boat. He was silent for a moment. "Your father tells me you asked about the eyes of the friends. He tells me you have learned much about the early believers and the hard times they had in Persia."

"Yes," said Ali. "I knew some of the stories before, but nothing like what Father told me."

"And it made you sad?"

"Later it made me feel good, but I don't know why. I didn't feel glad that people died. I suppose I felt proud, proud to be a part of it somehow."

"It is hard to feel too terribly sad when the martyrs themselves were so completely happy. Still, the stories of their pain are not easy to hear. But tell me this, Ali, since you have begun studying about Bahá'u'lláh as your dream told you to do, have you learned much about what happened after Ṭabarsí and the other battles?"

"You mean to Bahá'u'lláh?"

"Yes."

"I know that later He was put in prison in the Síyáh-Chál and then exiled to Baghdád."

"Very true, very true. But there's something important you are leaving out."

"What do you mean?" asked Ali as he tried to recall what he remembered about the life of Bahá'u'lláh.

"Bahá'u'lláh did not go directly from Ṭabarsí into prison. There were several years between those two events, and during that time Bahá'u'lláh did something important, something you need to know about if you are to be faithful to the assignment Shaykh Aḥmad gave you."

Ali was thrilled to hear the word *assignment* as if his task were not a vague exhortation, but a special duty entrusted to him alone. "About five months after the battle of Zanján, Bahá'u'lláh left for Karbilá in the neighboring country of 'Iráq."

"Was He trying to escape the persecution?" asked Ali.

"Bahá'u'lláh never ran from His enemies," said Moayyed, "even though He could have at any time. No, even more than before, Bahá'u'lláh began to direct the affairs of the Bábís, concealing the remains of the Báb from the officials, directing Nabíl and others to transcribe the Holy Writings of the Báb so that the Bábís could learn more about the teachings of their own religion. But the grand vizier already knew how Quddús, Mullá Ḥusayn, and other Bábís had turned to Bahá'u'lláh for advice. And when he saw how Bahá'u'lláh commanded the respect of these people, he decided he would send Bahá'u'lláh away so that He could not assist the very religion that the vizier was trying to destroy."

"Did Bahá'u'lláh obey him?" asked Ali.

"Bahá'u'lláh always obeyed the government officials wherever He lived," said Moayyed. "That way no one could ever accuse Him of being a lawbreaker or anything but an honest and faithful citizen. It's very important that you understand that. You see, the Prophet has the power to do whatever He wants. But just as God withholds His power to give us the chance to discover Him on our own, so does the Manifestation.

"So Bahá'u'lláh obeyed the orders of the grand vizier, and He left for the town of Kirmánsháh and then journeyed to Karbilá after staying for a few days in the city of Baghdád. But almost as soon as Bahá'u'lláh arrived in Karbilá, He began to attract attention. Bábís, and others who knew a little about the Bábí Faith, came to visit this wise young nobleman from Ṭihrán.

"Some were religious and political leaders. Many of these visitors later became Bábís as a result of their conversations with Bahá'u'lláh, for He did not simply tolerate those who were attracted to Him—He welcomed them, answered all of their questions patiently, talked with them for hours and hours about theology and philosophy.

"There are many stories about those meetings, but one of the most fascinating encounters occurred between Bahá'u'lláh and Shaykh Ḥasan-i-Zunúzí in the streets of Karbilá. Shaykh Ḥasan had been a devout follower of the Báb, and the Báb had told him that if he went to Karbilá and waited patiently, he would live to see the face of 'the promised Ḥusayn,' the Manifestation Whose advent the Báb had come to proclaim.

"Well, you can imagine how this promise must have excited Shaykh Ḥasan, and yet years had passed since then. The Báb had been executed. Most of the Bábí leaders had been killed, and Shaykh Ḥasan had forgotten the promise. But then in October of 1851, Shaykh Ḥasan, now quite aged, was walking beside the gate to the inner courtyard of the Shrine of the Imám Ḥusayn, a most holy place to Shi'ih Muslims. Suddenly the old man saw Bahá'u'lláh. Immediately he sensed in Bahá'u'lláh's face and in His penetrating glance and noble bearing the serenity, power, and beauty that made him immediately recall the promise the Báb had made. In his heart Shaykh Ḥasan was certain that Bahá'u'lláh was the One the Báb had described.

"Suddenly, for no apparent reason, Bahá'u'lláh came toward Shaykh Ḥasan and reached out and took his hand. 'Praise be to God that you have remained in Karbilá, and have beheld with your own eyes the countenance of the promised Ḥusayn,' said Bahá'u'lláh to the astonished old man."

"You mean that Bahá'u'lláh knew what the Báb had promised Shaykh Ḥasan?" asked Ali in amazement.

"Yes."

"So that means the Manifestations are not ordinary human beings—I mean, They have special powers?"

"Exactly."

"And Bahá'u'lláh already knew that He was a Prophet of God and that He was the One the Báb had talked about?"

"Most certainly."

"Then why didn't Bahá'u'lláh tell other people?"

"Good question. In fact, Bahá'u'lláh explained that very thing to Shaykh Ḥasan. Bahá'u'lláh told him that the proper time had not yet come to tell others. 'Not yet,' Bahá'u'lláh whispered to him. 'The appointed Hour is approaching. It has not yet struck. Rest assured and be patient.'"

Ali smiled. "I see. So, everyone has to be patient, not just me."

Moayyed laughed. "Yes, Ali, even we old men must learn the lesson of patience."

"Did things get better for the Bábís then?" asked Ali.

"For a while they did. While Bahá'u'lláh was in 'Iráq, He taught the Bábís about their religion, much as He had done several years before during the early days of the Bábí Faith when He was in Mázindarán. The future for the Bábís looked even brighter when the grand vizier of Persia, Mírzá Táqí Khán, the one who had been responsible for so many horrible things that had happened to them, was executed by the Persian government.

"The man who took his place, Mírzá Áqá Khán-i-Núrí, respected the Bábís, and he respected Bahá'u'lláh in particular. The new grand vizier immediately began to improve relations between the Bábís and the government. He even sent a letter to Bahá'u'lláh asking Him to come back to Persia.

"So Bahá'u'lláh agreed, and in the late spring of 1852 Bahá'u'lláh was formally welcomed by the brother of the grand vizier. For a whole month important dignitaries and government officials came to meet Bahá'u'lláh and kept Him so busy that He did not even have a chance to return to His own home. While Bahá'u'lláh was still a guest of the grand vizier, He went on to Lavásán, where He stayed on the vizier's estate and continued to meet with the many visitors who had heard of Bahá'u'lláh's uncanny wisdom and knowledge."

"I had no idea that such a thing ever occurred," said Ali. "But if Bahá'u'lláh received such respect, then how did He ever end up in prison?"

"I'm afraid that this period of felicity and progress came to an end because of the foolish behavior of two young Bábís. You see, Ali, all of the suffering and death your father told you about that had happened to the Bábís throughout Persia left many scars on the hearts of those Bábís who remained alive. And two young Bábís who could not put aside the intense anger they felt decided they would get revenge for all the suffering that the Sh̲áh had inflicted on the Bábís. They had seen so many of their friends and family tortured or killed that they decided they must kill the Sh̲áh himself."

"I don't blame them," said Ali.

"I am sure you don't blame them for what they felt, Ali, but listen to what happened because of their unwise actions. They managed to get an old pistol, not much of a weapon, really. Well, Bahá'u'lláh had been warned of what these two young Bábís were planning, and He reminded them that He had strictly forbidden the Bábís even to think of such a thing. He told them sternly that such acts of violence were completely opposed to the teachings of the Báb and would not help anything, but would only bring trouble to the Bábí community.

"But the two youths were unable to restrain their desire for revenge, and the entire Bábí community throughout Persia would pay for their disobedience. One morning, as the Sh̲áh went out riding, they approached him as if to ask a favor of the king. Suddenly they pulled out the awkward weapon and fired.

"Did the Sh̲áh die?" asked Ali.

"No. In fact, the wound was not terribly serious. But all of Ṭihrán was immediately in an uproar, especially when they learned that the two young men were Bábís. All the known Bábís, together with all those who were even suspected of having anything to do with the Bábís, were arrested or dragged from their homes by angry mobs that roamed the streets. Bábís—men, women, and children alike—were paraded through the streets of Ṭihrán. Some were whipped. Many were taken to the city gate, where they were ordered to recant their beliefs or be killed.

"These Bábís were unbelievably courageous. They refused to recant their belief in the Báb, and those who were executed faced death with dignity, even though members of their own family were being killed beside them. As they stood ready to be killed, they would chant one of the Báb's favorite verses: 'Verily, from God we come, and unto Him we return!'

"By nightfall, a heap of mutilated bodies lay in a pile by the town gate, and everywhere in the country the Bábís were once again in danger. In Nayríz and Shíráz a great number of Bábís were slain in ways too hideous and inhuman to talk about." Moayyed lowered his head and spoke in a muted voice. "Someday you will have to learn about it all so that these deeds will not be lost to history, but not now, not now."

Ali was surprised at his grandfather's suddenly changed demeanor. "Was it worse than at Ṭabarsí?" asked Ali meekly.

"Yes," answered Moayyed somewhat more forcefully. "What the believers endured at the hands of the fanatical mobs—the torture, the indignities and mutilation—could fill volumes. Indeed, there are accounts, books about that period, books that you must read when you get older, because that too is the history of the Bahá'í Faith—your history." He paused again, as if trying to control his emotions, and Ali was a little unnerved by his grandfather's seriousness.

Finally, Moayyed looked at Ali again, and his face softened. His voice became calmer. "Of course, except for Bahá'u'lláh, there were no Bábí leaders left alive for the government to blame for the plot to kill the Sháh. Because Bahá'u'lláh had gained so much respect while He was staying at the home of the grand vizier in Lavásán, the government at first left Him alone. But as the tumult mounted and the frenzied persecution of Bábís swept throughout the land, Bahá'u'lláh's own situation also became risky.

"For weeks and months Bábís were slaughtered. No Bábí was safe anywhere in Persia because the Sháh was determined to see that the religion of the Báb and all of its followers should be destroyed. You see, unlike his now deceased father, Muḥammad Sháh, who had respected the Báb and the Bábís, Náṣiri'd-Dín Sháh detested the Báb and His followers, and now that two Bábís had made an attempt on the Sháh's life, he could openly proclaim his hatred.

"In fact, it was but a few days after the attempt on the Sháh's life that Ṭahirih was martyred in Ṭihrán, strangled to death and thrown into a pit. Siyyid Ḥusayn-i-Yazdí, who had been the Báb's amanuensis in Máh-Kú and Chiríq and who had received the last instructions of the Báb, was also killed."

"What did Bahá'u'lláh do while all this was happening?" asked Ali.

"Well, as I said, when the attempt was made on the Sháh's life, Bahá'u'lláh was still in Lavásán at the home of the grand vizier. It was there that He received a message from His host, the brother of the grand vizier, who told Him that He was no longer safe there. 'The Sháh's mother is inflamed with anger,' the message said. 'She is denouncing you openly before the court and the people as the "would-be murderer" of her son.' He went on to tell Bahá'u'lláh to remain concealed where He was until the anger of the people quieted and a messenger would be sent to accompany Him to a safer place."

"Is that what Bahá'u'lláh did?" asked Ali.

"As I have told you, Ali, Bahá'u'lláh never tried to escape from His enemies, not once!" Moayyed emphasized his point by placing his hand firmly on the side of the boat as he spoke. "No, He ignored the message, and the very next morning, He set out toward the headquarters of the Imperial Army in the district of Shimirán. He went first to the home of His brother-in-law, who worked for the Russian minister. When the Sháh heard of Bahá'u'lláh's boldness, he demanded that the Russian minister hand Him over.

"But the minister had great respect for Bahá'u'lláh and refused. Instead, he sent Bahá'u'lláh to the home of the grand vizier because he thought that Bahá'u'lláh would be safe there. But he was wrong. The grand vizier was afraid to shelter someone whom the Sháh hated, and he allowed the soldiers to take Bahá'u'lláh.

"The soldiers had no respect for Bahá'u'lláh and forced Him to walk from Shimirán to Ṭihrán without shoes or headdress in the broiling midsummer heat. On either side of the road people gathered to see the Bábí leader Who, they believed, had been responsible for the plot to kill the Sháh. Many of the angry people threw stones or yelled at the Prophet of God, the very One Who had come to assist them. One woman stepped out from the crowd with a stone in her hand, intent on throwing it at Bahá'u'lláh, when a soldier grabbed her arm to stop her. Bahá'u'lláh turned to the guard and said, 'Suffer not this woman to be disappointed. Deny her not what she regards as a meritorious act in the sight of God.'

"Bahá'u'lláh was taken to the Síyáh-Chál, the 'Black Pit,' a dark dungeon where only the very worst criminals were placed. This foul-smelling place located in the center of Ṭihrán was three flights of steps below the ground and had not really been built to be a prison at all, but a water reservoir for one of the town baths. It had no windows and was completely dark. Nor were there separate cells, but one narrow room with an arched ceiling, like a low hallway. And since the prisoners could not move or clean themselves, you can imagine how filthy and disgusting a place it was.

"Bahá'u'lláh was chained in among the two rows of prisoners that faced each other, one against each of the two long walls. His feet were placed in stocks, and His neck was linked to the necks of the other prisoners by the massive Qará-Guhar chain, a chain so large and heavy that throughout Persia people knew its name."

"Was Bahá'u'lláh the only Bábí there?" asked Ali.

"No, there were other Bábís mixed in among murderers and other criminals. Naturally, the Bábís were grateful that Bahá'u'lláh was there among them to keep up their spirits, though I'm sure they were sad that this spiritual leader was being treated with such unbelievable indignity.

"At first, Bahá'u'lláh could not sleep or rest, and one of the executioners who watched over the prisoners was so touched by the sight of this respected and noble citizen being treated so abominably that he tried to get Bahá'u'lláh to take some tea which he had secretly brought in. But Bahá'u'lláh refused to drink it."

"Why, Grandfather? What was wrong with that?" Ali asked.

"Bahá'u'lláh wanted no special treatment. He wanted to be treated like all the other Bábí prisoners, and so He determined that He would endure whatever the other Bábís suffered."

"But He wasn't like the other Bábís," said Ali. "He was a Prophet of God!"

"That is true," said Moayyed, "But He had not told anyone yet, and besides, even after Bahá'u'lláh announced Who He was, He never asked for special privileges or treatment. He always endured whatever torture or hardship was inflicted on Him."

"But why?" asked Ali.

"Perhaps so that you and I can sit in this boat right now and realize that the Báb and Bahá'u'lláh accomplished what They did solely for our benefit and not to please anyone else and not to gain privileges or pleasure or assistance. So when Bahá'u'lláh was a prisoner, He wanted to be treated like all the other prisoners. You see, nothing physical made Him special. It was a power within Him that He wanted people to understand, and the way people treated Him was a sign of whether or not they recognized what He was.

"Let me explain it this way—if Bahá'u'lláh had been able to escape from the problems that faced others around Him, then people might have thought He was special because of His noble upbringing or political influence. You see, when the Sháh put Bahá'u'lláh and the other Bábís in the Síyáh-Chál, he expected them to be utterly miserable, because none of them had any hope of ever leaving the prison alive. The Sháh thought that if he took away their food, their light, their families and friends, the Bábís would lose their belief in the Báb.

"But spiritual power can thrive in a prison just as well as it can in a comfortable mansion, even better sometimes. Instead of crying out in pain and instead of giving in to the wretched conditions of the 'Black Pit,' the Bábís, under Bahá'u'lláh's leadership, prayed, sang, and rejoiced. Every night they would repeat certain verses that Bahá'u'lláh taught them. One row of prisoners would chant, 'God is sufficient unto me; He verily is the All-sufficing!' The row of prisoners on the opposite wall facing them would reply, 'In Him let the trusting trust.'

"Through the melodious tones of these chanted verses the prisoners could feel peaceful, even free, because these words reassured them that they were as close to God and God's protection in that dark prison as the Sháh was in his magnificent palace, so long as they believed in what they were doing."

Ali thought about the sound of the chant, how his mother's voice sounded when she would intone so beautifully the verses of Bahá'u'lláh. In particular he recalled how soothing and comforting those verses had been two years before when he lay sick in bed, his forehead burning with fever and his very bones seeming to ache. Over and over again he asked his mother to chant the prayers because while her voice was intoning the verses of God, the pain seemed to disappear.

Ali imagined how the voices of the prisoners chanting in this dark chamber would echo in the darkness, how the melody might comfort their hearts. "But what did the guards think of this, Grandfather?"

Moayyed leaned back a little, rested his elbows on the gunnels of the boat, and looked toward 'Akká at Bahá'u'lláh's cell. "The guards? The guards had no idea what to think. But it was not only the guards who were baffled by this behavior. During some gloomy cold nights and sometimes into the early morning hours these chanting voices, led by Bahá'u'lláh, would echo from the prison chambers up the stairwell and out into the courtyard so that even the Sháh in his nearby palace could hear their joyful sounds."

Ali's face lit up with excitement as he imagined how surprised the Sháh must have been. "What did the Sháh say?" asked Ali. "What did he do?"

"He was dumbfounded, Ali. At first he asked his men what the sound was, and when they told him this haunting music was from the Bábís in the Síyáh-Chál giving praise to God, the Sháh was shocked and angry—so angry that he took further steps to increase their misery. He had the prisoners tortured, and when that did not stop them, each day he would have one of the Bábís led out of the prison, where he would be executed if he did not recant his beliefs.

"Meanwhile, Bahá'u'lláh continued to guide these courageous men, to teach them and to buoy their spirits. For example, one day the guards brought the prisoners a tray of roasted meat. The prisoners almost never got any decent food, so this was indeed a treat, and the guards expected them to be eager for it. They looked at the meat, perhaps considering how good it would taste, but said nothing. Instead, they turned to Bahá'u'lláh to see what they should do.

"Bahá'u'lláh knew how hungry His fellow prisoners were, how they had been mistreated, but He also knew that the only way they could survive was to remain unified and to resist the Sháh's plans to taunt them and control them. Bahá'u'lláh looked at the guards who were holding the trays and said, 'We return this gift to you; we can well dispense with this offer.'"

Ali clapped his hands together with delight at the small victory.

His grandfather continued, "The guards could not understand this strange behavior. Neither could the Sháh, and so the executions and torture increased.

"Each day one of the guards would enter the dark prison, and, while each of the prisoners waited expectantly, the guard would call out the name of the Bábí who was to be executed that day."

"But why, Grandfather? Why would they kill them?"

"To try to break the spirit of the other Bábís. Another reason for this inhuman treatment was the anger of the Sháh's mother. She was convinced that Bahá'u'lláh had thought up the plot to kill her son, and each day she would request that Bahá'u'lláh be executed. She would tell the authorities, 'Deliver him to the executioner! What greater humiliation than this, that I, who am the mother of the Sháh, should be powerless to inflict upon that criminal the punishment so dastardly an act deserves!'"

"Did they ever try to execute Bahá'u'lláh?" asked Ali.

"Some tried. There was one of her supporters who heard her say these things and who wished to win her favor. Somehow he managed to put poison in Bahá'u'lláh's food."

"And what stopped Bahá'u'lláh from taking the poison?"

"Nothing," Moayyed said simply. "He did take it, but He didn't die. He suffered greatly because of the poison—for a long time afterward His health suffered, but Bahá'u'lláh endured the pain and hardship.

"But so did the other Bábís. When a prisoner was selected to be executed, he did not show any concern, and neither did the other prisoners. The selected prisoner would throw off his unlocked chains with joy and embrace each of his fellow prisoners. Each of the other prisoners would assure him of the eternal joy that awaited him in the next world and remind him that they would soon be there with him.

"He would then follow the guard out of the room to the gallows. There he would be tortured and killed." Moayyed looked at Ali. He could see that the young boy was trying hard to hold back tears. "After the prisoner had been killed," Moayyed continued, "the guard would return to the prison chamber and tell Bahá'u'lláh what had happened, how the prisoner had endured the torture bravely, even joyfully.

"And so the days passed in the Síyáh-Chál. It was only a matter of time before Bahá'u'lláh Himself would be killed. Many of Bahá'u'lláh's friends and family constantly asked the officials how He was being treated, but the officials would lie and say that Bahá'u'lláh was fine. Sometimes the family would try to get food to Him or to visit Him, but they were not allowed, and so they became more and more concerned that they might never see Bahá'u'lláh again.

"Of all of Bahá'u'lláh's friends and family, the saddest was His eldest son, 'Abdu'l-Bahá. He was about two years younger than you are, Ali—about nine—and He so wanted to see His father. Finally, when the young boy could stand it no longer, He persuaded the family's Ethiopian servant to take Him to the prison, and they got permission to see Bahá'u'lláh.

"What a sight they must have been—young 'Abdu'l-Bahá mounted on the shoulders of the tall black Ethiopian as they approached the entrance steps that went down to the dungeon. The guards pointed the way, and the two began to descend the steps, when all at once a commanding voice rang out from the prison room: 'Do not bring him in here!'

"It was the unmistakable voice of Bahá'u'lláh. He loved His son so dearly that He did not want the boy to see Him in this wretched condition. So 'Abdu'l-Bahá remained with the servant in the courtyard outside until the time when the prisoners were brought out for brief exercise. One by one the prisoners emerged, each chained to the other, their eyes flinching from the bright light of day, their malnourished bodies stooped from the weight of the huge links of chain, their faces gaunt, drawn, and pale.

"At last 'Abdu'l-Bahá saw His own dear father. It was a sight He would never forget. Bahá'u'lláh was barely recognizable and scarcely able to walk. His neck was scarred and swollen from the chains. His beautiful dark hair and beard were unkempt and tangled. His face, usually serene and strong, could not conceal the miseries of the prison life." Tears were now visibly streaking down Ali's face, and Moayyed had to stop his story long enough to comfort the boy.

"I was just thinking," Ali managed to say, "what I would feel if someone did those things to my father."

"That is why later on in their lives when Bahá'u'lláh finally got out of prison, 'Abdu'l-Bahá always tried to make a special place where His father could have some peace. But you are right. This is a very sad story, and yet, do not forget that something strange and wonderful also happened while Bahá'u'lláh was in the Síyáh-<u>Ch</u>ál. In fact, that's the most important part of the story!"

"Ali wiped his eyes and seemed to perk up a little. "What was that?"

"One night, as Bahá'u'lláh lay asleep in His chains, He had a dream, and in this dream He heard something strange and wonderful. All around Him He heard a beautiful and majestic voice saying, 'Verily, We shall render Thee victorious by Thyself and by Thy Pen. Grieve Thou not for that which hath befallen Thee, neither be Thou afraid, for Thou art in safety. Erelong will God raise up the treasures of the earth—men who will aid Thee through Thyself and through Thy Name, wherewith God hath revived the hearts of such as have recognized Him.'"

"What did these words mean?"

"They meant that Bahá'u'lláh should not worry or be afraid because He was in prison. The voice reassured Him that in time He would transform the world itself through His revelation and through His noble life. It was also promising Him that there would arise followers throughout the world who would believe in Bahá'u'lláh, who would become enlightened by His teachings and would assist Bahá'u'lláh in building the Kingdom of God on earth."

"And that's what we're doing, isn't it?" asked Ali with a smile.

"Yes, Ali. When we study Bahá'u'lláh's teachings and help others, we become those very 'treasures of the earth.' But more than one dream and one message was revealed to Bahá'u'lláh by the Most Great Spirit. Bahá'u'lláh heard these words many times, and when He would hear them, the burden of His imprisonment would seem to vanish and He would feel alive all over. He said that just as a mighty stream of water falls from a great mountaintop to the earth below, so this spiritual force seemed to flow through Him, to spread from the crown of His head over His breast.

"Bahá'u'lláh said that sometimes the voice was that of a beautiful Maiden who seemed to be calling above Bahá'u'lláh's head, and, turning His face, He could see her."

"Was it a real person who had come to visit him?" asked Ali.

"No, this was a vision, something Bahá'u'lláh said was a symbol of the remembrance of God. And in this vision the Maiden was suspended in the air before Him, and she pointed her finger at His head and announced to all creation that Bahá'u'lláh was the Appointed One Whom the Báb had talked about and described to His followers. She said, 'By God! This is the Best-Beloved of the worlds, and yet ye comprehend not. This is the Beauty of God amongst you, and the power of His sovereignty within you, could ye but understand. This is the Mystery of God and His Treasure, the Cause of God and His glory unto all who are in the kingdoms of Revelation and of creation, if ye be of them that perceive.'"

"How beautiful," Ali observed.

"Beautiful and very important, too," said Moayyed. "You see, these words were a signal to Bahá'u'lláh that He should now begin to carry out His mission. At this moment in the dark prison, Bahá'u'lláh knew that the time had come for Him to unleash His powers as a Prophet of God, powers that He had concealed until now, and He said that as this signal was given, He felt the power surge within Him to accomplish this immense task, a force that seemed to fill His entire being."

"Did the prisoners notice what was happening? Did He tell them Who He was?" Ali asked.

"It was not the time for that—not yet. You see, Ali, the Manifestations have the ability to look into the future, to know what events will occur before they happen, and Bahá'u'lláh knew that there would come a particular time when He would tell the Bábís Who He was, a time when they would be ready to understand."

Moayyed stopped. He looked at the sun in the sky. It was now at its highest point. He raised his still muscular arms and straightened his back, which was now stiff and a little tired from sitting in one position for so long. And as he reached upwards, stretching toward the sun, he seemed to grasp a little particle of the light with his fingers, and his wrinkled face seemed to drink in the power of the sun's radiance. Then he drew his hands down and looked at Ali knowingly.

"Let me explain it this way—Bahá'u'lláh knew that the Bábís could learn only so much at one time. You see, someone cannot become strong all at once, can they? No, one must exercise a little at a time for days and weeks and months before an important change takes place. Well, it's the same way with spiritual development. God did not send the Manifestations all at once, nor did one Manifestation teach us all we would ever need to know. One by one He sends us these Teachers. Piece by piece, He gives us the parts to the puzzle of world peace. That's how I think it will be—when the world is finally united and all the peoples are working in perfect harmony, it will seem as if it happened all at once, but actually the history of this small planet is a long and endless process of growth, like a beautiful flower come suddenly into bloom. We notice the bloom and we wonder at the suddenness of it, but the plant has been struggling for a long time to become ready for this moment. I guess we grow as quickly as we can, or as slowly as we must."

"Is that how I must learn, Grandfather, little by little?" asked Ali, thinking of his dream.

"That's how all of us must learn, my young scholar. There is no other way."

"Such patience is very hard for me, Grandfather, but I will try."

"Then let me give you a little bit of advice, Ali. Don't worry about what you have not yet learned. Enjoy however much you can learn today. Enjoy the art of learning itself. Learning is not something you ever finish, Ali. In your dream you finished the book, but you kept on learning, did you not? When the steed raced through the air and you saw the whole world being changed by the light of Bahá'u'lláh's teachings, were you not learning then?" Moayyed fell silent as Ali considered what his beloved grandfather had told him.

Ali stuck his hand in the cool blue salt water, then looked across the water at the old prison fortress. "That moment in the Síyáh-Chál, was that the beginning of the Bahá'í Faith?"

"It was the fulfillment of the Báb's promise that 'Him Whom God shall make manifest' would appear in the year nine."

"Because nine plus 1844 is 1853!" Ali concluded.

"That's right, except that the year Bahá'u'lláh was imprisoned in the Síyáh-Chál was the last few months of 1852, but it was nine years according to the lunar calendar that the Muslims use."

"It all fits together so mysteriously," said Ali pensively.

The two talked a little longer about the Báb and Bahá'u'lláh and of how happy the two Prophets must be to see what had become of the Bahá'í Faith. Afterward, Ali began to busy himself with raising the sail and tying off the rope while Moayyed lifted the anchor.

The small craft began to move as Ali steered the bow around so that the wind caught the sails and pushed the boat homeward. Ali looked into the distance at Mount Carmel. He thought he could make out the Shrine of the Báb on the side of the mountain. "Someday," he thought, "someday everyone will know about that building. Someday they will look to that mountain and they will know its holy secrets."

7

The Exile

It was getting late in the afternoon, and the three children sat on a large piece of driftwood by the shore near the spot where, several weeks before, Ali had listened to his father tell of the persecution of the Bábís in Persia. Ahmad and Neda were listening to Ali describe what Moayyed had told him in the boat, for though the two younger children knew something about what had happened to Bahá'u'lláh in the Síyáh-Chál, they wanted to hear all the details that Ali had learned.

They had not spent the whole day telling stories. After a long walk from town they had spent an hour or two building intricate little castles from sand, shells, and pieces of wood. Then Neda and Ahmad had grown tired of playing and wanted to hear Ali talk about Bahá'u'lláh, because Ali was an excellent storyteller, although he was not yet aware of it.

As Ali finished his story, Neda noticed in the distance a lone figure approaching. "It's your father, Ali," said Neda. "What do you think he wants?"

When Ali saw his father a short distance away, he suddenly realized that the sun was only a couple of hours from setting, and they were at least an hour's walk from the city walls. "He probably wants us to come home," said Ali, a little worried. "We should have started home an hour ago!"

"Will he be angry?" asked Ahmad.

"I wouldn't worry," said Neda. "He seems happy to me."

As Husayn approached the children, he said in a cheerful tone, "I thought it was you, but I wasn't sure from so far off."

"I'm sorry we're late," said Ali.

"Late? Oh, no, you aren't late. I didn't come after you, if that's what you're thinking. No, I like to walk along the beach when I have time. It settles my mind, the smell of the salt spray, the rhythm of the surf, the squeal of the gulls playing in the air."

"Would you like to sit with us and hear Ali's stories?" asked Neda. Ali immediately bowed his head with embarrassment.

"I would consider it a great honor to be accepted into your band." Ahmad laughed. "Ali was telling us the story his grandfather told him in the boat the other day."

"About the Síyáh-Chál?"

"Yes," said Ahmad. "He even told us the name of the chain that Bahá'u'lláh had around His neck."

"Very good, my son," said Husayn. "You are a good storyteller. Perhaps someday you will be a historian like Nabíl, eh?" Ali was pleased with his father's praise, and his smile showed it.

"So, what would you like to do now?" asked Husayn.

"Could you tell us a story?" asked Neda.

"Yes!" said Ali. "Could you?"

"Oh, I suppose I could tell you a little something as we walk back home. What would you like?"

There was only a brief silence as the three considered Husayn's question, then Ali spoke. "I would like to know what Bahá'u'lláh did after He realized He was a Manifestation. I know that after He got out of the Síyáh-Chál He went to Baghdád, but how did He get out of prison in the first place, and how did He get to Baghdád?"

"Yes," said Neda. "I was wondering about that myself. Ali told us that Bábís were being taken from the Síyáh-Chál each day and killed, so why wasn't Bahá'u'lláh killed?"

"I would like to know if the Bábís were still tortured and killed after Bahá'u'lláh was set free," said Ahmad.

"Very well," said Husayn. He was quiet for a moment as he pondered how to begin, and the three children got up from the sand and brushed themselves off. Then the four figures began walking on the hard-packed sand toward 'Akká, which seemed shadowy and magical in the setting sun of the summer afternoon.

"You must help me with this story if I am to tell it well," said Husayn.

"All right," said Ahmad enthusiastically, "we'll help!"

"As we walk, you must pretend that it is very cold." Husayn looked around and motioned with a sweep of his hand. "And this sand—it isn't sand at all, but snow!"

The children looked at each other and smiled.

"You must also imagine that the distance we must travel is not a mile or so, but hundreds of miles over steep hills and rugged mountain ranges."

The children liked the idea, and they began to lift their feet as if they were trudging through snow with the greatest of difficulty.

"I'm going to tell you about a journey," said Husayn," a journey like the one we're imagining, but first let me tell you how we came to be on this journey. So let's begin with Bahá'u'lláh while He was still in the Síyáh-Chál. Perhaps you wonder whether or not the other prisoners in that dark dungeon knew that Bahá'u'lláh was special. Well, many of the Bábís did. Perhaps they even knew that something special was happening when Bahá'u'lláh had the visions which told Him to begin His mission. But because He knew it was not the right time, He did not yet tell any of them that He was the Manifestation the Báb had described to His followers.

"Now, you might wonder why, if Bahá'u'lláh was a Prophet and had the special powers that only a Prophet has, He did not use those powers to escape or to influence others to get Him released so that He could carry out God's plan for His life."

"That's just what I was going to ask," said Neda.

"Well, Bahá'u'lláh was not really worried about these things. You see, He knew that if anything happened to Him, God would send someone else to complete His work. In fact, He said just that in one of His tablets. So He didn't try to get special treatment, because He knew that whatever happened would be for the best.

"Outside the prison, the Bábís were still being tortured and killed throughout the land. Troops had gone to Bahá'u'lláh's home in Tákur and destroyed it, and they had attacked many of the people in the village because they were friends of Bahá'u'lláh. Almost all of Persia was a land of sorrow for the Bábís."

"It still is, isn't it?" asked Ali.

"I'm afraid it is," said Husayn. "Bahá'ís are treated very badly, and occasionally they are killed—even here in 'Akká we must be careful. Well, while Bahá'u'lláh was in prison, 'Aẓím, the young Bábí who had originally thought of the idea to kill the Sh̲áh and who had told Bahá'u'lláh of his plan, was captured and questioned. In his confession He told the officials that Bahá'u'lláh had nothing at all to do with the plot. He told them, 'I alone conceived this plan and endeavored to execute it.'

"As a result of this information, Mírzá Áqá K̲h̲án, the grand vizier, commanded that Bahá'u'lláh should be released. Ḥájí 'Alí took the written order to the Síyáh-C̲h̲ál to give it to the guards. When he arrived at the prison and saw Bahá'u'lláh, Whom he respected and admired, he could not believe his eyes. Bahá'u'lláh's neck was weighed down by chains. His hair was unkempt and tangled. His face was haggard, and His clothes nothing but rags that smelled from the stench-filled dungeon air.

"Ḥájí 'Alí was stunned and told Bahá'u'lláh tearfully, 'God knows I had never imagined that you could have been subjected to so humiliating a captivity. I should never have thought that the Grand Vizier could have dared commit so heinous an act.' He quickly removed his own cloak and gave it to Bahá'u'lláh to wear in the presence of the minister and the counselors at court.

"But Bahá'u'lláh refused! He wanted everyone to see Him just as He was. So with Ḥájí 'Alí He walked to the court and appeared before the grand vizier.

"The vizier tried to defend what he had done. He said, 'Had you chosen to take my advice, and had you dissociated yourself from the faith of the Siyyid-i-Báb, you would never have suffered the pains and indignities that have been heaped upon you.'

"Bahá'u'lláh stared into the eyes of the vizier and, in spite of His weakened condition, announced in a clear, stern voice, 'Had you, in your turn, followed my counsels, the affairs of the government would not have reached so critical a stage.' Mírzá Áqá Khán was moved and impressed by Bahá'u'lláh's remarks. Bahá'u'lláh had indeed warned the vizier what would happen if the government tried to stop the Bábí Cause, and now Bahá'u'lláh's predictions were coming true as the country was being thrown into a chaotic state.

"'The warning you uttered has, alas, been fulfilled,' the vizier admitted. 'What is it that you advise me now to do?' He spoke as if he really would follow whatever advice Bahá'u'lláh gave, so Bahá'u'lláh instantly told him exactly what he should do. 'Command the governors of the realm to cease shedding the blood of the innocent,' Bahá'u'lláh told him, 'to cease plundering their property, to cease dishonoring their women and injuring their children. Let them cease the persecution of the Faith of the Báb; let them abandon the idle hope of wiping out its followers.'"

"That is amazing!" said Ali, astounded that even Bahá'u'lláh would speak so boldly under the circumstances. "Did the vizier get angry with Bahá'u'lláh for telling him these things?"

"Absolutely not," said Husayn. "With that answer the interview ceased, and Bahá'u'lláh left, but because of Bahá'u'lláh's advice, the grand vizier gave orders that same day that the governors of the various provinces in Persia should stop arresting and punishing the Bábís.

"However, I'm afraid that the government had not yet finished punishing Bahá'u'lláh. It still feared this young religion, and the Sháh in particular thought if he could only get Bahá'u'lláh out of the country and away from the people, there would be no trace left of these Bábís to bother him.

"So immediately Bahá'u'lláh was given an order that within a month He should take what few belongings He could gather, and leave the country forever, and with it all His lands and houses and friends. As soon as the Russian ambassador heard of this order, he offered to let Bahá'u'lláh go to his country, because he had such immense respect for Him. But Bahá'u'lláh chose instead to live in 'Iráq, where He could be closer to the followers of the Báb."

"So the persecution stopped after all?" asked Ahmad.

"For a while," said Husayn, "but things still looked very gloomy for the Bábí Faith. All the leaders except Bahá'u'lláh had been killed, and now Bahá'u'lláh was being removed from Persia. The temporary leader of the Bábí community was supposed to be Bahá'u'lláh's half-brother Mírzá Yaḥyá—the Báb Himself had given Mírzá Yaḥyá this distinction. But I'm afraid Mírzá Yaḥyá was not a very courageous individual. In fact, he had long since run away from the struggle in fear of being arrested and killed for being a Bábí."

"Where did Mírzá Yaḥyá go?" asked Neda.

"Most of the time he hid in the mountains of Mázindarán disguised as a dervish. But in addition to having a leader who was a coward, what made matters even worse for the Bábís was that the writings of the Báb were scattered among the disorganized Bábís."

"So they didn't know what to do?" asked Ali.

"Exactly. That's why it is easy to understand how the Sh̲áh thought that if he made Bahá'u'lláh leave the country, he would have finally succeeded in destroying the Bábí Faith itself. I'm sure that, to many of the Bábís, everything did seem bleak and hopeless. And, in fact, that's where our journey through the snow begins."

"I don't understand," said Ahmad. "What does our hike through the snow and the mountains have to do with all this?"

"I think I know," said Neda. "Bahá'u'lláh had to walk through the mountains on the way to exile in Bag̲h̲dád, didn't He?"

"Absolutely correct," said Husayn placing his hand on the young girl's shoulders. "Bahá'u'lláh and His family were forced to leave Ṭihrán on foot in the dead of winter and journey westward through the mountains toward the borders of 'Iráq. Bahá'u'lláh was not at all recovered from His suffering in the dungeon, so walking was even more difficult for Him. The icy cold winds and freezing snow battered the band of companions. With Bahá'u'lláh were His faithful brothers, Mírzá Músá and Mírzá Muḥammad-Qulí; Bahá'u'lláh's nine-year-old eldest son, 'Abdu'l-Bahá; Bahá'u'lláh's seven-year-old daughter Bahíyyih; and His wife Ásíyih K̲h̲ánum.

"Of course, Bahá'u'lláh knew that the Bábí Faith was far from dead. It was like a fire scattered into embers. By themselves the still-hot coals may not be strong enough to start a flame, but when they are gathered together a blaze can be rekindled. So it was that the same fire of faith that had burned so brightly in Persia and 'Iráq now desperately needed the guiding hands of Bahá'u'lláh to gather those embers."

"Did Bahá'u'lláh's family know what had happened to Him in the Síyáh-Chál?" asked Ali.

"I'm not sure. I suspect some of Bahá'u'lláh's family knew that something wonderful had occurred while He had been in the prison, but their primary concern was to help Bahá'u'lláh get well. And of course, Bahá'u'lláh knew how much work lay ahead for Him—not only would He have to reveal all the teachings to guide humanity until the next Manifestation of God appeared; He would also have to teach the Bábís about their own religion before He could even begin."

"I don't understand," said Neda. "Didn't the Báb teach the Bábís with His own writings?"

"Yes, He did. But as I told you, most of the Bábís had no chance to study the teachings of the Báb. Most understood that He was the Promised Qá'im, but they had never had an opportunity to study His writings and teachings to prepare themselves for the coming of Bahá'u'lláh.

"You see, the Báb wrote over 500,000 verses, more than all the teachings of the previous Manifestations combined. And almost all of these writings were preparing the Bábís for the coming of 'Him Whom God shall make manifest,' Bahá'u'lláh Himself."

"In other words, before Bahá'u'lláh could tell anyone that He was the Promised One the Báb had talked about, He had to teach them what the Báb had said about the next Manifestation?" said Neda.

"Exactly. When He left Ṭihrán and Persia, the community of Bábís was scattered and confused, so Bahá'u'lláh knew He would have to wait to tell the believers Who He was until they had had a chance to understand their own beliefs as Bábís. And in His heart He knew that there was no one left to do this job but Himself. In fact, in a tablet addressed to Bahá'u'lláh, the Báb asked Him to wait nineteen years 'as a token of Thy favor so that those who have embraced this Cause may be graciously rewarded by Thee.' You see, the Báb had told His followers that the Promised Manifestation would appear in the year nine, the ninth year of the Báb's revelation, 1853, the same year that Bahá'u'lláh was in the Síyáh-Chál. But because the Báb was a Prophet, He also knew the future and understood everything that would happen to His followers and to His religion. For that reason, He asked Bahá'u'lláh not to reveal Himself until the year nineteen—ten years later in 1863—so that the Bábís would have a chance to become prepared to recognize Him, even though some had already recognized Bahá'u'lláh's station."

"Like Shaykh Ḥasan?" said Ali.

"Yes, and probably some of the Letters of the Living as well. Many others would also come to understand during the next ten years as Bahá'u'lláh worked to rebuild the Bábí community."

"I think I understand now," said Neda. "I wondered why Bahá'u'lláh didn't tell everyone right away that He was the Manifestation."

"The Bábís had suffered quite a lot and were probably already confused," said Husayn. "If Bahá'u'lláh had told them right away that He was a Manifestation, they might have become even more confused." Husayn slackened his pace a little when he noticed that Ali seemed to be limping a little. "What's wrong with your foot, Ali?"

"Oh, nothing, Father. I must have stepped on a piece of seashell this morning, and my foot is starting to sting."

"Can you walk the rest of the way to the town? We still have over a mile to go until we get to the city walls."

Ali looked up at the white city of 'Akká, which seemed tinted orange in the late afternoon sun. He knew that if he couldn't walk, his father would have to carry him, so, even though his foot didn't feel very good at all, he pretended it didn't hurt. "It's just a small cut," he said.

But Husayn looked into his eyes to be sure that the boy wasn't hiding the pain. "I suspect it hurts more than you say, Ali. We'll rest here a few minutes and then we'll walk back."

They found a large old tree trunk that had washed ashore, and they sat down facing the water. The breeze off the water was exhilarating, and their hair danced in the wind.

"How far have we walked today?" asked Neda. "Oh, a few miles, I suppose," said Husayn. "Why do you ask?"

"When they had to leave Persia, how far did Bahá'u'lláh and His family have to travel?"

"You mean, how far was the entire journey?"

"Yes."

"From Ṭihrán to Ba<u>gh</u>dád was about five hundred miles, Neda, and the way was rough, across a mountain range and through the winter snow."

"But how could Bahá'u'lláh do that if He had just come out of prison?" asked Ahmad.

"Well, they tried to give Bahá'u'lláh a little time to heal from his months inside the dungeon, but they were only given a few weeks to prepare for the journey."

"Was that enough time for Bahá'u'lláh to get well?" asked Ali.

"Not at all, Ali. The scars from the heavy chains never went away, and He was quite ill for most of the journey. As soon as He got out of prison, He went to stay at the home of His half-brother Mírzá Riḍá-Qulí, who was a physician."

"Was His half-brother a Bábí?" asked Ahmad.

"No, His brother's wife, Maryam, was a Bábí and loved Bahá'u'lláh very dearly, so she and Bahá'u'lláh's wife Ásíyih <u>Kh</u>ánum took care of Bahá'u'lláh until He was somewhat better—well enough to begin the journey. When at last Bahá'u'lláh's children were allowed to see their father, they noticed immediately the marks that four months in prison had left on Him. They saw the deep scars on His neck where the chains had cut His delicate skin, and they saw the wounds on His feet from the bastinado.

"And when they wept as they tended His wounds, He told them stories about the brave Bábís who has suffered in the prison with Him. He spoke of their faith and courage, how many had endured torture and then courageously faced martyrdom."

"Did they know what it was?" asked Ali.

"I'm not sure, Ali. I know that 'Abdu'l-Bahá knew. 'Abdu'l-Bahá was really the first to believe in Bahá'u'lláh, the first to understand that He was a Prophet sent from God. So 'Abdu'l-Bahá's love was even greater than the love of a son for a father. His love was coupled with the awe and reverence that one has in the divine presence of a Manifestation of God. Consequently, the nine-year-old 'Abdu'l-Bahá decided to dedicate the rest of His life to serving Bahá'u'lláh in whatever way He could.

"When Bahá'u'lláh was well enough, Ásíyih Khánum tried as best she could to gather provisions for the arduous journey. She sold almost all that was left of her marriage treasures, including her jewels and elegant garments, and any other belongings which might bring in enough money to buy what they needed. But she could manage to get only about 400 túmáns. With that money she bought food and a few other things they needed for the journey. The government would give them nothing.

"Well, as you can imagine, the family was in a pitiful condition as they set out, and no doubt the Sháh felt quite victorious at their departure. As far as he knew, all of the Bábí leaders had been killed or imprisoned. And now, sick from imprisonment and ill-prepared for this difficult journey in the middle of winter, the last leader of the Bábís was being removed from Persia.

"Indeed, the future looked bleak and hopeless to the family. 'Abdu'l-Bahá had suffered from tuberculosis so horribly that the doctors had given up hope, but before they departed He suddenly became well. But perhaps the journey was most wretched for Ásíyih Khánum because she had to take command, even though she was hardly prepared for such a thing."

"Why do you say that?" asked Neda.

"It's hard to explain," Husayn answered, "but I will try. You see, Ásíyih Khánum was from a noble family, so she had received a courtly upbringing. She had always had servants and elegant surroundings. Now, suddenly, she was deprived of all assistance and had to be responsible for an arduous journey in the dead of winter with a young family and a sick husband. In fact, she not only had to leave behind all the beautiful jewels and clothing she had been used to, the houses and lands that the family had owned for so many years, but she also had to leave her youngest son, Mihdí, who was only two years old.

"Fortunately, she could leave him with her grandmother where he would be safe, but she had no way of knowing if she would ever see her precious son again. Imagine how miserable she must have been, to be deprived of her child at the same time she was being exiled from her native country. What is worse, she was seven months pregnant!"

"Then how could she possibly walk all that way?" asked Neda.

"Well, she did ride a little, but in a *takht-i-raván,* a rough sort of seat placed on the back of a mule."

"I've seen one," said Ahmad. "I think I would rather walk!"

"Perhaps so," said Husayn. "Nevertheless, this most noble of women did not once complain, nor did any of Bahá'u'lláh's family, in spite of the cold and having to leave behind everything they owned or held dear.

"When they departed, they were accompanied by an officer of the Imperial Guard and an official representing the Russian legation. As they headed south to Qum it was already cold, but soon they traveled westward toward the town of Hamadán and the high mountain paths. Towns were few in that region, and there were not many places to stay indoors. Ásíyih Khánum, who was a delicate woman and greatly burdened by her pregnancy, would wash the clothes at the public baths in the villages they passed through while the others washed themselves. She would then carry the cold clothes away in her arms and try to dry them, though in the moist winter air it was extremely cold, and very soon her hands became tender and raw.

"The terrain along the way was barren, with only a few settlements. Sometimes there would be a caravansary where they could stay indoors. But you have seen these, and you know that they are far from comfortable. What is more, they could stay in them only one night with one room for the whole family, and after dark they were not allowed to have any lights, nor were there any beds."

"Sometimes they were able to have tea or a few eggs, or some cheese and coarse bread, but Bahá'u'lláh was still so ill that He could not eat this rough food. Before long Ásíyih Khánum and the others began to worry that Bahá'u'lláh was becoming dangerously weak from the lack of good food.

"One day, after Ásíyih Khánum had managed to obtain some flour, she returned to the caravansary where they were staying that night. Without any proper cooking utensils, she labored to make a sweet cake for Bahá'u'lláh. But there was a problem—in the dark caravansary room, she had mistaken salt for sugar, and the small cake was ruined and could not be eaten.

"And so the trip went, day after day with little or no rest, until after they had gone through some of the mountains, they passed the town of Hamadán and journeyed into the territory of the Kurds."

"Who are the Kurds?" asked Ahmad.

"They are a tribal people who live an independent sort of life in the mountainous region of Ádhirbáyján. Well, these tribes are mortal enemies of the Persians, but when the family reached the Kurdish town of Karand, a small village nestled between two sawtoothed ridges on the most western frontier of Persia. Here at last they found decent lodging and a needed rest because, as it happened, Bahá'u'lláh was an old friend of the governor.

"As a result of this stay, Bahá'u'lláh's health gradually improved because they were allowed to stay as guests in the governor's mansion with its lovely courtyard in the shade of giant poplars. From there they could hear the peaceful sound of a nearby river. In fact, it was to these same lovely mountains Bahá'u'lláh would return within the year.

"A few days later the band of exiles traveled on, and shortly they reached the border of 'Iráq, where the Persian soldiers left them in the charge of Turkish soldiers. The land in 'Iráq was quite different from what they were accustomed to. It was arid, dusty, and barren.

"Finally, after a long and difficult journey that had taken three months, they arrived in Baghdád on April 8, 1853. And in this ancient city, the capital city of the Turkish province of 'Iráq, they sensed a hope that perhaps the fortunes of the Bábí Faith might be reversed. In this city on the Tigris River, which was once the cradle of civilization, they hoped that after five years of ceaseless bloodshed somehow the fortunes of the new religion might be changed for the better.

"After a few days the family moved to the village of Kaẓimayn, a Persian settlement about three miles north of the city. When they arrived there was great excitement, for even though few of the Persians in Kaẓimayn were Bábís, they had heard of Bahá'u'lláh and were anxious to see Him and talk with Him.

"Before too long, the consul-general of Persia became disturbed by the number of visitors who came to Kaẓimayn to see Bahá'u'lláh, and he suggested to Bahá'u'lláh that the family should move into a house in the old section of Ba<u>gh</u>dád. Thus, in the month of May, after the difficult journey from Ṭihrán, Bahá'u'lláh rented the house of 'Ali Madad, a house which is very important to Bahá'ís today."

"Bahá'ís make pilgrimages there," said Neda. "I know because my uncle has been there."

"That's right," said Husayn. "In fact, the only place more important to Bahá'ís is . . ." Husayn paused.

"'Akká!" said Ahmad proudly.

"Correct," said Husayn. "Yes, over the next ten years after Bahá'u'lláh arrived, that house became a very important place, because even this painful journey into exile could not defeat the destiny of the Faith of God. Once more it seemed that Bahá'u'lláh and His followers were able to endure whatever people tried to do to destroy the Bábí religion, to transform mysteriously what seemed like certain defeat into victory.

"But it wasn't an easy victory. It didn't happen overnight, as you all know—but that's another story. Eventually Bahá'u'lláh did change the hearts of the people in Ba<u>gh</u>dád, and people came from all over the city, even from other cities far away, to seek His advice or simply to enjoy meeting Him. But before any of these changes could happen, Bahá'u'lláh had more basic things to accomplish."

"Like what?" asked Ali.

"Well, first He had to regain His health. Then He had to begin reorganizing the Bábí community so that He could teach them about their own religion. And, of course, all these things took time and an incredible amount of work."

Husayn stopped for a moment. He looked at the faces of the three children. He marveled at how attentive they were, how eager and bright. "So the journey from Ṭihrán to Ba<u>gh</u>dád was painful and difficult, but at the journey's end was waiting a city which a Muslim tradition calls the 'Abode of Peace' and which Bahá'u'lláh Himself called the 'City of God.'"

"Then the journey really had a happy ending?" asked Ali.

"Well, I am not so sure if the rest of the family knew when they first arrived that it would be happy, but for those who were patient enough to see how it would all turn out, there was a happy ending."

"Must there always be patience?" said Ali smiling.

"I'm afraid so," said his father. "And, speaking of patience, how is your foot now?"

Ali stood up to see how his foot felt. To his surprise, the pain had completely gone. He could tell there was a cut, but it didn't hurt anymore. "It's fine! I could run back to 'Akká . . . if I had to."

"What about it, children? Shall we make Ali run back, or do we plod through the deep snow?"

They all laughed and began the last part of their journey hand in hand as Neda sang in a sweet melodic voice a Persian song her mother had taught her.

It had been a memorable day for the children. After that, when ever the three of them walked along that same part of the beach, they remembered Bahá'u'lláh's long journey to Ba<u>gh</u>dád. And whenever they came to that same big log where they had listened to Ali's father tell them about the journey, they would call it the story tree.

8

The Nameless One

'Akká was a poor town. Its streets were usually quite dirty, and most of the people who daily dwelled within its ancient walls were the downtrodden from various lands. Many were prisoners and exiles of the Turkish government.

In ages past, the town had been a stronghold, a magnificent fortress against attack. At another time it had been a bustling seaport where Syrians sold their goods. But now the fame and beauty of 'Akká seemed a thing of the past. The atmosphere of the town had greatly improved since Bahá'u'lláh and the other Bahá'í exiles had arrived there some forty-four years before in 1868. But now in 1912 most of the people in 'Akká were still quite poor.

Across the bay the growing town of Haifa was cleaner, its townspeople more prosperous. Perhaps many of the people in 'Akká longed to live across the bay or in some other place, but Ali thought of this ancient walled town with its many secret places as a special place to live. After all, it was close to the Shrine of Bahá'u'lláh, and for all this time it had been the home of 'Abdu'l-Bahá. But Ali also liked 'Akká for itself—the old walls so huge and grand, the constant sound of the sea washing against the old fortress, the small fishing boats that skimmed across the bay or bobbed out toward the horizon on a sea that reached out endlessly to lands that Ali could only dream about.

Sometimes when Ali and Ahmad were fishing off the seawall, and other children, who weren't Bahá'ís, talked about how nice it would be to move away, Ali and Ahmad would tell them what a special place 'Akká was. Occasionally, the children from Muslim families would make fun of Ahmad and Ali or the other Bahá'í children, though some had admiration for the Bahá'ís. Certainly almost all the citizens loved and respected 'Abdu'l-Bahá, Who had become known to them as "Father of the Poor" because He was so kind and generous to everyone He met.

One afternoon, however, when Ali was making his way through the shadowed streets that fit narrowly between the old stone houses, he came upon Bijan, his seven-year-old cousin. The small boy was sitting sadly on the doorstep in front of his apartment. His face resting on his hands, he stared blankly at the street.

"Bijan," said Ali, "would you like to go fishing with me down on the wall?"

Normally the young lad would have been quite honored to be invited to go anywhere with his older cousin, for whom he had the greatest admiration.

"No, thanks," said Bijan softly.

"Come on! I'm going to get Ahmad and Neda."

Bijan looked up. "Well . . . if I can get permission."

As Bijan spoke, Ali noticed that his cousin's eyes were red as if he had been crying. "What's the matter? Are you hurt?"

"No," said Bijan quickly, looking down with embarrassment.

"What is it then?"

"It's the kids down the street, Omar and his friends. They did it again. They . . . well, they said things!"

"About you?"

"About Bahá'u'lláh!"

"What did they say?"

"That He . . . that He was . . . a coward."

"A coward?" said Ali, almost laughing at the ridiculous idea. "After all the things that Bahá'u'lláh suffered? They should know better than that!" But Ali's comment did not cheer Bijan.

"They said that He ran away to the mountains, just like His brother Mírzá Yaḥyá. Is that true, Ali?"

"It's true that both went to the mountains, Bijan, but Bahá'u'lláh was never a coward, not at all. Look, go ask permission to come with us, and while we fish off the wall, I'll tell you the true story. I'll explain why Bahá'u'lláh went to the mountains, and you'll see."

Bijan's face cheered a little, and he turned and scampered into the house.

Within a few minutes Ali and Bijan were meeting Ahmad, and the three of them walked toward the place on the wall where they always fished when they did not have time to go to the docks or could not walk to the beach to cast their lines in the surf. Bijan felt proud as he walked between the two older boys.

When they reached the wall, he pretended to check his handline like Ahmad and Ali, but he was not really sure what he was supposed to be doing. His father always helped him unravel the line and bait the hook. Now the old line had many knots and was wrapped tightly around a stick. But by watching the older boys and doing what they did, he managed to get his line ready by himself, which made him feel quite proud.

The three of them had just finished settling down on a warm part of the stone wall and casting their lines below them into the surf when Ali saw his grandfather walking toward them with Neda beside him. The boys smiled when they saw Moayyed because he always had a surprise. Perhaps it would be a handful of pistachio nuts or some fresh dates, but there would always be something. But even more important to them were the stories he could tell. Even the simplest stories became exciting when Moayyed told them.

Ali was especially glad to see Moayyed because he thought his grandfather might help him explain the answer to Bijan's question.

"Greetings, my brave fishermen," said Moayyed as he sat down beside them. "Neda and I bring you greetings from the Garden of Riḍván." And with that he reached into the small pouch that Neda was carrying over her shoulder and pulled out several tangerines.

As the fruit was being passed around, Ahmad asked, "Are these really from the Garden of Riḍván?"

"Yes," said Neda. "We left early this morning and just returned."

"And you're just in time to tell a story," said Ali. He explained to his grandfather what Omar had said to Bijan.

"Well, I think we can clear up this problem without too much trouble," said Moayyed as he peeled away some of the rind from the sweet sections of fruit, "that is, if you will help me, Ali, for you know this story almost as well as I do."

Moayyed sat down on the wall and stretched his back, which always became sore when he went on long walks. "Let me see," he began, "where do I start?" He paused, rubbed his chin with his hand, then spoke again. "Bijan, as you know, Bahá'u'lláh and His family were forced to leave Persia because they were Bábís."

"Yes," said Bijan. "Mother and Father have explained that to me."

"And did they also explain to you who Mírzá Yaḥyá was?"

"I heard my parents say that he died last month on an island."

"That's right, the island of Cyprus. You see, when the government sent Bahá'u'lláh here to 'Akká, they sent Mírzá Yaḥyá to the city of Famagusta in Cyprus. But we're getting ahead of ourselves. Let me explain to you exactly who Mírzá Yaḥyá was.

"In 1850, after the Báb had been martyred in Tabríz, the country was a very dangerous place for all Bábís. As you know, many Bábís had already been killed at Ṭabarsí and Nayríz, at Zanján, and in many other places. Every day Bábís were being arrested or persecuted, even women and small children. But even when their lives were threatened, few would deny that they were followers of the Báb, even though they could have saved their lives by doing so.

"Mírzá Yaḥyá was a half-brother of Bahá'u'lláh, and when their father, Mírzá Buzurg, died in 1839, Mírzá Yaḥyá was only eight years old, so Bahá'u'lláh, Who was twenty-two, cared for Mírzá Yaḥyá, raised him like a son. So you might think that Mírzá Yaḥyá would be strong and brave, like Bahá'u'lláh. But he was not. Unlike most of the Bábís, who were brave and courageous about being followers of the Báb, Mírzá Yaḥyá was terrified that someone might discover he was a Bábí. When the persecutions became very severe, Mírzá Yaḥyá, who was now nearly twenty, ran in fear to the mountains of Mázindarán, where he hid and disguised himself."

"I think I might run too," said Bijan softly.

"So might we all," said Moayyed, putting his hand on the child's arm. "We never know how brave we are until we are tested. Until then, we can never be certain. But we can still understand what was wrong with the way Mírzá Yaḥyá behaved. You see, Mírzá Yaḥyá wasn't just any Bábí. Before the Báb was executed in 1850, He designated Mírzá Yaḥyá as the temporary head of the Bábí community.

"Why was it temporary?" asked Ahmad.

"Because the Báb told His followers that when the next Prophet appeared, everyone should immediately follow Him."

"And did Mírzá Yaḥyá lead the community?" asked Ali. "Sadly, he did nothing of the sort. He was nineteen years old when the Báb was executed, and instead of becoming a leader, he disappeared, not just for a few days or weeks. He stayed in the mountains for several years, wandering through Mázindarán and the province of Gílán, often wearing disguises. He dressed himself up to look like someone else so that the authorities would not know who he was and the Bábís would not attract attention to him by coming to him for advice and guidance.

"So it was that in 1852 when Bahá'u'lláh was arrested and put in the dark dungeon of the Síyáh-Chál and suffered so horribly for four long months, Mírzá Yaḥyá, whom Bahá'u'lláh had loved like a son and educated to become a most eloquent and gifted writer, remained hidden. But when Bahá'u'lláh was released from prison and exiled to Baghdád, Mírzá Yaḥyá did not want to be left alone in Persia. He found out where Bahá'u'lláh was headed and went secretly to Kirmánsháh, a town near the Persian border in the west, on that same road to Baghdád that Bahá'u'lláh and the family were traveling. He knew that Bahá'u'lláh would be passing through this town on the way to Baghdád. So that winter in 1853, when Bahá'u'lláh and His family came to Kirmánsháh, Mírzá Yaḥyá was there waiting."

"Did he join the family in their journey?" asked Neda.

"No, he did not. You see, even though he was now a young man of twenty-two, Mírzá Yaḥyá was deathly afraid someone would find out who he was. So he followed the family, but he did not travel with them. He didn't even visit Bahá'u'lláh or the other Bábís when they came to Kirmánsháh. In fact, when the family discovered that Mírzá Yaḥyá was in Kirmánsháh, they sent Mírzá Músá to find him so Mírzá Yaḥyá could join them. But when Mírzá Músá found him, Mírzá Yaḥyá became very angry. He was afraid people would now know that he was a Bábí."

"There's something I don't understand," said Ahmad. "If Bahá'u'lláh was the One the Báb had come to tell about, then why was Mírzá Yaḥyá supposed to be the leader?"

"That's a good question, Ahmad. Can you answer that, Ali?" said Moayyed, turning to his grandson.

"I'll try," said Ali. "Mírzá Yaḥyá was appointed to lead the Bábís, but he was not the promised Manifestation, not 'Him Whom God shall make manifest,' even though I think he later said he was. The Báb indicated Who the Manifestation was when He sent His pen-case, His seals, and His writings to Bahá'u'lláh."

"And I am sure," added Moayyed, "that Bahá'u'lláh would certainly not have minded if Mírzá Yaḥyá had led the Bábís as he was asked to do. I am sure that would have made Bahá'u'lláh immensely proud of His younger brother. But Mírzá Yaḥyá not only refused to assume his proper responsibility, he became a source of unbelievable pain and suffering for both Bahá'u'lláh and His family."

"What sort of things did he do?" asked Bijan.

"Not long after Bahá'u'lláh and the family arrived in Baghdád and settled in a house in the old quarter of the city, there was a knock on the door one day. Bahá'u'lláh's faithful brother Mírzá Músá went to the door, and when he opened it, he saw a strange dervish with an alms box over his shoulder. And do you know who that dervish was?"

"I know," said Bijan with a smile. "It was Mírzá Yaḥyá, wasn't it?"

"Correct!" said Moayyed. "When the dervish spoke, Mírzá Músá realized that it was Mírzá Yaḥyá in disguise once again. Well, the pitiful young man begged the family not to tell anyone that he was in the city. He then found a secret house in the Arab quarter where no Persians lived, but during the nighttime he would visit Bahá'u'lláh's house."

"Didn't that make the family angry?" asked Neda.

"No doubt it displeased them, but Bahá'u'lláh instructed them always to treat Mírzá Yaḥyá with respect, no matter what he did. So they would always welcome him. But during the day he would not meet with any of the Bábís for fear of being recognized."

"Even though he was supposed to be the leader of the Bábí community?" observed Ali.

"That's right," said Moayyed. "And the Bábís desperately needed leadership, too. For almost three years they had been without the Báb, and they had hardly any of His writings to guide them in how they should behave or organize themselves.

"As you can imagine, this upset Bahá'u'lláh terribly. As Bahá'u'lláh roamed about Ba<u>gh</u>dád and the neighboring villages, He discovered that almost no one claimed to be a Bábí. In all of Ba<u>gh</u>dád He found just one Persian Bábí. In the nearby Persian settlement of Káẓimayn there were only a few others, and even they were afraid and confused."

"You mean all the work of the martyrs was for nothing?" asked Ahmad.

"Not at all," said Moayyed. "The seeds of faith which the martyrs planted and nourished with their own blood would later yield much fruit, but for now things seemed very hopeless. Consequently, with great care and the utmost love Bahá'u'lláh began to talk with the Bábís, to encourage them, though He knew it was not yet time to tell them that He was the Manifestation the Báb had promised would come to them.

"Of course, 'Abdu'l-Bahá knew Who He was, and there was a young Bábí who discovered Bahá'u'lláh's identity in a dream. The Bábí's name was Mírzá Áqá Ján, a young man who had traveled a great distance from his home in Persia to serve Bahá'u'lláh. Because of this young man's devotion, Bahá'u'lláh chose him to become His secretary. In fact, many of the tablets of Bahá'u'lláh were copied down by Mírzá Áqá Ján.

"But other than telling these two, Bahá'u'lláh thought it best to keep His secret hidden and to teach people what the Báb had to say so that later on they would be ready for Bahá'u'lláh's own teachings. So Bahá'u'lláh began organizing the Bábís and teaching them. Little by little He began to breathe life into the Bábí community in Baghdád.

"However, at the same time Bahá'u'lláh was beginning to revive the Bábí community, someone else was trying to stir up trouble for Bahá'u'lláh and to put a stop to the wonderful work He was doing. His name was Siyyid Muḥammad of Iṣfahán."

"Wasn't he the one who gave Mírzá Yaḥyá the idea of claiming that he, not Bahá'u'lláh, was the Prophet the Báb had promised?" asked Ali.

"That's right. You see, just before Bahá'u'lláh had been put in the Síyáh-Chál, He had visited 'Iráq and the town of Karbilá, where Siyyid Muḥammad was staying. When Bahá'u'lláh spoke there among the scholars and wise men of the town who had once followed Siyyid Káẓim in searching for the Promised Qá'im, He won their complete respect and devotion. And when they heard Him speak about the Báb, they felt such reverence for Him that Siyyid Muḥammad became very jealous.

"Bahá'u'lláh could tell that Siyyid Muḥammad was jealous, and He tried to be especially nice to him. But it is strange the way jealousy makes people behave. The more patient Bahá'u'lláh was with Siyyid Muḥammad of Iṣfahan, the more jealous and angry the young man became.

"So now, as Bahá'u'lláh began to teach the Bábís in Baghdád, Siyyid Muḥammad heard about Bahá'u'lláh's increasing popularity, and he came to see if he could put a stop to Bahá'u'lláh's success. That's when Siyyid Muḥammad of Iṣfahan came up with an idea about how he could hurt Bahá'u'lláh. He found out where Mírzá Yaḥyá was living and made friends with him. Of course, Mírzá Yaḥyá was already jealous of Bahá'u'lláh, especially when Bahá'u'lláh began doing the job that the Báb had appointed Mírzá Yaḥyá to do."

"What was Siyyid Muḥammad's plan?" asked Ali.

"He had several plans," said Moayyed, shaking his head in disgust. "Over the years that followed, he devoted his whole life to hurting Bahá'u'lláh and those who followed Him, and he almost always used Mírzá Yaḥyá to carry out his schemes."

"But why?" asked Neda with a puzzled look. "Why would anyone want to hurt a Prophet of God?"

"I'm not sure I can answer that, my child. I suppose the simplest explanation is that when you have been in the darkness and a bright light shines on you, you can be patient until you become accustomed to the benefits it brings, or you can turn away. And if you continue to turn away, you may grow to hate the light itself and continue living in the darkness.

"Of course, if you choose to abide in darkness, you will become miserable. What is more, you will become jealous of those who enjoy the light. So it was with Siyyid Muḥammad of Iṣfahan. He was jealous of Bahá'u'lláh, and yet he had no power to subdue Him. I suspect in his misery he thought that if he could turn Mírzá Yaḥyá against his own brother, he would at least inflict some injury on this Source of light. So he tempted Mírzá Yaḥyá by telling him that if he claimed to be the Promised One and told others that Bahá'u'lláh was trying to take his rightful place as the chosen one of the Báb, he would receive all the honor and respect that Bahá'u'lláh was receiving."

"But how could he do that?" asked Ahmad.

"Remember, Ahmad, the Bábís did not have many of the Báb's writings. They were not yet very deep in their beliefs. So, when the very same young man whom the Báb had designated to lead them started telling such lies, many became confused. Of course, they loved Bahá'u'lláh and knew He was not a greedy man. They could also tell that Bahá'u'lláh was wise and Mírzá Yaḥyá was not. Still, they did not want to disobey the Báb.

"Let me give you an example of what I mean." Moayyed paused to eat a section of a tangerine. "One well-known, honorable, and learned Bábí was very disturbed by what had happened to his religion after the Báb died. When he heard that Mírzá Yaḥyá was claiming to be the Promised One, this Bábí traveled to Baghdád to talk with him and to get advice. But Mírzá Yaḥyá would not meet with him because, as usual, he was trying to hide."

"Finally, Mírzá Yaḥyá agreed to see the man. When he did, the visitor asked Mírzá Yaḥyá to explain a certain passage in the Qur'án. At first,

Mírzá Yaḥyá refused, but the visitor pleaded again and again until Mírzá Yaḥyá agreed to write down an explanation of the verse. When this wise Bábí took the tablet Mírzá Yaḥyá had written and read it, he became very sad. He could tell that Mírzá Yaḥyá did not really understand the passage. In fact, he could tell that Mírzá Yaḥyá was not even particularly intelligent.

"In his sadness, the Bábí went to Bahá'u'lláh and told Him what had happened and asked Him if He could explain the verses. Bahá'u'lláh immediately began to explain what the verses meant, and the Bábí became happy and excited because he knew that it was Bahá'u'lláh Who was the Promised One, not Mírzá Yaḥyá.

"There were also other Bábís who knew that Bahá'u'lláh could help them, and even other people in Ba<u>gh</u>dád, such as public officials and the governor of the city, who came to visit Him. But the more popular Bahá'u'lláh became, the more Siyyid Muḥammad of Iṣfahan plotted with Mírzá Yaḥyá to cause trouble for Bahá'u'lláh by telling the Bábís that Bahá'u'lláh was trying to destroy their religion!"

"But how could Mírzá Yaḥyá say such a thing when he was the one who was trying to destroy it!" said Bijan angrily. "Why didn't Bahá'u'lláh do something?"

"What could He do?" said Moayyed. "Bahá'u'lláh could hardly tell Mírzá Yaḥyá to stop talking to the other Bábís. And how could He tell the Bábís not to pay attention to the very one whom the Báb Himself had designated as the temporary leader of the Bábí community? That was the problem, Bijan. The more things Bahá'u'lláh did to help the Bábís, the more Mírzá Yaḥyá would claim that Bahá'u'lláh was simply trying to replace Mírzá Yaḥyá as leader."

"I imagine Bahá'u'lláh must have been very angry!" said Bijan, "especially since Bahá'u'lláh had helped raise Mírzá Yaḥyá."

"I think He was more sad and disappointed," said Moayyed. "But soon Bahá'u'lláh realized that there was nothing He could do to straighten out this situation, that the only way He could prove He was not trying to take power away from Mírzá Yaḥyá was to leave and let Mírzá Yaḥyá show what he could do.

"That was when He decided to leave Baghdád. Without telling anyone, not even His wife or His children, He left the city in April of 1854 accompanied by one servant."

"Where did He go?" asked Bijan.

"He headed toward the rugged mountains of the north in the land of the Kurds, near the village of Sulaymáníyyih."

"Then He *didn't* go because He was afraid," said Bijan.

"Afraid!" said Moayyed. "I should say not! The mountains of Kurdistán are no place for anyone who is afraid, especially for a Persian. The Kurdish people are not particularly fond of Persians. No, Bijan, Bahá'u'lláh had good reasons for going, but fear was not one of them. I recall two places in His writings where He talks about His reasons. In fact, in one of His tablets He says very clearly why He left. 'The one object of Our retirement,' He said, 'was to avoid becoming a subject of discord among the faithful, a source of disturbance unto Our companions, the means of injury to any soul, or the cause of sorrow to any heart.' And in another tablet He said, 'I shunned all else but God, and closed Mine eyes to all except Him, that haply the fire of hatred may die down and the heat of jealousy abate.'"

Already Bijan felt better. His question had been answered. But now he wanted to know more. He wanted to know what happened to Bahá'u'lláh in the mountains. "Can you tell us what happened to Him in the mountains?" asked Bijan.

"Yes, and I would like to know what happened back in Baghdád with Mírzá Yaḥyá while Bahá'u'lláh was gone," said Ahmad.

"Very well," said Moayyed. "First let me tell you what happened in the mountains. Bahá'u'lláh took only one change of clothes and a begging bowl when He went into the wilderness. The only food He had was a little rice now and then and perhaps some goat's milk. The one servant who accompanied Bahá'u'lláh was soon killed by a band of thieves. And so, now completely alone, Bahá'u'lláh disguised Himself as a dervish and called Himself Darvísh Muḥammad."

"Why did He do that?" asked Bijan, once again concerned that the Muslim boys were right and Bahá'u'lláh had indeed tried to hide.

"Bahá'u'lláh knew the family and other Bábís would try to find Him and seek advice from Him, and He knew it was important to give Mírzá Yaḥyá a chance to do the job the Báb had given him so that if Mírzá Yaḥyá failed, no one could claim Bahá'u'lláh was behind it.

"For a while Bahá'u'lláh lived in total isolation on a mountain called Sar-Galú, a desolate place visited only twice a year by the people of the region. Sometimes He dwelled in a cave, and sometimes out in the open or in a crude hut. His only companions were the birds and beasts of the wilderness."

"What did He do there?" asked Ali.

"Most of His time He spent in prayer and meditation. Sometimes He chanted aloud prayer after prayer, or He might compose beautiful odes praising God. At other times He thought about the problems that had come to the Bábís and considered what other problems would come to pass in the future.

"Meanwhile, in Baghdád, Bahá'u'lláh's family was grief stricken, especially ten-year-old 'Abdu'l-Bahá. He could hardly bear the sorrow He felt over the disappearance of His father. He would occupy His time with copying the tablets of the Báb or trying to help His mother with the many tasks she had, rough chores which she was not at all used to doing. Sometimes 'Abdu'l-Bahá would help her with the cooking, as Bahá'u'lláh had done before He had left. Occasionally, Mírzá Músá would take 'Abdu'l-Bahá to the meetings of the Bábís. At these meetings 'Abdu'l-Bahá amazed the other Bábís with His wisdom and eloquence.

"Of course, more than anything else, 'Abdu'l-Bahá longed to have His father back, and every day He prayed that someday Bahá'u'lláh would return. And the fervor of his prayers increased when another unexpected problem occurred."

"What was that?" asked Neda.

"I bet I know," said Bijan. "Mírzá Yaḥyá came to stay with Bahá'u'lláh's family, didn't he?"

"Absolutely correct," said Moayyed. "Mírzá Yaḥyá knew that Bahá'u'lláh had told the family to be kind to him, and so he began to take advantage of this situation. He was a ruthless guest, a tyrant. No matter how hard they tried to please him, things were never just right. He would complain about the food, even though he always insisted that he receive the best things they had. What was worse, he wouldn't let the children go outside to play with other children because he was still afraid that people would discover where he was.

"In fact, he kept the door locked and would not allow the family to go to the public baths for fear that he might be arrested one day. He wouldn't even let anyone visit to help with housework, though the housework was hard. For example, the water had to be raised bucket by bucket from the well. And, naturally, Mírzá Yaḥyá never helped with anything.

"Then a very tragic thing occurred. Bahá'u'lláh's youngest son, who had been born soon after they arrived in Baghdád, became very sick. But Mírzá Yaḥyá would not allow the family to get a doctor. And without care, the baby became worse each day. Without medical help the child soon died.

"Well, as you can imagine, Bahá'u'lláh's wife Ásíyih Khánum was brokenhearted with sorrow. But that's not the saddest part of the story. Because Mírzá Yaḥyá would not allow the family to go outside the house and prepare the child for burial, they were forced to give the child to a stranger, who took the body away to be buried, and the family was never able to discover where the burial site was." Moayyed looked at the downcast children. He wished he could simply skip over the sad parts of his stories, but he knew in his heart that these young Bahá'ís needed to know all of their history, not just the victories and the happy parts. So he decided he should now tell them about Bahá'u'lláh's return.

"Meanwhile, Bahá'u'lláh continued His rough existence in the mountains, where in spite of the rough existence, He found great joy in living a simple life and being in constant communion with God. For even though His food was scarce, He might occasionally obtain a tiny bit of sugar, which He would boil with some rice and milk to make a kind of pudding. But usually He was lucky just to get a bit of cheese and some coarse bread.

"No one knows exactly where He went in the mountains, but we do know that the few people He met were greatly changed by Him. In fact, before too long the people of that region began to hear stories about a wonderful dervish, a Nameless One who possessed great wisdom and love. For example, one evening some Ṣúfís were gathered together to discuss a very difficult poem. Suddenly, the nameless dervish stood among them and spoke about the poem. He explained it to them so beautifully and clearly that everyone was astounded by Bahá'u'lláh's wisdom. They were instantly enthralled by this stranger and gathered around Him to ask if He would teach them more. 'In a time to come,' Bahá'u'lláh answered, 'but not yet. Go to the city of Ba<u>gh</u>dád. Ask for the house of Mírzá Músá Írání. There shalt thou hear tidings of Me.'

"On another occasion, the Nameless One was walking near a mountain village when He met a young boy sitting beside the pathway. When Bahá'u'lláh saw that the boy was crying, He asked, 'Little man, why art thou weeping?' The boy looked up at the dervish and answered, 'The schoolmaster has punished me for writing so badly.' The lad showed Bahá'u'lláh his work. 'See, I cannot write, and so I have no copy! I dare not go back to school.

"Bahá'u'lláh smiled and sat down beside the boy. He took the pen in His hand and said, 'Weep no longer. I will set a copy for thee, and show thee how to imitate it. The dervish then began writing in a script so magnificent that the boy was astonished. He had never seen anything like it, not even from his own teacher.

"When Bahá'u'lláh had finished, He handed the tablet to the boy and said, 'And now thou canst take this and show it to thy schoolmaster.'

"The boy thanked Bahá'u'lláh several times and then ran off to his school. After he arrived, he showed the copy to his teacher. When the teacher saw the exquisite calligraphy, he asked the student, 'Who gave this to thee?' The boy replied, 'He wrote it for me, the dervish on the mountain.' The teacher then said, 'He is no dervish, the writer of this, but a royal personage.'

"So once again, as it had happened several times in His mountain wanderings, people heard about this marvelous man who went from place to place, living in solitude in the wilderness. But eventually two things happened that changed the situation. First, two holy men from the town of Sulaymáníyyih came to Bahá'u'lláh and pleaded with Him to move where they could be with Him and learn from Him. And so He agreed to go and live for a while in the town of Sulaymáníyyih, where He was given a room in a theological seminary, which is a school for studying religion.

"The second important thing happened in Baghdád. As you can imagine, Bahá'u'lláh's family had been trying for some time to find out what had happened to Bahá'u'lláh, but with little success. 'Abdu'l-Bahá prayed constantly that He might discover some news of His beloved father. On one occasion he prayed one prayer over and over the whole night long."

"What was the prayer?" asked Ali.

"It was a prayer asking God that Bahá'u'lláh be allowed to return to them. On the next day, as 'Abdu'l-Bahá and Mírzá Músá were walking in the streets of Baghdád, they overhead two people speaking of a wonderful dervish who lived in the mountains of Sulaymáníyyih, a man called 'the Nameless One,' who had changed the hearts of many people in that mountain region. 'Abdu'l-Bahá instantly knew that this must be His beloved father, for surely this dervish was the same 'Darvísh Muḥammad' to Whom Bahá'u'lláh's murdered servant had left his belongings in his will.

"Without delay the family sent a faithful friend, Shaykh Sulṭán, to find out if this dervish was Bahá'u'lláh. And so Shaykh Sulṭán journeyed toward the mountains of Kurdistan to find Bahá'u'lláh and to beg Him to return.

"Meanwhile, in Sulaymáníyyih the stories about the Nameless One continued to spread. Like a magnet, Bahá'u'lláh attracted people through His words, through His great wisdom, and through the love they found in His presence. No one was sure who He was, but that didn't matter. Even the teachers in the seminary, together with some of their best students, visited Bahá'u'lláh to see if He was really as wise as everyone said. When they visited Him, He would let them ask whatever questions they wished. And to their complete satisfaction He answered every question they asked, no matter how difficult the question was.

"Once as a test of His wisdom, they asked Him to do something no one else had been able to do, though many had tried to write a complicated poem using the same patterns of rhyme and meter as the famous mystical poem by Ibnu'l-Fáriḍ, a poem called 'Qaṣídiy-i-Tá'íyyih.' Without even hesitating, Bahá'u'lláh wrote down a poem just as they had asked. It was two thousand couplets long, and it is called 'Qaṣídiy-i-Varqá'iyyih.'

"Naturally, the news of this learned dervish spread to other villages, and scholars, doctors, holy men of all kinds, even princes and men in high political positions came to meet Bahá'u'lláh. For even though Bahá'u'lláh was still dressed in the clothing of a poor beggar, everyone was attracted to Him and knew He must be a holy person.

"Well, you can imagine how shocked Shaykh Sulṭán was when he found Bahá'u'lláh dressed in the clothes of a dervish and living in this small room at the seminary. But he was also overjoyed to find Bahá'u'lláh at long last, because the Bábís in Baghdád now desperately needed the help that Bahá'u'lláh alone could bring.

"But when Shaykh Sulṭán saw how much the people of the town and the teachers and students had grown to love Bahá'u'lláh, he was afraid they might not let Him leave. He also was not sure that Bahá'u'lláh would consent to go with him, and so he began to tell Him all the sad news of what had happened in Baghdád. He told Him that Mírzá Yaḥyá had ordered the deaths of several important Bábís whom he thought might give him trouble. Mírzá Yaḥyá had also sent Mírzá Áqá Ján to Persia to try to kill the Sháh. But worst of all, Mírzá Yaḥyá had dishonored the name of the Báb by marrying the Báb's second wife, Fáṭimih, and then a month later giving her in marriage to Siyyid Muḥammad."

"I had no idea that Mírzá Yaḥyá did such horrible things as that," said Neda.

"Much worse than that," Moayyed continued. "Shaykh Sulṭán informed Bahá'u'lláh that Siyyid Muḥammad had organized a band of robbers in Karbilá who would steal from people visiting the holy shrines. Furthermore, Shaykh Sulṭán told Bahá'u'lláh that more than twenty-five different people had now claimed to be the Promised One the Báb had foretold in His writings.

"When Bahá'u'lláh learned that the Bábí community was split into various groups and that the name of the Faith itself was getting a horrible reputation, He feared that the self-sacrificing acts of such martyrs as Mullá Ḥusayn, Quddús, Vaḥid, Ḥujjat, Ṭáhirih, and many other early Bábí heroes and heroines would be wasted. In fact, the Bábí community was in such a dreadful state that even Mírzá Yaḥyá did not know what to do and sent word that he, too, wished for Bahá'u'lláh to return.

"Now Bahá'u'lláh knew the time had come for Him to begin to show His true power and authority, for even though He would personally have preferred to stay in this mountain retreat, He knew it was God's will that He go back to Baghdád and carry out His mission.

"So it was that Bahá'u'lláh gathered together the friends He had made in Sulaymáníyyih, and He gave them the sad news. But when He told them He had to leave, He also assured them of His great love, and later, after He returned, He would send special tablets to several of them. The people bid a tearful farewell to their beloved visitor, this dervish Who had changed the lives of so many of them and had brought such tranquility to their mountain village, though in their hearts many of them suspected that this nameless dervish had far greater work to do.

"As Bahá'u'lláh started back on the path to Baghdád with Shaykh Sulṭán, He contemplated the trials and hardships He would have to face in the years to come. His days of solitude and wandering, the tranquility of His private communion with God, and the peaceful communion with these students of religion—all this was over. And so, as Bahá'u'lláh and Shaykh Sulṭán neared the city of Baghdád, Bahá'u'lláh told His companion that the time spent in seclusion in the mountains were days of peace and tranquility which would never be His lot again.

"Ah, but the joy at His return!" continued Moayyed, raising his hands. "Who could describe it? All the Bábís were suddenly filled with hope when the word reached the communities that Bahá'u'lláh was coming back. His daughter Bahíyyih and His wife Ásíyih Khánum sewed together a beautiful red coat from pieces of Persian cloth which Ásíyih Khánum had carefully guarded from her marriage gifts for just such a purpose.

"When they received word that He was on the way, each day seemed an eternity and each hour was filled with expectation. Finally one afternoon, they heard the familiar footsteps and immediately opened the door. There stood a strangely dressed dervish, but through the unfamiliar clothes they recognized their beloved Bahá'u'lláh.

"Each one clung to Him with tears of joy. His lovely wife tried to remain calm, though her heart overflowed with joy and thanksgiving. Young 'Abdu'l-Bahá held fast to His father's precious hands as if He would never let go."

Bijan smiled broadly as Moayyed finished the story, and tears welled up in Neda's eyes.

"After two long years of wandering Bahá'u'lláh was home at last! The family was together again. And for the first time in almost six years the Bábí community had a leader they could turn to without fear or hesitation. All the Bábís knew that only Bahá'u'lláh could save their precious Faith from extinction."

Bijan looked across the bay toward Mount Carmel, where the Báb was buried and where Bahá'u'lláh had pitched His tent on His several visits to the holy mountain. Now he understood why Bahá'u'lláh had left, and now he knew exactly how different were the actions of Mírzá Yaḥyá and Bahá'u'lláh. And now the young boy knew why he should always be proud to be a Bahá'í and never ever be ashamed about anything Bahá'u'lláh had done.

9

The Master Builder

Weeks had passed since Ali had dreamed about riding the black stallion into the heavens, but his memory of the dream was vivid and clear, as if he had actually done the things that he had imagined in the dream. So it was that one bright morning as Ali and his grandfather Moayyed walked the last part of the path that led from ‘Akká to the Garden of Riḍván, Ali looked intently at Napoleon’s Hill, where Ali had fallen asleep.

After several minutes of silence, something uncommon for this talkative lad, Moayyed looked at his grandson and wondered what was on the boy’s mind. For a while Moayyed was silent, not wishing to interrupt the boy’s reverie. Then he could resist no longer. “We are going to the Garden of Paradise,” said Moayyed, “and you walk like one who is being led away to prison.”

Ali laughed. “I’m sorry, Grandfather.”

“No need to apologize. But I still have one good ear, you know. I may be getting too old to do some things, but I can still listen.” Moayyed laughed at himself, and so did Ali.

For a moment, it seemed strange to Ali to hear his grandfather speak of himself as old, as if he had ever been anything else. To Ali, his grandfather had always been an old man. But for some reason on this morning as Moayyed spoke of himself as getting old, Ali considered for the first time that this same man, walking beside him, who in the boy’s mind had always been old, a grandfather, had once been a boy like himself, a boy with dreams, a boy who had looked to the future with wonder and expectations just as Ali now did. Of course, what really startled Ali was the sudden realization that he, too, would someday become as old as his grandfather and would be saying similar things to his own grandchildren.

Ali gazed at Moayyed's stooped shoulders, the eyes deep-set and worn, the face deeply creased with wrinkles like well-worn leather. Ali wondered if his grandfather still remembered the feelings he had felt as a boy. "Did you ever have a special dream?" Ali said at last.

"Many of them." Moayyed replied.

"I mean one particular dream that you still remember, one that changed your life?"

"Is that what you are thinking about—your dream?"

"Yes."

"You want to find that key, don't you, the key to the gates of 'Akká?"

"That's part of it. But there's something else, too. I've been studying about the life of Bahá'u'lláh—the way the dream said I should. And the more I have learned about the Bábí heroes—about Quddús, Mullá Ḥusayn, Ṭáhirih, and the rest—the more I feel like . . . well, that I could never be like them, that I could never do the things they did."

"Are you afraid?" asked Moayyed.

"What do you mean?"

"Are you afraid that someday your own faith will be tested, that you may be asked to perform heroic deeds like the ones they did?"

"I guess—maybe so. Except that . . . well, it's not just them. I know they were very special people. They were Letters of the Living, after all. But all of those early believers, all of them faced so much hardship, and yet they continued to have faith, to believe, to follow. I'm just not sure I could do what they did. I'm not even sure if I would want to!"

"Do you feel ashamed because you don't want to give up your life? Is that what's bothering you?"

Ali looked down at his feet. His grandfather was right, at least partly right, and it made Ali feel even worse to hear someone else say what had been going through his mind for the last several days. "I suppose so," he said softly. Then he reached down and picked up a small, flat rock that looked particularly good for throwing. He reached back, cocked his arm, and sailed the stone high in the air with a quick snap of his wrist.

Moayyed did not say anything, and Ali looked up at his grandfather. "Did you think you were special when you were my age?" he asked.

"Special?"

"Did you think that you might be something no one else had ever been, that you might do something important, something that might change the world?"

Moayyed was touched by Ali's question. He understood what Ali meant, and he remembered all too well the feelings that Ali was talking about. "I think everyone wants to be important, to make a difference in this world. Everyone wants to be remembered—that's one way we can become immortal, by doing something that those who live after us will remember. Why else would the powerful rulers of the earth never think they have quite enough, and why else would they build monuments to themselves, name cities after themselves, have paintings and statues made showing how magnificent they were?"

"And you think that's wrong? You think that's silly and prideful?"

Moayyed laughed in deep and boisterous tones. "Silly? I should say not, not so long as people want to be remembered for the right reasons. Because it's all quite true, you see? Each person can be famous, at least to those who matter—the family they leave behind, the lives they touch."

He paused for a moment as he touched his chin. "I guess I believe that each person has some special talent, some particular gift to give this world." In years to come Ali would often recall this walk and his grandfather's words, particularly when he told his own children about his grandfather and the gifts of knowledge he had given Ali. For now, Ali thought mostly about himself as he wondered if his dream really had been special, or just a fantasy that fades into ashes or faint memories.

"And did your dream come true, Grandfather? What was your gift, Grandfather?"

"What do *you* think it was, Ali?"

"I think your gift is what you are giving to me right now, when you tell me stories about Bahá'u'lláh."

"Yes," said Moayyed, "you are exactly correct. Because I am old I have seen much, and I remember most of what I have seen. This I can share with others—the lessons I have learned, the people I have known, the places I've seen. And it all has one purpose, to serve the servants of God in whatever way I can."

"That's what I want!" said Ali. "I want to know what my gift is, what I can do that's special."

"Well, if you keep studying and thinking, I am certain you will discover what your gift is."

As they walked the rest of the way to the garden, Ali wondered if his gift, his special talent, might be the key that had opened the gates of 'Akká in his dream. But he wondered how long would he have to search and study, and he also wondered if he would be able to be patient until he discovered the answer.

They were now only about a hundred yards away from the entrance to the Garden of Riḍván, and both were looking forward to sitting beneath the shade in this special garden that Bahá'u'lláh had called His "verdant isle." It was not a huge park, an island about 100 yards long and fairly narrow, with the river Na'mayn splitting into two streams that ran on either side. The garden was sheltered by two giant mulberry trees and scattered palms, beneath which were rows of well-tended flowers as well as tangerine trees and other kinds of fruit trees. The path was decorated by the colors of various sorts of flowers, and the air was wonderfully scented with the mingled fragrances.

At one end of the path was a small, one-room summerhouse where Bahá'u'lláh would sit on hot summer afternoons or sleep when He stayed overnight. On either side of the path were long wooden benches where visitors could sit and meditate or say prayers while taking in the sensual delight of this quiet oasis.

One bench, the spot where Bahá'u'lláh was wont to sit, was surrounded by potted flowers to indicate to the visitor that this spot was special. So many Bahá'ís would sit across from the bench to say prayers as they imagined what it might have been like to see Bahá'u'lláh sitting there and to be in His presence.

The rustling of a gentle breeze rustling the leaves of the mulberry trees blended with the gurgling sounds from the stream and from a beautiful fountain situated in the middle of the garden.

This tranquil place always made Ali feel peaceful inside, though most of his visits were made on holy days when he had come with his parents and many other Bahá'ís. Today, with Moayyed, he felt that the garden was reserved just for him and his grandfather.

They greeted the gardeners as they entered, and they spent several minutes strolling down the pathway while one of the gardeners who knew Moayyed pointed out which flowers were special or newly blossomed. Ali heard names like "narcissus," "heliotrope," and "anemones," but except for the violets and roses, he could not tell which was which.

Before long Moayyed and Ali were by themselves sitting on the bench directly across from where Bahá'u'lláh would sit. In the background through the leaves of the trees they could see the stream and the golden fields of the countryside glistening in the distance.

"You were speaking about the heroes, Ali," Moayyed said, "and it started me thinking about courage, about what it means to be courageous. And it occurred to me that having courage does not mean that we should not be afraid."

"I always thought it did," said Ali.

"Perhaps it seems so," said Moayyed, "because the heroes don't complain or seem to mind what they endure. But I wonder if having courage doesn't mean that we do what we know is right even though we are afraid. I mean, if the path we choose is not difficult, if it does not test us, then how will we grow and change? Do you understand what I mean?"

"I'm not exactly sure, Grandfather."

"Let me put it this way, Ali. You may never know if you could have done the amazing things those early believers did. None of us knows how we will do until the time comes and our courage is tested. The kind of faith that requires instant reaction —without stopping to think things over, without being able to ponder how much to give—that kind of faith demands total devotion. Perhaps you will never face that kind of a test, though I suspect you may.

"But there are other kinds of courage and faith which I guarantee you will need, a kind of patient courage that is a daily battle each Bahá'í must wage, not against soldiers, but against ourselves, against our desire to stay just as we are.

"This is the kind of courage that Bahá'u'lláh taught the believers to have after He returned from His sojourn in the mountains of Sulaymáníyyih. In fact, this very same sort of daily struggle was the main tool with which Bahá'u'lláh built an entire community out of the disorganized and confused Bábís He found upon His return. Do you understand what I am talking about?" Moayyed asked.

"I think so," said Ali.

"Let me put it this way. It is certainly a fine thing to do a good deed. But it is finer still to do that good deed every day, over and over, until it becomes part of you, until you become changed, until your very soul is gradually transformed."

"You mean that the deed becomes a habit?"

"Exactly!" said Moayyed placing his gnarled hand on Ali's knee. "What Bahá'u'lláh needed to do when He returned was to build a whole community of believers, but not by showing them how to endure pain or to fight in a battle. He had to show them how to change their daily lives—slowly, patiently, little by little, until everyone in Baghdád would recognize the Bábís not by how well they endured torture or by how well they could defend themselves against the swords of the Sháh, but by their high moral standards and their noble character, by their courtesy and kindness, by their meekness and cleanliness.

"Do you remember from your lessons how long it was before Bahá'u'lláh told the Bábís that He was the One the Báb had promised, 'Him Whom God shall make manifest?'"

"I think it was about seven or eight years," said Ali.

"And do you have any idea why Bahá'u'lláh waited that long?"

"I suppose it wasn't the right time at first."

"That's very true, but why wasn't it the right time? Have you ever thought about that? Remember now, the Bábís were like you. They were also searching for a key, a key that would lead them to the One the Báb had promised.

"But Bahá'u'lláh knew that the Bábís were not yet ready or prepared for the next step in their education. They were like students whose new teacher, the Báb, had been taken from them before they could learn the lessons He had prepared for them. So the next teacher, Bahá'u'lláh, could not very well give them His own lessons until they had learned the lessons that the Báb had brought them, because those were the very lessons that were to prepare them for the coming of Bahá'u'lláh."

"I remember once during the summer when I went away with my parents and I forgot how to do multiplication. So when I began studying again, I could not learn division until the teacher showed me again about multiplication."

"That's right. First Bahá'u'lláh had to teach the Bábís about what the Báb had said before He could tell them about the teachings He Himself had brought. So, in a way, He had two jobs to do.

"You see, when Bahá'u'lláh returned to Baghdád in March of 1856 with Shaykh Sulṭán, the Bábís had not had a leader for a long time, and the religion of the Báb was nearly extinct. What was worse, the reputation of the Bábís had become dreadfully tarnished by the wicked deeds of Mírzá Yaḥyá and Siyyid Muḥammad. I am sure that to many Bábís it seemed as if the heroic sacrifices of the martyrs had been wasted, and many of them knew the only hope they had was in the leadership of Bahá'u'lláh. So when Bahá'u'lláh returned, all the Bábís were eager to do whatever He said."

"But how did He do it?" asked Ali. "How did He build the Bábí community?"

"Well, He didn't do it in one or two days. I can tell you that much," said Moayyed with a chuckle. "But He did begin immediately, and He worked in several different ways at once. First of all, He began to reveal tablets, writings which could guide them in their daily life. At the same time He opened His doors to whoever wanted to see Him, whether they were Bábís or not, because for the first time, He could reveal His power completely to anyone who had the spiritual eyes to recognize that power."

"I don't understand what you mean by 'spiritual eyes,'" said Ali.

"Well, not everyone who met Bahá'u'lláh knew Who He was. Not everyone was impressed by Him—only those people who could recognize spiritual qualities." Moayyed could tell Ali still did not quite understand. "For example, if someone played a flute more beautifully than anyone else in the world, but you had your ears covered, the music could not stir your heart. Or take this garden," he said, motioning toward the nearby flowers. "If only money or jewels made you happy, this garden might not make you feel peaceful, for there is no money here, only blossoms, birds, and trees.

"But there were many people who *could* recognize the wisdom and power of Bahá'u'lláh. For example, the Kurds who had met Him in the mountains traveled great distances to find the wise dervish and the house of Mírzá Músá as Bahá'u'lláh had told them to do. And when these strangers came to find the wise One, the religious leaders of Ba<u>gh</u>dád began to wonder what attraction He had that would cause people to come so far just to talk with Him.

"Soon they too asked permission to talk with Bahá'u'lláh, and most who came into His presence were amazed at the dignity and learning of the Persian exile. Eventually, government officials came, poets came; mystics and all manner of townspeople.

"Of course, not all of these people became Bábís, but most of them were never the same after their visit with Bahá'u'lláh, and many did become Bábís. Of course, those who were already Bábís visited Bahá'u'lláh as often as they could because their belief in the Báb and their understanding of what the Báb had said in His writings was only now becoming clear to them.

"And Bahá'u'lláh was loving to all who came, loving and patient. He would teach them whatever they wanted to know, and in time, even princes of royal blood and other dignitaries traveled to meet Bahá'u'lláh. Why, within a few years after His return from the mountains, Bahá'u'lláh's house perched on the western bank of the Tigris River—'the Most Great House,' as Bahá'u'lláh called it—became a center of activity for Persians and Arabs, for Turks, Muslims, Jews, and Christians alike.

"Many Bábís left homes in Persia and walked over the mountains or through the deserts to meet Bahá'u'lláh, the One Who was reviving their religion, breathing the breath of life into the teachings the Báb had brought for them. In fact, some of these Bábís refused to go back to their homeland and stayed with Bahá'u'lláh in Baghdád. Some even followed Him when He had to leave the city years later. Others went back to Persia to teach the Bábís there what they had learned. Some of these took back to the other believers the tablets that Bahá'u'lláh had given them.

"At last the Bábís had someone they could trust and follow. They came before Bahá'u'lláh like empty vessels, ready to be filled with His love and wisdom, like thirsting desert wanderers discovering an oasis, and soon the community of Bábís began to grow and develop. The Bábís who moved to Baghdád to be with Bahá'u'lláh usually brought few belongings with them. But they did bring faith and a determination to work, to rebuild their precious Faith.

"Nabíl the historian was one of these people. And so was Aḥmad, the one to whom Bahá'u'lláh wrote the beautiful 'Tablet of Aḥmad.' Aḥmad had searched from village to village in Persia looking for the Promised One, and when he did not succeed, he went to India and patiently continued his search. Later he came back to Persia, where he finally met a Bábí who told him about the new Manifestation, but only after he had searched for more than twenty years."

"More than twenty years?" asked Ali.

"That's right," said Moayyed, smiling. "Let's see now, you've been on your search for how long?"

"I don't think I could wait as long as Aḥmad, Grandfather."

"You might surprise yourself," said Moayyed. "You'd be amazed how patient we can become when we know the value of what we are looking for."

"Who were some of the others in Baghdád?" asked Ali.

"Well, there was Nabíl-i-Akbar, the learned Muslim scholar who had come from Najaf to visit Baghdád. When he heard of Bahá'u'lláh, he went to visit Him and almost immediately became a Bábí himself. Soon he began to teach others with such excitement that when he returned to Persia, the government tried to arrest him. Eventually he went to 'Ishqábád, where he wrote five essays demonstrating the truth of the Bábí Faith."

"Wasn't he a Hand of the Cause of God?"

"Yes, and that title was also given to a few others who visited Bahá'u'lláh in Baghdád. Mullá Ṣádiq, for example, was a Hand of the Cause. He had become a believer in Shiráz very early and fought at Ṭabarsí. He was taken prisoner and then tortured several times, but through all the pain and hardship he never once wavered or stopped teaching others about the Báb.

"Another important visitor was Shaykh Salmán, who came to see Bahá'u'lláh, not once, but every single year. He would travel on foot from Persia carrying a large bundle of letters from the believers there. He would deliver these messages to Bahá'u'lláh, and then, after he had spent some time with Bahá'u'lláh, he would return to Persia taking with him all the tablets that Bahá'u'lláh had written for the Persian believers. In fact, he continued to do this wherever Bahá'u'lláh went.

"And there were others. There was Muḥammad-'Ali of Iṣfahán, who received many bounties from Bahá'u'ilah. He always seemed to have a bright, cheerful spirit, no matter how poor he was or how difficult things became for the Bábís. As I mentioned, there was the historian Nabíl-i-Zarandí, who also continued to follow Bahá'u'lláh and to record all the important events that occurred so that future generations of Bahá'ís would know the story of their religion. Later on, Bahá'u'lláh sent Nabíl on many important missions—to Kirmánsháh and to other places in Persia—where he taught many people about the Báb and Bahá'u'lláh.

"Ah, there were so many pure souls, Ali. Darvísh Ṣidq-'Alí, who had been a Ṣúfí mystic, and then 'Abdu'lláh, who was called Pidar-Ján, or 'Beloved Father,' because he was so kind and gentle to everyone. Pidar-Ján met with Bahá'u'lláh almost every day, and when he was not with Bahá'u'lláh, he was chanting prayers.

"There was Ṣádiq, who had come from Yazd to be with Bahá'u'lláh. While he was in Baghdád, Ṣádiq became so ill that he was near death, so Bahá'u'lláh sent 'Abdu'l-Bahá to him, and he was healed instantly. When this happened Ṣádiq vowed never to leave Bahá'u'lláh's company, even when Bahá'u'lláh advised him to stay in Baghdád—he simply could not bear the separation. So when Bahá'u'lláh left, Ṣádiq ran on foot toward the town where Bahá'u'lláh was camped, but before he could reach it, he fell down exhausted and died.

"Some were old, some were young, some were peasants, and others were learned noblemen. Some could not bear to leave the presence of Bahá'u'lláh, so they followed Him the rest of their days, while others felt so inspired that they traveled back to Persia to teach others what they had learned. Some were simple craftsmen, like Áqá Muḥammad-Ibráhím, who became a believer as a very young man. He was a coppersmith, and with his brothers he opened a shop in Baghdád. There were carpenters, like Mírzá Ja'fari-Yazdí, who had been a well-known scholar in Persia and had learned carpentry just so he could live in Baghdád near Bahá'u'lláh. Ghulám-'Alíy-i-Najjár was another carpenter who came to be with Bahá'u'lláh—he was the one who designed and built the roof which covers the courtyard of the Shrine of Bahá'u'lláh."

"He's the one who made it so the sunlight can shine on my face when I'm in the outer room of the shrine," said Ali with a bright smile.

"The very same," said Moayyed. "And there were many, many more, names that in times to come will be familiar to everyone who studies about that period in Baghdád, that time when so many people flocked to see Bahá'u'lláh.

"But that is only part of the story of Bahá'u'lláh during the period He was in Baghdád. As I told you, perhaps the most important thing Bahá'u'lláh did was to teach the Bábís to live in such a way that everyone in Baghdád would know they were special people."

"But how would they know that?"

"In many ways. By the love and kindness they showed each other, by their manners, their friendship with the other townspeople, by their honesty and humility, by their refusal to gossip about other people or to become involved in arguments about the government or to join secret groups, by the way they cooperated to help others, by the fact that they were never violent or angry. They were honest, hard-working citizens who lived very simply and were kind and patient with others.

"Of course, as I said, these changes did not happen overnight. They had to work hard to become good people by following carefully the teachings that Bahá'u'lláh gave them. In fact, some of the Bábís were so determined to follow these teachings that they made an agreement with one another. They decided that if one of them violated a teaching, the other would have to punish him by hitting him on the bottom of his feet.

"Of course, the other Bábí would not want to punish his friend, but if the Bábí who had broken the rule did not receive his punishment, he would not eat or drink until he had been given his punishment."

"You mean they wanted to be punished?" asked Ali with surprise.

"What they wanted was to follow the teachings, to change themselves completely. I suppose they thought the punishment would help them remember."

Moayyed shifted himself on the bench and looked into the trees to catch a glimpse of a small songbird that was chirping loudly on a branch above. Moayyed made a whistling imitation of the bird, then listened for an answer. When the bird called back, Moayyed smiled so broadly that his face looked as if it had never frowned. Then Moayyed looked at Ali.

"You know the happiness that you sometimes feel when Bahá'ís get together for a feast or a holy day celebration?"

"Especially when 'Abdu'l-Bahá is here!" said Ali.

"Exactly. Well, I imagine it was like that all the time in the house of Bahá'u'lláh. There was such joy and peace for those Bábís, especially after all the confusion they had gone through during the persecutions. Even the visitors who weren't Bábís could feel how special the place was. In fact, one of the princes who visited Bahá'u'lláh there said, 'Were all the sorrows of the world to be crowded into my heart they would, I feel, all vanish, when in the presence of Bahá'u'lláh. It is as if I had entered Paradise itself.'

"Sometimes the Bábís would have grand feasts which would last far into the night. They would chant prayers and poetry, or they would tell stories and sing songs. But they were always happy, even though most of them had almost nothing to live on and sometimes had little to eat.

"Some nights as many as ten of them might eat no more than a few dates. Many of them had few clothes, and some had no shoes—for a time Bahá'u'lláh Himself had only one shirt. Many of the Bábís would live together in small rented rooms and share what food and clothes they had. But of all the things Bahá'u'lláh did to build the community, do you know what was the most important?"

"I'm not sure," Ali said.

"His writings, His tablets. You see, Ali, this is the main gift the Manifestation brings to us, the Word of God, the divine utterance. In fact, Bahá'u'lláh tells us that the utterance of the Prophet is the most important proof that He is sent by God. Because when the Prophet is no longer physically on the earth, we still can read His words, the very same words that the Prophet receives from God.

"So as soon as Bahá'u'lláh returned from the mountains, He began dictating tablets with such energy that no one could describe it. Sometimes 'Abdu'l-Bahá, Who was now a young man, would transcribe the words that His father revealed. But there was also Mírzá Áqá Ján, Bahá'u'lláh's amanuensis who wrote down most of Bahá'u'lláh's tablets for many years to come.

"Until this time in Baghdád Bahá'u'lláh had written only a few tablets for the believers, because the time was not right to do more. But now Bahá'u'lláh knew that the time had come for Him to unleash the full power of His pen. And the words poured forth in torrents, words to teach and guide the Bábís who were in Baghdád, as well as people all over the world. In fact, the book which inspired your dream, *The Seven Valleys*, that was written then.

"Like so many other tablets, it was originally a letter to a particular individual who had asked Bahá'u'lláh questions, a student of Ṣúfism, a man named Shaykh Muḥyi'd-Dín who was a judge in the town of Kháníqayn.

This learned man admired Bahá'u'lláh and had sent Him questions about the relationship of man to God. So Bahá'u'lláh wrote *The Seven Valleys* to explain how one learns about God through the Manifestations, the Teachers that God sends."

"Didn't Bahá'u'lláh also write *The Book of Certitude* in Baghdád?"

"Yes, He did. In fact, *The Book of Certitude* is one of the most important tablets Bahá'u'lláh wrote, because in that book He explains very clearly how each individual can recognize the Manifestation."

"Was that tablet also written for someone?"

"Yes, He wrote *The Book of Certitude* to an uncle of the Báb who had not yet become a Bábí. And I'll tell you something else very interesting about that tablet. He wrote the whole book—over two hundred pages—in only two days and two nights."

"But how could anyone do that?" asked Ali in disbelief.

"Not just anyone can, Ali. You must understand that the Manifestation is not an ordinary human being like you or me. God has given Him powers and abilities far beyond anything you and I will ever fully understand. Why, several times during the first two years after He returned from the mountains, He would reveal in one day and night as many verses as are contained in the entire Qur'án."

"But how could He even think that fast?"

"Ali, the only answer I can give you is that Bahá'u'lláh was a Manifestation, and a Manifestation of God is able to do whatever needs to be done. In fact, Bahá'u'lláh could have done much more than He did. In one of his books about the history of our Faith, Nabil says that Bahá'u'lláh ordered Mírzá Aqá Ján to throw away hundreds of thousands of verses which Bahá'u'lláh did not feel humankind would be ready for during this dispensation."

"What is a *dispensation*, Grandfather?"

"A dispensation is the period of time that a religion endures."

"So that means Bahá'u'lláh knew things that the next Prophet will teach?"

"Exactly. You see, Ali, the Prophets know each other, are aware of each other, and in the world of the spirit associate intimately with each other."

"Then They are like a team?" asked Ali.

"Very true, very true—very much like a team."

Ali was amazed. He had known for a long time that Manifestations were special, but to Ali that had meant that a Manifestation was simply a very good person Whom God had chosen to deliver a message. Now he was beginning to understand more about what truly distinguished the Manifestations and made Them able to change the whole world.

"And let's not forget about *The Hidden Words*," continued Moayyed, "those elegant and beautiful poetic verses He revealed as He walked along the Tigris River."

"Oh, yes!" said Ali. "I have memorized many of those. Neda and I are going to memorize all of them—at least, we are going to try."

"Very good, very good," said Moayyed with pride.

"But tell me something about how Bahá'u'lláh lived. Would He just sit in His house and meet visitors? Didn't He ever do anything else?"

Moayyed laughed heartily at his grandson's question. "Good question," he said. "Very good. My, my, yes. Bahá'u'lláh was like you, Ali. More than anything else, He loved the countryside, the fields, the streams, the birds, the flowers, the infinite beauty of God's creation. That is one of the few ways He could relax a little. So when He was not busy in Baghdád, He and 'Abdu'l-Bahá, together with a few other believers, would visit the countryside. In particular, they loved to go to Salmán-i-Pák, a village several miles from Baghdád. There they would sit and watch the birds sporting in the trees, or they would talk about nature. On one occasion when the believers discovered they had brought nothing to eat, Bahá'u'lláh cooked them a Kurdish dish of pitted dates, buttered and cooked in a pan.

"On another visit to the park, Ḥájí Muḥammad-Taqí of Shíráz, who was a great hunter, traveled with them. After they arrived, Ḥájí Muḥammad-Taqí decided he would show his great skill, and he shot some of the birds just for sport. This upset Bahá'u'lláh, and Bahá'u'lláh told him, "Don't kill these innocent birds!"

"But Ḥájí Muḥammad-Taqí did not think Bahá'u'lláh was serious, and he once again fired his rifle, only this time he missed. Well, this proud hunter *never* missed, and he was quite embarrassed, so he quickly took more careful aim and tried again. Again he missed.

"Again and again he aimed and fired, and the more he fired and missed, the more frustrated he became. After a while, when the proud hunter had fired many rounds of ammunition without killing a single bird, Ḥájí Muḥammad-Taqí learned a great lesson—he realized that his only true power came not from himself. He understood that his personal power was unleashed only when he was completely obedient to the teachings and principles of Bahá'u'lláh."

"It sounds like Bahá'u'lláh had a sense of humor," said Ali with a smile.

"Did you not know that? Yes, certainly He had humor. He had wit and charm and affection. That was why people were drawn to Him—not merely because He had profound things to say about God and religion. People felt happy in His presence. They felt loved and accepted in a way they had never known before. That's how He changed their hearts. That's how He built the Bábí community. Little by little, with words and with His own actions, Bahá'u'lláh was like a magnet that brought together the scattered pieces of the Bábí community, gathered the believers, organized them, and built something so solid and so firm that when He told them in 1863 that He was the Manifestation the Báb had promised, none of them had any trouble believing Him because they had experienced firsthand the wonders He could perform. They had seen their lives changed by His presence and by His teachings.

"Bahá'u'lláh had attracted the hearts so that few who met Him did not sense the spiritual power He possessed. Fugitives came, Persians of high rank. Why, the British consul-general, Colonel Sir Arnold Burrows Kemball, offered Bahá'u'lláh the protection of British citizenship. Bahá'u'lláh even won the heart of Námiq-Páshá, the governor of Baghdád. In fact, during the last years of this period, the governor loved Bahá'u'lláh so dearly that he tried to protect Him from His enemies."

"What enemies?" asked Ali.

"Ah, yes, this period of growth and love and unity does come to an end, doesn't it?" said Moayyed, shaking his head as if he wanted the story to end happily. "I tell you what, Ali, let us save that part of the story until after we eat something. That way we can enjoy the peace and beauty of this wonderful place without worrying about what happened to shatter that glorious time. But before we eat, let me ask you something. Do you understand now what Bahá'u'lláh accomplished during those years in Baghdád?"

"I think I do," said Ali.

"And what would you think was the most important tool Bahá'u'lláh used to do that work in Baghdád?"

"Patience!" said Ali forcefully.

"And what does all this have to do with your dream?"

Ali did not answer right away. He wasn't sure what Moayyed meant, but he ventured a guess. "Does it mean that I must be like those Bábís who had to wait to find out Who Bahá'u'lláh really was? Does it mean that I may have to wait a long time until I am ready to find the answer to my search?"

"Yes, but it also means that you can do more than wait, my son. Like the Bábís in Baghdád, you can grow and improve little by little, day by day. That way, when the time comes and the gates of 'Akká swing open for you, you will not come tumbling down from your steed. You will be ready to be whisked away to your appointed tasks."

Moayyed stood up and stretched a little. "So do not worry about whether you have the courage to be a hero today. There are all kinds of heroes. Every age needs its own sort of hero. You might not fight at Fort Ṭábarsi, but you will be a warrior of some sort, I assure you. Just be sure you use as much today as you know how, and then your tomorrows will never be wasted."

Ali stood beside his grandfather. He put his arms around Moayyed and gave him a gentle hug. "Thank you, Grandfather," said Ali softly. "Thank you for giving me one of your todays."

10

The Garden of Riḍván

Moayyed walked beneath the shade of the mulberry tree to the fountain in the middle of the garden. There an old gardener was resting from his labors of tending the flowers. Ali remained seated for a while, thinking over the story of the Bag͟hdád period that his grandfather had just told him.

The boy looked intently at the bench where Bahá'u'lláh would sit. He imagined that Bahá'u'lláh was there, looking back at him and smiling. It was an unusual feeling. He has always considered Bahá'u'lláh a lofty figure, someone far beyond such casual intimacy. But now he felt close to Bahá'u'lláh. He felt loved, cared for. And he sensed that so long as he kept himself open to that love, he would always be protected, no matter what happened in his life.

It was a fleeting thought, an instant of insight, but he never forgot it. In fact, in moments of worry or sorrow or doubt, he would remember the pure delight of that moment, and his spirit would be relieved.

Ali looked up through the mulberry leaves that seemed to spread in a canopy over the whole garden. He inhaled the commingled scent of lemons, tangerines, and oranges. It seemed to the boy a holy scent, the fragrance of nearness to God.

After a short while Moayyed returned, walking beside Abu'l-Qásim, the old gardener who had served the Cause of Bahá'u'lláh his whole life.

"Can this be Ali?" asked the old man as Ali got up. "My, my! The years go more swiftly than the days used to. I remember when you were a mere bundle of blanket in your mother's arms. Now you sit here and converse with your wise grandfather." Abu'l-Qásim reached out his wrinkled hand and gave Ali a freshly picked tangerine.

"Ali, Abu'l-Qásim has a treat for *us,*" said Moayyed. "He will take us to the summerhouse for some prayers, and then we'll have some tea."

"Oh, thank you, sir," said Ali.

"I will tell you something else, Ali," said Abu'l-Qásim. "Come here one day early in the morning, before I start my work, and I will tell you stories of the Blessed Perfection and what it was like when He used to come to these gardens."

"That would be wonderful!" said Ali. The thought of such a day already intrigued him. But right now he was even more excited about visiting the little summerhouse where Bahá'u'lláh had often stayed when He lived outside the city walls of 'Akká. Ali had been inside before, but usually there had been many adults present, and he felt as if he were visiting a museum rather than communing with God. Now, with just Moayyed and Abu'l-Qásim, the visit seemed to hold special promise.

The three of them walked down toward the end of the pathway where the little summerhouse stood like a guardian of the trees and flowers. The three removed their shoes, climbed the several steps to the front door, and entered slowly, reverently.

On the right, beside the bed where Bahá'u'lláh would rest, was a small but beautiful rug on which the three of them kneeled. Each chanted a prayer in turn, and Ali felt very grown-up praying beside the two men.

Ali remained inside after Moayyed and Abu'l-Qásim left. In the quiet he scrutinized every part of the room. He tried to imagine Bahá'u'lláh walking in the room, or lying on the bed, or sitting in the chair. He wondered, if he had been there when Bahá'u'lláh was alive, if he had actually seen Him, would he have known Who this was without anybody telling him? Would he have known or guessed that this person was special, something more than an ordinary human being?

The idea excited Ali. But for some reason it also worried him. What if he had not liked the way Bahá'u'lláh looked? Would he have allowed some unimportant thing to prevent him from seeing the truth—a look, a gesture?

As he pondered this question, he realized that what he really wondered is whether or not he would be a Bahá'í were it not for the fact that his family were Bahá'ís and he had been raised as a Bahá'í. It would have been wonderful to meet Bahá'u'lláh, Ali thought, to be in His presence, to hear His words. At the same time, Ali was a little bit thankful that he would never have to face such a test.

He arose and walked out of the room and into the garden. He sat down under the single mulberry tree near the cottage where an Arab woman had cheerfully served each of them a cup of tea. Ali was surprised when he tasted the tea. It had an exotic taste of spices and fruits and cloves, like Russian tea, but milder. It was almost lunch time, but the tea and a few sections of tangerine were all Ali wanted for now. His mind was too busy to think of food.

After the tea and some light conversation, the three strolled around the garden while Abu'l-Qásim showed them his most prized flowers. It delighted Ali that Abu'l-Qásim spoke of the plants as if they were dear friends or cherished pets.

After they had finished Abu'l-Qásim's guided tour, Ali and Moayyed returned to the same seat they had occupied before lunch. The sun was at a different angle now, and as they looked out toward the stream that passed beside the slender island, the colors of the distant plains seemed softer and more vivid.

"So," began Moayyed, "you want to know how the Baghdád period ended?"

"Yes, Grandfather. I don't want it to end, but I want to know everything I can."

"Well, it's quite a story, and perhaps it is not so sad as you might think. The trouble began with a Muslim priest in Baghdád named Shaykh 'Abdu'l-Ḥusayn. As you can imagine, this Mullá was terribly jealous of Bahá'u'lláh—of the attention He got and the love that the people showered upon Him. So the cleric joined forces with Mírzá Buzurg Khán, the newly appointed Persian consul-general who was just as jealous and corrupt as Shaykh 'Abdu'l-Ḥusayn.

"These two men were not terribly bright, but they were very persistent. When one plan failed, they would try another. First they told lies about Bahá'u'lláh to the governor of Baghdád so that he would send Bahá'u'lláh and the other Bábís back to Persia. But by this time he was well acquainted with the character of Bahá'u'lláh and the other Bábís, and he considered them an asset to his community. He would not even consider the request of these mischievous troublemakers.

"When Shaykh 'Abdu'l-Ḥusayn saw that the governor was too fond of Bahá'u'lláh to help plot against Him, he began to spread rumors among the townspeople. But they would pay no attention either because they, too, knew by now the remarkable qualities of Bahá'u'lláh, and they were happy to have Him in their midst.

"Meanwhile, Mírzá Buzurg Khán was trying to stir up the hatred of the rougher people in the town, those who might do anything for a sum of money. He paid them to confront Bahá'u'lláh in the streets."

"What did he want them to do?" asked Ali.

"His hope was that when these people said annoying things, Bahá'u'lláh would say something back in anger, something that these two villains could then use against Him.

"When the friends of Bahá'u'lláh heard about this plan, they begged their Beloved not to walk the streets alone. But, of course, Bahá'u'lláh was afraid of nothing and no one. So He continued to walk the streets by day and by night without any fear whatsoever. And when these ruffians would find Him and insult Him, He would simply be courteous and kind to them. In fact, sometimes He would approach them first, so that instead of trying to hurt Him, they would become totally disarmed by Bahá'u'lláh's courage and friendliness.

"Needless to say, this plan soon failed, so Mírzá Buzurg Khán decided to do something far more reprehensible. He decided that if he could not make Bahá'u'lláh angry, then he would simply have Bahá'u'lláh murdered."

"Murder Bahá'u'lláh?" asked Ali in disbelief.

"Yes, Ali. And this would not be the last time such a thing was tried. Mírzá Buzurg Khán hired a Turk named Riḍa, promising the poor soul

100 túmáns if he would kill Bahá'u'lláh. He then gavc him a horse and two pistols and told this ignorant villain that if he would kill Bahá'u'lláh, he would not be arrested by the government. Instead, he would get the money and his freedom.

"Well, several days later, Riḍa found out that Bahá'u'lláh was at the public baths. By this time, however, the Bábís were aware that Buzurg Khán and his followers meant to harm Bahá'u'lláh. Consequently the Bábís tried their best to guard Bahá'u'lláh. But on this day Riḍa was able to sneak into the public baths with one of the pistols hidden beneath his cloak. The pitiful assassin waited for the opportunity to strike. At last he saw the opportunity and reached into his cloak.

"But as his hand was ready to grasp the gun, he looked directly into the face of Bahá'u'lláh and stopped. He was so astonished by the dignity of this noble Figure before him that he could not move. Finally, he turned, and without speaking, he quickly left the baths.

"But Riḍa was poor and desperately wanted the money that Mírzá Buzurg Khán had promised him. So a few days later he again tried to carry out the mission. He mustered his courage thinking, no doubt, that he would have the courage this time. Riḍa waited in the street for Bahá'u'lláh to come by, though he was quite nervous because of what had happened in the baths.

"Before long Bahá'u'lláh approached, and as He got nearer, Riḍa reached into his cloak, grabbed his weapon, and pulled it out. Once again he looked at the face of the Manifestation, and once again he was so humbled by what he saw that he let the pistol drop from his hand."

"What did Bahá'u'lláh do when He saw the pistol?" asked Ali.

"He told Mírzá Músá, who was with Him, to pick it up and hand it back to Riḍa and take the wretched man to his home. Needless to say, the bewildered assassin never bothered Bahá'u'lláh again.

"Thus far all of the attempts to injure Bahá'u'lláh accomplished absolutely nothing, except to increase the jealous rage that these two clerics felt. Shaykh 'Abdu'l-Ḥusayn in particular was far from giving up. He decided to take a new course of action. He would try to have Bahá'u'lláh taken back to prison in Ṭihrán by writing false reports about Bahá'u'lláh and sending them directly to people who were close to the Sháh. He also promised Mírzá Buzurg Khán that he would be promoted to a higher position if he could get the government to move Bahá'u'lláh back to prison in Persia."

"What did the letters say about Bahá'u'lláh?" asked Ali.

"He told the Persian government that Bahá'u'lláh was gathering a large army among the Kurdish tribes in northern 'Iráq, and he said that Bahá'u'lláh was plotting to take over the Persian government."

"Did the government believe these lies?" asked Ali.

"Not at first," said Moayyed. "But you must remember that the government didn't like Bahá'u'lláh to begin with. That's why they had exiled Him from Persia. So after a while, when the letters continued, the Sháh gave Shaykh 'Abdu'l-Ḥusayn authonty to investigate the matter, and he told all the Persian 'ulamás in 'Iráq to help him.

"The Shaykh immediately sent a message to these relgious leaders, asking them to meet in Kaẓimayn, where he was living. At first the power-hungry 'ulamás thought of a plan for launching a war against the Bábí community, but, their leader spoke out against this idea. After a long debate, the ulamás finally decided on a scheme. They would embarrass Bahá'u'lláh by asking Him such difficult questions that He would not be able to answer them, and in that way Bahá'u'lláh would lose the respect of the people of Baghdád and the Bábís as well.

"So these clerics made a list of the most difficult questions they could think of."

"What sort of questions?" asked Ali.

"Questions about religion or about the traditions in Islám which are very mysterious and hard to understand. They gave the list to a very wise and respected man, Ḥájí Mullá Ḥasan-i-'Amú, and asked him to deliver the questions to Bahá'u'lláh.

"Now because Mullá Ḥasan was very learned, he listened carefully to the answers Bahá'u'lláh gave when he presented the questions to Him."

"That reminds me of the story about Muḥammad Sháh sending Vaḥid to question the Báb."

"Exactly," said Moayyed. 'And in the same way that Vaḥid was overcome by the learning and wisdom of the Báb, so Mullá Ḥasan was astounded at Bahá'u'lláh's eloquent and brilliant response. In fact, he quickly became quite embarrassed at his presumption in testing one so profoundly brilliant and spiritual. Consequently, as he started to ask the final question which the gathering of religious leaders had called for, Mullá Ḥasan hesitated for fear that Bahá'u'lláh might be angered."

"Why?" asked Ali. "What was the question?"

"They asked Bahá'u'lláh if He could perform a Miracle."

"A Miracle?" said Ali with surprise.

"Yes," said Moayyed. "They said that if He was a Prophet of God, He should be able to perform a Miracle."

"Did Bahá'u'lláh get angry?" asked Ali.

"He became stern," said Moayyed with a smile. "He told Mullá Ḥasan, although you have no right to ask this, for God should test His creatures, and they should not test God, still I allow and accept this request.'"

"You mean Bahá'u'lláh actually agreed to perform a Miracle for these religious leaders?"

"Yes," said Moayyed, enjoying Ali's excitement. "He certainly did."

"But what was it? What Miracle did He agree to?"

"Ah," nodded Moayyed, "that is where the wisdom of Bahá'u'lláh once again became evident. He instructed Mullá Ḥasan that the 'ulamás must meet together and come to an agreement as to what they wanted Him to do. Then they should sign a pledge, an agreement, that if Bahá'u'lláh should actually perform the Miracle they asked for, they would no longer doubt that He was indeed a Prophet of God—they would agree that His Cause was true.

"Well, as you can imagine, Ḥájí Mullá Ḥasan was full of joy and excitement when he heard Bahá'u'lláh's words. He left hurriedly to give this message to the 'ulamás, for never before had anything like this occurred. When Mullá Ḥasan gave Bahá'u'lláh's answer and read the agreement to perform a Miracle, the gathered religious leaders were shocked into silence. They were truly astounded at Bahá'u'lláh's confidence. And, of course, they were quite worried.

"After their consternation had passed, they began to consult on what Miracle He should perform. Some wanted one thing, some another. But there was little agreement as to what act would prove that He was indeed a Manifestation of God. For three whole days they talked and argued amongst themselves, but they could not agree. Finally, exasperated by their own confusion and disunity, they gave up on the whole matter, perhaps because deep down inside they really did not want to face the truth that was before them."

"But why would they be afraid of the truth? Why wouldn't they be happy about discovering the new Prophet?" asked Ali.

"Perhaps they also knew that if Bahá'u'lláh really was a Prophet, they would have to follow Him, *and* they would lose their position as the religious leaders."

"I understand," said Ali. "So they didn't bother Him anymore?"

"Bahá'u'lláh won this battle, but these wicked men, pitiful and absurd as they were, had still managed to damage Bahá'u'lláh with their mischief. You see, while all this was taking place, there were other events happening that would work against Bahá'u'lláh. For nine long months Mírzá Buzurg Khán and Shaykh 'Abdu'l-Ḥusayn had been trying everything they knew to destroy Bahá'u'lláh and His popularity among the people of Baghdád. Finally, one of their plans actually met with some success.

"You remember I said that they had been sending letter after letter to the Sháh, asking him to remove Bahá'u'lláh from Baghdád, where they said He was still an evil influence on the Persian people? Well, after so many letters and accusations against Bahá'u'lláh, the Sháh finally gave in. He used whatever methods he could to influence 'Abdu'l-'Azíz, the new Sulṭán of the Ottoman Empire, to remove Bahá'u'lláh from Baghdád.

"The Sulṭán had no way of knowing that these statements about Bahá'u'lláh were all lies. So he approved the Sháh's request that the governor of Baghdád invite Bahá'u'lláh to Constantinople, the capital city of the Ottoman Empire."

"And did the governor tell Bahá'u'lláh to go?" asked Ali.

"Not at first. Námiq Páshá was the governor, and because he had come to know Bahá'u'lláh very well, he had great love and respect for Bahá'u'lláh. So when he received the instruction from Sulṭán 'Abdu'l-'Azíz to arrange for Bahá'u'lláh to leave his city, he simply refused. He didn't even tell Bahá'u'lláh that the order had been given. Námiq Páshá knew that Bahá'u'lláh and the other Bábís were law-abiding citizens, not troublemakers. But what was even more important was that this community of Bábís had brought about a changed atmosphere in the city itself, and so naturally the governor wanted them to stay.

"Well, as you know, nothing can be hidden from a Manifestation of God. Even though the news had been kept from Bahá'u'lláh for a while, He knew what was going to happen. Therefore, for a period of months Bahá'u'lláh had begun to hint that changes would soon occur, and He started preparing the Bábís for that time.

"What do you mean, Grandfather? How did He do that?"

"In some of the tablets He revealed for them, He hinted at the problems that were about to occur. Then sometimes when He would talk to the Bábís, He would refer to approaching trials and tribulations, and His tone would become sad so that some Bábís became quite frightened.

"For example, Bahá'u'lláh would talk of ominous dreams He had had. In one of these He had seen all of the Manifestations of the past gathered around Him. They were crying and moaning with such a grief and lamentation that Bahá'u'lláh asked Them why They were so sad. They answered that They were weeping for Him because of the things that He was going to have to endure. He also told the Bábís that He had dreamed He heard a voice from on high which said that He would soon experience hardship and sorrow such as no other Manifestation had ever experienced." Moayyed paused and looked sternly at Ali. "And the voice told Him something else, Ali. It said, 'Be patient, be patient.'"

Ali thought he understood exactly what Moayyed was saying to him. If a Manifestation, Who is perfect, had to be reminded to be patient, then how much harder it would be for 'Alí-Riḍáy-i-Mashhadí to learn this quality. To Ali this message meant that his dream of finding the key to 'Akká might not come true in a few days or weeks. He might have to wait months or even years to know his destiny.

"Did the Bábís really know that something was about to happen to end that time of peace and happiness?" asked Ali.

Moayyed stroked his chin once. "I think they must have known something as soon as Bahá'u'lláh's mood changed and He Himself became concerned. But if they had any doubts as to what was going to happen, these doubts were removed at Naw-Rúz of that same year. On the occasion of that New Year's celebration, Bahá'u'lláh pitched His tent in a field outside the city of Baghdád. Spring was just beginning, and the believers who accompanied Him felt happy to be with the Beloved of their hearts in this lovely spot which Mírzá Músá had rented for them to celebrate the beginning of a new year.

"However, on the fifth day of this happy occasion Bahá'u'lláh's amanuensis, Mírzá Áqá Ján, emerged from Bahá'u'lláh's tent with a somber look on his face. In his hand was a tablet Bahá'u'lláh had just revealed. And as Bahá'u'lláh had requested, Mírzá Áqá Ján began to chant aloud the verses from the Tablet of the Holy Mariner."

"I have heard Father chant that tablet many times," said Ali, "though I never understood exactly what it means."

"To Bahá'u'lláh's followers the meaning was *very* clear, Ali. It was a dreamlike portrayal of the problems that were about to descend on Bahá'u'lláh and the community itself. The last passage describes how the heavenly spirits wept when they heard what was happening to Bahá'u'lláh. It says, 'they bared their heads, rent their garments asunder, beat upon their faces, forgot their joy, shed tears and smote with their hands upon their cheeks, and this is verily one of the mysterious grievous afflictions.'"

"As Mírzá Áqá Ján chanted these verses to the assembled believers, the Bábís knew that this special period in Baghdád with their Beloved had suddenly and unexpectedly come to an end. Many of the Bábís wept and looked at each other in dismay. Then Bahá'u'lláh emerged from His tent and immediately ordered all the believers to fold up their tents and return to Baghdád.

"Then a rather mysterious thing occurred, Ali. Before they had even finished removing the tents, a messenger arrived from the city with a letter from the governor. Because the Prophets know the future, Bahá'u'lláh no doubt knew the letter would be coming—probably this is why He had told the believers to prepare to go home."

"But what was in the letter?" asked Ali impatiently.

"The letter was from the governor, and it requested that Bahá'u'lláh proceed to the headquarters of the government to meet with Námiq Pá<u>sh</u>á."

"So the governor gave in after all," said Ali.

"He could refuse the Sulṭán's command only so long, Ali. And, as always, Bahá'u'lláh courteously accepted the invitation, but He told the messenger that the meeting should take place at a mosque instead of at the governor's headquarters."

"Was this when the governor told Bahá'u'lláh about the Sulṭán's orders?"

"Yes, it was. The governor had delayed telling Bahá'u'lláh for three whole months. But now for the *fifth* time the prime minister of the Sulṭán had ordered Námiq Pá<u>sh</u>á to inform Bahá'u'lláh, so the governor had no choice. The governor had done the best he could, but he felt so ashamed at the prospect of having to tell Bahá'u'lláh to leave his city that he could not face Him. Instead, he sent his deputy to the meeting in his place.

"At the mosque the next day, the deputy handed Bahá'u'lláh the letter which 'Ali Pá<u>sh</u>á, the prime minister, had sent to the governor. The letter was courteous in tone. It 'invited' Bahá'u'lláh to travel to Constantinople as a 'guest' of the Ottoman government. It even offered Bahá'u'lláh a generous sum of money to help Him in His travel. It further designated a mounted guard of soldiers to go with Him on the long and difficult journey.

"But, of course, the real meaning of the letter was quite clear to Bahá'u'lláh. He was being removed from Ba<u>gh</u>dád and from His friends so that His influence on the growth of the Faith might be stopped."

"Did He agree to leave?" asked Ali.

"Bahá'u'lláh was always faithful to the laws and commands of the government in whatever land He lived. No matter how cruel or dishonest they were with Him, He was ever a faithful and dutiful citizen. So He agreed to go, but He refused to accept the money which the deputy tried to give Him. When the deputy insisted again and again, Bahá'u'lláh finally took the money, but to the complete dismay of the officials, He gave away every bit of it to poor people in Baghdád that very same day."

Ali laughed at Bahá'u'lláh's trick.

"Thus it seemed that the enemies of Bahá'u'lláh and the Bábí Faith had won again, and the believers in Baghdád were in a state of confusion and grief when they heard what the government had done. In fact, all of the citizens of the town were disturbed by the news that this wise and noble friend would soon have to leave them.

"That night, after they learned of this decree, the Bábís could not eat or sleep. They simply could not accept the idea that Bahá'u'lláh would actually be gone. Some even talked of killing themselves, but Bahá'u'lláh talked to them and comforted them as best He could.

"In the days that followed, Bahá'u'lláh continued to comfort the believers and shower His love upon them. For each believer—for the children as well as for the adults—He revealed a tablet in His own handwriting. In most of these tablets He tried to prepare them for the problems that would be coming, especially the troubles that Mírzá Yaḥyá would cause.

"But Bahá'u'lláh's stay in Baghdád was not yet completely over. One of the most important events of the Baghdád period was about to occur, an event for which Bahá'u'lláh had been patiently preparing them during all the years in Baghdád."

"Riḍván?" asked Ali, unable to contain himself.

"Yes, Ali, Riḍván. Twenty-seven days after He had revealed the Tablet of the Holy Mariner, Bahá'u'lláh began the first part of His journey to Constantinople. That was also the first day of the period we now celebrate as the Festival of Riḍván, the most important festival of the Bahá'í calendar. For on this first day, as He was departing from the city, and after He had bidden farewell to countless visitors, Bahá'u'lláh appeared in the courtyard of His house. There the believers gathered before Him, and in their grief they prostrated themselves at His feet. He told them that He would see them once more, for in the coming twelve days He would stay across the river in a specially prepared garden where He would meet with each one of them to bid them farewell.

"This assurance did little to soothe the aching hearts of the Bábís. As Bahá'u'lláh walked along the streets of Bag͟hdád toward the river, the townspeople crowded around Him. Some tried to touch Him or see His face. Others knelt before Him as He proceeded to the river bank. When He arrived at the ferryboat that was to take Him across to the garden that had been rented for Him, He spoke once more to the assembled believers and friends. In this farewell speech He said it was now up to them to keep the city as He had left it, full of love and harmony.

"When He arrived on the other side of the river and entered the beautiful garden, Bahá'u'lláh seemed joyful. The garden was filled with spring roses. The warbling songs of nightingales poured forth from many branches. The time had come to make His announcement to His followers, though probably many already suspected what He would say. You see, during the final month or so in Bag͟hdád, Bahá'u'lláh had changed His behavior."

"In what way?" asked Ali.

"It's hard to say exactly," said Moayyed. "Perhaps He seemed a little more serious, more formal, perhaps. I'm really not sure. I do know that on the day He left the city He began to wear a different type of headdress as a sign of this change. Instead of a turban, He wore a tall felt taj.

"But as soon as He arrived at the garden, He told the few believers and members of His family who were present that He, indeed, was the Promised Manifestation the Báb had described 'Him Whom God shall make manifest.' He also told them that this very day was the beginning of a festival that would be commemorated every year as the Festival of Riḍván. And that was why the garden where all of this took place was called the Garden of Riḍván, the Garden of Paradise."

"The same name as this garden," said Ali.

"Exactly, because paradise is not really a place, but a condition of the heart. So when He told this wonderful news to the believers, that their waiting was over, that the Latter Resurrection had at long last arrived, the sadness and sorrow of the Bábís seemed to melt away. One and all, they were filled with immense joy that the promise of the Báb had been fulfilled and that a new era in the divine education of humankind had now begun.

"The few days that followed in the garden were a time of complete celebration and happiness for everyone. The first day, the day of His arrival, He called the 'Day of supreme felicity.' On this day, besides telling the believers Who He was, He revealed to them three particularly important things. First, He told them that they could no longer use any kind of arms or weapons, that they should give up their lives rather than resort to killing those who persecuted them. This, of course, was a change in what the Báb had taught.

"The second thing He told them was that no other Manifestation would appear before at least a thousand years had passed. The third thing He told them was that a New Day had come with a fresh outpouring of spiritual power for all humankind. He also said that at the very moment He revealed these new teachings, all created things now could fully reflect the attributes of God.

"And that was just the first day," said Moayyed continuing. "During the days that followed He would reveal for the believers tablets to assist them after He had left. In one of the most important of these, He described in great detail how the believers in Nayríz more than ten years before had endured all the tests that the enemies of the Bábí Faith could inflict on them. He praised their courage, their steadfastness, especially that of Vaḥid, their leader, and Ḥájí Muḥammad-Táqí, who had helped Vaḥid teach the Cause in Nayríz."

"But why would Bahá'u'lláh talk so much about what had happened ten years before?" asked Ali. "It seems to me that He would want to tell them how important His announcement was."

Moayyed smiled and leaned forward. "This long tablet was preparing these unsuspecting followers for what they themselves were going to have to endure in the coming years. He knew that their own lives would become very difficult because of their beliefs, that they, too, would have to endure great suffering. He knew they would need courage and a strong character to survive these tests and trials. Above all else, Bahá'u'lláh knew they would need the particular virtue which is named in the title of the tablet itself." Moayyed paused to see if Ali would guess what that virtue was.

"Courage?" Ali offered.

"Patience!" Moayyed said with a knowing smile. "He called this important work the Súrih of Patience!"

Ali smiled and shook his head. Somehow, it seemed, all of the stories and all of his searching kept leading back to this singular quality.

"The believers had already shown patience in building the Bábí community in Baghdád," Moayyed continued, "but soon they would need the same caliber of steadfastness that the heroes of Nayríz and Ṭabarsí had shown years before.

"And so it was that the extraordinary days in the Garden of Riḍván passed—peacefully, festively, but with hearts and minds always aware of what was about happen in the future. Wave after wave of believers and non-believers alike visited Bahá'u'lláh during these twelve precious days. They would pay their respects to Him, and every day He would reveal even more about the beautiful secret which He had kept hidden for ten long years.

"Every morning before dawn, gardeners would pick roses from the garden and place them in the center of Bahá'u'lláh's tent. When the believers would enter and sit down for morning tea, they could hardly see each other across the tent because the flowers were piled so high. Then Bahá'u'lláh would give to each of them one of the flowers, and He would also give them flowers to take back to the friends who remained in Baghdád.

"At night, after the believers had met with Bahá'u'lláh and listened in rapt ecstasy to His melodious voice and the wonderful news He had to tell them, they would sleep among the fragrant rosebushes as the nightingales sang out their praise. As the believers lay sleeping, Bahá'u'lláh would frequently emerge from His tent and pass among them during the night as a loving parent might fondly gaze at a sleeping child.

"So you see, Ali, the end of the period in Baghdád was not a time of sorrow. It was a time of celebration. It was the very time that the Bábís had longed for. And, most wondrous of all, once again the enemies of Bahá'u'lláh who had tried so desperately to destroy Him and the Bábí religion witnessed (as they would time and time again in the future) how all of their efforts to deter this divine force would, in the long run, serve only to help Bahá'u'lláh and the Cause of God. There could be no greater demonstration of the power of Bahá'u'lláh and what He had accomplished than this glorious festival in the Garden of Riḍván."

11

The Clarion Call

Several days after the trip to the Garden of Riḍván, Ali wandered down to the place on the seawall where he and the other children had listened to Moayyed tell about Bahá'u'lláh's journey to the mountains. Ali sat on the wall by himself watching the waves crash on the jagged layers of rock beneath him, and he mused about how when he went to a place where he had heard a story, he would automatically remember the events in the story. It worked in reverse, too. When he thought about Bahá'u'lláh in the mountains, he remembered the day at the seawall with his grandfather and his friends.

Now, as he thought about his walk back to 'Akká from the Riḍván garden, he recalled the questions that had been forming in his mind, questions that had not been clear enough to him to ask his grandfather that afternoon. Besides, they had both been tired and were simply enjoying the picturesque landscape of bright blue Mediterranean Sea spread out behind the ancient buildings of 'Akká.

Now that the questions had become clearer in his mind, his grandfather was in Haifa for a few days. And since his mother and father were both busy, there was no adult Bahá'í he might ask, and, as usual, Ali was having a difficult time being patient.

Ali turned away from the wall and ambled slowly down the street toward the sea gate as he tried to think of someone he might ask. After all, the two questions were really fairly simple matters of fact: When did the Bábís begin calling themselves Bahá'ís, and what had been Mírzá Yaḥyá's reaction to the announcement in the Garden of Riḍván?

As he turned up the street that passed by the building where Neda and her family lived, Ali thought again about how the period in Baghdád had ended. Mulling over the events in the life of Bahá'u'lláh, he realized that he could detect a pattern there. The more he thought about it, the more he seemed to sense a pattern in all of the early history of the Bahá'í Faith. It went something like this: When everything seemed to get more and more hopeless, Bahá'u'lláh would do something to make everything all right again. But then, after Bahá'u'lláh had solved the problems and made everyone hopeful and happy again, some jealous or mischievous person would always try to hurt Him and to destroy the religion itself. Ali wondered if that same pattern had continued after Bahá'u'lláh left Baghdád.

Ali was so deep in these thoughts as he walked that he did not notice the broom that suddenly poked out in front of him, almost tripping him. He glanced up at the broomstick holder to see the smiling face of Neda.

She was pleased with her little joke. "What's wrong, Ali?" she said. "You weren't sleepwalking, were you?"

Ali laughed and realized how silly he must have looked.

"Perhaps you were having another one of your strange dreams," she said.

"You shouldn't make fun of my dream," said Ali. "Even Grandfather thinks it means something important."

"I know," said Neda. "I heard him talking with your father about it. 'Yes, it *is* remarkable—so simple yet so powerful!'" Neda spoke in a mockingly deep voice and pretended to stroke her chin as if she were Ali's grandfather. Then she broke into a giggle, and Ali laughed as well.

"Okay, okay," said Ali. "That's enough!" Ali knew that Neda was not trying to hurt his feelings. She was only reminding him that he had suddenly become so very serious at a time of year when most children of his age were more concerned with playing games or walking in the countryside. "Haven't you ever had a strange dream?" asked Ali.

"Yes, as a matter of fact I have," she answered with an unexpected seriousness.

"Well, . . . wouldn't you like to tell me about it?" asked Ali.

"I think not," she said decisively. "At least, not now. Another time perhaps."

Ali wanted to insist, but he knew that once Neda made up her mind about something, it stayed made up. "All right," said Ali. "But if you ever want to tell me, I'd like to hear it."

"Where are you going?" she asked, intentionally changing the subject.

"Oh, nowhere really," he said, shrugging his shoulders. "I was just thinking about a couple of things."

"What sort of things?" asked Neda.

"Well, if you really want to know, I wanted to asked Grandfather a question about something we were discussing the other day, except that he's in Haifa, and Mother and Father are busy."

"What's the question?"

"We were talking about how Bahá'u'lláh met with the believers before He left Baghdád to tell them He was the Promised Manifestation, and it made me wonder if that's when the Bábís started calling themselves Bahá'ís. But I also wanted to know what happened when Bahá'u'lláh arrived in Constantinople."

"I know!" said Neda, to Ali's surprise.

"You mean you can tell me the answers?" he asked.

"No, but I know how we can find out. My great-uncle was in Constantinople and Adrianople when Bahá'u'lláh was there. He has often told us stories about the journey to Constantinople and about the troubles with Mírzá Yaḥyá in Adrianople."

"Can you remember enough to tell me?" asked Ali.

"I can do better than that," said Neda with a smile. "My great-uncle will be here tomorrow for a visit. If you can come by in the afternoon, after he has had a chance to be with Mother and Father for a while, I'm sure he would be happy to tell you whatever you want to know."

"Would he really?" asked Ali excitedly.

"I'll ask Mother and Father first, but I don't think they'll mind." With that, Neda dashed into the house. She returned shortly to tell Ali that he would be welcome in their home to meet Neda's uncle.

That night Ali slept fitfully, and he was glad when the morning came. The morning was light and airy, the sky, a crisp blue. Already Ali was anticipating talking to Neda's uncle, though he was a bit nervous. To meet someone who had actually been with Bahá'u'lláh, in His presence during those eventful times—it was as if he were meeting Quddús or Mullá Ḥusayn.

He passed the morning hours by helping his mother with various chores around the house, though he was so preoccupied that he was probably more a nuisance than a help. Finally, the afternoon arrived and he found himself knocking at the door of Neda's house.

He was welcomed in by Neda's mother, who took him upstairs to a sitting-room where a stocky, rough-hewn old man was already deep in conversation with Neda's father. They were talking about the difficulties of coming to 'Akká from Baghdád, where her uncle lived. Ali sat down and watched the two men. He guessed that Neda's uncle was at least seventy-five or eighty years old, though he had the clear voice and quick movements of someone much younger.

Then, to Ali's surprise, the elderly man turned toward Ali with an inviting smile and said, "And you must be Ali, the young man Neda told me so much about." Neda blushed in her chair across the room, but Ali didn't notice. He was too intrigued by the man's eyes, which seemed to peer into Ali's very soul. "I am Uncle Ibráhím 'Abbás, but you must call me 'Uncle.' All the children in Baghdád do."

The others laughed, and Neda's mother came into the room carrying a tray of tea and small pastries which Neda herself had made. Ali had not expected so many people, nor had he expected this to be such a formal occasion. "Uncle" sensed Ali's nervousness and tried to make the boy feel more at ease. He made a few jokes, and, in spite of the hardships he had known and the suffering he had endured, he had soon transformed the formal air of respect that everyone felt in his presence into the warmth one feels among an intimate gathering of friends.

"So you want to know about Constantinople and Adrianople, do you?" he said, looking at Ali. The young boy felt embarrassed, as if he had no right to suggest what this venerated Bahá'í should talk about.

"Anything, sir. I would love to hear about anything at all," Ali said courteously.

"My son," said Uncle Ibrahim, "I have lived many years, long enough for two lives at least. If I start talking about everything I have seen and done, I might waste the rest of your remaining years. If it is Constantinople and Adrianople you wish to know about, then so you shall." Then without waiting for approval from the others, who were paying close attention to him, he began telling his story with the same enthusiasm and assurance with which he seemed to do everything else.

"Of course, you all know about the joy the friends felt when Bahá'u'lláh made His marvelous announcement in the Garden of Riḍván. Such a joyous occasion you cannot imagine. Then there was the journey from Baghdád to Sámsún. My, that was a journey unlike any other.

"I was but a young man then, about thirty years old. I had become a Bábí in Baghdád and had been fortunate enough to visit Bahá'u'lláh in the Garden of Riḍván. I also remember that fateful day of His leaving when He began His journey toward the capital city of Constantinople.

"It was noon, I believe. It was the third of May, 1863. The friends were gathered around Him hoping against hope that somehow He would not have to go, that some last-minute change in plans could keep Him in their presence. Then the Blessed Perfection majestically mounted a beautiful red roan stallion which the believers had bought for Him."

When Ali heard about the stallion his face lit up with a smile.

"Then there was a great commotion. All the people flocked around, some with their heads bowed in the dust before the feet of the approaching horse. A few even threw themselves in front of the steed, wanting to die rather than be separated from Bahá'u'lláh. And the tears . . . I have never seen such tears and such love in all my long life.

"Many of them feared they might never see Bahá'u'lláh again because none of us knew what fate awaited the Beloved of our hearts. We were just heartbroken. Only a few were allowed to go with Him. My family and I could not go on the journey, but we were allowed to accompany Bahá'u'lláh's entourage as far as the town of Firayját, the first stopping-place. That's where the caravan was formed. Oh, it was a magnificent sight—ten soldiers with their officer, seven pairs of howdahs, fifty mules.

"Most of the people who were allowed to go with Bahá'u'lláh were members of His family, together with Mírzá Músá, Mírzá Muḥammad-Qulí, and about two dozen other close followers. A few others joined along the way, including Nabíl-i-A'ẓam and Mírzá Yaḥyá, that infamous half-brother who was soon to be causing trouble again.

"After the group was assembled and all the provisions were gathered, the caravan began the long journey northward toward the port of Sámsún on the coast of the Black Sea.

"Well, I have talked to some who made this journey, so I can tell you a little about how the journey went. Bahá'u'lláh stayed about a week in Firayját while everything was being prepared, and then the glorious troop proceeded to the town of Judaydah, where they were given a friendly welcome by the townspeople. In fact, they were greeted like that at nearly every stop along the way. You see, many people had already heard about Bahá'u'lláh. Also, the governor of Ba<u>gh</u>dád had sent ahead of the caravan a written order to each village along the way, telling the people they should treat this noble Visitor with honor and respect.

"Sometimes Bahá'u'lláh would ride on horseback and sometimes in a howdah. At some villages the townspeople would send out a delegation of citizens to meet Bahá'u'lláh, and often there would be arranged in the villages grand feasts to celebrate the arrival of this special Guest.

"There were over twenty stops like this during the journey, which lasted 110 days and covered a thousand miles or more. Most of the companions on the journey were completely devoted to Bahá'u'lláh so that they were always lively and happy. And to make the journey even more special, along the way Bahá'u'lláh would sometimes reveal tablets to commemorate the journey. For example, you all have heard of the Tablet of the Howdah? Well, that was composed as the caravan approached Sámsún.

"On other occasions Jináb-i-Muníb would chant in his melodious voice odes and poems expressing the boundless love that he and the other friends felt for Bahá'u'lláh. Some stops were brief, and the caravan would spend only one night. But in other towns, such as Karkúk, Irbíl, Mosul, Nísíbín, Márdín, and Díyár-Bakr, they might stay two or even three nights.

"Day after day they traveled northward, enjoying the hospitality of villagers and the presence of Bahá'u'lláh. You can be sure, though, that in the back of their minds they were always wondering what problems lay ahead. Finally they reached the port city of Sámsún. There they were also treated with respect by the government officials, and they stayed there for seven days where they enjoyed great hospitality.

"When the time came to depart, Bahá'u'lláh and the rest were taken to the docks, where they were put on board a Turkish steamship headed for Constantinople. For three days the ship sailed along the coast of the Black Sea until it reached the majestic city of Constantinople, the capital city of the Ottoman Empire, where the ruler of the empire, Sulṭán 'Abdu'l-'Azíz, lived.

"When Bahá'u'lláh and His companions arrived on August 16th, 1863, they were still treated with dignity, though you can be sure that Bahá'u'lláh knew all too well the true purpose behind the Sulṭán's 'invitation.' Two carriages were waiting at the dock to take Bahá'u'lláh and His family to the house of Shamsí Big, a man who had been asked to take care of Bahá'u'lláh as a guest of the Ottoman government."

"Then they weren't prisoners?" asked Ali, forgetting for a moment that the adults might not think it polite for him to interrupt Uncle's story by asking questions as he usually did with his parents or his grandfather. But Uncle broke the nervous silence that followed Ali's question with a kindly smile at Ali, and he answered the question.

"In a way they were, of course. But naturally the government officials wouldn't say so at first. No, they treated Bahá'u'lláh with respect, pretending that He really was a guest instead of someone they wanted to remove from Baghdád.

"And so it was that for the first month there the family lived in the two-story house of Shamsí Big. Then Bahá'u'lláh did what may seem to us a curious thing, especially since we know the trouble that Mírzá Yaḥyá would soon cause. He invited Mírzá Yaḥyá, who had already caused so much trouble for Bahá'u'lláh and His family in Baghdád, to come and live with them in the house."

"Why did He do that?" asked Neda.

"I don't really know," said Uncle Ibrahim, looking affectionately at Neda. "Perhaps He wanted to give Mírzá Yaḥyá a chance to change. Perhaps He thought that if He showed His half-brother forgiveness, then Mírzá Yaḥyá would not be so jealous anymore."

"But I thought the Manifestations know everything," said Ali, "even the things that haven't yet occurred. Didn't Bahá'u'lláh know what Mírzá Yaḥyá was going to do?"

Uncle smiled again, then looked at the faces of Neda's parents, both of whom seemed somewhat embarrassed by the difficult questions that Neda and Ali were asking. "That's an excellent question," said Uncle, as if to signal to the parents that he welcomed the inquisitive minds of these two young Bahá'ís. "Yes, that is true. I have no doubt that Bahá'u'lláh knew exactly what Mírzá Yaḥyá was going to do, and I am also sure that Bahá'u'lláh knew He could not force Mírzá Yaḥyá to change. So I suspect that this gesture was for the other believers, . . . and for us," said Uncle, punctuating his observation with his index finger, pointing at his own heart. "I suspect that Bahá'u'lláh wanted His followers to know that when Mírzá Yaḥyá began to cause trouble again, it wasn't because of anything Bahá'u'lláh had done to him.

"Well, the family stayed in the house about a month. Then 'Abdu'l-Bahá—Who, though only about twenty years of age, was a most wise, able, and respected young man—talked with the governor and managed to have the family moved into a house with a little more room. This was the house of Vísí Pá<u>sh</u>á.

"Of course, those who had followed Bahá'u'lláh to this further exile were not all members of the holy family, nor were all of them believers. There were merchants, tradesmen, learned mullás, and noblemen. Naturally, the nobles and others who might be recognized by the government officials disguised themselves. Some presented themselves as tailors or bakers or members of some other common trade or lowly office so that they would be allowed to come with Bahá'u'lláh without arousing the suspicions or concerns of the officials.

"As you can imagine, soon people flocked to meet Bahá'u'lláh just as they had in Baghdád. Soon the people in Constantinople were talking about this noble Guest, about His great wisdom and vast knowledge. Before too much time had passed, the city officials began to hear about all this attention as well, and it made them curious about Bahá'u'lláh. After all, the Sulṭán had invited Bahá'u'lláh not because he thought this Persian was truly wise, but just to remove Bahá'u'lláh from Baghdád, where the Muslim religious leaders had become so jealous.

"Soon some of the government officers came to visit Bahá'u'lláh, and many were so overcome by His wit, charm, grace, and affection that they became His friends. One who was particularly fond of Bahá'u'lláh—the Persian consul-general himself—tried to help Bahá'u'lláh and His followers."

"How did he do that?" asked Neda.

"It was the custom then for visitors to Constantinople to pay a visit to Sulṭán 'Abdu'l-'Azíz to present him with gifts and show him their respect for his great power. The consul-general knew that if Bahá'u'lláh would make such a visit and pay homage to the Sulṭán's power, Bahá'u'lláh, with all His knowledge and warmth, would surely win the Sulṭán's affection, and things would be easier for the believers.

"But Bahá'u'lláh persistently refused. 'I have no wish to ask favor from them.' He told the consul-general during one of their discussions. 'I have come here at the Sulṭán's command. Whatsoever additional commands he may issue, I am ready to obey.' You see, Bahá'u'lláh was ever obedient to the laws and rulers of the lands where He was forced to live. But He wanted to make it clear that His success and the success of the Bahá'í Faith was not due to any external influence or assistance. 'My work is not of their world; it is of another realm, far removed from their province,' He told the consul-general. 'Why, therefore, should I seek these people?'

"When the consul-general heard these responses he was proud of Bahá'u'lláh, but he was also worried. He knew that among the government officials were enemies, people who feared Bahá'u'lláh or who were jealous of Him as the religious clerics in Baghdád had been.

"Sure enough, when Bahá'u'lláh did not visit the court, the Persian ambassador, who was one of those officials so very jealous of Bahá'u'lláh, told members of the court that Bahá'u'lláh was a proud, arrogant, and very dangerous person. For several months these enemies of Bahá'u'lláh at the court spoke against Bahá'u'lláh until, finally, the Sulṭán himself sent a message—an edict—to Bahá'u'lláh, announcing that the exiles would be banished from Constantinople."

"But why?" asked Neda. "I don't understand why he did that."

"He did not give any reason," said Uncle Ibrahim. "He was the Sulṭán. He didn't need to give a reason. He simply sent a messenger to meet with Bahá'u'lláh. Of course, Bahá'u'lláh had little patience with the arrogant and the proud, even if they were kings. So Bahá'u'lláh would not meet with the messenger. Instead, He sent 'Abdu'l-Bahá and Mírzá Músá to meet the messenger.

"After the messenger read the announcement of the further exile, he told Mírzá Músá and 'Abdu'l-Bahá that he would return in three days for a response. Now, as you can imagine, the government officials fully expected Bahá'u'lláh to ask for a meeting with them so that He might beg for forgiveness and plead to stay.

"Once again Bahá'u'lláh did the unexpected. On that very same day, Bahá'u'lláh revealed a tablet to the Sulṭán, a very long tablet. And on the following morning He gave the tablet to Shamsí Big in a sealed envelope and told him to take it to 'Alí Páshá, a chief minister of the Sulṭán. What is more, Bahá'u'lláh told Shamsí Big to tell the minister that the tablet was sent to Sulṭán 'Abdu'l-'Azíz from God!"

Ali and Neda looked at each other and smiled, leaning forward on their chairs as they listened.

"Shamsí Big took the letter to the court as Bahá'u'lláh had instructed him, and he gave the tablet to the grand vizier. This haughty official of the Sulṭán opened the letter and began reading. But as he read, his face turned pale. He looked up at Shamsí Big. At first he was speechless. Finally he mumbled in a startled tone, 'It is as if the King of Kings were issuing his behest to his humblest vassal king and regulating his conduct!'"

"What did the letter say?" asked Neda.

"I suppose we will never know exactly," said Uncle, his eyes wrinkling at the corners from his smile. "The tablet was lost. But we do know that in this lengthy epistle Bahá'u'lláh explained to Sulṭán 'Abdu'l-'Azíz and his officials exactly how they should correct their behavior and how they should become just rulers.

"Well, while this small victory of Bahá'u'lláh is indeed delightful to hear, it meant that Bahá'u'lláh and His family had to leave again, and this time in the dead cold of winter. So they gathered what few belongings they could carry and quickly prepared to depart. But before they left, Bahá'u'lláh sent another message, this time to the Persian ambassador. He informed this inveterate enemy of the Cause of God that no matter how far away Bahá'u'lláh was exiled or how many believers the government might kill, the Revelation of God would not be stopped.

"Nevertheless, the rulers of the world once again thought they were getting rid of Bahá'u'lláh and the Bahá'í Faith, and they sent Bahá'u'lláh and His family to the desolate city of Adrianople only four months after their arrival in Constantinople. So Bahá'u'lláh, His family, and a few followers gathered what belongings they could carry, put them into wagons or on pack animals, and began their journey.

"It was not a very long distance, not compared to the journey from Ba<u>gh</u>dád to Constantinople. But it happened in the midst of a particularly harsh winter, and the travelers were poorly clothed. On this journey there were no celebrations, no cheering townspeople. For twelve miserable days they marched across the drab, freezing land in the middle of fierce winter storms. Sometimes they had to travel at night without winter clothing, stopping only at a few small towns along the way.

"When they finally arrived in Adrianople, they had no house to stay in, only a drafty two-story caravansary. After staying in that cold and miserable shelter for three days, Bahá'u'lláh and His family were moved to a small, flimsy house, a building that was not meant to be a winter dwelling at all. A week later they moved once more, this time to a house that was not much better, where they stayed for six months.

"Finally, they were moved to a larger house more suited to their needs, the place that in time became known as the house of Amru'lláh, the House of God's command.'"

"Why was it called that?" asked Ali.

"I will tell you why very soon," said Uncle Ibrahim. "You see, during the five years that Bahá'u'lláh stayed in the remote city of Adrianople, some very important things happened in the history of our religion—in fact, two of the most important events you can imagine. The first of these involved Mírzá Yaḥyá once again. It had been almost ten years since the mischievous Siyyid Muḥammad had incited Mírzá Yaḥyá to cause so much trouble for Bahá'u'lláh and for the Bábí Faith. Now, after Bahá'u'lláh had forgiven him and welcomed him back into the family, Mírzá Yaḥyá began once again to plot with Siyyid Muḥammad against Bahá'u'lláh. This time, however, Mírzá Yaḥyá decided he would do more than simply tell lies about Bahá'u'lláh. This time he intended to get rid of Bahá'u'lláh for good."

"Murder Him?" asked Neda.

"Yes, exactly so. You see, the first year in Adrianople went well. No one suspected that any trouble was brewing. Perhaps the believers had forgotten about the events foretold in the Tablet of the Holy Mariner, or else they thought that the exile to Adrianople was the turmoil the tablet had predicted. So in the house of Amru'lláh all seemed quite happy. The friends would gather at night to hear Bahá'u'lláh speak, and in the daytime the believers went about their trades.

"A few actually served in the house itself. For example, Áqá Muḥammad-Baqír-i-Qahvih-chí and Ustád Muḥammad 'Alíy-i-Salmání made sure the tea, the coffee, and other refreshments were prepared. No thought of trouble ever entered their minds.

"But about a year after their arrival, Mírzá Yaḥyá got a place of his own and began learning all he could about deadly poisons. Soon after, he started inviting Bahá'u'lláh to his home, pretending to be loving and friendly, as a brother should be. But on one of these visits Mírzá Yaḥyá secretly smeared Bahá'u'lláh's teacup with a most deadly poison.

"Bahá'u'lláh quickly became quite ill. He was immediately taken to His home, and a doctor—a foreigner named Shíshmán—was rushed to Bahá'u'lláh's bedside. But when the doctor saw how pale Bahá'u'lláh was, he was sure there was no hope for survival. And because the doctor knew Bahá'u'lláh and had the utmost respect and love for Him, he fell at the foot of Bahá'u'lláh's bed in sorrow. Finally, he got to his feet and left without even prescribing any medicine, because he thought there was no hope that Bahá'u'lláh might be cured.

"Day by day over the next month, Bahá'u'lláh began to improve. He had great pain and often a high fever, but eventually He could move about and do some work. But even when He was almost completely over the sickness, His hand shook from the effects of the poison. He could no longer write in the exquisite penmanship He had learned as a young Man—not then or even for the rest of His life."

"What happened to Mírzá Yaḥyá?" asked Ali. "Was he arrested?"

"No, he wasn't arrested. How could Bahá'u'lláh explain to the authorities that one of His own followers was trying to kill Him? No, I'm afraid Mírzá Yaḥyá was not even sorry for what he had done, nor did he intend to stop trying to destroy Bahá'u'lláh. When he failed to kill Bahá'u'lláh, he poisoned the well from which the family got its drinking water. No one died, but many of them became seriously ill.

"No, when one plan would fail, Mírzá Yaḥyá would simply think of another. For example, he talked to Bahá'u'lláh's barber, Ustád Muḥammad-'Alí, a man to whom Mírzá Yaḥyá had given extravagant gifts. He told the barber how horrible he thought Bahá'u'lláh was, and he finally told the barber of a plan to kill Bahá'u'lláh in the public baths."

"Did the barber agree?" asked Neda.

"Absolutely not!" said Uncle, slapping his knee. "Mírzá Yaḥyá had picked the wrong man. Ustád Muḥammad-'Alí loved Bahá'u'lláh with all his heart, and so at first he didn't believe Mírzá Yaḥyá was serious. When he finally realized that Mírzá Yaḥyá was serious, the poor man ran weeping from the bathhouse where he had been talking with Mírzá Yaḥyá.

"Once outside he saw Mírzá Músá and, enraged by Mírzá Yaḥyá's proposal, he told him what had happened. He said that at first he wanted to kill Mírzá Yaḥyá. He said that he certainly would have done so, except that he knew Bahá'u'lláh would not have wanted him to do such a thing."

"But why didn't the family do something to stop Mírzá Yaḥyá?" asked Neda.

"I know it's hard to understand," said Uncle. "But remember, the believers were Persian exiles, prisoners in a foreign land. If they suddenly started fighting amongst themselves, what would the government think?

"Bahá'u'lláh did do one thing, though, something extremely important! Remember that when Mírzá Yaḥyá had caused trouble in Bag͟hdád, Bahá'u'lláh went to the mountains to avoid becoming a source of confusion to the Bábís. And, of course, Bahá'u'lláh wanted them to see for themselves what Mírzá Yaḥyá would do if he were given a chance to lead them.

"But now Bahá'u'lláh was in a different position. He had officially announced to the believers that He was the Promised Manifestation Whom the Báb had foretold. The time allotted for Mírzá Yaḥyá to function as the 'nominee' of the Báb had long passed. Now Bahá'u'lláh spoke as the appointed Prophet of God. He determined that the time had come to make it perfectly clear to Mírzá Yaḥyá that any further attempt to stop Bahá'u'lláh's leadership would be the same as trying to stop the Cause of God itself.

"So Bahá'u'lláh wrote a tablet to Mírzá Yaḥyá, the Súrih of the Command. In this tablet Bahá'u'lláh stated emphatically that He was the One Whom the Báb had promised and that His purpose was to reveal a new religion.

"After He had written the tablet, He told His secretary, Mírzá Áqá Ján, to go to Mírzá Yaḥyá, to read the tablet aloud in his presence and then demand an answer. So Mírzá Áqá Ján took the tablet to the house of Mírzá Yaḥyá and read it aloud as Bahá'u'lláh had instructed. But when he asked for a reply, Mírzá Yaḥyá could say nothing. Finally, after some delay, Mírzá Yaḥyá asked for a day or so to think about his answer.

"Naturally, this was only another trick. He never did answer. Instead, he wrote a tablet of his own in which he claimed that he, Mírzá Yaḥyá, had received a revelation from God and that everyone should follow him!"

Ali and Neda were both shocked. Neither had had any idea that Mírzá Yaḥyá had done such things.

"What did Bahá'u'lláh do then?" asked Neda.

"Bahá'u'lláh determined that the time had come for decisive action. He knew that He could no longer tolerate Mírzá Yaḥyá's wretched actions with forbearance and kindness as He had done over and over again through the years. That was when the 'most great separation' began."

"What was that?" asked Ali.

"Bahá'u'lláh and His family moved from the house of Amru'lláh, the house He shared with the other exiles, and they moved to the house of Riḍá Big. This was in March of 1866. For two whole months Bahá'u'lláh refused to see anyone outside the family."

"Not even the faithful believers?" asked Neda.

"Not even the closest believers. Only His family. You see, He wanted the believers to decide for themselves once and for all whom they would follow—Bahá'u'lláh or Mírzá Yaḥyá. As a symbol of this separation, Bahá'u'lláh also divided up all His belongings into two portions. He then ordered Mírzá Músá to see that half of the belongings were given to Mírzá Yaḥyá, including all of the various rings and tablets that Mírzá Yaḥyá had always desired.

"Bahá'u'lláh was not really concerned about dividing these objects, you understand. This was a gesture, a symbolic way of separating himself officially and finally from Mírzá Yahyá, regardless of how much consternation this caused the other believers and no matter how strange it might have seemed to the local officials. That was the way Bahá'u'lláh acted. He was more tolerant and kind and forgiving than any ordinary human being could ever possibly become, but once a different sort of action was required, Bahá'u'lláh was decisive as the blade of a sword.

"Bahá'u'lláh did not enjoy this act—I'm sure you understand that. But it was a necessary thing to do at this period of confusion. That's why He called this period the "Days of Stress," because this was the period that fulfilled the turmoil described in the Tablet of the Holy Mariner. For while it didn't last long, it was a very difficult time for the believers, and it appeared to the government as if the religion itself had suddenly become divided. This idea was supported by the lies told to the Persian ambassador in Adrianople by Siyyid Muḥammad. He had said that Bahá'u'lláh was depriving Mírzá Yaḥyá of his rights and that Bahá'u'lláh was planning to kill the Sháh of Persia. Furthermore, the stress caused by this separation lasted far beyond the two-month period during which Bahá'u'lláh refused to see anyone.

"Well, as you can imagine, the strain of seeing His own half-brother whom He had raised as a son turn against Him again was very hard on Bahá'u'lláh. This grief added to the pain and torment of His exile and aged His once youthful appearance. His hair became white, and gradually the brightness of His face seemed to fade.

"Then, about a year after His withdrawal to the house of Riḍá Big, Bahá'u'lláh moved back into the house of Amru'lláh where He stayed for about three months. In September of 1867 He moved again, this time to the last place in which He would live in Adrianople, the house of 'Izzat Áqá.

"While Bahá'u'lláh was living there, a very interesting thing occurred that has always been for me a most revealing story. A certain believer from Shíráz named Mír Muḥammad, who had become very angry at Mírzá Yaḥyá for claiming to be a Prophet of God, decided upon a plan to prove publicly once and for all the true nature of Mírzá Yaḥyá. You see, outwardly with others, Mírzá Yaḥyá appeared meek and humble, the image of a loving servant of God. All the vicious and cruel things he did went unobserved since he usually employed others to do his dirty work.

"Mír Muḥammad knew the one way to unmask Mírzá Yaḥyá, to show others what he really was, would be to arrange for a public meeting between Bahá'u'lláh and Mírzá Yaḥyá. This would allow people to decide for themselves who was telling the truth. Well, my children, one of the great weaknesses of the corrupt ones of this world is that they assume everyone else responds with the same selfish motives that they do. Thus Mírzá Yaḥyá was certain that Bahá'u'lláh would never be so humble as to participate in such a confrontation. He was sure Bahá'u'lláh would not come. Therefore, this scheming brother who had inflicted such incalculable pain and suffering on One Who had never given him anything but love and forgiveness agreed to the public meeting.

"When word reached Bahá'u'lláh that this meeting had been arranged, He did not hesitate for an instant. He walked in the midday heat to the mosque where the meeting was to take place, accompanied by Mír Muḥammad himself. So composed and resolute was Bahá'u'lláh as He paced through the streets of Adrianople that He began to chant aloud some of His own revealed verses."

"Do you know what those verses were?" asked Ali, eagerly wanting to know every detail of how Bahá'u'lláh at long last confronted His ungrateful brother.

"As a matter of fact, I do," said Uncle, pleased that this bright youth was so enthralled by the story. "One such verse went like this: 'Were all the divines, all the wise men, all the kings and rulers on earth to gather together, I, in very truth, would confront them, and would proclaim the verses of God, the Sovereign, the Almighty, the All-Wise. I am He Who feareth no one, though all who are in heaven and all who are on earth rise up against me.'"

As Ali heard these powerful verses, he unconsciously clasped his hands together as if he were applauding. "As Bahá'u'lláh walked, Mír Muḥammad hurried on ahead to the mosque to announce the arrival of Bahá'u'lláh. But when he arrived, he discovered that Mírzá Yaḥyá had changed his mind and had not come. Dear friends, for the next three days Bahá'u'lláh came to that spot and waited, ready for this long-awaited confrontation with Mírzá Yaḥyá."

"He never came, did he?" said Neda, remembering how Mírzá Yaḥyá had in his cowardice disguised himself rather than risk being discovered as a Bábí.

"Quite correct," said Uncle. "He never came, and so the few followers Mírzá Yaḥyá did have were very disappointed by his cowardly behavior. Once and for all Bahá'u'lláh had proved to the believers that He was the Promised Manifestation, and Mírzá Yaḥyá was officially cut off from the rest of the believers. Indeed, it was from this time forward that the followers of Bahá'u'lláh called themselves 'Bahá'ís'—'followers of Bahá.' The few followers of Mírzá Yaḥyá were called 'people of the Bayan,' or sometimes 'Azalís,' because Mírzá Yaḥyá's title was Ṣubḥ-i-Azal, or 'Morning of Eternity.'"

"Such a beautiful name for one so corrupt," said Neda's mother almost to herself.

"So true, so true," said Uncle. "And perhaps that's the point of it all. Perhaps the name says what he could have been had he only made the right choices. But the truth is not always easy and obvious. Certainly it was not obvious to the government officials who learned of this internal strife among the Persian exiles. No, Mírzá Yaḥyá's rebellion had done terrible damage to the reputation of the Cause of God, especially in the eyes of those who did not understand all that had happened. But at least within the community of believers the issue was resolved—their religion had been given a new name, the Bahá'í Faith."

"But you mentioned *two* important events that occurred in Adrianople," said Ali. "What was the other one?"

"Ah, yes, that is the truly wonderful part of the story of the years in Adrianople. That is the most *important* thing. During this period, in fact during the entire life of Bahá'u'lláh from the time God told Him in the Síyáh-Chál to reveal Himself, the Pen of the Blessed Beauty never stopped. But His writing was not always the same, you see. Everything Bahá'u'lláh wrote was written in a particular style, at a particular time, for a particular purpose. And His writing in Adrianople was a clarion call to the entire world, announcing that the long-awaited Lord of Hosts had come to redeem the world!" Uncle spread out his hands as he said this, as if he were embracing a descended angel.

"For while Bahá'u'lláh had already announced to the believers in the Garden of Riḍván that He was the Prophet Whose advent the Báb had foretold, it was now time to tell everyone else!"

"But how could he tell *everyone?*" asked Ali.

"Quite right. Bahá'u'lláh obviously could not send a personal letter to every human being on earth, could He?" observed Uncle. "So Bahá'u'lláh did the next best thing possible. He wrote to the kings and rulers and religious leaders of the world and made them responsible for telling the people."

"But what exactly did He tell these leaders of the world?" asked Neda.

"He said different things to different individuals, things that only those particular individuals could understand. But in most of these letters was one clear message. Bahá'u'lláh told each of them that God had revealed Himself again and that He, Bahá'u'lláh, lowly Prisoner and Exile that He seemed to be, was the Manifestation of God sent to transform the face of human civilization.

"I must tell you that it was truly an amazing event. Why, in future ages, historians will marvel at the importance of these letters, even though the leaders themselves scarcely noticed them. Yes, even in the midst of the heartrending problems He had with Mírzá Yaḥyá, Bahá'u'lláh kept Mírzá Áqá Ján, 'Abdu'l-Bahá, and a number of other secretaries busy almost every day copying down His words.

"There were thousands of verses, almost every single day. Tablet after tablet poured forth, announcing to the world that the day had come at last when the earth would be united under one universal law and one religious faith, one clear vision of who we are and how we can all work and live together to fashion the Kingdom of God on earth."

"Who exactly did He write to?" asked Ali.

"To kings and princes, to the Sháh of Persia and to Sulṭán 'Abdu'l-'Azíz, to Napoleon III, to the Czar of Russia, to the Emperor of Austria, the Queen of England, to the American government, to the Pope, and to many others. What is more, in these letters Bahá'u'lláh said that the people of the world were in great danger unless the rulers worked together to stop preparing for war. Bahá'u'lláh said that He had come to unite the world because the peoples of the world were entrusted to these rulers by God. Therefore it was the rulers' responsibility to see that the people in their care were treated with justice and kindness."

Uncle Ibrahim stopped. He sat back in his chair. He was clearly exhausted. Everyone in the room showed immediate concern. Then, unexpectedly, a knowing grin appeared on Uncle's face, and he spoke. "The Súrih of Kings was one of the greatest tablets of that period. It was intended for *all* the world leaders of the East and the West. It said that their only hope was to heed the laws and teachings that Bahá'u'lláh was presenting to them. And that, you see, is one reason the house in Adrianople is called the house of Amru'lláh, the House of God's Command.

"But just imagine," he said, speaking more slowly and looking around the room into the eyes of everyone there. "Just imagine how it might have been to be a king, to receive one of those letters, a letter from a Manifestation of God. How would you feel? What would you think?" He paused and looked at Ali in particular. "What do you think those kings and leaders feel right *now* in the world of the spirit, where all that was hidden is made clear and apparent, and all the empires they thought they possessed are only faint memories of their wasted lives and lost opportunities?"

The elderly man leaned forward again. "Think on it, my friends. Here we are as living examples of the power of Bahá'u'lláh. The kings did not heed Him. The religious leaders ignored Him or persecuted Him. But the ordinary people, people like you and me, we heard and recognized the truth, and we followed. And yet how many more, perhaps right here in 'Akká, perhaps next door, are patiently waiting, waiting to hear what only we can tell them?"

Neda's Uncle stopped. His face was stern now. His eyes gazed ahead, as if his thoughts were suddenly somewhere else, as if he might be looking beyond this room and into the future.

At last Neda's mother, who had been sitting slightly past the doorway, got up quietly from her chair and began to prepare some more tea. Then Neda got up to help her. Gradually, others began to talk or move about the room, but Ali noticed that Uncle Ibrahim did not rise. He smiled and began to talk with Neda's father about the Bahá'í community in Bag͟hdád.

Soon a steady mumble of voices filled the room while Ali sat and watched. It was a cozy sound, those voices. The voices seemed to blend with the refreshing aroma of spiced tea and warm pastries, and Ali felt a peace within himself that he had seldom known before.

When she had finished serving the others, Neda sat down next to Ali, who was still watching the old man with awe and reverence. "He is so joyous, so strong!" Ali said to her at last. "I hope someday I can be like that."

The words were no sooner out of his mouth than Ali saw Uncle Ibrahim trying to stand, but not by himself Neda's father almost lifted Uncle to his feet. Then slowly, one shaking and painful step at a time, Uncle was helped into the adjoining bedroom where he would lie down and rest.

Ali looked at Neda. A tear ran down her cheek. "The bastinado," she said softly to Ali.

12

The Most Great Prison

The pace of summer days quickened. For Ali, autumn seemed to be arriving more rapidly than usual. He enjoyed the bright, dear, warm days, and more and more often he took his sailboat past the seawall, out into the open waters of the Mediterranean. He ventured out in the mornings while the sea was calm. In the afternoons, when the offshore winds would become stronger, he found himself reading the writings of Bahá'u'lláh on his own, something he had done in the past only when he was being instructed by his parents or his teacher, Dr. Bushrú'í.

He continued to talk with his grandfather and his parents about the life of Bahá'u'lláh and about other stories of those who had rendered great service to the Bahá'í Faith. It seemed that the more answers he discovered, the more new questions he found there were to ask. He did not yet feel he had discovered the "key" he had dreamed about, and he was beginning to wonder if he ever would.

But sometimes it didn't seem to matter so much because he was beginning to enjoy the search itself. He was starting to have a much dearer sense of what it meant to call himself a Bahá'í, and he found that he liked that feeling very much.

Sometimes out in the boat with his makeshift sail taut in the wind, pulling the little craft across the blue water, Ali felt strong and self-confident. He had rarely known such feelings before his dream—this sense that he was growing up, that he was already preparing himself for a future that, though concealed from him, now held out a promise of adventure and meaningful service. What he would do or how he would do it—all this he would leave in Bahá'u'lláh's hands. But he no longer doubted that there was a special task for him.

There was another change beginning in this youth. Things that had once been troubling or frightening did not seem to bother Ali anymore. As he learned about the courage of the early believers and met Bahá'ís like Neda's uncle who themselves had suffered because of their beliefs, these feelings of confidence and determination grew.

Often he thought about the visit to Neda's house and the sight of Uncle Ibrahim struggling to his feet. He still marveled at how the real power within the man had been completely untouched by the iron rods of the bastinado.

One morning Ali lowered his sail and set the anchor a short distance from the seawall. He baited a handline and threw it out. As he waited for the cork to bob and for the unmistakable tug at the line, he thought back over some of the stories about Bahá'u'lláh that he had heard. He thought once again about the pattern he had observed in the life of Bahá'u'lláh—that as soon as people recognized the power, the dignity, the love of Bahá'u'lláh, in whatever place He happened to be, something would always happen to interfere with the peace and progress of the community. Intrigues, persecutions—some problem or other—would always occur. The temporary tranquility would be interrupted, and Bahá'u'lláh would once again be imprisoned or banished.

Ali's thoughts were interrupted by a plaintive voice. In the distance across the water was the rising and falling of the muezzin's voice calling Muslims to the noon prayer. Ali stopped his fishing to say his own obligatory prayer. When he finished praying, he thought how strange it was that each day the streets of 'Akká would echo with that call, the voices from the tall spires, exhorting the townspeople to the worship of God. And yet these same townspeople still remained unaware that in their very own city, God had revealed Himself again.

He remembered Neda's uncle telling of Bahá'u'lláh's letters announcing Who He was to the kings and rulers. Once more Ali wondered what he might have felt had he been such a king and received such a letter from Bahá'u'lláh. Would he have known?

He looked at the prison behind the city walls. "If I'd been sailing my boat when Bahá'u'lláh was in that prison," he thought, "would it have looked any different? Would I have known that the prisoner in that very same building was special, or would I have been like the other townspeople? Would I have believed the bad things that were being said about the strange Persians who came as prisoners to 'Akká?"

Then Ali thought of something he had not considered before. He looked out toward Haifa, where Bahá'u'lláh and the other Bahá'ís had landed on their way to the prison, and he tried to imagine that he was on that boat. He wondered what the Bahá'ís must have felt as they saw for the first time the place where most of them would spend the rest of their lives.

He looked again at the prison. "The Most Great Prison," he repeated several times. To Ali, it seemed a beautiful place, a sacred place where Bahá'u'lláh had stayed. But if Bahá'u'lláh gave it such a stark name, it must have been a horrible experience indeed.

As he sailed back an hour or so later, he turned his boat in toward the seawall and the shore. He decided he wanted to know what it was like when the Bahá'ís came to 'Akká. He wanted to go with Moayyed to all the places where the Bahá'ís had first lived. He wanted to find out as much as he could about how they were treated. He wanted to understand what they had experienced.

On the following day, the day when Moayyed always had dinner with the family, he told his grandfather of the plan. To the young boy's delight, Moayyed was as excited by the idea as Ali.

"A grand tour of the city, eh? Well, I think we can manage that," said Moayyed. "In fact, after such a huge meal, a walk around 'Akká would be just what we both need."

After dinner Moayyed and Ali walked down the ancient streets toward the wall that guarded 'Akká from the sea. The boy and his grandfather were a familiar sight to all who passed by them, and most of the townspeople nodded with a smile or greeted them. They walked past the house of 'Abbúd, taking the long route to the sea gate, the place in 'Akká where the Bahá'ís had landed.

Moayyed spread his arms as he took in several deep breaths to indicate his pleasure with the afternoon sea breeze. "So you want to know about how the Bahá'ís came to 'Akká? I think I can help you. Let's see, it's been almost forty-five years since then, and 'Akká has changed a great deal."

"In what way, Grandfather?"

"It's still a humble place. I sometimes think of it more as a museum than a city. But back then it was a miserable prison city. City water came into the moat, and when the tide went out, it left a most awful stench. There was hardly any fresh water.

"But I'm getting ahead of myself. Do you know how Bahá'u'lláh was made to come here in the first place?"

"Not exactly."

"Then let me begin there, for the story of 'Akká really begins in Adrianople with the problems Mírzá Yaḥyá caused."

"I know about those," said Ali. "I heard Neda's uncle talk about them."

"Then you know that Bahá'u'lláh wrote to all the leaders and peoples of the world to announce His Prophethood?"

"Yes, Grandfather."

"In fact, during this period, around 1867 and 1868, His pen never stopped, and believers no longer called themselves Bábís, but began using the title 'the people of Bahá,' or 'Bahá'ís.' And in place of the Muslim greeting *'Alláh-u-Akbar,'* Bahá'ís began using the greeting *'Alláh-u-Abhá,'*— 'God is Most Glorious.'

"But in spite of all the work that Bahá'u'lláh was doing to advance the Cause of God and reveal the teachings for a new day, Mírzá Yaḥyá and Siyyid Muḥammad never stopped their dreadful activities.

"Even after Mírzá Yaḥyá refused the challenge to debate Bahá'u'lláh at the mosque?"

"So you know about that, do you?" said Moayyed with a smile. "You have been studying well indeed. Yes, I'm afraid, even after that. They continued to send letters to government officials, charging Bahá'u'lláh with every crime they could think of. Even in Baghdád and Persia troubles reignited. The persecutions, which had subsided for a while, began once more throughout the towns and villages where Bahá'ís lived. There was once again horrible bloodshed and suffering. And as before, the Bahá'ís were brave and faithful to their beliefs, even when they were faced with death.

"But in Adrianople the actions of Mírzá Yaḥyá and Siyyid Muḥammad were about to have an important effect on the entire future of the Bahá'í Faith. The government officials who had received all the anonymous letters from these two villains had decided that the time had come to destroy this offensive religion once and for all. They decided that the best way to do this was to remove Bahá'u'lláh to a place where He would either die or, at least, never be heard from again. The Sulṭán decided to exile Bahá'u'lláh to a dreadful penal colony, a place where they thought He would most surely die."

"Where was that?" asked Ali.

"Why, right here, Ali! Right here in your very own town of 'Akká. Back then, 'Akká was a dreadful place, a prison city where only the very worst criminals were sent." The two climbed a few steps and then sat down beside a corner of the wall where they could look across the bay to Haifa and Mount Carmel. "Yes, your very own 'Akká was a wretched place then, full of sickness and misery. Only criminals lived here, criminals and the poorest of the poor.

"But let me tell you how it all happened. The Bahá'ís did not know about the Sulṭán's decree until one morning troops of soldiers surrounded the house of 'Izzat Áqá where Bahá'u'lláh was living. The soldiers told the startled Bahá'ís that they would have to prepare to leave at once. The house was guarded so closely that Bahá'u'lláh's family was not even allowed to leave to get food to take with them."

"They must have been terrified."

"They were not told where they were to be taken or what would happen to them. Most presumed they were going to be tortured and killed. When the neighbors saw the troops surrounding the house, they all became extremely upset, because whether they were Christians or Muslims, they all loved and respected Bahá'u'lláh, Whom they now considered their most trusted friend.

"Shortly they were ready—what belongings they could not carry with them were auctioned off. Quickly the word spread to official representatives of other countries who were living in Adrianople, who became immediately concerned about the safety of Bahá'u'lláh, so they met at Bahá'u'lláh's house. Several of them offered to try to help Bahá'u'lláh, but He refused."

"But Why?" asked Ali. "Why didn't Bahá'u'lláh want them to help Him?" There was a long pause before Moayyed spoke. It was a subtle thing to explain.

"Ali, to understand the answer to your question, you have to think again about how the Prophet chooses to teach us. He tries to show that His powers have nothing to do with politics or earthly possessions, all of which He could control in a minute, if that were His purpose. But the mission given to Him by God is to teach us, to lead us, and to challenge us, to see if we can discover His hidden gifts, powers that only the pure in heart can detect.

"I've tried to explain this to you before, but it must be explained many times before it is clear. You see, Bahá'u'lláh never tried to run away, because He never wanted it said in the future that He manipulated events, that He arranged for things to turn out the way they did, because every single event that occurred in His life fulfills ancient prophecies and traditions."

"You mean it was predicted in past religions that Bahá'u'lláh would end up here in 'Akká?" said Ali in disbelief.

"Precisely!"

"But how could the Prophets have known that hundreds of years ago?"

"Because, my bright young grandson, there is no time or limitation to what can be known in the world of the spirit. Besides, Bahá'u'lláh knew that God would arrange things to turn out for the best, regardless of what the religious or political leaders tried to do. Bahá'u'lláh knew that no matter what His enemies did to Him or to His followers, they could not stop the spread of the Bahá'í Faith. He even said that if He were killed, God would raise up another to finish His work, so Bahá'u'lláh was utterly fearless about these decisions.

"When Khurshíd Páshá, the governor of Adrianople, received the order that he must banish Bahá'u'lláh, he reacted the same way as the governor of Baghdád had. He was so ashamed that he could not bear to face Bahá'u'lláh to tell Him these things. You see, the governor had been defending Bahá'u'lláh against the lies and false reports that the officials in Constantinople had concocted because Khurshíd Páshá had great admiration and love for Bahá'u'lláh. So when he received the command that Bahá'u'lláh must be exiled, the governor sent another official to tell Bahá'u'lláh of the sad decree that Sulṭán 'Abdu'l-'Azíz had issued.

"When the Bahá'ís heard the edict, that they would be banished to the prison city of 'Akká, there was great fear and sorrow among them. They were given a list of those Bahá'ís who would be allowed to go with Bahá'u'lláh. When some of the Bahá'ís discovered that they were not on the list, they were so grief-stricken that some contemplated suicide. One of them tried to cut his own throat.

"It was a time of grief and panic. It even looked as if some would be forced to be separated from their families, and none of them knew whether they would live or die, whether they would be sent back to Persia to be tortured or put in prison.

"Bahá'u'lláh and His family set out from the city on August 12th, 1868, accompanied by government soldiers. As they departed from Adrianople on their four-day journey to the port of Gallipoli, people in the section of the town where they had lived gathered to bid Bahá'u'lláh an emotional farewell. They had come to love this family of exiles, and as Bahá'u'lláh passed by, some wept openly or knelt to kiss the hem of His robe because they knew He would never return.

"When they arrived at Gallipoli, some of the Bahá'ís from Constantinople were waiting to find out what was to be the fate of Bahá'u'lláh. It was only then that they learned the extent of the horrible decree. Bahá'u'lláh would be banished to 'Akká with His two brothers, Mírzá Músá and Mírzá Muḥammad-Qulí, and one servant. The rest were to be sent back to Constantinople.

"As you can imagine, the believers were horrified. Even Bahá'u'lláh was unable to accept this decision. He insisted to the officials that at least some of the Bahá'ís be allowed to go with Him.

"As a result of His protest, the decision was changed so that about seventy believers were allowed to accompany Bahá'u'lláh to 'Akká. However, while the government officials relented a little, they also decided to give one final insult to Bahá'u'lláh and the believers. They included in this group several followers of Mírzá Yaḥyá who were to act as spies for the officials, and among these spies was none other than Siyyid Muḥammad himself, the very one who had instigated most of the problems in the first place.

"But amidst the sorrow and fear and consternation was one minor victory, something I've always thought of as a sort of divine trick. It concerned Mírzá Yaḥyá himself. As you know, this further exile was caused in no small way by the ceaseless lies and intrigues of Mírzá Yaḥyá, by his continuous accusations against Bahá'u'lláh. No doubt this faithless brother hoped that all his deceit would cause the government to have Bahá'u'lláh killed or at least removed from the community so that Mírzá Yaḥyá could take over."

Moayyed paused and shook his head from side to side. A wry smile appeared. "What this false one definitely had *not* counted on was that the government viewed him as one of these same Persian Bábís whom they had come to find so troublesome. After all, it was the Bábí religion that the officials wanted to exterminate, not simply one or two individuals. And if Mírzá Yaḥyá considered himself a leader of this group, then he, too, should be exiled."

"So Mírzá Yaḥyá was exiled to 'Akká as well?" asked Ali.

"Exiled? Yes, indeed he was! To 'Akká? Much to the amazement of the pitiful soul, he was not. Instead, Mírzá Yaḥyá and his dependents, together with four Bahá'ís, were removed to Cyprus to live in perpetual exile."

"And that's why he died there a few months ago, in Famagusta?"

"April 29th, to be exact. For forty-four years he was cut off from everyone—from the believers, from the loving brother Whom he had treated so cruelly, so unnaturally."

"So that ended the problems with Mírzá Yaḥyá once and for all," observed Ali with a sigh of relief.

"With Mírzá Yaḥyá, but not with Siyyid Muḥammad of Iṣfahan—something I'll explain later. But let me tell you about the journey from the seaport of Gallipoli. The Bahá'ís who were able to go with Bahá'u'lláh felt very fortunate, though Bahá'u'lláh told them in no uncertain terms before they departed that this journey would be far more severe than any of the previous exiles. But the believers chose to stay with Him in spite of these warnings, and on the morning of August 21, 1868, they set sail in an Austrian steamer heading for Alexandria, a seaport in Egypt.

"It was a wretched voyage, from the beginning to the end—ten days of going from ship to ship, from seaport to seaport. They did not have proper clothing, and they had only the most meager supply of food—a little bread and cheese that they had managed to bring aboard.

"After only a day on the sea, one of Bahá'u'lláh's dearest companions, Jináb-i-Munír, became seriously ill, and he had to be removed from the ship when it reached Smyrna. 'Abdu'l-Bahá took Jináb-i-Munír to a hospital on shore and then quickly went to purchase some fruit to help him recover. However, when 'Abdu'l-Bahá returned to the hospital, He discovered that Jináb-i-Munír had died.

"When 'Abdu'l-Bahá returned to the ship, the Bahá'ís on board were greatly saddened by the news of this devoted believer's death. You see, this noble soul had become a Bábí as a youth, and he had been with Bahá'u'lláh since early in the Ba<u>gh</u>dád period.

"But there was little time for grieving. Two days later they were forced to resume their journey to the port of Alexandria. The journey was rough, and when they reached Alexandria, they were removed from the ship without any idea of what was to be done to them or where they were headed. What was worse, no one knew who would be allowed to continue with Bahá'u'lláh and who would not.

"The travelers were exhausted from the rough seas, and many were quite ill. But the hand of God is always at work in such things—within view of that port was a prison where Nabíl was being held."

"Nabíl the historian?" asked Ali.

"The very same. As Nabíl looked out the narrow window of his cell, he was astonished to realize that he recognized one of his dear Bahá'í friends. Then he realized that the entire band of prisoners was family and close companions of Bahá'u'lláh. He called out in excitement to one of those nearest to the window and asked what was happening. It was then he learned that Bahá'u'lláh and His companions were being taken to prison in 'Akká.

"You can imagine how he longed to be free so that he could go with them! But, alas, he was not. He would have to wait until he was released before he could make his own way to 'Akká to be with his Beloved, but at least he now knew where he would travel as soon as he obtained his freedom.

"Before long the Bahá'ís were transferred to a second ship. This ship was even more uncomfortable than the first. There was no place to lie down. The believers were weak from lack of food as they sailed along the Egyptian coast, arriving at Port Said by the next morning. Then that same evening the ship set sail for Jaffa and finally to Haifa."

Ali looked out across the water toward the cluster of buildings at the foot of Mount Carmel. He wondered what the ship had looked like as it entered the port of Haifa that day. He tried to imagine what the Bahá'ís on board the ship might have thought as they looked for the first time at Mount Carmel and the white walls of 'Akká across the bay.

Moayyed continued, "They were allowed to leave the boat when it arrived in Haifa, but only for a few hours. But before I tell you what happened next, let's walk toward the sea gate, since that's where Bahá'u'lláh and His companions first set foot in 'Akká."

Even though Ali had been to the sea gate many times, he became excited as he and his grandfather approached the site. He found it exciting to walk over the same stones that the feet of Bahá'u'lláh had touched, and in his mind's eye he envisioned how it must have been that day almost half a century before as the sick and bewildered Bahá'ís, some of whom were his own kin, ascended the steps and entered the walled prison city of 'Akká.

Haifa had changed greatly over the years, but 'Akká was very much the same as when Bahá'u'lláh had arrived—at least the ancient walls and buildings were the same, even if the atmosphere had become transformed over the years.

"When they arrived at the sea gate," Moayyed said, "it was terribly hot that day. Everyone was completely exhausted. Many were extremely ill. And as they were being taken to the landingstage in Haifa, a very sad thing happened. 'Abdu'l-Ghaffár, a most devout believer, discovered that he was among four faithful Bahá'ís who were going to be exiled to the island of Cyprus with Mírzá Yaḥyá."

"But why, Grandfather? Why did they do that to him?"

"I suppose for the same reason they made Siyyid Muḥammad of Iṣfahán and a few of his companions go with the faithful Bahá'ís to 'Akká. They probably thought that this way each group would make the other group miserable. But whatever their reasons were, 'Abdu'l-Ghaffár was so distraught by this horrible news that he immediately leaped into the water and tried to drown himself, preferring death to being deprived of nearness to Bahá'u'lláh."

"Did he die?" asked Ali.

"No. Some of the friends pulled him out of the sea before it was too late. Then Bahá'u'lláh tried to cheer up this hapless soul. He said to him in jest,

'Why did you jump into the sea? Did you wish to give a banquet to the fishes?' But 'Abdu'l-Ghaffár could not be consoled. The idea of being separated from Bahá'u'lláh and the other Bahá'ís was more than he could bear.

"After several hours in Haifa, they were put into a small sailing vessel to take them the last few miles across the bay. But the wind was slight, and it took several hours in the hot sun before the boat arrived here. And by the time they arrived, all the townspeople of 'Akká had come to watch the Persian prisoners arrive. They wanted to see this 'God of the Persians,' as some of the crude citizens of 'Akká mockingly called Bahá'u'lláh.

"The townspeople gathered here at the sea gate," said Moayyed gesturing with his hand as he led Ali through the arched stone portal. Then, standing at the dock where several fishermen were working at their boats, preparing their nets for the next day, Moayyed continued, "Some had to be carried from the boat, but the citizens of 'Akká had little pity for the Bahá'ís, for they had been told that these exiles were infidels, nonbelievers, criminals, troublemakers.

"Later the farmán, the edict of the Sulṭán, was read aloud to the townspeople at the Mosque of Jazzár Páshá shortly after the Bahá'ís arrived." Ali thought about his dream, how he had stood in the courtyard of that same mosque trying to announce to the townspeople that the Promised One had come. Then he looked back through the sea gate and pretended that he was entering 'Akká for the first time. He tried to imagine how that might have felt. Then he turned to Moayyed.

"Were the Bahá'ís afraid?" the boy asked.

"They were completely exhausted and miserable," said Moayyed, "and I have no doubt that most of them were afraid. How could they not be? They had no way of knowing what would happen next. The people were cursing them, yelling at them. They had been sentenced to lifelong imprisonment in a place hundreds of miles from their homeland and from anyone they knew. And when they were led through the streets of 'Akká to the barracks prison, you can be sure that any hope for relief that they may have had soon vanished."

Moayyed motioned that they should walk back toward the prison, taking a route through the center of town past the Mosque of Jazzár Páshá, the way that Moayyed thought the Bahá'ís might have taken. Before long, Moayyed and Ali arrived at the barracks which had served as the prison for Bahá'u'lláh and the companions, a building which Ali had seen all his life, but which now took on a special meaning.

Moayyed stopped and said to Ali, "I have a surprise for you, my son. During the past months I have made friends with a guard here. He is on duty now, and he told me that it may be possible for us to take a quick walk up to the second floor so that we can see where Bahá'u'lláh and the other Bahá'ís were imprisoned."

Ali's face lit up—he had never imagined that his grandfather had prepared such a special treat for him.

Moayyed approached the guard at the entrance to the old prison, spoke with him briefly, and both of them smiled as they looked at Ali. Then Moayyed looked back and signaled for Ali to come with him. The guard had talked on several occasions with Moayyed, and he had now come to respect Ali's grandfather and the Bahá'ís in general. So as Ali passed by him and greeted the guard, the tall soldier with his military hat and huge rifle smiled at the youth, and Ali felt a shiver run the length of his spine as he and his grandfather walked to the wooden bridge that crossed the moat and led into the courtyard.

As Ali followed his grandfather into the courtyard, he felt as though he were entering a different world, an enchanted place. For while he had seen this same building a thousand times from every direction, he had never been inside the precincts of what, to Ali, was a most sacred place.

Moayyed knew exactly where to go, and he led Ali to the steps that ascended the outside of the rough stone building. Ali immediately thought about the Síyáh-Chál, where Bahá'u'lláh had also been imprisoned, but that was hundreds of miles away in Persia. So with each step that brought Ali closer to this place where Bahá'u'lláh had dwelled for over two years, Ali's heart pounded more forcefully.

At last they reached the top of the stairs, and Ali could see that they were almost next to the room where Bahá'u'lláh had been imprisoned. They could not go all the way inside, but Ali could see through a window in the door to the inside of the second-story room. Then, unexpectedly, a voice from behind the door said, "Care to come in?" A dark face appeared at the window. "The guard at the gate said you might come by. You may come inside if you wish." The voice was stern, but friendly enough, and so Moayyed and Ali cautiously pulled at the door and quickly went inside.

It was hard to see at first. It was cool and dark. But Ali could make out the room well enough. It was vacant and larger than he had imagined. There were windows with bars across them looking out toward the sea, the same windows he had seen from the other side when he sailed his boat.

"We dare not stay long," Moayyed whispered to Ali, "so look carefully, and remember what you see." Almost immediately Moayyed pointed in the opposite direction from the windows, toward the back of the room. "Remember that spot," he said softly. Then he nudged Ali toward the left of the door they had entered. The guard seemed occupied with other business and left them alone.

"This is the room?" Ali asked with awe.

"Yes," Moayyed whispered, "this is the Most Great Prison."

Bahá'u'lláh's feet were on this floor, Ali thought. For two years He was actually in this room. Ali felt a tingling sensation in his feet, and the room seemed to take on the same atmosphere and spirit he had sensed at the summer house. Ali surmised that he felt these things only because of his love for Bahá'u'lláh, yet the sensation was quite palpable.

They stayed in the room for only a few minutes, though they were minutes Ali would always treasure. Then they thanked the guard and quietly left. They walked again across the courtyard, but when they got to the bridge, Ali stopped and looked down, trying to imagine how the moat looked in the time of Bahá'u'lláh when the seawater would rush in at high tide.

After they crossed the bridge, Moayyed and Ali went down the path that led to the seawall. When they reached the wall, which was only about two hundred yards away, they turned around and looked back at the prison building they had just left. For a moment they were both silent.

"Now that you have seen the prison you will understand better what I am about to tell you," said Moayyed, sitting down on a large stone step. "All of the believers, all seventy of them, were crowded together in the confines of that top floor. It was gloomy and filthy, and all of the horrible smells from the outgoing tide in the moat below sent up a sickening smell. The prisoners were completely exhausted from the hardships of their ten-day journey from Adrianople to 'Akká. And, to add to all this misery, they were not allowed to have any food or drink that first night."

"Not even water?" asked Ali.

"No, nothing at all. And something else. 'Akká was not then as it is now. There was a saying that if a bird flew over 'Akká, it would die from the foul-smelling air that rose from this prison city. In fact there was no fresh water in the whole town. The water in the courtyard pool which the prisoners had to use was so rank that no one could drink it.

"In the days that followed, the meager food they each received consisted of just three loaves of black, salty bread. Within a few days all except two of them became horribly sick with malaria, dysentery, or one of the many other diseases that infested the dank air of the prison. When three of the Bahá'ís died soon afterwards, Bahá'u'lláh gave the guards His own carpet that He had brought with Him as a payment for them to give a proper burial to the friends. Later Bahá'u'lláh learned that the guards had kept the money they got for the sale of the carpet and buried the three believers without coffins or ceremony. Furthermore, because the edict of the Sulṭán had said that the Bahá'ís should be strictly imprisoned and kept from contact with the townspeople, the guards kept a close watch over the Bahá'ís.

"It was several months before the governor of 'Akká saw fit to loosen these severe restrictions. By then he had spoken several times with 'Abdu'l-Bahá, Who was now a strikingly handsome young man of twenty-four. The governor was very impressed with 'Abdu'l-Bahá's wisdom and sincerity. The governor had also talked with a Greek doctor who had become a friend of the Bahá'ís and who had told the governor about their sincerity and about the hardships they had endured. The governor gave the prisoners a little money so that one of them might go into the town, accompanied by a soldier, in order to buy some food fit to eat.

"The prisoners were still completely isolated from the townspeople and from the other Bahá'ís throughout 'Iráq and Persia. But when the Bahá'ís in other places received word that Bahá'u'lláh and the family were imprisoned in 'Akká, almost immediately many began traveling to this remote place in order to see their Beloved.

"In spite of the long journey—in some cases a thousand miles or more—and in spite of the restrictions which the Sulṭán's edict had placed on the prisoners, Bahá'ís came, often on foot, to this faraway village in Syria to be close to the Manifestation of God."

Moayyed stopped his story for a moment. "Come with me. I want to show you something." With that Ali followed Moayyed over to the wall of the second moat, where Moayyed pointed toward the fortress. "This is as close as those pilgrims could get to Bahá'u'lláh," said Moayyed.

Ali looked at the prison, still more than a hundred yards away. The afternoon sun was in Ali's eyes so that it was difficult even to see the windows on the second story. It would have been even more difficult to see a face from such a distance.

"What was worse for these faithful souls is that not too many of them were even able to get through the city gates," said Moayyed. "If the guards at the gates knew they were Bahá'ís, they were not allowed to enter. And to make matters still worse, Siyyid Muḥammad of Iṣfahan and Áqá Ján—two of Mírzá Yaḥyá's followers had been placed in a dwelling near the gate so that if they recognized any Bahá'ís, they would tell the guards and the friends would be kept out of the city.

"The Bahá'í pilgrims had such devotion, such a longing to be near Bahá'u'lláh, that they did whatever they could just to see His face at the prison window, or perhaps only His hand waving, sometimes with a handkerchief to show where He was. But many had to leave the city and walk all the way back to their villages without ever being able to see Bahá'u'lláh after their long and difficult journey.

"One faithful soul, Ustád Ismá'íl-i-Káshání, walked all the way from Mosul in 'Iráq. He gazed for hours as he stood right here on this very spot. The Bahá'ís inside the prison recognized the old man and waved to him, but his failing sight was too feeble to see them. His devotion caused tears to flow from the eyes of the prisoners as they watched the sorrow and frustration on the face of the old man.

"Similar was the anguish of Nabíl after he was released from prison in Egypt. He journeyed secretly in disguise to Mount Carmel, where he stayed in a cave at the bottom of the mountain, as Elijah had once done. Then he walked the ten miles to 'Akká so that he might catch a glimpse of Bahá'u'lláh from the moat wall. But when he reached the city gate, he was recognized by Siyyid Muḥammad, who immediately reported him to the authorities, and Nabíl was forced to flee."

Moayyed became silent and stared at the vacant window where Bahá'u'lláh had spent two sorrowful years. The sun was now close to setting, and Moayyed slipped his arm around his grandson's shoulders and gave a gentle squeeze.

As they walked back toward Ali's house, Moayyed observed, "Well, that is how it was at first, Ali. It was so difficult that in one of His tablets Bahá'u'lláh said, 'From the foundation of the world until the present day a cruelty such as this hath neither been seen nor heard of.'"

Ali said nothing. He almost felt guilty that he had ever thought of 'Akká as a good place to live, and he wondered if he should be ashamed that 'Akká was his home.

"I suppose I shouldn't like 'Akká," he said somberly.

"No, never say that, Ali," said Moayyed. "That is not so at all! The city was not responsible for what the Sulṭán did. 'Akká is a sacred spot for having seen the face of Bahá'u'lláh. The presence of the Prophet of God sanctified this place and made it a holy dwelling. And there is much more to this story than I have yet told you, Ali." Moayyed paused and observed the lateness of the hour.

"But that will have to wait for another day. For now I'll simply tell you this much—in the Old Testament writings of the Jewish people, our town is called the 'Strong City' and the 'door of hope' and the 'gate that looketh toward the East.' And in the Muslim traditions it is said that 'Akká is a city in Syria 'to which God hath shown His special mercy,' and 'Blessed the man that hath visited 'Akká, and blessed he that hath visited the visitor of 'Akká.'"

Ali was heartened by what he heard, and it showed on his face. After all, it was good to feel that 'Akká was his city, something to be proud of. But he still wondered exactly how things had gotten better, how the Bahá'ís got from the prison to Bahjí, the beautiful mansion several miles outside the city.

"Tomorrow!" said Moayyed emphatically. "Tomorrow I shall tell you the rest of the story about the prison years—that is, if your mother and father don't have too many jobs for you to do."

Ali thanked his grandfather several times as they approached Ali's house. "Someday," thought Ali, "someday I will repay Grandfather for these stories. Someday I will make him proud of me."

13

The House of 'Abbúd

On the same day that Ali had gone with Moayyed to the prison, he walked to Neda's house after the evening meal to tell her about the tour of the city. He described to her some of the more interesting details he remembered, particularly the way he had felt while standing in the part of the prison that Bahá'u'lláh had occupied.

"Tomorrow," said Ali, "Grandfather is going to take me to see some more."

"You are a lucky one!" said Neda.

Almost without thinking, Ali said, "Would you like to come with?"

"Do you think I could?" asked Neda with an enthusiastic smile.

"If your parents don't mind. I'm sure Grandfather would like you to come, and I . . . I'd like you to come too," said Ali, a little embararassed.

Neda went inside to ask her parents while Ali waited at the door. Within a few minutes a smiling Neda returned with their answer, that she could join them.

Early the next morning, before her mother could nudge her awake for dawn prayers, which the family had together whenever they could, Neda was already open-eyed, listening to the early morning noises of the town streets. As she lay in bed, she tried to remember if it had been the noises outside, the excitement about the day ahead, or her dream, which had gently eased her from sleep.

She doubted that it had been the noises. They were there every morning. No, probably it was anticipation of her day with Ali and his grandfather, because the dream was the same one she had dreamed twice already, and it had never wakened her before.

This was not *exactly* the same dream, but very similar all the same. She was on a boat, or what seemed like a boat. She was out on the boat, and the ship was close enough to land that she could see the buildings of a city. The city looked much like 'Akká, except that she was leaving, going slowly out to sea. She was leaving, but she did not feel frightened or sad, because she was aware of someone standing beside her.

The first two times she had dreamed about the ship, there was no one else on board, and she had felt a bit lonely and a little frightened. Or if there had been someone else, she was not aware of it. But this time she was aware of a presence, of another person standing beside her, and all the loneliness and fear had vanished.

"Neda, are you awake?" said her mother's voice in a hushed tone as she tapped on her daughter's door. "Time for prayers."

"Yes, Mother, I'll get dressed," said Neda. She quickly slipped into her favorite dress and brushed her hair until it was smooth and shining. She looked at herself in the small mirror on top of the old wooden chest, the only piece of furniture in her little room except for the bed. She wondered if she should tell her dream to her mother and father. In a way, she wanted to share it, but she decided not to, at least not right away.

The family gathered in the sitting room to chant their morning prayers. Afterward Neda had some tea and a little breakfast. Then came the knock on the door signaling the arrival of Ali and his grandfather. Neda's mother and father talked briefly with Moayyed about the latest news of 'Abdu'l-Bahá's travels in America. Then Moayyed, Ali, and Neda stepped out into the morning streets of 'Akká to begin their adventure.

Because the narrow passageways that honeycombed the old quarters of the city were hidden from sunlight by the buildings on either side, they were still cool. The morning was pleasant enough—misty and quiet—and they walked toward the prison on the western border of the town, exchanging cordial greetings with cartdrivers and others who were preparing for work.

When they reached the wall a few hundred yards west of the old citadel where Bahá'u'lláh had been imprisoned, they found a comfortable and private spot where they could talk without interruption and without worrying about what they said. The Bahá'ís still had to be cautious about their activities, even though relations with the local inhabitants had greatly improved during the past years, because the town was still governed by Muslim authorities.

As they looked eastward toward the prison and listened to the thrashing of the surf against the rocks and wall, the rays of the morning sun came over the tops of the buildings, as if the light were streaming from the prison itself.

"See how the light of the world comes from that ancient building?" Moayyed said with a grin. "You see," he said to Ali, "there's no need to be ashamed of 'Akká. The sun itself lives here."

"Did Ali say he was ashamed of 'Akká?" asked Neda, unaware of the conversation Moayyed and Ali had had the day before.

"Not exactly," said Moayyed. "He was disturbed that the Bahá'ís were treated so badly when they arrived here and that Bahá'u'lláh called 'Akká 'the Most Great Prison.' It is true that the years Bahá'u'lláh spent within the walls of this city were not easy, but some wonderful and exciting things also happened during that time."

"Can you tell us what they were?" asked Ali.

"Tell us *everything,*" said Neda.

"Very well, then, I will try to tell you a little bit about all of the things that happened while Bahá'u'lláh and the companions dwelled here, the good and the bad, because all of it is important, isn't it? And someday this small town will be known throughout the world as the place where Bahá'u'lláh spent nine whole years of His precious life.

"The happier days of Bahá'u'lláh's stay in 'Akká came later on. As I was telling Ali yesterday, the first period was full of pain and misery—sickness and sorrow. Neither of you has ever been a prisoner, so you can't know how it feels not to be free, to be watched over, to be treated like a flock of sheep. But I'll tell you what we can do. For this morning, at least for a while, I'm going to make you my prisoners."

"What?" said Ali.

"Oh, yes!" said Neda.

"You mean you want us to pretend we are in the prison with Bahá'u'lláh?" asked Ali.

"Exactly. That will be the very best way for you to remember the things I am going to tell you—to imagine that you are with the other Bahá'ís in the prison. Remember now, the townspeople all think of you as evil foreigners who are trying to destroy the Faith of Islám. They do not respect you or trust you in any way. Remember, too, that for the fourth time you have been made to live farther away from your homeland. What is more, you speak a language that most people here don't understand, and you believe in a Manifestation of God Whom officials hate and are trying to kill.

"After an unbelievably miserable voyage, crowded together on an uncomfortable boat, you are brought to a smelly and cold stone prison. You are marched through the courtyard, which is ankle-deep in mud, and you are locked in a single large room with seventy others. There is little light. There is no privacy. There is no fresh water or food, and within a day or so, almost everyone is quite ill.

"But there are no doctors, and the guards don't care whether you live or die. And even though you have been in the hot sun, you are given nothing to drink or to eat. When you finally do get to drink, it is brackish, foul-tasting water that has collected in the courtyard cistern.

"Now, my little prisoners," said Moayyed, "tell me, how long do you think you would like to stay in such a place?"

Ali and Neda looked at each other.

"It would be hard for me to stay more than a few days," said Neda at last.

"Yes," said Ali. "She's right." "Even if you were in the presence of a Manifestation of God?" asked Moayyed.

"I don't know. I mean, it would be wonderful to be near a Manifestation," said Ali, "to be able to talk with Him, to ask Him questions. But if I were tired and sick and afraid, I am not sure how much I would be able to enjoy even that."

"Now you can appreciate what these Bahá'ís experienced when they were in the prison you see before you. Except they didn't stay for a few days. They were in the barracks prison for two years, two months, and five days."

"Then they were set free?" asked Neda.

"No," said Moayyed. "They were still prisoners long after that, but that is how long they had to live bunched together in that old building."

"Did they know that someday they would get out?" asked Neda.

"No, they didn't. I don't mean to say that they were miserable and sad all the time. After all, if the Bahá'ís had to be in prison, at least they were able share this ordeal with their beloved Bahá'u'lláh and other inspiring souls such as Bahá'u'lláh's faithful sons—twenty-year-old Mihdí, who helped his father in many ways, and twenty-four-year-old 'Abdu'l-Bahá, Who was now the recognized spokesman for the group of prisoners.

"In fact, from this point on, 'Abdu'l-Bahá made it His duty to help His father by taking care of all the business with the local officials and the outside world in general. In this way 'Abdu'l-Bahá was able to help shield Bahá'u'lláh from annoyances that might prevent Him from doing the all-important work of revealing the teachings of God for humanity."

"So it wasn't all bad?" said Ali.

"It had its rewards—let's put it that way," said Moayyed. "I'm sure it was always uncomfortable, but I imagine that Bahá'ís would have preferred being in prison with Bahá'u'lláh to being anywhere else in the world without Him. After all, remember that many of them had made exactly that choice. Perhaps they also felt some relief when they saw through the prison bars the distant faces of pilgrim friends who had sacrificed so much to trudge across mountains and wilderness on the mere chance that they might catch a glimpse of One Whom these prisoners could see every day.

"One thing that is particularly interesting in this is that these pilgrims were not only a sign of the staunch faith and fearless devotion of the Bahá'ís. Their devotion was also a proof of what Bahá'u'lláh had told the Persian ambassador in Adrianople—that no matter where they put

Bahá'u'lláh or how many Bahá'ís they killed, the Cause of God would survive and prosper."

"Were they never allowed outside the prison during all that time?" asked Neda.

"After a while they were allowed to go to the public baths now and then," said Moayyed. "But even then they were under close watch by the prison guards. And as if all this weren't enough, toward the end of the second year, something occurred that saddened Bahá'u'lláh for the rest of His life. One evening the Purest Branch, Bahá'u'lláh's young son Mírzá Mihdí, climbed to the prison roof where he would sometimes go to chant prayers. As was his custom, he paced back and forth while he said his devotions, when suddenly his feet slipped near one of the skylights on the rooftop. With a crash he fell through the opening and landed on a wooden crate on the floor below. Members of the holy family rushed to his side and found that he was still alive, but he was fatally injured. You see, a piece of wood from the splintered crate had pierced his ribs.

"As you can imagine, Bahá'u'lláh, Who loved His son so dearly, was grief-stricken to see the young Mihdí near death. As the dying youth spoke with his beloved father, he asked Bahá'u'lláh that his life might be accepted as a ransom for those Bahá'ís who were not able to be with Bahá'u'lláh as he had been. Two hours later, Mírzá Mihdí died."

"I don't understand," said Ali. "What did Mírzá Mihdí mean?"

"What Mihdí meant was that he hoped God would accept the sacrifice of his life as a payment to give the other Bahá'ís a chance to visit Bahá'u'lláh again—as they had done in Baghdád and in Adrianople before Bahá'u'lláh was imprisoned.

"Bahá'u'lláh promised Mihdí that his request would be granted. You see," Moayyed continued, "because Bahá'u'lláh was a Manifestation of God, He had the power to save Mihdí, and Mihdí knew this. But Bahá'u'lláh agreed to accept His son's request, even though it pained Bahá'u'lláh immensely to lose the companionship of this precious and beloved son, something Bahá'u'lláh states in a special prayer revealed in honor of Mírzá Mihdí. The prayer says, 'I have, O my Lord, offered up that which Thou hast given Me, that Thy servants may be quickened, and all that dwell on earth be united.'

"This happened on June 23, 1870. His body was then washed and prepared for burial. The Bahá'ís were allowed to take him beyond the city walls to a spot that you have both visited several times with your parents."

"Is that when they were allowed to leave the prison?" asked Neda.

"Not then," said Moayyed. "Not for good. That would occur several months later—about four months later, to be exact. But don't get the idea that they were set free then. You see, the Turkish army needed to make the building a barracks for their soldiers, and so they had to move the Bahá'í prisoners elsewhere.

"But they were still prisoners and still kept under arrest in cramped quarters—first in one house, then in another. Many people had to live in one room, first in the house of Malik for three months, then in the house of Khavvám across from it for a time, then in the house of Rábí'ih for four months, and then finally—"

"To the house of 'Abbúd!" said Ali, pointing his finger down the street to where the two-story building could be easily seen by the three.

"Yes, Ali, the house of 'Abbúd. They were there for six long years. Of course, not all seventy could fit into that one small building, so most of the Bahá'ís were placed in other houses or in the large caravansary of Khán-i-'Avámíd. But it is the house of 'Abbúd that we are interested in this morning, because that is where some of the most important events occurred in the life of Bahá'u'lláh and the holy family."

Before Moayyed continued with his story he led the two young children down the street, toward the house of 'Abbúd. As they walked, with the wall and the sea on their right, they passed by the house where 'Abdu'l-Bahá lived in later years, when Bahá'u'lláh had moved outside the city and before He Himself had moved to Haifa. Shortly they were in front of the house of 'Abbúd, with its arched entrances and porch on the second floor.

As they looked at the house, Neda said, "It must have been nice to be able to walk out onto that porch and look at the sea."

"Oh, they were not allowed to live in the front part of that floor at first," said Moayyed. "They lived only in the back part, the eastern part. The front was occupied by the owner, 'Abbúd. It was separated from the back part by a wall. No, I'm afraid this dwelling wasn't that much better than the barracks. Thirteen people of both sexes had to live in one room while Bahá'u'lláh worked in a small room in the back."

As he talked, Moayyed led Ali and Neda toward the side of the house and pointed to the windows on the second floor, the windows of Bahá'u'lláh's room. Then Moayyed approached the side-door of the house and knocked. A custodian opened the door and immediately smiled when he saw Moayyed, who once again had worked his magic by arranging for Ali and Neda to see the inside of the house.

Moayyed talked softly now, and the three of them, accompanied by the custodian, walked into a small courtyard. As they climbed the steps to the upper story, the bright blue sky seemed glorious through this open space in the middle of the building. Quietly, Moayyed showed them around the house—where the wall had been that originally separated the two parts of the house, the small room in the back that Bahá'u'lláh had occupied, and the front room where He later lived.

They didn't stay very long. Moayyed exhorted the children to take one last look around, then he thanked the custodian and led the children back down the steps and out of the house. They went across the street to the wall where they could see the house and talk about it some more.

"Well, what do you think now that you have seen where Bahá'u'lláh and His family lived? I am sure it was nicer than living in the prison barracks. But remember, they were still under house arrest, still prisoners, and at first they lived only in the back of the house, so they could not observe the sea or leave the house when they pleased."

"Did the townspeople still hate them?" asked Ali.

"They had no reason not to," said Moayyed, "at least not until later, when 'Abdu'l-Bahá was free to begin making friends and showering His kindness on everyone He met. After that, the people of 'Akká gradually began to realize that the Bahá'ís were not criminals or godless infidels, but courteous and dignified people to be welcomed and admired, not to be scorned and feared.

"Yes, little by little things became more relaxed. The guards were not so strict, and later there were no guards around the house at all. It seemed once again that by showing love and respect, the Bahá'ís had won over the hearts of the townspeople and the town officials as well.

"But just as this change was beginning to take hold, another tragedy struck the community. This time, however, the culprit was not from outside the community of Bahá'ís."

"It wasn't Siyyid Muḥammad of Iṣfahán or the Sulṭán?" asked Ali.

"No. The problem came from among the Bahá'ís themselves. You remember how the young Bábís had thought they could help the believers by killing the Sháh? Well, something similar occurred in 'Akká. Remember, Ali, how I told you yesterday that the government officials had placed Siyyid Muḥammad of Iṣfahán and Áqá Ján Big in a dwelling beside the town gate, where he and his companions could point out to them any Bahá'ís trying to enter the city? Well, Bahá'u'lláh knew how much the believers detested the presence of these inveterate enemies of the Bahá'ís, and Bahá'u'lláh also knew that a few of the Bahá'ís wanted to kill these informers. In fact, on several occasions Bahá'u'lláh had warned these believers not to disobey His laws by resorting to violence. He had even ordered one Arab Bahá'í who had trouble keeping his temper to go back to Beirut so that he would not cause trouble with the townspeople. Bahá'u'lláh knew how important it was to maintain harmony with the people of 'Akká.

"In spite of these clear warnings, some of the Bahá'ís decided to take matters into their own hands. Seven of them plotted together to rid the Bahá'í community of these Azalís once and for all. Without telling the other Bahá'ís about it, they decided to attack these informers at their house near the gate. Late one afternoon they broke into the apartment and killed Siyyid Muḥammad, Áqá Ján Big, and another Azalí who had helped them.

"When it was discovered what had happened, all of 'Akká was in an uproar. The town officials immediately sent troops to surround the house of 'Abbúd. The citizens of 'Akká suddenly wondered if the Bahá'ís might try to kill them, too. Even 'Abbúd, who lived in the front part of the house, became so frightened that he reinforced the wall between the two parts of the house.

"While Bahá'u'lláh was in the midst of dictating a tablet, the soldiers entered the house with their swords drawn and ordered Bahá'u'lláh to go with them to the government office. 'Abdu'l-Bahá was arrested and taken to the jail, where He was put in chains. Twenty-five other Bahá'ís were also put in prison and shackled.

"That evening the authorities questioned Bahá'u'lláh over and over again. He told them He was not responsible for the acts of these misguided believers. 'If one of your soldiers were to commit a reprehensible act,' He said to one official, 'would you be held responsible, and be punished in his place?' "The officials soon realized that Bahá'u'lláh was not to blame for the murders, and they let Him return to the house. But that was not the end of the problem. The seven guilty men were imprisoned for seven years. The others were held for six months, but all of the Bahá'ís were affected. The townspeople now distrusted them. Even Bahá'í children would be jeered at and pelted with stones when they walked in the streets of 'Akká. Perhaps the most unfortunate result was that the good reputation that the Bahá'ís had earned with such great difficulty was now shattered. The citizens of 'Akká now feared that all of the bad things they had been told about the Bahá'ís was true."

"It reminds me of the early years in Baghdád," said Ali, remembering how Bahá'u'lláh had found the Bábís when He returned from the mountains.

"Yes," said Moayyed. "It was similar, except that now Bahá'u'lláh did not have the freedom or the time to devote His energy to winning the hearts of the townspeople in 'Akká. His primary task was to reveal those teachings that would guide humankind for hundreds of years to come. Consequently, this burden of changing the reputation of the Bahá'í community among the citizens of 'Akká fell to 'Abdu'l-Bahá.

"Every day 'Abdu'l-Bahá would mingle with the townspeople, talking kindly with them, helping them in any way He could. Naturally, not everyone responded to His efforts, but most of the citizens were impressed with His wisdom and gentleness, no matter how they might have felt in the beginning.

"Meanwhile, Bahá'u'lláh was busy every day, dictating more tablets to the rulers of the world and revealing other works that would guide the Bahá'í community in every aspect of their lives. But amid all this activity, Bahá'u'lláh was also planning something special for His beloved son."

"What was that?" asked Neda.

"A marriage!" said Moayyed. "You see, Bahá'u'lláh in His wisdom knew of a young woman in Persia, Munírih Khánum, whom He knew would be the perfect wife for 'Abdu'l-Bahá. But Bahá'u'lláh also knew that arranging to bring this young Bahá'í to 'Akká would be quite difficult, because the Bahá'ís were under such close scrutiny everywhere they went. So Bahá'u'lláh sent His trusted messenger, Shaykh Salmán, to Iṣfahán, where Munírih Khánum lived. Then, on the pretense of going on pilgrimage, Shaykh Salmán traveled with Munírih Khánum and her brother to Mecca and visited the Muslim holy shrines. But instead of returning to Persia afterwards, they proceeded to the town of Jiddah, and from there to Alexandria. There they waited until they felt it was safe to leave, then they sailed from Alexandria to 'Akká.

"Bahá'u'lláh sent word to Shaykh Salmán to wait at the boat until someone came for them. So the other passengers disembarked, and soon it began to get dark. By this time, they were becoming quite worried. At long last Bahá'u'lláh's brother Mírzá Músá appeared with a citizen of the town who had told the officials he was expecting some friends on the boat."

"But if the citizens of 'Akká were so afraid of Bahá'ís, who would dare to help them like that?" asked Neda.

"'Abbúd!" said Moayyed with a grin, "the very same man who had once been so afraid of the Bahá'ís that he had reinforced the wall between his residence and theirs. In a short time 'Abdu'l-Bahá had been able to melt the heart of this man, and 'Abbúd was more than willing to return the favor by assisting this young woman, because, you see, he knew she had come so that 'Abdu'l-Bahá might ask her for her hand in marriage. In fact, for a brief while, Munírih stayed at the house of 'Abbúd. Then she went with her brother to stay in the house of Mírzá Músá for several months.

"On occasion she would chance to see 'Abdu'l-Bahá swimming in the bay, and she quickly came to admire this young man, Who at twenty-eight was a strong and graceful swimmer. In the afternoons, she would often go with the wife of Mírzá Músá to visit Bahá'u'lláh at the house of 'Abbúd.

"Now you should know that before this time many lovely daughters had been offered in marriage to 'Abdu'l-Bahá, but He had refused them all. But when He met Munírih and came to know her, He knew that this was the woman He wanted to marry. So you see, even though Bahá'u'lláh Himself knew that this beautiful young woman would be the perfect wife for 'Abdu'l-Bahá, Bahá'u'lláh still left the decision to the two of them." Moayyed paused and looked at the two attentive children, and he could not help smiling. In his heart he sensed that if these were the Bahá'ís of the future, then the Bahá'í Faith was in good hands.

"So, did they get married?" asked Ali impatiently.

"I should say they did!" said Moayyed with a broad smile. "But not right away, because there was a slight problem."

"Not *another* problem," said Ali.

"They had no place to live," said Moayyed. "The entire family lived in only a small part of the house, so there was no spare room for 'Abdu'l-Bahá and Munírih Khánum to have a room for themselves. So the wedding was postponed. But when the wedding did not take place, 'Abbúd, who had come to love 'Abdu'l-Bahá like everyone else, went to Bahá'u'lláh and asked, 'Wherefore the delay in the marriage?' When Bahá'u'lláh told him the problem—that there was not enough room—he smiled at Bahá'u'lláh and said, 'I can arrange about the room. I pray Thee, let me have the honor of preparing a place for the Master and His bride.'

"Without delay, 'Abbúd had a door opened in the wall that separated the two parts of the house, and he furnished and decorated a room in his own part of the house for them to use.

"The very next day, Bahá'u'lláh asked His beloved daughter Bahíyyih Khánum to help prepare the bride. She and Bahá'u'lláh's wife Navváb had already made a dainty white dress for the young bride. A few guests were then gathered for the occasion, and 'Abdu'l-Bahá and Munírih were married on March 8, 1873.

"There was no grand feast, no elaborate ceremony, no decorations. Bahá'u'lláh chanted several prayers. Then He told Munírih how fortunate she was to receive the greatest gift that Bahá'u'lláh could possibly give her, His Greatest Branch, 'Abdu'l-Bahá."

"That would be enough of a gift!" said Neda enthusiastically.

"Yes," agreed Moayyed, "I should think so."

"Then things finally got better?" asked Ali with a hopeful tone.

"Much better," answered Moayyed, patting Ali on the shoulder. "In fact, not too long after that, during that same year, there occurred what was one of the most important events in the life of Bahá'u'lláh and in the life of the Bahá'í community itself. Can you imagine what it was? I'll give you a clue. Something Bahá'u'lláh did in the small wood-paneled room we saw in the back of the house was made known to the Bahá'ís."

"I think it must have been something that Bahá'u'lláh wrote," said Ali.

"Was it the Kitáb-i-Aqdas?" said Neda.

"Precisely," said Moayyed. "Bahá'u'lláh informed the community that He had revealed His Most Holy Book. Yes, in that small, seemingly insignificant room that we saw, Bahá'u'lláh penned a work that would establish the laws and worldwide institutions that will guide humankind until the appearance of the next Manifestation of God. In fact, He established in that work the foundation for a system that will govern this planet forever. But there is something else in the Most Holy Book besides Bahá'u'lláh's statement about laws and institutions."

"The Covenant!" said Ali, remembering what he had learned in his Bahá'í classes.

"Yes, Bahá'u'lláh describes how the Bahá'í Faith should be organized after His passing, how the peoples and leaders of the world should turn to

His Revelation for guidance, and, in particular, He says that they should turn to 'Abdu'l-Bahá."

"My mother translated that part from the Arabic and helped me memorize it," said Neda. Then she recited the verse: "When the ocean of My presence hath ebbed and the Book of My Revelation is ended, turn your faces toward Him Whom God hath purposed, Who hath branched from this Ancient Root."

"So you see, in that simple house standing before us, a dwelling that most of the great rulers of the world would disdain to stay in for a single evening, the entire destiny of the world was established."

Ali was utterly delighted by this thought, and he now understood clearly for the first time why talking about the past, about history, excited him so. He also understood why it thrilled him to visit these places where Bahá'u'lláh had lived and worked and touched the hearts of the faithful. He realized that these stories and these places connected him to his own story because this was not the history of an ancient people or some remote place. This was his personal story, and the more he learned, the more he felt a vital connection to his own sense of who he was and what he would become.

Neda was feeling much the same thing and observed, "I think that in the years to come people all over the world will know about this street and will travel hundreds and thousands of miles to visit this little house."

All three studied the house in silence for several minutes until Ali decided he wanted to hear the rest of the story.

"When did they leave the house, Grandfather?"

"Not until several years later," said Moayyed. "I believe it was in the summer of 1877. You see, as time passed, the people of 'Akká began to respect Bahá'u'lláh again. There were still severe problems for the Bahá'ís in Persia and in other places, but in 'Akká, 'Abdu'l-Bahá managed to win respect not just from the citizens, but also from the governor and other officials.

"So it happened that one day 'Abdu'l-Bahá heard His father lament that it had been nine long years that He had been confined to 'Akká without being able to see the greenery of the countryside or to take long walks among the fields and streams. Well, as I have told you, 'Abdu'l-Bahá's entire life was devoted to Bahá'u'lláh, Whom He adored both as His father and as a Prophet of God. Therefore, when He heard Bahá'u'lláh express these sentiments, He rented the beautiful Garden of Riḍván just outside the city and also the house of 'Abdu'lláh Pasha, the house called Mazra'ih, several miles north of the city."

"I bet Bahá'u'lláh was pleased," said Neda.

"'Abdu'l-Bahá didn't tell Bahá'u'lláh He had done this—at least, not right away, not until everything was ready and He had obtained permission from the guards to be sure they would be permitted to leave the city. When all of that was done, He went to His Beloved and told Him, 'The palace at Mazra'ih is ready for You and a carriage to drive You there.'"

"What did Bahá'u'lláh say?" asked Neda with a smile.

"He refused to go!" said Moayyed.

"But why?" asked Ali.

"He said to 'Abdu'l-Bahá, 'I am a prisoner.' Of course, He was right. Officially, the Bahá'ís had been condemned to spend the rest of their lives in prison, and Bahá'u'lláh did not want to disobey the government. Later 'Abdu'l-Bahá asked Him again, but the answer was the same.

"Then 'Abdu'l-Bahá devised a plan. He went to the Muftí of 'Akká, Shaykh 'Alíy-i-Mírí, a man who loved Bahá'u'lláh a great deal. He told this learned man the problem, and together they devised a plan. That evening the Muftí went to Bahá'u'lláh and fell on his knees before Him. He took hold of Bahá'u'lláh's hands and kissed them. Then he asked, 'Why do you not leave the city?' Bahá'u'lláh answered, 'I am a prisoner.' Then Shaykh 'Ali said, 'God forbid! Who has the power to make you a prisoner? You have kept yourself in prison. It was your own will to be imprisoned, and now I beg you to come out and go to the palace. It is beautiful and verdant. The trees are lovely, and the oranges like balls of fire!'

"Bahá'u'lláh refused again. But as often as He refused, Shaykh 'Ali simply held on to Bahá'u'lláh's hands and kissed them and repeated his request. For a whole hour Shaykh 'Ali continued to plead with Bahá'u'lláh until, at long last, Bahá'u'lláh agreed.

"The excited Shaykh hurried out of the room to tell 'Abdu'l-Bahá the news, and the very next day, 'Abdu'l-Bahá took a carriage and drove His beloved father to the house of Mazra'ih, a peaceful dwelling amid fields and trees and flowers, a refuge where Bahá'u'lláh was to spend the next two years.

"Who can imagine the joy that 'Abdu'l-Bahá must have felt on the carriage ride? What utter delight He must have felt as He took His father through the city gate for the first time in nine years. How content He must have been, sitting there beside Bahá'u'lláh as the Beloved of His heart experienced for the first time in so long the sights and sounds so precious to Him—the smells of the country fields, the sounds of songbirds on the bright June day, the beautiful trees spread out before Them across the plains of 'Akká.

"'Akká, this Most Great Prison, was no longer the home of Bahá'u'lláh, nor would it ever be again. 'Abdu'l-Bahá continued to live here. He lived in the house of 'Abbúd for over thirty years, and then He lived for eleven years in the house of 'Abdu'lláh Páshá up the street." Moayyed pointed toward a house which was closer to the prison. Then he looked to his right across the bay at the city of Haifa. "It certainly doesn't seem like three years have passed since the Master moved from 'Akká to the house in Haifa."

Moayyed seemed lost in thought for a moment, then he smiled and shook his head slowly from side to side. "It's hard to believe how quickly it all goes by," he said, talking to himself more than to the children.

Neda touched his arm and handed him a small purple wildflower. "What? Oh, thank you, dear Neda. It's quite lovely. Where did you find such a beautiful little flower in 'Akká?"

"Right here," said Neda, pointing to a crack in the stone wall. "Somehow it managed to grow between the stones."

"Just like the Bahá'í Faith!" said Ali.

"Indeed," said Moayyed, stroking a smooth stone on the ancient wall with the palm of his hand. "From the ancient stones of the Most Great Prison of 'Akká '. . . a Flower hath begun to bloom, compared to which every other flower is but a thorn, and before the brightness of Whose glory the very essence of beauty must pale and wither.'"

14

The Last Link

In the weeks that followed the tour of 'Akká with Moayyed, Ali began to change. It was not the kind of change that casual friends would have noticed, but his mother and father commented about it several times—not to Ali, but to each other and to Moayyed, who had noticed it too.

"He seems so quiet lately," Nahid had said to Husayn.

"Yes," Husayn replied, "but he seems happy enough. I don't think anything is wrong, do you?"

"I suppose you are right. He seems content, but he's so quiet, always mulling over his books or just staring into space, almost as if he were in another world."

"You would like to ask him what's on his mind, wouldn't you?" observed Husayn.

"Naturally." Then she added quickly, "But perhaps he needs his privacy right now. He's probably not even aware that we've noticed anything."

"I've thought the same thing," said Husayn, reaching for a late-night cup of tea. "Perhaps if we wait a bit longer, he'll tell us anyway—when he's ready, that is."

Weeks passed, but Ali continued his quiet, pensive walks and his study of the Bahá'í writings and Bahá'í history. Then, unexpectedly, around the middle of September the boy, who was now almost as tall as his mother, came into the parlor room where his parents were preoccupied with several miscellaneous tasks. Nahid was making a type of headdress called a *niqáb,* and Husayn was writing a letter to his cousin who had remained in

Mas͟hhad. Without waiting for his parents to look up, an animated Ali blurted out, "A chain! It's like a chain, that's what!"

Husayn was startled by the sudden outburst, and Nahid turned toward Ali in surprise. When they saw the joyful look on the young boy's face, they relaxed. "Is it really?" said Husayn. "I always thought it was more like a gray goose."

"More like a fish, I should think," said his mother in mock seriousness.

"What?" said the confused lad.

"Ali!" said his father. "*What* is like a chain?"

"Oh!" said Ali when he realized the joke. "The Bahá'í Faith, that's what. Or at least the story of Bahá'u'lláh. Look! Let me show you!"

He placed a large scroll-like sheet of paper on the tabletop and unrolled it for his parents to see. On the paper was an elaborate drawing depicting the links of a great chain. In each link, Ali had written in very small lettering descriptions of events from the life of Bahá'u'lláh, together with the date of each event. In the first link were listed things that happened before Bahá'u'lláh received the letter from the Báb. In each successive link was another period in the life of Bahá'u'lláh—the sojourn to the mountains of Sulaymáníyyih, the building of the Bábí community in Bag͟hdád, the journey to Constantinople, the Adrianople period, and, finally, Bahá'u'lláh's life in 'Akká (life in the barracks prison, then in the house of 'Abbúd, and finally at Mazra'ih).

Husayn and Nahid were amazed at the intricate work Ali had done. "You did this by yourself?" asked Nahid.

"Yes," said Ali with a smile, anxiously wanting to explain his idea. "But do you see what I mean? Each time it seemed that the chain had ended, Bahá'u'lláh added another link. And if you wanted to, you could go backwards in time and link Bahá'u'lláh to the Báb, and the Báb to Muḥammad, and Muḥammad to His Holiness Christ, and on and on."

'And the same thing into the future," said Nahid.

"Exactly!" said Ali, pleased that she understood his idea. "The whole thing, the whole plan of God is like a never-ending chain that links everything together."

"So *this* is what you've been doing with your time," said Husayn, more to himself than to Ali. Then he looked up at Ali with great affection. "Your mother and I have been wondering." The concern that Husayn and Nahid had been harboring for months now vanished in an instant. Husayn examined the chart more closely. In fact, that evening Nahid, Husayn, and Ali looked at the intricate work and discussed what Ali had done for almost two hours.

Several times the proud parents observed how clearly the chart laid out the web of events surrounding the life of Bahá'u'lláh, and often they commented about what careful and exquisite work Ali had done.

"Well?" said Ali later, "Is this not a sort of key?" Now the parents understood the true source of Ali's excitement—the key in his dream. "I mean, isn't my chart a key to understanding the life of Bahá'u'lláh?"

Husayn looked at Nahid. "Yes," he said, "I think it very well may be!" He leaned over to scrutinize the work again. Then he rubbed his chin the way that Moayyed did when he was thinking deeply about something. "Of course . . ."

"What?" asked Ali impatiently. "Is something wrong?"

"It's just that . . . you may have left out an important link in this magnificent chain."

Ali looked at his chart. "But what? What more is there to say? I suppose I could link the end of Bahá'u'lláh's life to the time when 'Abdu'l-Bahá became the Center of the Covenant. Is that what you mean?"

"Not exactly. There's actually another period in Bahá'u'lláh's life, perhaps worthy of another link."

Ali looked at the last link, in which he had described how Bahá'u'lláh finally left the city of 'Akká. "What more is there?" he asked. "Bahá'u'lláh left 'Akká and was no longer a prisoner. He lived at Mazra'ih and Bahjí."

"But in what year did Bahá'u'lláh leave 'Akká?" asked Husayn, sitting down in his chair and setting his teacup on his lap.

Ali quickly consulted his chart and found the date written neatly in his best penmanship. "1877," he said proudly.

"And in what year did Bahá'u'lláh die?"

Again he scanned his chart and placed his finger on the date. "In 1892."

"That's fifteen years," said Husayn. "That's a long period in someone's life, particularly in the life of a Manifestation."

"That's true," said Ali as he looked at how many years each of the other links lasted. "Perhaps I should put in another link."

"Look at it this way," said Nahid. "Even though there might have been no more major catastrophes in Bahá'u'lláh's life after He left 'Akká, some extremely important things occurred all the same, events that shaped the future in many ways."

"Your mother is absolutely correct, Ali. Those years were hardly a period of retirement or rest. Bahá'u'lláh spent them writing, preparing the Bahá'ís for the time when He would no longer be in their presence to answer their questions or to tell them what to do."

"I know He wrote a lot at Bahjí," said Ali, "but I don't remember hearing about anything in particular that He did or anything exciting that happened to Him, at least nothing like being put in prison or going off to the mountains, nothing like that."

"Ah, but He did go to the mountains," said Husayn with a smile.

"He did?"

"Certainly. Several times He visited Mount Carmel during those years."

Ali laughed, thinking his father was joking. "Father, that's a small mountain, and it's only about ten miles away."

"Ah, perhaps, but it's the most important mountain of all, is it not?" said Husayn. "What is more," he continued, "Bahá'u'lláh did not go there simply to have a pleasant outing. Of course, almost everything Bahá'u'lláh did in His life was filled with symbolism and significance, but His visits to Carmel were among the most important gestures of all."

"I don't understand," said Ali. "What sort of 'gestures' and 'symbols'?"

"For example, on one of those trips Bahá'u'lláh showed 'Abdu'l-Bahá where the Shrine of the Báb should be built," observed Nahid.

"I see," said Ali, sitting down on the arm of the chair where Nahid had resumed her work on the headdress. "So there is a part of Bahá'u'lláh's life I don't know about yet."

"My son, there are parts that no one knows yet," said Husayn. "We are all but simple students trying to understand. I think that's why we begin our lives on this planet—to begin learning. If we already knew everything, we could go straight to the Abhá Kingdom without even bothering to stop off on the way." All three laughed at Husayn's remarks. "But that doesn't mean you have not found your key, my son."

Ali looked again at the chart he had worked on for so long. "Still, I want my chart to be complete," he said. "Could you two tell me about those years at Bahjí? Then I could put them on my chart, and I would be finished!"

"There's someone who can tell you better than I, someone who has already promised to help, as a matter of fact."

"Abu'l-Qásim, the gardener at Riḍván?" asked Ali.

"Yes, Abu'l-Qásim. He was with Bahá'u'lláh during those years."

"Indeed he could," agreed Nahid, looking up from her sewing. "He loves to talk about Bahá'u'lláh and the years at Bahjí, especially about the trips Bahá'u'lláh made to the Garden of Riḍván."

"But there is one part of that last link that I would like to tell you about myself," said Husayn.

"The trips to Mount Carmel?" asked Ali excitedly.

"Why, yes, but how did you know?" asked Husayn.

"Mother told me you were going to Mount Carmel in a few days! Does that mean I can go too?"

Husayn smiled across the room at Nahid. "Yes, I will be happy to take you," said Husayn.

"Then when can I go to Bahjí?" asked Ali.

"The day after tomorrow," said Husayn. "I will arrange for a carriage to come here and pick you up early in the morning and take you to spend the day with Abu'l-Qásim."

In spite of his excitement at showing his parents the chart he had made and the prospect of a day with Abu'l-Qásim and another with his father on Mount Carmel, Ali slept well that night and the following night too.

He had several dreams, all of them pleasant. In one, he saw a huge golden chain suspended in the air, a little like the one he had drawn, only larger. In each link of the chain were beautiful pictures. One showed the Garden of Riḍván full of beautiful roses. In another were the mountains of Sulaymáníyyih. All of these were clear, even in the world of his dream, and it delighted him to see his chart brought to life. Then, when he looked at the last link, he saw only an open door. In the dream Ali opened the door, and there before him were steps. He followed the steps upward until he reached a corridor that looked as if it meandered endlessly. He woke up before he had a chance to explore where the corridor went.

In another dream, Ali was running faster than horses along the beach beside 'Akká. He was running so fast and so easily that his feet barely touched the sand. Suddenly he began to fly, and he was amazed that it seemed so effortless—he simply held out his arms and off he went. First he was gliding low, skimming across the water. Then, as he approached Haifa, he swooped up toward Mount Carmel with just enough momentum to carry him up to the roof of the Shrine of the Báb, where he landed ever so softly.

The next morning, his marvelous dream still fresh in his mind, Ali sensed it was going to be a special day. He was up earlier than anyone else in the house. He prepared his own breakfast, though he was too excited to eat much. Then he sat patiently on the front steps, waiting for the sound of carriage wheels on the morning streets. He had not been waiting more than about fifteen minutes when he heard the unmistakable sound of the carriage.

When the carriage came to a stop, he saw that the driver was not Abu'l-Qásim but a young man in his twenties. "You must be Ali," the young man said with a cheery smile. "Climb aboard and we can get started!"

Ali scampered onto the carriage seat, which was wooden and not very comfortable. "I thought Abu'l-Qásim was going to take me," said Ali.

"He had work to do this morning and sent me instead. He'll meet us later. My name is Abdu'l-Muhammad."

"Nice to meet you. Do you work at the gardens too?"

"Yes, my father works with Abu'l-Qásim, and I help him. In fact, I saw you in the garden several months ago when you visited with your grandfather, but you were busy talking and didn't see me.

"How long have you worked there?" asked Ali.

"Since I was sixteen." The young man looked confident as he held the reins and guided the horses past the house of 'Abbúd and up the street toward the prison. "Abu'l-Qásim told me to take you to Mazra'ih first. Later we will meet him at Bahjí."

Abdu'l-Muhammad slowed the carriage down as they neared the house of 'Abdu'lláh Pá<u>sh</u>á, with its long steps that crossed over an arched entrance and mounted to the upper story. "Of course, you probably know that although 'Abdu'l-Bahá arranged for Bahá'u'lláh to live at Mazra'ih, He Himself stayed here in 'Akká. He lived there in the house of 'Abdu'lláh Pá<u>sh</u>á until He moved across the bay to Haifa."

"Yes," said Ali, "my grandfather told me. My father said that the first Bahá'í pilgrims from the West stayed in that house before they went to Bahjí to see the Shrine of Bahá'u'lláh."

"You've learned a lot!" said Abdu'l-Muhammad. "That's right. That's also the house where Shoghi Rabbani, one of the grandsons of 'Abdu'l-Bahá, was born."

"I have seen him," said Ali. "Didn't he go with 'Abdu'l-Bahá on the long journey across the sea?"

"He was supposed to," said Abdu'l-Muhammad, "but I have heard that the authorities in Italy would not let him go. They said he was sick and had to return. He is now north of here, in Beirut, studying at the university there."

Abdu'l-Muhammad shook the reins for the horse to quicken its pace and looked back as they moved away. "There must be many memories in that house. I often wish that the houses could speak to me and tell me everything that happened in them. Sometimes I think they do."

"Yes," said Ali, "I know exactly what you mean." And Ali smiled to hear that his own feelings were shared by someone he had just met.

"When I'm in the summerhouse at the gardens and nobody else is there," said Abdu'l-Muhammad, "I feel I hear the distant whisper of conversations, but it's usually the faint sound of the fountain."

He looked at his young passenger, who was paying careful attention to what he was saying. "Did you know that it was in the house we just passed that 'Abdu'l-Bahá concealed the remains of the Báb until just three years ago, when He was able to transfer them to the vault of the Shrine on Mount Carmel? In fact, I remember the month—it was Naw-Rúz day of 1909."

"I didn't know it had happened so recently!" said Ali. Then he remembered about visiting the Shrine of the Báb. "My father and I are going to visit Mount Carmel in a few days."

"Is that right? Haven't you ever been there before?"

"Once, but I don't remember much. I felt ill that day, and I had to rest in the shade with my mother while my father and grandfather walked up the mountain to visit the Shrine of the Báb."

"Well, now that you're studying about what all these holy places mean, your trip will mean much more to you."

"Yes," said Ali as he thought about his chart. "Yes, it will."

The morning sun grew brighter as the carriage jostled along the main road heading north from 'Akká. After a while, Ali could see the old stone aqueduct which used to bring water to the city from the country streams. He remembered being told by his mother that the governor of 'Akká, Aḥmad Big Tawfíq, had repaired the old structure on Bahá'u'lláh's advice, and how for the first time in many years the city had had fresh water.

When the carriage had gone about four miles it turned off to the right, and a few minutes later they arrived at the two-story dwelling where Bahá'u'lláh lived for two years after He was released from 'Akká. It was a simple country house with several tall cypress trees beside it. To the north was a view of the Lebanon Mountains, and behind the house was a multicolored plain that stretched eastward toward a Druze village.

For a while Ali and Abdu'l-Muhammad walked around the grounds of the house, and then they entered through a back door. After Abdu'l-

Muhammad led Ali inside, they approached the foot of a stairway leading up to the second floor where Bahá'u'lláh's room had been. They climbed the steps and at the top turned left into a small hallway.

"That is Bahá'u'lláh's room," said Abdu'l-Muhammad. Then he and Ali removed their shoes as a sign of respect and went through the doorway into a very small room where there was a simple bed and a few other pieces of furniture. They knelt down on the rug beside the bed, and Abdu'l-Muhammad began to recite a prayer.

Ali tried to concentrate on the words, but soon found himself imagining the voices that Abdu'l-Muhammad had described. It was enchanting to Ali to think about Bahá'u'lláh's voice speaking in this room. He wondered if Bahá'u'lláh's voice had sounded like his father's—smooth and mellow—or deep and a little raspy like his grandfather's. Abdu'l-Muhammad had an eloquent voice, strong and controlled, and as he chanted, Ali closed his eyes and imagined that Bahá'u'lláh was in the room at this very moment.

They stayed in the house about twenty minutes or so while Abdu'l-Muhammad described for Ali what life was like for Bahá'u'lláh at Mazra'ih. Then they walked around outside for a while longer. Abdu'l-Muhammad described for Ali how much Bahá'u'lláh loved this peaceful countryside abode after spending so many years in the prison or confined within the walls of 'Akká in small houses. And when Abdu'l-Muhammad spoke of Bahá'u'lláh's leaving the walls of 'Akká, it made Ali remember again his own escape on horseback in his dream.

Ali picked a few wildflowers to take back to his parents, then Abdu'l-Muhammad suggested that they begin the journey back toward the road that led to Bahjí. Ali climbed aboard, and soon they were once again rumbling along the country road at a steady pace. At first, neither said very much. They enjoyed the pleasant view, the sweet-smelling air, the songbirds that could be heard even above the steady noise of the carriage wheels.

After a few minutes, Ali said, "Wouldn't it be wonderful if we could go into Bahá'u'lláh's room at Bahjí?"

"I'm sure someday Bahá'ís from around the world will be able to do just that, but only God knows when that will be. For the time being it is in the hands of the Covenant-breakers." Abdu'l-Muhammad and Ali talked about Muḥammad-'Ali, the younger half-brother of 'Abdu'l-Bahá who had, after Bahá'u'lláh's death, claimed the position that Bahá'u'lláh had clearly conferred on 'Abdu'l-Bahá.

"I don't understand," said Ali. "How could anyone turn against 'Abdu'l-Bahá, especially someone like Muḥammad-'Ali, who knew what Bahá'u'lláh had said in the Book of His Covenant? How could he disobey Bahá'u'lláh like that?"

Abdu'l-Muhammad smiled. "You are forgetting that Mírzá Yaḥyá was Bahá'u'lláh's own brother, yet he rebelled. He did things much worse than trying to steal a mansion or claiming to be the Center of the Covenant."

"That's true," said Ali, shaking his head with a puzzled look.

"I suppose some people want to feel important, Ali. Sometimes this kind of ambition, this desire to feel better than other people, can become more powerful than the desire to be faithful or spiritual or even happy. I suppose that's why we must be very careful to follow the teachings Bahá'u'lláh has given us, because we never know when we might be infected with that same desire." To Ali it sounded strange to hear an evil action described as something contagious.

"You make it sound like being a Covenant-breaker is a disease. Are Covenant-breakers just bad people?"

"No one is born evil, Ali. We all have things that tempt us to do the wrong thing. We all have choices, every day of our lives. It may be the desire to have power or prosperity, or it may be something else entirely. But we are all tested—make no mistake about that."

Ali found it strange to hear this advice coming from such a young man. "Don't worry," said Abdu'l-Muhammad, changing the subject. "Abu'l-Qásim will describe the rooms at Bahjí for you in such detail that you'll feel as if you had visited them yourself. You see, he visited Bahá'u'lláh there, and he can tell us enough so that our eyes won't suffer much loss."

"I suppose I should be thankful that I can visit the Shrine of Bahá'u'lláh and not worry about what I can't see," said Ali.

"Exactly!" said Abdu'l-Muhammad. And they both laughed as they talked about seeing the mansion of Bahjí and hearing the stories Abu'l-Qásim had to tell.

Before too long they could see the red-tile rooftop of the huge mansion in the distance. It was surrounded by other smaller buildings and beautiful tall pines. Ali was always surprised by the size of the place. It seemed to grow larger while the rest of the buildings around 'Akká seemed to become smaller the older Ali grew.

As the carriage approached the path leading from the Garden of Riḍván, they saw Abu'l-Qásim walking toward them. He had just come from the garden, where he had been working since sunrise. He smiled when he saw Ali and Abdu'l-Muhammad and raised his arms in a welcoming gesture.

After Abdu'l-Muhammad secured the horse, the three walked toward Bahjí and the Shrine of Bahá'u'lláh. "By the way," said Abu'l-Qásim, stopping and turning to Ali, "the garden gave me a message for you." The old man reached behind his back mysteriously and handed Ali a rose, the most beautiful blossom Ali had ever seen. It was slightly golden in the center, with white petals and a sweet, delicate fragrance. "This was one of Bahá'u'lláh's favorite flowers," said Abu'l-Qásim.

"Thank you, sir," said Ali. He took the stem in his hand and brought the rich, full blossom to his nose. He inhaled deeply. It was an incredibly lovely fragrance, like the inside of the Shrine of Bahá'u'lláh itself where daily the custodians would place fresh rose petals.

"As we walk down this path, which has known the feet of travelers from many distant lands," said Abdu'l-Qásim, "you must try to think of all the many pilgrims through the years, all the footsteps that have trod this trail, of all the sacrifices they made to come here, and of all the love they received when they arrived. More important, you would do well, my young ones, to think on the heroic deeds these same pilgrims performed after they left here and went about teaching the Cause throughout the world."

Abu'l-Qásim stopped and pointed to the upper floor of the mansion. "You see those windows at the far corner? That's the room where the pilgrims would meet Him. That's the room where Bahá'u'lláh stayed during the last twelve years of His life." Abu'l-Qásim made sure Ali knew which room he meant, then they resumed walking. "It is a large room," he continued, "and when Bahá'u'lláh was there, it had a divan along one side and beautiful carpets."

"But how could Bahá'u'lláh afford such a place?" asked Ali.

"A very rich man named 'Údí Khammár built the mansion in about 1870, while Bahá'u'lláh was still in prison. Then, while Bahá'u'lláh was at Mazra'ih, an epidemic spread throughout this area. 'Údí Khammár decided to take his family elsewhere, and so 'Abdu'l-Bahá was able to rent the mansion for a relatively small sum of money.

"That was in 1879, two years after Bahá'u'lláh moved to Mazra'ih. Of course, 'Abdu'l-Bahá, Munírih Khánum, and their young children, together with Navváb and Bahíyyih Khánum, stayed in 'Akká."

"Is it true," asked Ali, "that Bahá'u'lláh had them stay in 'Akká to protect them from the Covenant-breakers who lived with Him in the mansion?"

"Moayyed is right," said Abu'l-Qásim with a broad grin as he placed his hand on Ali's shoulder. "It is no wonder you were born in Masá'il, the month of questions. Oh, I suppose there were many reasons that Bahá'u'lláh had those he cherished most stay behind in 'Akká while He lived here. No doubt, what you say may be one reason. Certainly Bahá'u'lláh did not trust those who lived with Him at the mansion. In fact, the person who prepared Bahá'u'lláh's food kept the keys to the larders where the food was stored so that no one in the household would have a chance to poison Bahá'u'lláh. And, as you know, the very reason we can't go into the mansion now is that when Bahá'u'lláh died, these same family members became Covenant-breakers, took over the mansion, and have remained there ever since, refusing entrance to the Bahá'ís and even to 'Abdu'l-Bahá.

"Another reason that 'Abdu'l-Bahá, Bahá'u'lláh's wife Ásíyih Khánum, and Bahá'u'lláh's faithful daughter Bahíyyih Khánum remained in 'Akká was to allow Bahá'u'lláh to have the privacy He needed in order to continue His writing. You see, when pilgrims would come to visit Bahá'u'lláh, they would first stay with 'Abdu'l-Bahá and the family in 'Akká. 'Abdu'l-Bahá would prepare them for their meeting with Bahá'u'lláh and then, when the time was right, He would escort them here to Bahjí. This arrangement also allowed 'Abdu'l-Bahá to take care of His beloved mother and to meet all the governmental officials and conduct all the business affairs for Bahá'u'lláh."

"So 'Abdu'l-Bahá was like Bahá'u'lláh's business director?" said Ali, trying to understand.

"Yes, I suppose that's one way of putting it."

When they arrived at the Shrine of Bahá'u'lláh, they ceased talking. They removed their shoes, then reverently entered the inner courtyard with its lovely glass windows surrounding the roof. Ali smiled as soon as he smelled the fragrant rose petals in the room, and he looked again at the blossom he still held in his hand.

Each of the three went in turn to the threshold of the burial room, and after several minutes of silent prayer and meditation, Abdu'l-Muhammad chanted the Tablet of Visitation. Then Abdu'l-Muhammad and Abu'l-Qásim rose and slowly walked out. Ali wanted to stay awhile longer.

After a few minutes of silence, he stepped to the threshold and knelt down. He took a last smell of his flower and then placed it on the threshold. "Oh, Bahá'u'lláh," he said softly, "help me find the key so that I may serve Thy Cause."

That was all he said, but it felt sufficient. He remained with his head bowed, waiting until he felt the vibrations from his voice filter throughout the chamber. He then rose and went outside again where the two men were waiting for him.

After Ali put on his shoes, they walked several hundred yards away from the mansion and sat beneath the shade of one of the great pines. "Let us talk here for a whilem" said Abu'l-Qásim. "Then we shall go to the Garden of Riḍván."

The old gardener settled himself in a comfortable position, his tired back against the trunk of the tree, and he looked at Bahjí. "The years here were many, but they went swiftly for me," he began. "Much happened, of course, but not the sort of dramatic things that had happened before—no exiles, no more prison, at least not for Bahá'u'lláh. But there was so much work to do that a schedule had to be established. It was not absolutely rigid or unchangeable, understand, but it was usually followed."

"What was the schedule?" asked Ali.

"First of all, there were the pilgrims and other visitors. As I mentioned, they would meet first with 'Abdu'l-Bahá, Who would schedule a time that would be convenient for them to come visit with the Blessed Beauty. And, of course, Bahá'u'lláh had such love for 'Abdu'l-Bahá that when He knew His son was coming to visit Him, His face would glow. Why, I remember one pilgrim, Ṭarázu'lláh Samandarí, who was but a young lad at the time—about sixteen years of age—He had stayed with 'Abdu'l-Bahá for several days until finally he was able to see Bahá'u'lláh. Naturally, when he finally got to meet the Blessed Beauty, he exclaimed how ecstatic he was to be with Him at long last." Abu'l-Qásim chuckled as he anticipated the rest of his story. "Well, Bahá'u'lláh said to the young man, 'Do you not meet the Master every day?' The young man responded that he did. Bahá'u'lláh told him, 'Then why do you speak of not having been here in My presence for several days, you who meet the Master every day and receive the honor of His company?'

"That's the sort of love and affection Bahá'u'lláh had for 'Abdu'l-Bahá. In fact, sometimes when Bahá'u'lláh missed 'Abdu'l-Bahá too much, He would send a message to Him asking Him to come to Bahjí to share a meal with Him. Naturally, 'Abdu'l-Bahá was all too happy to oblige and would eagerly walk to see His beloved father.

"But, as I was saying, a routine was arranged. At certain times Bahá'u'lláh would see the pilgrims, and then at certain other times during the week He would meet with regular visitors. For example, Nabíl might see Bahá'u'lláh on Tuesday, and then on another day Bahá'u'lláh would meet with 'Abdu'l-Bahá, Who would tell His father which Persian believers had settled in 'Akká and how the people of 'Akká were treating the Bahá'ís.

"Overall, things got progressively better for us during those days. 'Abdu'l-Bahá became known more and more to the citizens of 'Akká as a friend and counselor. The Christians and Muslims alike came to Him for advice and help because they admired Him so much. Much of the time, 'Abdu'l-Bahá worked to help the poor and the needy of the town, or He would tend to the sick or the helpless.

"Even the officials of the court asked for His assistance in complicated cases. So it was that the reputation of the Bahá'ís was assisted by the selfless deeds and great wisdom of 'Abdu'l-Bahá, while Bahá'u'lláh stayed here to fashion the blueprint for the education and development of the world at large.

"Ah, it was a miraculous thing, let me tell you! It was like nothing you could imagine, though few people ever had the chance to see it take place. As you know, during the early years, Bahá'u'lláh Himself wrote many tablets in His own hand. But after He was poisoned by Mírzá Yaḥyá, He did not write as much. Instead, He would dictate tablets to others, who would then write them down. Bahá'u'lláh would review what they had transcribed, make any necessary corrections, and then affix His seal.

"It was Mírzá Áqá Ján who did most of the copying. He devised a special script that only he could read whereby he could copy Bahá'u'lláh's words with great speed and accuracy. He could write almost as quickly as Bahá'u'lláh would speak the words. So Mírzá Áqá Ján would always have ready his ink pot, many pens, and large sheets of paper. As Bahá'u'lláh would speak, Mírzá Áqá Ján would scribble down the words in that hurried and strange script. His pen would scratch the surface of the paper so quickly and with such a noise that it could be heard at twenty paces. Then Mírzá Áqá Ján would take these odd-looking notes, rewrite them into verses in an exquisite calligraphy, and show them to Bahá'u'lláh.

"But what was even more amazing about this revelation process was that Bahá'u'lláh's words poured forth like a mighty torrent of water gushing from a holy fountain, for such is the power of a Manifestation of God. And He could have revealed even more than He did, but He gave us only as much as we are ready for." Abu'l-Qásim paused, his eyes staring blankly across the fields, his thoughts fixed steadfastly on his memory of Bahá'u'lláh. For a moment he forgot about his companions.

"Then those were very happy years?" asked Ali at last.

"What?" said Abu'l-Qásim. "Oh, yes—happier than the years in 'Akká. There were picnics with the family at the garden, and 'Abdu'l-Bahá's daughters were so happy to see their grandfather. Affection and love showed in their smiles and their eyes. To them He was like a loving father.

"But of course there were some sad times, too, for life is not life without sadness. About 1886 Ásíyih Khánum, the beautiful and saintly wife of Bahá'u'lláh, finally succumbed to all the hardships she had been made to endure through the years. Her death caused much grief to everyone who had known her, but especially to Bahá'u'lláh, Who had given her a special title. He called her 'Navváb'—the 'Most Exalted Leaf'—and He said she would be His 'perpetual consort in all the worlds of God.'

"In all those years of exile and imprisonment when she had to work harder than any peasant woman, she never once complained or became impatient, even though she had been raised to be an elegant lady of the court. But of all the things she did to serve Bahá'u'lláh, perhaps the most marvelous gifts she gave Him were the faithful and beloved children she bore—'Abdu'l-Bahá, Bahíyyih Khánum, and Mírzá Mihdí."

Abu'l-Qásim said no more. He stood up slowly. With a broad smile he motioned that they should return. As they walked toward the carriage the old man said, "So many beautiful times, so many lovely stories. Would that they had never ended!" The old gardener chuckled softly to himself. "By the way, did you know that Bahá'u'lláh loved to laugh, Ali?"

"Really?" said the boy, finding it difficult to imagine that a Prophet of God, Whose life and mission were so deadly serious, could find anything amusing in His arduous and thankless task.

"Who would have thought that with all the pain He suffered and all the work He had to do there was room for laughter?" said Abu'l-Qásim. "But there was, not just for the little children, mind you, but for all of us. I remember early in the mornings when He stayed at the garden in the summerhouse, others would be in their tents, and He would rise before everyone else and then go among the little tents and wake them up and chide them for being so lazy. It was another way for Him to show His love for us.

"I remember another time at the garden when locusts came. There were so many of the creatures swarming all over the garden and over the tall trees and beautiful plants that I ran to the summerhouse where Bahá'u'lláh was working. 'My Lord,' I said, 'the locusts have come, and are eating away the shade from above Thy blessed head. I beg of Thee to cause them to depart.' But Bahá'u'lláh was not bothered. He smiled at me and said, 'The locusts must be fed. Let them be.' So I went back to the garden and tried to be patient.

"But I simply could not. All those little insects were destroying the beauty of the garden which gave such peace to Bahá'u'lláh. Again I went to Him and begged Him to do something."

"I don't understand," said Ali. "What did you expect Bahá'u'lláh to do?"

Abu'l-Qásim looked at Abdu'l-Muhammad with a knowing grin. "Someday you will understand more completely, Ali. For now I will simply tell you that the Prophet is able to do whatever He wants. He is not limited like ordinary human beings. He is not like you and me."

"Then what did He do?"

"Well, as a favor to me He left the tranquility of the summerhouse and went out into the middle of the garden. He stood there beneath the trees, which by now were completely covered with these pests. He looked up at them and said, Abu'l-Qásim does not want you; God protect you!' Then He lifted the hem of His robe, shook it once, and suddenly all the locusts arose from the garden and flew away!"

"Is that true?" asked Ali.

"Please," said Abu'l-Qásim, "this was but a small, little Miracle. Think about the Miracle that Almighty God sent us a Savior! That's the Miracle! Yes, of course it is true. And there is so much more, Ali, so much more. It would be hard for me to describe all of one day in the life of a Manifestation, but twelve years—that's impossible.

"It was the last period of His life, and I suppose in a way it was quite different from the earlier periods. It was a time of putting everything together, a time of preparing to place the guidance of His Cause in the capable hands of 'Abdu'l-Bahá. For example, during this time He wrote a long tablet reviewing the things He had done and the works He had written during His life. It is called the Epistle to the Son of the Wolf.

"And, of course, there were the trips to Mount Carmel! But Moayyed said your father is going to tell you about those when you go with him to the that blessed spot." The old gardener stopped talking as if he were suddenly lost in thought, and there was an interval of awkward silence.

"Thank you," said Ali as the three climbed aboard the carriage. "Thank you for—"

"Please, please!" said Abu'l-Qásim before Ali could finish. "My joy is to tell you these stories. My joy is to share with everyone what was given to me with such complete love. It would be a burden to keep such happy memories inside me or to take that gift with me to the next world without having given it a few times."

15

The Mountain of God

For several days after his visit to Bahjí, Ali talked with his parents about Mazra'ih and Bahjí, recounting for them the stories that Abdu'l-Muhammad and Abu'l-Qásim had told him. They listened eagerly, and afterwards Husayn began to explain to Ali more about the last years in the life of Bahá'u'lláh. He discussed with his son how the Blessed Beauty made certain that the Cause of God would be safeguarded when He was no longer present to guide it.

"All of the Manifestations of God had covenants with their followers. All of the Prophets left behind laws and other kinds of guidance to direct the believers," said Husayn. "But never before had a Prophet left a written document designating exactly who would be the head of the religion after the Prophet had died."

"But what exactly is a covenant?" asked Ali. "I thought it was simply an agreement."

"That's right. A covenant is a promise, an agreement, usually between two parties. For example, there is the Greater or Eternal Covenant, that agreement between God and humankind—what we sometimes call the Ancient Covenant.

"I know what that is" said Ali. "That's God's promise that He will always send a Manifestation when we need one."

"Exactly," said Husayn. "At least, that's God's part in the agreement, but what is our part?"

"That we will try to recognize the Prophets when They come and that we will follow the teachings They give us."

"You've learned your lessons well, Ali. Then there is the second sort of covenant, the agreement between the Prophet and His followers—what we sometimes call the Lesser Covenant. For example, the Covenant of Bahá'u'lláh appoints 'Abdu'l-Bahá as the Center of the Covenant, or head of the Bahá'í Faith."

"And our part in that agreement is to follow 'Abdu'l-Bahá?" Ali suggested.

"Correct. But by specifying this in writing, Bahá'u'lláh made certain that the religion of God would not become divided and splintered as happened in the past with Christianity and with Islám."

Ali mulled over what his father had said and what Abdu'l-Muhammad had said about Covenant-breaking being like a contagious disease. "There's something I don't understand, Father. God is perfect, is He not? And He is All-Powerful—He can do whatever He wants?"

"Yes, certainly."

"Then if God is perfect and if the Manifestations are like Him—if They also have power and are perfect—why did God wait so long before He allowed one of His Messengers to leave a written Covenant?"

"Well, you see—"

"And one more thing," continued Ali before his father could begin his answer, "if Bahá'u'lláh's Covenant is so clear and so powerful, why is it that right now Mírzá Muḥammad-'Alí and his family live in the mansion at Bahjí and mock 'Abdu'l-Bahá and the pilgrims who come to worship at the Shrine of Bahá'u'lláh?"

Husayn took a deep breath and looked at his wife, who was slowly shaking her head from side to side with a wry smile. Without words she was saying to Husayn, "This soul we have nurtured is no longer merely our offspring, no longer merely a reflection of our thoughts and views. He has become his own person." Ali, however, was too engrossed in thought to perceive this silent communication between his mother and father.

Husayn looked back at his son with a new kind of respect. "I don't know for certain all the answers to your questions, Ali. But I can tell you what I think."

"That's good enough for me," said Ali with a smile.

"There is such a thing as timeliness in the plan of God. Each of the Prophets says so. Each One says to His followers that He cannot tell them all there is to know, but He will teach them all they can understand until the next Teacher comes. Bahá'u'lláh says the same thing."

"I understand that," said Ali.

"Well, in this day it is time for all the peoples throughout this planet to understand that there is but one God and one people and that all the Manifestations have come for the same purpose."

"But what does that have to do with the Covenant?"

"Now is the time for such a Covenant, a written one, one that will stand the test of time. And perhaps the reason it has not happened before is so that all the people can look back at the history of religion—which, after all, is the history of our human family on this earth—and see what happens to religion when there is no covenant written down or when individuals break that covenant."

"The religion becomes divided?"

"Exactly."

"And what about the Covenant-breakers living at Bahjí? Haven't they divided the Cause of Bahá'u'lláh? Haven't they defeated 'Abdu'l-Bahá and taken over the mansion?"

"They most certainly have *not* divided the Cause," said Nahid sternly. "They have divided *themselves* from the Cause of Bahá'u'lláh. You have studied the life of Bahá'u'lláh. Where are the followers of Mírzá Yaḥyá today? True, Mírzá Muḥammad-'Alí and his family occupy Bahjí and cause problems for 'Abdu'l-Bahá, but who commands our hearts? Who is at this moment traveling throughout the world to teach the Cause of Bahá'u'lláh? And who is named to be the Center of the Covenant of Bahá'u'lláh? Be patient, Ali, and you will see how history will demonstrate the power of Bahá'u'lláh's Covenant."

"Your mother is absolutely right, Ali. Fifty years from now, a hundred years from now, this blessed Cause will be spread throughout the world, but no one will know anything about Mírzá Muḥammad-'Alí."

"I guess that's when the Covenant is most important,' Ali observed, "when the Prophet goes back to the world of the spirit."

"Yes," said Husayn. "That's when the Covenant undergoes its greatest tests, at these points of transition when power is transferred from one person to another or from one institution to another. At those times, the followers feel a little bit lost. They are used to following one person, and suddenly that face, that voice, that presence is no longer there. And when people who are ambitious sense that weakness, they become like predators in the jungle who think they have discovered wounded prey. They think they have discovered an opportunity to have power and control, to be head of the religion or to use it for their own gain."

"Or perhaps the believers may start quarreling among themselves about who should run things," said Nahid. "But that's the point, Ali. Bahá'u'lláh did not abandon us to work these things out for ourselves, and in the long run that Covenant will make all the difference. He appointed 'Abdu'l-Bahá to be the Center of the Covenant, and then someday there will be a Universal House of Justice to guide us when 'Abdu'l-Bahá is no longer here."

"And all of that is part of Bahá'u'lláh's Covenant?" asked Ali lying down on the carpet, his chin propped on his hands.

"Yes," said Husayn. "That's why your idea about the chain is such a good one. Each Manifestation is linked to every other Manifestation on the chain that is the Eternal Covenant, and each Manifestation is linked to the next Manifestation through His own Covenant, which will guide His followers until the next Prophet comes."

"But why exactly is Mount Carmel so important? What does it have to do with all of this?" asked Ali.

"Mount Carmel is essential in the Covenant of Bahá'u'lláh and the whole future of the Bahá'í Faith. It is perhaps the most important part of this last link in your story of Bahá'u'lláh. But to understand why, you will have to wait until we go there for the day."

"And do you know what we are going to do there?" said Nahid.

"Go inside the Shrine of the Báb?" Ali responded.

"Yes," said Nahid. "And we will be able to look across the bay at 'Akká from the top of Mount Carmel."

Ali got up and gave both of his parents an affectionate hug. Then, later, as the boy lay in his bed looking at a half-moon that shone through his window, he thought about the trip to Carmel, and he wondered how close he might be to discovering the gold key.

Husayn and Nahid lay awake in the next room, talking about Ali. Both found it remarkable that Ali had learned so much in so short a time, especially since his dream.

"I don't remember knowing that much when I was a child," said Husayn.

"Perhaps he is no longer just a child," Nahid responded as she thought about the changes that had occurred in her son.

"You're right," said Husayn. "It's hard to describe, but he seems so sure of himself now."

"I honestly think that dream had a lot to do with it," said Nahid.

"All I know is that ever since the dream, the Faith has come alive for him," said Husayn.

"And there's something else," said Nahid, "something in his manner, in the way he is with others, especially with older people. He seems to respect them more, to value them."

The proud parents continued to talk about Ali late into the night and over the course of the next several days. By Sunday, Husayn and Nahid were as excited about the visit to Mount Carmel as Ali was.

The day broke cloudy, but by mid-morning the sun had burned away the mist that hung like a veil over the bay. The three finished packing some food for lunch, and Ali helped his mother put everything into the carriage while Husayn checked the horse's bridle and saddle girth.

Shortly afterwards, the carriage left the city and headed down the beach toward Haifa and Mount Carmel. The wheels made a soft crunching sound as the carriage rolled along the sand, and the fall breeze felt cool as it gusted in from the sea.

Soon they crossed the Na'mayn River, which flowed gently into the sea just outside the city, and as the horse pulled the carriage through the stream, Ali wondered if the water was special water, sanctified water, because it had flowed around the Riḍván Garden before making its way to the seaside.

The sun soon arched over the mountains as the carriage jostled over the furrowed beach. The pounding sound of small breakers mingled with the distant cry of gulls. The steady rhythm of the horse's hooves and the music of the carriage had a hypnotizing effect on Ali, and before too long, the boy closed his eyes and let his face bask in the morning sun.

After a while the carriage crossed another stream, the Kishon. This water was deep, and Ali watched his father guide the horse cautiously as he looked for a place where the river bed was firmer and water more shallow. After they had passed through the water, Ali looked back and saw 'Akká, now gleaming white beside the blue Mediterranean water that seemed to surround it.

Before too much longer, Ali and his parents were on the streets of Haifa, a village quite different from 'Akká. It was cleaner, newer. There were pretty trees along some of the streets, and the buildings weren't all pushed together.

"There it is!" exclaimed Ali as he got his first glimpse of the white rectangular building halfway up the mountain directly in front of them.

"We'll be up there soon!" said Husayn.

Ali felt proud as he looked up at the Shrine of the Báb. It was one of the few structures on the otherwise rocky, mostly barren mountainside. It stood out above the city as if to say, "Something important is happening here!" Ali wondered how many people who came to Haifa wanted to know what that solitary building was. And when they learned it was a holy shrine, did they wonder who the Báb was or what He had done?

"Do you remember those houses with the red tile on the roof from your first visit?" asked Husayn pointing toward several dwellings at the foot of the mountain.

"I remember seeing them," said Ali, "but I don't remember what they are."

"About fifty years ago, when Bahá'u'lláh was in the prison, a group of German Christians built them. They were called Templars, and they built homes at the foot of Mount Carmel because they had studied the scriptures and believed that the time for the return of Christ was near."

"But why did they come here all the way from Germany?" asked Ali.

"Because they believed the scriptures indicated that Christ would appear on Mount Carmel."

"It was the same with the monks who live in the monastery on top of the mountain," said Nahid.

"They also believe that this is a holy place. They call themselves Carmelites because their religious order began here over seven hundred years ago."

"Are they also waiting for the return of Christ?" asked Ali.

"Not exactly," said Nahid. "This mountain was a holy place for early Christians who settled here, and also for the Jewish people because the prophet Elijah's cave is here. In fact, several thousand years ago the Egyptians also believed this mountain to be a holy pace.

"Did any of the Templars or Carmelites become Bahá'ís?" asked Ali.

"Not that I know of," said Husayn. "No doubt some of them saw Bahá'u'lláh on His visits to the mountain. Still, let me show you something very curious." Husayn pulled on the reins and the carriage stopped in front of one of the Templar houses. "Do you see the words over that door?"

"I can't read them, but I see the writing," said Ali.

"Well, the words are in German, but they say, 'The Lord is near.'"

"And yet they never heard about Bahá'u'lláh?"

"Not that I know of," said Husayn.

"And what about the monks?" asked Ali.

"As far as I know, they aren't even aware that the Bahá'í Faith exists. You see, it is their belief that they can best serve God by staying inside the monastery and praying. So they aren't very aware of what happens outside."

"They never come out?" asked Ali.

"Not very often," replied Husayn. "They believe in staying secluded, away from the things of this world."

"But didn't Bahá'u'lláh say that people shouldn't do that?"

"Yes, on several occasions. He says that in the Most Holy Book and also in another tablet called the Words of Paradise. He says that these devoted souls are needed in the world, that they should use their spiritual understanding to help others."

"How strange it all is," said Ali, looking at the house, wondering what the Templar would have said had he known how close he had been to the One he was awaiting.

"The holy land is like a vast puzzle waiting to be assembled," said Nahid. "So many Prophets have lived in this land. It is a holy place to Christians, Jews, Muslims, and Bahá'ís alike, and yet so few people here understand the one simple truth that can assemble all the pieces of this puzzle, the fact that all of these different Teachers were trying to lead us to the same truth, the same God, the same spiritual reality."

Husayn shook the reins and the carriage rattled along, but instead of going up the mountain, he headed the horse by the road around the base of the mountain. "Carmel is not a single hill, but a long mountain range which ends in Haifa as it drops off into the sea," said Husayn. "First we will go around to the very foot of the mountain so we can see Elijah's Cave."

Ali had not been to this part of the mountain before, and he looked ahead, wondering what the cave would be like. Husayn slowed the carriage as they neared an odd brick building perched on the slant of the mountainside. "That building arching over the pathway is where there is an entrance to the cave of Elijah," said Husayn. "I am told that on one of His visits to the mountain, Bahá'u'lláh stayed in that building for three days."

"How many times did Bahá'u'lláh come to Mount Carmel?" asked Ali.

"Four times," said Nahid. "He came two times during the last two years of His life."

"But why did He wait so long before He came here?"

"I'll tell you what," suggested Husayn, "why don't we take our lunch under those trees over there, and before we investigate this holy mountain, we'll prepare our bodies and answer some of your questions. How does that sound?"

They agreed, and Husayn pulled the carriage off to the side of the dirt roadway. Nahid and Ali prepared the food while Husayn tied the horse under a shade tree and poured some water from a leather pouch into a pan he had brought along.

As they ate the bread, cheese, and several kinds of fruit, Husayn talked to Ali about Bahá'u'lláh's trips to Mount Carmel. "You were asking why Bahá'u'lláh waited until the last years of His life to come here," said Husayn. "As I have told you so often, we can really only guess why a Manifestation does things in a certain way because there are many, many reasons behind every single thing They do. But I do know some of His reasons.

"On these visits Bahá'u'lláh explained to 'Abdu'l-Bahá what would happen here in the future. It was all part of the Covenant that I was explaining to you the other night. I suspect Bahá'u'lláh knew He had almost finished the work He needed to do on earth, and so He instructed 'Abdu'l-Bahá about such things as where to bury the remains of the Báb and how the world center of the Bahá'í Faith would in time be constructed here."

"Did They always stay in that building when They came here?" asked Ali.

"No. Usually They stayed in houses near the German Templar colony, and sometimes in the colony itself. I know that on at least one occasion Bahá'u'lláh stayed in His tent, which He called the Tabernacle of Glory."

"When can we climb the mountain?" asked Ali impatiently.

"After we have cleaned up here, then we can take a look inside the cave," said Nahid. "After that, we can visit the shrine." Within a few minutes they had packed the baskets in the carriage and walked up the pathway to the cave.

When they first entered the cave it was hard to see, and Ali was just a little scared—he had never been inside a cave before. After his eyes became accustomed to the dark, Ali could see that the cave was wide but not very deep. It had a low ceiling, blackened by the smoke from centuries of ritual fires. Ali's imagination ran wild thinking of what strange things had taken place in this ancient shelter, what biblical figures had been here, what miraculous events had occurred.

There was not much to see, really, except with the mind's eye, and Ali tried to picture what the holy men through the centuries might have looked like as they visited this spot seeking shelter or safety. It was easier to imagine Nabíl the historian who had hid here, because Ali had seen a picture of him.

Nahid chanted a brief prayer at the entrance to the cave, and then the family returned to the carriage and began the ride back around to the mountain road. Husayn drove a short distance beyond the Templar houses and stopped the carriage. All three got out of the carriage, and Husayn tied the horse beside a path which wound up the mountainside.

The three then began walking along the pathway up the steep slope of the mountain. Refreshed as they were from their lunch, they made the climb easily, and within fifteen minutes or so they were about halfway up the slope where the shrine was located. The sun was already past its zenith, but the day was still quite warm, and Ali felt glad that the sea breeze was still blowing.

As he walked behind his parents amid the rocks and scrub trees, he looked out to his right toward 'Akká. "Father!" he said, pointing toward the city. "Look at how 'Akká glistens!"

"White as ivory," said Nahid, surprised herself at how clear the city seemed on this bright autumn day. "Imagine how Bahá'u'lláh felt as He looked for the first time across the bay at the place that had been His prison," she continued. "How many times He must have looked from the house of 'Abbúd at this mountain as He made His plans for the Bahá'í Faith."

"Imagine how He must have felt," Husayn added, "to have lived through all the hardship and suffering, and finally to be here in the open countryside He loved so dearly and to know that He had finally accomplished everything that God had set out for Him to do. He had revealed all the teachings the world would need. And here on this very spot He would add the finishing touch by showing 'Abdu'l-Bahá where to place the remains of the Báb and showing Him where the world center of the Bahá'í Faith would be built."

"But there's nothing else here," said Ali.

Husayn looked out toward 'Akká as he spoke. The three were only a short distance from the shrine now. "The history of this Cause, *our* history, has only just begun, Ali. Before your life is done, you will witness more changes here than you can imagine."

As they approached the shrine, Ali could see the cypress trees which towered behind the simple building, the spot where Bahá'u'lláh had stood with 'Abdu'l-Bahá to show where the shrine should be built. The building itself had a flat roof and was wider than it was deep. There were two doors on either side and one in the front, and Ali wondered which door they would enter.

"First let's go behind the shrine to the spot where Bahá'u'lláh stood," said Husayn. Nahid and Ali agreed, though Ali was anxious to see the inside. They went up the path behind the shrine and stood together among the clump of cypress trees. "I am going to recite a prayer, Ali, and as I do, remember that only about twenty years ago, Bahá'u'lláh stood on this very ground and told 'Abdu'l-Bahá where to build this shrine. Now we are here, the shrine is here, and inside the shrine are entombed the remains of the Báb."

Ali listened carefully to his father, who spoke softly and clearly to show the reverence he felt for this holy spot. And as his father intoned the verses of Bahá'u'lláh, his voice blending with the rustling cypress leaves, the mountain itself seemed to sing, as if it understood the precious treasure it cradled. When he was through, the three went down to a side door where they removed their shoes, and Ali felt his heart beat a little faster in anticipation.

He wondered what the building would be like inside and whether he would feel the same sort of emotion he felt when he visited the Shrine of Bahá'u'lláh. They stood, and Husayn opened the large metal door. As they entered, the room seemed cool, quiet, and serene. The simple walls were white and smooth. The floor was covered with Persian carpets. The room they entered was separated from the room beside it, but through an arched threshold in front of them they could see into a center room, and beyond it through a similar arched threshold into another room that was like a mirror image of the one they were in. There were six rooms altogether, two rows side by side of three rooms each.

The burial place was in the center of the back row of rooms, covered by a simple stone. Ali walked slowly across the thick carpet to the threshold between the room they had entered and the burial chamber. He looked at the stone. He thought about how the remains of the Báb and Anís, the youth who had been executed with Him, were actually entombed not more than a few feet from where Ali stood. It seemed almost incredible, and yet it was true, that the light and life the Sh͟áh had thought to obliterate was more alive than ever.

The more Ali considered this thought, the more he understood with a final clarity that the stories he had heard all his life about the Báb, about Mullá Ḥusayn, Quddús, Ṭáhirih—stories that had once seemed more myth or legend than fact—were all terribly real. No, these were not just stories. This was the history of real people who had faced what had seemed to be insurmountable obstacles with a courage and faith sufficient to secure the Revelation of God's guidance for all the peoples of the world.

Ali slowly knelt at the threshold, and almost as soon as his knees touched the carpet, Nahid's melodious voice began to chant in exquisite tones the Tablet of Visitation. As the words reverberated through the vaulted chambers, Ali felt warm tears trickle freely from his eyes and down his cheeks. The boy was not sad, and he made no noise. The tears flowed easily as though they had been trapped inside for a long time.

Ali stayed in the room for several minutes after his parents had left, and when he emerged from the building, they were waiting for him with proud faces. He could not help smiling when his eyes met theirs. Husayn suggested that they stroll around as he explained to Ali, "Someday people will come here from all over the world. There will be beautiful gardens that will call out from this mountain to tell the people of the world that something important has happened."

"I hope it doesn't change too much," said Ali. "I like it the way it is." Nahid and Husayn both laughed with Ali, and the three of them decided to walk toward the head of the mountain where Bahá'u'lláh had revealed the Tablet of Carmel near the Carmelite monastery.

The path led further up the mountain and then along toward the promontory, almost directly above the Cave of Elijah. The walk took about half an hour, but they all agreed that the climb was well worth their trouble because the view was breathtaking. They could see for many miles on both sides of the mountain. The sea spread out before them on one side, and on the other they could view 'Akká and the bay. They could see the Shrine of the Báb to the right and the Carmelite monastery to their left.

"It is said that when Bahá'u'lláh chanted the Tablet of Carmel on this spot, His voice was so loud that the monks came out of their building to see what was happening," said Husayn.

"I do not know the Tablet of Carmel," said Ali.

"That's because it's in Arabic," said Husayn. "But let's rest here awhile, and I'll tell you about it," said Husayn, and the three made themselves as comfortable as they could sitting on the cloth that Husayn had carried. "On one of those four trips to Carmel," Husayn began, "Bahá'u'lláh pitched His tent very near this spot. And during that visit, He stood here and revealed a tablet which describes how important this mountain will be in the future of the Bahá'í Faith."

"Is that why you were saving this visit for the last part of my study?" said Ali. "Is that why this is really the last link?"

"In a way," said Husayn. "But the Covenant which Bahá'u'lláh left us has many parts. As you know, He left 'Abdu'l-Bahá to lead us, but He also designed the foundation of the religion itself, an institution that will guide humankind long after 'Abdu'l-Bahá is gone. Of course, Bahá'u'lláh left us laws and hundreds of tablets to give us spiritual insight and advice. But He also left us this mountain as well, and He foretold that gift in the Tablet of Carmel.

"For example, one verse says, 'Haste thee, O Carmel, for lo, the light of the countenance of God, the Ruler of the Kingdom of Names and Fashioner of the heavens, hath been lifted upon thee.' Then in another place it says, 'Rejoice, for God hath in this Day established upon thee His throne, hath made thee the dawning place of His signs and the dayspring of the evidences of His Revelation.'"

"Does that mean that the Shrine of the Báb is the 'throne' He talks about?"

"I think it means more than that," said Nahid. "It seems to say that the world center for the Bahá'í Faith will someday be here to guide all humankind, though I'm sure it will take time and patience, just as it took time and patience for 'Abdu'l-Bahá to build the Shrine of the Báb."

Ali wanted to believe his mother, but it seemed such a far fetched notion that in his heart he wondered if such a thing could really happen.

Sensing Ali's doubt, Husayn said, "Look at it this way, Ali, what do you think the people of 'Akká would have said if you had told them forty-four years ago that the same Prisoner Who was being taken to the prison in chains would someday leave the walls of 'Akká with great respect, that He would go across the bay to Mount Carmel to show His son where to build a beautiful shrine, and that His followers would spread throughout the world?"

Ali laughed. He understood his father's point. "Or who would have thought that the remains of the Báb and Anís that had been left in the streets of Tabríz for the wild dogs to devour would have ended up here on this mountain," said Ali.

"Quite true. So you see that this mountain is not the last link, but it is a very important one."

"How long after He came here did Bahá'u'lláh die?" asked Ali.

"About nine months before He died Bahá'u'lláh told 'Abdu'l-Bahá that His mission was almost over and that He was ready to leave this world. Then, in the spring of 1892, 'Abdu'l-Bahá received a message from His father, saying, 'I am not well, come to Me and bring Khánum.' At the time, Bahá'u'lláh was at Bahjí, and He wanted to see 'Abdu'l-Bahá and Bahíyyih Khánum, who had served Bahá'u'lláh so faithfully all her life."

"Was He dying?" asked Ali.

"He had a fever that would not go away. It continued for about twenty days, and when it worsened, it was clear that He was not going to recover. Naturally, all the Bahá'ís around Him were sorrowful and afraid, but Bahá'u'lláh was very calm and peaceful. You see, the Bahá'ís didn't know what would happen to their Faith when Bahá'u'lláh died, but Bahá'u'lláh did, because in the Book of His Covenant, He had left clear instructions for them to turn to 'Abdu'l-Bahá.

"During the final days, Bahá'u'lláh called into His room members of His family and some of the other Bahá'ís who were there at the time. He was very weak, but with some help He managed to sit up in bed and talk to them. 'I am well pleased with you all,' He told them. 'You have rendered many services and have been very assiduous in your labors. You have come here every morning and every evening. May God assist you to remain united. May He aid you to exalt the Cause of the Lord of being.'

"Most of them didn't understand why Bahá'u'lláh should speak to them about being united, but others among them did, because already there had been talk about which of them might lead the Bahá'ís after Bahá'u'lláh died. What they did not know was that they would never be able to talk with Bahá'u'lláh again. Six days later, on the 29th of May, 1892, at about 3 A.M., the hour of dawn, Bahá'u'lláh departed from this world. But soon afterwards His followers learned that He had not left them alone.

"That afternoon, a telegram was sent to the Sulṭán saying simply, 'The Sun of Bahá has set.' They were then given permission by the government to bury Bahá'u'lláh at Bahjí."

"But why did they need permission?" asked Ali. "Because officially Bahá'u'lláh was still a prisoner of the Ottoman government," said Nahid. "Bahá'u'lláh's body was laid to rest shortly after sunset that same day."

"What did the Bahá'ís do then?" asked Ali.

"They did not know what to do. For the next week crowds of visitors came to the shrine to show their respect for Bahá'u'lláh. Rich and poor, Christians, Jews, Muslims, all who knew of the kindness and love which Bahá'u'lláh had brought to their land. Everyone who knew Him was greatly saddened by His death, and Nabíl, who had loved and served Bahá'u'lláh since the early days in Baghdád, was so grief-stricken that he drowned himself in the sea.

"On the ninth day after the Ascension of Bahá'u'lláh, however, the cloud of confusion and turmoil lifted, because according to the instructions of Bahá'u'lláh, on this day His Will was opened. In front of nine witnesses—some of them members of the family, together with a few of His companions—the Kitáb-i-'Ahd was unsealed.

"That afternoon the Will was taken to the outer room of the shrine, where many Bahá'ís had gathered. The son of Mírzá Músá held the tablet and began to read to the anxiously waiting believers, who listened to hear what instructions Bahá'u'lláh had given them. As the tablet was read, the doubts and confusion evaporated like a mist in morning sunlight. The troubled hearts and minds of the Bahá'ís were calmed as they heard that Bahá'u'lláh had appointed 'Abdu'l-Bahá, His Most Great Branch, to be the Center of the Covenant, the One to Whom all the Bahá'ís should turn for guidance and leadership."

"Muḥammad-'Alí didn't say anything?" asked Ali.

"I'm sure that in his heart he was already plotting what to do, but no one there questioned the tablet. How could they? Its meaning was absolutely clear. No, everyone was immediately obedient to 'Abdu'l-Bahá," said Husayn. "And the chain of the Covenant continued as another link was added."

"So, in a way, the story of Bahá'u'lláh never stops, does it?" asked Ali. "There is no last link."

"The religion of God never stops," said Nahid. "His Covenant is never-ending, and we are all a part of that never-ending story."

"That means we are links too—in a way we are!" said Ali with a sudden sparkle in his eyes. "We are part of the history of the Bahá'í Faith!"

"Certainly," said Husayn. "That's why we must always consider our role in that history as we live our lives, because while it is a privilege to be a part of that history, it is also a serious responsibility."

For Ali the summer had been a long journey from the hill of Tell al-Fakhkhár to Mount Carmel, but it had been a joyful one, a journey the boy would never forget. He still did not know whether he had found the key that would unlock the gates of 'Akká for him, but for the moment it did not seem to matter. His belief, his faith, his understanding of who he was had now become something clear and vital to him in a way that it never had been before.

Bahá'u'lláh was no longer a shadowy hero. He was a figure of flesh and bone Who had walked the earth, and Ali felt proud to follow in those hallowed footsteps along the streets of 'Akká. For Ali, this discovery was well worth all the study, all the thinking and praying. He was no longer simply the member of a Bahá'í family, the son of Bahá'í parents. He himself, 'Alí-Riḍáy-i-Mashhadí, was a Bahá'í in his own way. Ali now knew that he, too, was a part of the story of Bahá'u'lláh.

16

The Golden Key

Hand in hand, Ali and Neda climbed the hill of Tell al-Fakhkhár. Because both of them were so busy these days, they rarely found time to spend an afternoon doing as they pleased. But Neda had insisted, and once Ali was out of the city and away from the routine of his work, he realized once again how wise Neda was. Almost as soon as he had passed through the city gates he felt more relaxed. He even took note of how beautiful the trees were, swaying in the November wind.

It had been a long time since he had visited the hill. At twenty-three years of age he had so many responsibilities that he never had enough time to do everything that needed to be done. He worked hard at his father's store. And when he had time, he studied so that he might become a doctor someday. But today he had taken Neda's advice, and he was glad of it.

As they reached the top of the hill, he noticed the sheen of her long black hair blowing from beneath her scarf. And as he observed her grace when she walked, Ali found himself marveling again at her rare combination of qualities—her beauty and wit combined with her unmatched charm and wisdom. Often he thought how lucky he had been to marry her, even though they had barely enough money to live on and almost no furniture in their little two-room apartment. Both families had been surprised when Ali and Neda had asked for permission to get married, not because the parents objected in any way, but because they sometimes still thought of Ali and Neda as youngsters or as little friends playing games on the beach with Moayyed.

Ali and Neda found a grassy spot on the hilltop, and Ali spread out the cloth he had brought along. They sat down and looked out over the old buildings of 'Akká. "It's changed so little," said Ali. "I can't really see much difference between the way it looks now and the way it looked eleven years ago when I used to come here."

"When you had your dream?" asked Neda.

"My dream?" said Ali.

"Don't tell me you could have forgotten!" she said. "How could you possibly forget such a dream?"

Suddenly Ali remembered his dream about the gold key. He had not really forgotten it, but it had been such a long time since then, and so many things had happened that it rarely came to mind any more. In 1913 after 'Abdu'l-Bahá's return from the journey to Europe and America, there had been the year of war when the Turkish government once again treated 'Abdu'l-Bahá and the other Bahá'ís with suspicion and hatred. The government had even threatened to execute 'Abdu'l-Bahá, and the Bahá'ís feared for His life.

Then over the next several years the conflagration of the First World War inched ever closer to the Holy Land. In June of 1914 when Ali was fourteen, 'Abdu'l-Bahá instructed the Bahá'í pilgrims to leave the Holy Land. Soon afterwards 'Abdu'l-Bahá directed the Bahá'ís living in 'Akká and Haifa to move to the countryside—to the nearby Druze villages—where they would be safe. Most went to the village of Abú-Sinán.

During that same time Ali's cousin, Hasan, whose parents had been martyred in Yazd, came to live with Ali and his family and went with them to Abú-Sinán. Ali and Hasan soon came to look upon each other as brothers, and the two spent what would be one of the most delightful years of their lives together with Ali's parents in the small farming village of 'Adasíyyih. Then, in May of 1916, the Bahá'ís received word from Haifa that it was safe for everyone to return to their homes.

But the threat of tragedy had not diminished for 'Abdu'l-Bahá. Over the course of the next two years the Holy Land itself became a subject of contention as the British expeditionary force contended with the Turkish forces in Gaza and the Holy Land. 'Abdu'l-Bahá became a hero to the local populace by using the Bahá'í farms around the Sea of Galilee to grow wheat to feed the local citizens.

In the meanwhile, the Covenant-breakers had convinced the Turkish officials who governed the Holy Land that 'Abdu'l-Bahá was a dangerous enemy. As a result of these accusations, Turkish authorities threatened to crucify 'Abdu'l-Bahá and His family on Mount Carmel. But when General Allenby, the head of the British forces, received word that the Turks were threatening 'Abdu'l-Bahá's life, he immediately sent his troops to Haifa and captured the city, thereby saving 'Abdu'l-Bahá's life.

After the war ended in 1918, Ali and Hasan worked in Husayn's shop in 'Akká. Ali had decided he wanted to become a physician, but he knew he would have to delay his plans until the aftermath of the war had subsided and he had saved enough money to go to a university somewhere.

Less than three years later, the local Bahá'í community was shaken to the core by the unexpected death of 'Abdu'l-Bahá. After a funeral attended by a mass of citizens who had come to love the Master, 'Abdu'l-Bahá's body was taken up Mount Carmel, where it was entombed in the Shrine of the Báb in the chamber next to that where the remains of the Báb lay.

Fortunately for the Bahá'í Faith, 'Abdu'l-Bahá, like His father before Him, had left written instructions for the Bahá'ís in His Will by appointing as Guardian of the Bahá'í Faith His eldest grandson, the twenty-four-year-old Shoghi Effendi Rabbani. Now the Bahá'ís began to turn to the young Guardian for guidance, just as they had done previously with Bahá'u'lláh and 'Abdu'l-Bahá.

Perhaps because the Guardian was such a young man, some of the Bahá'ís who had been accustomed to the leadership of 'Abdu'l-Bahá had difficulty in accepting this appointment, even though it was made by 'Abdu'l-Bahá Himself. Nevertheless, under the strong and able direction of the Guardian, the institutions which Bahá'u'lláh had designed in His writings were being formed with patient care all around the world. Often word came to Haifa of new territories where the Bahá'í Faith had been accepted and where spiritual assemblies had been formed.

As he sat on the hill considering all of the things that had taken place since his dream, Ali shook his head in wonder and smiled. These days he was usually so busy that he rarely had time to think about how much change he had seen since that summer in 1912 when he had devoted himself to studying the story of Bahá'u'lláh's life. But now as he recalled the vivid images from his remarkable dream, he remembered the glowing points of light that he had viewed from the stallion, and he also remembered the halos of light that had emanated from 'Akká.

"What *are* you thinking about?" said Neda, noticing the pensive look on her husband's face.

"About that dream—about how much has happened since then. Remember how anxious I was to find all the answers then, to discover the gold key that would release me from the walls of 'Akká?"

"Who could blame you? It was a magnificent dream!"

"Perhaps that steed of patience is a beast I've finally learned to ride," said Ali.

Neda smiled tenderly and placed a gentle hand on Ali's arm. "You are a fine man, Ali. You are indeed patient. Perhaps that was the key after all, the patience you learned."

"I don't know," said Ali. "But what does it matter? After all, we are happy here, and the dream helped me learn about Bahá'u'lláh in a way that I might never have done otherwise."

"Still, I'll never forget it," said Neda. "I always felt as if it were my dream too. Of course, my dreams were always much clearer."

"What do you mean?" asked Ali.

"There were never many symbols in my dreams. There was rarely any need to ask anyone what my dreams meant. I knew as soon as I dreamed them."

"I remember once when we were standing on your doorstep," said Ali. "It was the day you invited me to meet your uncle. You told me then you had dreamed something important, but you wouldn't tell me what it was. Do you remember that?"

Neda smiled broadly, and her face reddened slightly with embarrassment. "Yes, I most certainly do remember."

"Well?"

"Well what?"

"Don't you think I've waited patiently long enough? Can you tell me now what the dream was?"

"I'll give you a hint," she said coyly. "It came true."

Ali looked puzzled. "Was it something about your family?"

"It was about you!" she said emphatically.

"About me?"

"About the two of us—I dreamed that we were going to be married!"

Ali immediately broke into laughter and embraced his wife. "You're the secretive one," he said. "All the time you knew and didn't say a single word?"

"I knew what I had dreamed. I didn't know it would come true," said Neda.

The two continued to talk about Neda's dream for a while, and then she rested her head on Ali's lap. It had been an extremely hard day for her, and before too long she was asleep. Ali folded the cloth over her feet to ward off the cool autumn air. Then he scanned the countryside and watched the small clouds that hurried over head.

Ali thought about his beloved grandfather, who was now confined to a bed. "How imperceptibly time passes," he thought.

"How like a thief it is, stealing our youth, our loved ones, some of our memories. Even when things seem the same, they aren't. They're always changing."

He thought about his parents. He realized that he did not picture them as being any different from the way they were a decade before, but when he would look at a photograph from those years, he could see the changes in their faces.

It was difficult to see his grandfather in bed. He could never get used to that. For someone so alive, so spirited, so animated to be confined to one room seemed so unnatural, so unjust. Moayyed could still read, but only with great difficulty. Yet every time Ali visited him, his grandfather would have something new and exciting to share that he had discovered in the writings of Bahá'u'lláh or 'Abdu'l-Bahá.

Ali looked down at Neda. He thought once more about the dream, the strange and marvelous vision that had meant so much to him during his twelfth year. He wondered why he had not thought of it for so long. It was not because he no longer believed in dreams. Perhaps because he was content where he was and because he was already doing important work for Shoghi Effendi, he had set aside those romantic visions of his youth. Soon he and Neda hoped to have children, and someday it might be possible for them to go to a place that had a university where Ali could study medicine and become a doctor.

Suddenly Neda opened her eyes and sat straight up as if something had startled her. Her eyes were wide open and she took Ali's hand. "Ali!" she said.

"What's the matter?" he asked, surprised by the intense look on her face.

"Nothing is the matter!" she said. "Everything is fine! The key has come!"

"What?" he said.

"The key!" she repeated. "The key in your dream. It's here! I know it is!"

"On the hill?"

"No, no. In 'Akká!"

Ali smiled and took Neda's hands. "You aren't awake yet," he said. "We were talking about the key before you fell asleep."

"I know we were talking about it," said Neda, "but I tell you, it has come! I know it!"

"Neda, Neda," said Ali, trying to calm her, "not all dreams come true, you know. Not all dreams tell the future."

"I know that," she said insistently, "but this is no dream. I'm sure of it!"

Ali tried to assure her that the key in his dream was but a symbol. But Neda would not be convinced, and so they immediately got up, folded the cloth, and walked back toward 'Akká.

In about half an hour they had reached their apartment, and as Ali was unlocking the front door, Neda noticed the corner of an envelope on the threshold. "What's that?" she said, and picked up what appeared to be a letter. Ali recognized the envelope as being the kind of stationery that the Guardian used.

"I think it's from Shoghi Effendi," said Ali as he opened the letter. Then Ali looked at Neda and said in mock seriousness, "I think I feel a key inside!"

She smiled back. "Don't be surprised if there is, my young Persian friend!"

Ali scanned the letter, and his face became more serious.

"What is it?" she asked.

He took Neda's hand. "It's a copy of a letter from the Guardian to the Bahá'ís of America. It was sent a few days ago to commemorate the Ascension of 'Abdu'l-Bahá."

"What does it say?" she asked.

"It's dated November 24, 1924. It has this quotation from 'Abdu'l-Bahá: 'It behooveth them not to rest for a moment, neither to seek repose. They must disperse themselves in every land, pass by every clime, and travel throughout all regions.' Then the Guardian says, 'Let us make it the dominating passion of our life. Let us scatter to the uttermost corners of the earth; sacrifice our personal interests, comforts, tastes and pleasures; mingle with the divers kindreds and peoples of the world; familiarize ourselves with their manners, traditions, thoughts and customs. . . .'"

Both Ali and Neda were silent for a moment. Then Ali took her hands in his and looked deeply into her eyes.

"Are we thinking the same thing?" said Neda.

"That we must leave here?" asked Ali.

"Yes!"

"Do you think we should?" asked Ali.

"Do we have any choice?"

"No!" said Ali, and they embraced.

That evening they said many prayers together and talked for long hours about where they might go and what they would have to do to prepare for such a journey. They wondered how their parents would react to the idea and what it would be like to leave their native land and all the people and places they loved so dearly.

They could not sleep because of the excitement. The more they talked, the more they realized that it would not be easy to leave so much behind, to make a new home in a strange land far away from 'Akká and Mount Carmel, far away from all the holy places and all their friends and family.

First one would be awake, then the other. Several times they picked up the letter again and read it through, and each time they read it, any traces of doubt that remained about whether or not they should go began to fade. Finally, just before dawn, Neda made a fresh pot of tea, and they discussed what they knew would be the most difficult step in their decision—telling their parents.

"I'm sure they will understand, don't you think so?" Ali said.

"I know they will understand how important the Guardian's letter is, but my parents have so few family here in 'Akká. It will be very hard for them. I'm afraid they may be very upset." She looked across the table at Ali. Her eyes were moist. "Of course, it's not as if we will never see them again," said Neda.

"That's true," said Ali, "and yet, who knows where we'll go? It may be to the other side of the world."

Neda stood up from the table and walked to the window. It was getting light outside, and streaks of rose-colored clouds brightened the morning sky. "Then they'll just have to come with us," said Neda almost inaudibly.

"What?" said Ali, not quite sure he understood her. Neda turned around and with a smile of relief repeated, "Then they will simply come with us—that's all there is to it!"

"Of course!" said Ali, standing up and embracing Neda. "That's perfect! That's the answer!"

For a while they stood holding on to each other in the quiet of the morning. Then Neda looked up at Ali and whispered, "Do you think we could take a few more friends and perhaps the Shrines as well?"

And so the morning went, with Neda and Ali making plans and writing out lists of what they would need to do. Later in the day, they paid a visit to his parents and afterwards to Neda's, but they did not tell them the news. Instead, they invited them for dinner that evening to partake of "Neda's famous pilau and a 'grand surprise,'" they told them.

All four parents thought they knew what the surprise was. They were sure that Neda and Ali must be expecting a baby. And so, when the evening came, the parents arrived together trying to act as if they didn't know the young couple's secret, even though they were positive they did.

Because they were all so excited, no one could eat very much of the pilau. At last, when the dishes were removed and tea and spice cake had been served, Ali stood and announced, "As I told you, we have an announcement for you." But when he saw the beaming faces of all four parents, he stopped and looked at Neda with his hand to his mouth. He suddenly realized what they were thinking.

For an instant he wanted to stop and prepare them, to tell them that what they were expecting was *not* the surprise. But there was no way to do that except to tell them the truth.

"Neda and I have decided to pioneer to another country."

Faces dropped. Nahid grabbed Husayn's hand. Neda's parents looked at each other in shock and disbelief. There was complete silence in the room. Neda quickly tried to explain about the letter, how it seemed to be the answer to Ali's dream. But the parents were only half listening. In one instant they had lost the grandchild they had expected, and now, instead of a grandchild, they were having to face the possibility of losing Ali and Neda as well.

"I . . . I suppose we knew this might happen someday," said Nahid. "I think we knew that twelve years ago when you had your dream. But it always seemed like something far off, something in the distant future." She tried to smile a little. "I suppose the future has finally come."

"We are all proud of your dedication," said Husayn, "but do you really think this is wise or prudent?"

Neda's parents reiterated Husayn's concern, and soon Ali and Neda found themselves being lectured about the perils of going out into the world and leaving the sacred precincts of the Holy Land. Even when Ali got the Guardian's letter and read it to them, they commented that the Guardian's advice was really intended for the Americans, not for them.

Finally, Neda, who had been silent through all the commotion, could take no more. She stood, held up her hands to halt the discussion, and said emphatically, "Wait!" She paused until everyone was quiet. "But there's something else. We want all of you to come with us!"

There was silence again. The parents looked at one another. Finally, Husayn said, "You want us to come?"

"Yes," said Neda. "All of you. Ali and I have decided."

"Do we have nothing whatever to say about this?" said Neda's mother with a smile. "Nothing at all?"

"Nothing whatsoever," said Neda, taking her mother's hands.

"What kind of consultation is that?" said Husayn.

"The very best kind," said Ali.

"If only we *could* go," said Neda's father.

"But why can't you?" said Neda, seeing that he was serious.

"How will you go to your new home?" asked Husayn.

"By boat, I suppose," said Ali.

"And how will you buy your tickets?" asked Husayn.

"We have some money saved," said Neda. "Not much, but enough to . . ."

"Enough to buy four more tickets?" asked Nahid.

Ali and Neda looked at each other. In their enthusiasm and excitement, they had not even considered such practical matters, especially the fact that neither family had much money. It would be hard enough for Ali and Neda to pay for themselves and to find work once they reached their destination. But Husayn's father and Neda's father both had businesses to run. They could not simply close up their shops and expect to start over again.

"Now, now, my children," said Nahid, comforting the young couple, "once you get settled, then we will see. Why, when you become a famous doctor, Ali, you will have enough money to come and get us in your own private boat!"

"You mean you accept their decision?" asked Husayn.

"How can I not accept it?" said Nahid, reaching to pick up the letter. "The Guardian has given his advice, and they are following it. How can they go wrong?" She went to Neda and embraced her.

Soon almost everyone was embracing or crying or both. When the emotions had subsided a little, the parents helped Ali and Neda decide how they could go about planning for such an uncertain future. But the main issue was settled to the satisfaction of everyone. The parents would not go with them immediately, but there was the hope that later they might be able to follow. Then they would all be together again.

The next few days were filled with much activity. Ali informed Shoghi Effendi of his desire to go pioneering, and the Guardian suggested some places they might go. He even gave Ali a list of towns and villages where it would be useful for Bahá'í families to settle. Some of the places were in large cities, while others were small villages. Some of the localities were in Persia, while others were in distant lands.

Ali studied the list with Neda, looking for some sign that would let them know which would be the best place for them. They knew they wanted to go where Ali could study medicine. But there were so many other things to consider. They borrowed books which had information on some of the cities on the list that had universities, and for several evenings they studied what was written about each of these places. On one of these evenings as Ali was thumbing through a book on India, he stopped suddenly on a page that had a picture of buildings that looked familiar to him. "Where have we seen this picture before?" he asked Neda.

She studied the picture carefully. "I don't think I have ever seen this picture before," she said.

"It looks so familiar to me, especially those buildings," said Ali, pointing to one particular part of the picture. But he could not remember where he had seen them or why they should be familiar to him, so he put the book aside and continued to work until late that evening, when they finally went to bed.

Neda went to sleep quickly, but Ali still could not get the picture out of his mind. He had the feeling that if he just thought long enough and hard enough, it would come to him. Suddenly he said aloud, "My dream!"

"What?" said Neda, awakened from sleep.

"In my dream, the dream about the gold key, when I was coming back toward the earth, I saw those buildings!"

"What buildings?" she said, rubbing her eyes.

"As I came down, I was heading toward one of those spots of light, remember? And I got closer and closer until I woke up. But before I woke up, I did see something very clearly. It was those very same buildings that are in the picture I showed you today!"

"Are you quite sure?"

"I'm positive. The buildings in that picture are the same buildings!" Ali got up from the bed and stumbled in the dark to light the lantern in the room.

"What are you doing?" asked Neda.

"I must find that picture," said Ali. "I want to find out what city it was. Do you remember?"

"No, I don't," said Neda, who got up and joined him in searching through the book. Together they turned pages nervously until at last they found it.

"Bombay!" said Neda. "Here it is—Bombay, India!"

"What do you think?" said Ali.

"I think we may have found our new home," said Neda.

Several weeks passed as Neda and Ali confirmed that Bombay would indeed be a good place for them. Then they began to make all the many preparations necessary for their journey. There were passports to obtain and a whole array of other official documents. There were arrangements to make for the voyage and a few belongings to pack.

As the time for their departure drew near a month later, the Bahá'ís in 'Akká and Haifa held several feasts in their honor at which many farewells were said and many more tears were shed. Ali and Neda visited the Shrine of Bahá'u'lláh and all the other special places so dear to their hearts, places they knew they would miss in their travels. Most important of all, they spent as much time as they possibly could with their parents and friends.

"I think Ali's dream has come true at last," said Nahid to Husayn one evening after one of their visits.

"Yes," said Husayn. "I would have to agree. I suppose all of his study and patience have at last won for him his golden key."

"I'm glad we will still have Hasan here with us in 'Akká," said Nahid. "Though you know how he admires Ali. I imagine this decision will cause him to think about leaving. He is already talking of pioneering."

"Even if we had children here, I would miss Ali just as much," said Husayn. "He was always a special child—always asking questions, always so full of curiosity." Husayn stopped. A tear rolled down his cheek. "And now, now that he is grown and works with me, I find that he has also become my friend and companion." Husayn stopped. He could talk no more and embraced Nahid.

"I will miss his smile," said Nahid, her eyes welling up. "I will miss that face and smile."

Husayn looked across the room at a photograph on the table. It showed several Persian children and an old man. They were sitting on a stone wall, and they were all smiling and waving their hands, looking for all the world as if they would never grow up or grow old. But they had.

The time neared for Ali and Neda to leave, and, unavoidably, the day of their departure arrived at last. They were to set sail in the evening, and so that same morning when Ali was sure everything was in order, he went to visit one whom he suspected he would never see again.

Ali walked alone down the ancient streets of 'Akká that he knew so well, streets that had echoed his footsteps for so many years. His pace slowed as he approached the apartment that had been magical to him as a child. He took a deep breath, sighed, then knocked softly on the familiar wooden door.

An elderly serving woman opened the door and smiled when she saw Ali. Without a word, she took him down a musty hallway and into a dimly lit bedroom where a very old man lay. He was reading with great difficulty through a magnifying glass. The old man was hard of hearing and looked up only slightly darkened by Ali's appearance.

When he recognized his visitor, a radiant look transformed the wrinkled, tired face, and Moayyed stretched out his feeble arms to his grandson. Ali walked over to give his beloved grandfather a firm hug.

"So, you have found your gold key at last," said Moayyed.

"Yes, Grandfather. With your help, I have."

"With my help and the help of a few thousand martyrs, not to mention your noble parents," said Moayyed, chuckling.

Ali laughed. Then his face became serious again. "You know what I mean, Grandfather. You know how much I love you. Someday I hope I can be half the teacher you are."

Moayyed looked proudly at his grandson and patted his arm as Ali sat on the bed beside him. "You were a good student, Ali, you and Hasan. I will miss you terribly. But when I have passed on to the next world, remember that you represent more than just yourself. You represent all of us who have loved you and taught you."

"I will remember, Grandfather. I promise."

"You are never alone, Ali. Don't forget that. No matter how far away you and Neda go, no matter how lonely you will feel sometimes in that strange land. Nothing in this world can take away the love we have for you. But no matter what happens, no matter how difficult life becomes for you, you must never allow anything to interfere with your faith in Bahá'u'lláh. You can't control many things in this life, but over that, over your faith, you have command."

Moayyed stopped talking. His serious look turned once more into a wrinkled smile. "You are my treasure, Ali. You are my *greatest* treasure."

It was not a dark steed with a short-cropped mane. It was an old steamer on which 'Alí-Riḍáy-i-Ma<u>sh</u>hadí left 'Akká to begin the first leg of his journey to Bombay. Early that evening as the ship hoisted anchor and began moving out from the Bay of Haifa, Ali and Neda watched the lights from the town gradually fade in the distance, but they did not say much. They stood against the railing not wishing to turn away from what might be their last glimpse of this precious land for a long time.

"Well, I suppose I never did become a great hero, did I?" said Ali wistfully as he looked across the water.

"What do you mean?"

"When I was on the hill—the time I had the dream—I wanted more than anything to be a hero, like Mullá Ḥusayn, or Badí', or Quddús."

"But you found the key, didn't you?"

"Yes," said Ali, "I suppose I did."

"And you rode the steed for twelve long years."

"What do you mean?"

"The steed of patience," said Neda with a smile.

"Oh, that. I'm not so sure I was patient, really. I just forgot about it—the key and the dream."

"Perhaps that's the whole idea," said Neda, "to become so patient that it no longer requires much effort. That's when patience has become a part of you."

Ali looked at his wife as she spoke. As usual, she was right. What was more, with the full moon across the water reflecting off of her face, she looked darkly beautiful.

"Besides, you *are* a hero," she continued. "In fact, we both are."

"Why do you say that?" asked Ali.

"I'll show you," she said. She pulled from a bag she was holding a folded piece of paper. "This is a gift to us from your grandfather. He told me to show it to you, but only after we had left."

"Have you already seen it?" asked Ali.

"Yes," said Neda with a grin.

"You're good at finding letters, aren't you? What does it say?"

She moved over under a deck light. "It's not very long. It's a quotation from Bahá'u'lláh. It reads, 'They that have forsaken their country for the purpose of teaching Our Cause—these shall the Faithful spirit strengthen through its power. . . . By my life! No act however great can compare with it, except such deeds as have been ordained by God, the All-Powerful, the Most Mighty. Such a service is, indeed, the prince of all goodly deeds and the ornament of every goodly act.'"

"Well we're not quite heroes yet," said Ali. "We have left our country, but we really haven't taught anybody in Bombay yet."

"But we will," said Neda, taking his hand. "We will."

Glossary

'Abá: A cloak or mantle.

'Abdu'l-Bahá: "Servant of Bahá." Bahá'u'lláh's eldest son, and the first to believe in Him. He was appointed by Bahá'u'lláh in His Will and Testament to be His successor and the Center of His Covenant.

Abu'l-Qásim: The gardener of the Riḍván Garden near 'Akká in this story, based on a Bahá'í of the same name.

A<u>dh</u>án: "Announcement." The Muslim call to prayer, proclaimed five times each day by the muezzin.

'Akká: An ancient city north of Mount Carmel in present-day Israel that serves as the setting for the story. It is here that Ali lives, and it was here that Bahá'u'lláh spent the last twenty-four years of His life.

Alláh-u-Abhá: "God is Most Glorious." The Greatest Name, used sometimes as a greeting among Bahá'ís. It was adopted during the period of Bahá'u'lláh's exile in Adrianople to replace the Muslim *Alláh-u-Akbar,* which means "God is the Most Great."

Amanuensis: One who copies manuscripts or takes dictation. Bahá'u'lláh's sons 'Abdu'l-Bahá and Mírzá Mihdí served in this capacity, as did others, but the person who served continuously for the longest period as Bahá'u'lláh's amanuensis was Mírzá Áqá Ján.

Ásíyih <u>Kh</u>ánum: The wife of Bahá'u'lláh and the mother of 'Abdu'l-Bahá, Bahíyyih <u>Kh</u>ánum, and Mírzá Mihdí. She was surnamed Navváb (meaning "Highness") by Bahá'u'lláh, and He paid her the tribute of naming her His "perpetual consort in all the worlds of God."

Azalís: The followers of Ṣubḥ-i-Azal (Mírzá Yaḥyá), a half-brother of Bahá'u'lláh who attempted to destroy Bahá'u'lláh and the Bahá'í Faith.

Báb: "Gate." The title taken by Mírzá 'Alí-Muḥammad (1819–50), the Prophet and Forerunner of Bahá'u'lláh. A young merchant from <u>Sh</u>íráz, He declared His mission in 1844 and was executed in 1850.

Bábí: A follower of the Báb; of, or pertaining to, the religion of the Báb.

Bábíyyih: A house in Mas͟hhad belonging to Mírzá Muḥammad-Báqir-i-Qá'iní, an early convert to the Bábí Faith, who died at Fort S͟hayk͟h Ṭabarsí. Here people could learn about the Bábí religion.

Badas͟ht: A small village in Mázindarán where Bahá'u'lláh conducted a conference lasting twenty-two days, in June–July 1848, to proclaim the independence of the Bábí Faith from Islám, thus making clear that a new Dispensation in religion had begun.

Badí': A seventeen-year-old youth who delivered a tablet from Bahá'u'lláh to the S͟háh, knowing that this mission would result in his own death.

Bag͟hdád: The capital city of 'Iráq, then a province of the Ottoman Empire, to which Bahá'u'lláh was exiled in 1853. He lived there, except for a period of two years, until His further exile in 1863, recreating the Bábí community and revealing some of His most important writings. He called Bag͟hdád the "City of God."

Bahá: "Glory" or "Splendor." An Arabic word with the numerical value of nine, which is referred to in many prophecies of this Day. It is the title of Bahá'u'lláh and the root word of the Greatest Name, *Alláh-u-Abhá.*

Bahá'í: A follower of Bahá'u'lláh; of, or pertaining to, the Bahá'í Faith.

Bahá'u'lláh: "The Glory of God." A title of Mírzá Ḥusayn-'Alí (1817–92), the Prophet designated by the Báb as "Him Whom God will make manifest."

Bahíyyih K͟hánum: The devoted daughter of Bahá'u'lláh, entitled by Him the "Greatest Holy Leaf." Her entire life was spent assisting those around her—Bahá'u'lláh, 'Abdu'l-Bahá, and later the Guardian, Shoghi Effendi.

Bahjí: "Delight." Originally, the name given to a beautiful garden north of 'Akká. The name is now used to designate the mansion nearby, where Bahá'u'lláh lived from 1879 until His ascension in 1892. His shrine is adjacent to the mansion. Built by 'Údí K͟hammár for his own residence, after his death it was rented by 'Abdu'l-Bahá for a meager sum when it was abandoned during an epidemic. Later, it was purchased and is now a place of pilgrimage for Bahá'ís.

Blessed Perfection: One of the many titles used to designate Bahá'u'lláh.

Bombay: A major port city on the west coast of India.

Calligraphy: Beautiful penmanship, which, in Persian and Arabic writing, is treated as an art and is considered indicative of the writer's education and social status.

Caravansary: A place for travelers to stay; an inn, often a crude structure with little to offer but some shelter from the elements.

Carmel: See "Mount Carmel."

Certitude: Certainty or confidence. In discussions of religion, the term relates to a state of faith in which a person no longer has doubts about the validity of his or her beliefs.

Chant: A method of reciting holy scripture in which the verses are sung or intoned.

Covenant: A pact or agreement.

Darvísh Muḥammad: A name assumed by Bahá'u'lláh during His wanderings in the mountains of Kurdistán, April 1854–March 1856. He stayed in caves on a mountain called Sar-Galú and in a theological seminary when He came into the town of Sulaymáníyyih.

Dervish: "Poor one"; usually refers to a religious mendicant who lives simply and practices a mystical approach to religion. There are many orders of such mystics.

Exemplar: Refers to 'Abdu'l-Bahá.

Farman: An order, edict, or royal decree, such as that exiling Bahá'u'lláh and His companions to 'Akká and stating the conditions of their imprisonment. It was publicly read in the principal mosque of 'Akká.

Fort Shaykh Ṭabarsí: A Muslim shrine where 313 Bábís built a makeshift fort to defend themselves against the onslaught of the people of that vicinity, and later the attacks of government troops. Their defense lasted from October 12, 1848, until May 9, 1849.

Guardianship: An institution anticipated by Bahá'u'lláh and delineated by 'Abdu'l-Bahá in His Will and Testament, wherein He appointed Shoghi Effendi the Guardian and the Interpreter of the teachings. Shoghi Effendi served in these capacities after the passing of 'Abdu'l-Bahá in 1921 until his own death in 1957.

Haifa: A modern city at the foot of Mount Carmel, across the bay from 'Akká. In 1912, at the time of the story, it was only a small town.

Howdah: A litter or covered seat for travelers that is mounted on the back of a camel, mule, or other pack animal.

Ḥujjat: The Bábí leader who heroically rallied the Bábís at Zanján to defend themselves against the far superior forces of the government troops.

Imám: One of the twelve hereditary successors of the Prophet Muḥammad, according to Shí'ih Muslim belief.

'Írán: The country formerly called Persia.

Islám: The religion of Muḥammad.

Kitáb: "Book."

Kitáb-i-Aqdas: The Most Holy Book of Bahá'u'lláh, in which the laws and institutions of His future World Order are preserved. It was completed in 1873 while He was living in the house of 'Abbúd.

Kitáb-i-Badí': A book written by Bahá'u'lláh in Adrianople to defend His Faith and demonstrate the truth of His mission. It was addressed to a judge in Constantinople.

Kurds: Independent tribespeople who reside principally in Kurdistán. These proud people have often been unfriendly to Persians but became fast friends of Bahá'u'lláh during His sojourn there, 1854–56.

Lawḥ: "Tablet."

Lawḥ-i-Hawdaj: "Tablet of the Howdah," revealed by Bahá'u'lláh on the journey from Baghdád to Constantinople, when He first sighted the Black Sea.

Letters of the Living: The first eighteen disciples of the Báb. Among the better known are Mullá Ḥusayn, the first Letter; Quddús, the last, but the first in rank; and Ṭáhirih, the only woman of the group and a well-known poetess.

Maiden: The symbol of the "Most Great Spirit," the figure through whom the Voice of God revealed Itself to Bahá'u'lláh; analogous to the Burning Bush (Moses), the Dove (Christ), and the Angel Gabriel (Muḥammad).

Manifestation: A Prophet or Messenger of God. His purpose is to further the divine education of humankind by renewing spiritual teachings and revising social ordinances to comply with the changing conditions of humanity. The Manifestations live exemplary lives, have innate knowledge, and are the means by which we on this plane of existence come to know God and make both individual and social progress. Manifestations mentioned in this story are Christ, Muḥammad, the Báb, and Bahá'u'lláh.

Martyr: One who willingly gives up his life rather than renounce his religious beliefs.

Mashhad: The capital city of the province of Khurásán in northeastern 'Írán. In our story, the hometown of Ali's parents. For Muslims it is a holy city, as it has within it the shrine of the eighth Imám. The word means "a place of martyrdom." It was here that Mullá Ḥusayn did much of his teaching, and it is thought that the three Magi (Zoroastrians) set out from here in their search for the infant Jesus.

Masjid: A mosque, temple, or place of worship for Muslims.

Mázindarán: A province in the north-central part of 'Írán where Bahá'u'lláh sometimes lived.

Mazra'ih: "Farm" or "field"; refers to the house about seven kilometers north of 'Akká where Bahá'u'lláh lived immediately after leaving the confines of the city of 'Akká in 1877. He stayed there for about two years.

Mihdí (Mahdí): "The One Who is guided"; the Promised One of Islám.

Mírzá: A title meaning "the son of Amír." When used before a name, it simply means "Mr."; when added to a name, it signifies a prince.

Mírzá-'Alí-Muḥammad: See "Báb."

Mírzá Áqá Ján: The amanuensis of Bahá'u'lláh for forty years.

Mírzá Buzurg: The father of Bahá'u'lláh, also called Mírzá 'Abbás.

Mírzá Ḥusayn-'Alí: The given name of Bahá'u'lláh. It combines the names of the third and first Imáms.

Mírzá Mihdí: A son of Bahá'u'lláh and younger brother of 'Abdu'l-Bahá, known as the Purest Branch. He died at twenty-two years of age in June 1870 after falling through the roof of the prison of 'Akká.

Mírzá Muḥammad-'Alí: A half-brother of 'Abdu'l-Bahá. He broke the Covenant of Bahá'u'lláh by openly refusing to accept the appointment of 'Abdu'I-Bahá as Center of the Covenant.

Mírzá Músá: The faithful brother of Bahá'u'lláh who was a constant source of assistance and support to Him and the other members of the family.

Mírzá Yaḥyá: Entitled Ṣubḥ-i-Azal, "Morn of Eternity"; a faithless younger half-brother of Bahá'u'lláh. Urged on by Siyyid Muḥammad of Iṣfahán, he was a constant source of disruption and distress to the Bahá'í community. Although the "nominee" of the Báb and the "recognized chief" of the Bábí community until the appearance of "Him Whom God will make manifest" (Bahá'u'lláh), he consistently rejected and misused his responsibility.

Mosque: A place of worship for Muslims; see Masjid.

Mount Carmel: A mountain long regarded as a holy place by Egyptians, Jews, and Christians alike. The mountain ends abruptly at the sea at Haifa. The Shrine of the Báb, a well as the World Administrative Center of the Bahá'í Faith, is located on the mountain overlooking the center of Haifa and the bay beyond.

Muezzin: In Islám, one who calls the faithful to prayer. He mounts the tower or minaret of the mosque and chants the call at five specified times each day.

Muḥammad: The Prophet or Manifestation of God (A.D. 570–632) Who founded the religion of Islám and revealed the Qur'án. His name means "highly praised." His followers are known as Muslims.

Mujtahid: A doctor of Islámic law; these men usually receive their diplomas from eminent jurists of Karbilá and Najaf in 'Iráq.

Mullá: A Muslim priest, theologian, or judge.

Mullá Ḥusayn: The first to believe in the Báb, hence the title Bábu'l-Báb ("Gate of the Gate") given to him by the Báb. Born about 1813, he was a student of Siyyid Kaẓim for nine years, then taught the Bábí Faith for nearly five years until his martyrdom in 1849 at Fort Shaykh Ṭabarsí.

Munírih Khánum: The wife of 'Abdu'l-Bahá.

Muslim: A follower of Islám, the religion of Muḥammad.

Nabíl: References in this book are to Nabíl-i-A'ẓam (Mullá Muḥammad-i-Zarandí), author of *The Dawn-Breakers,* a history of the Bábí Faith. He was a faithful Bahá'í who performed numerous missions for Bahá'u'lláh.

Náṣiri'd-Dín Sháh: The Sháh of Persia from 1848 to 1896, who was responsible for much of the severe persecution of the Bábís and Bahá'ís.

Naw-Rúz: "New Day." The name applied to the Bahá'í New Year's Day; according to the Persian calendar, the day on which the sun enters Aries, usually March 21.

Nayríz: A town southeast of Shíráz in 'Íran, where Vaḥid and his followers defended themselves against the government troops.

Pilau: A dish of rice, served with a meat or fowl sauce usually highly spiced and often with raisins. It is a common dish in Persian cuisine and is variously prepared.

Pilgrimage: A journey to a shrine or other holy place; in general terms, a long search which has moral implications.

Qá'im: "He Who ariseth." The designation in Shí'ih Islám of the Promised One, a prophecy fulfilled by the appearance of the Báb.

Qiblih: "Point of Adoration"; the direction toward which people turn in prayer. It was changed by Muḥammad from Jerusalem to Mecca. For Bahá'ís it is the Tomb (Shrine) of Bahá'u'lláh at Bahjí.

Quddús: The Letter of the Living who was first in rank among the Letters. He went with the Báb on pilgrimage to Mecca and led the Bábís in defending themselves at Fort Shaykh Ṭabarsí. He was martyred in his native town of Bárfurúsh (known today as Bábul).

Qur'án: The Holy Book of Islám, revealed by Muḥammad during His ministry of twenty-two years (A.D. 610–32). It is divided into súrihs, or chapters.

Revelation: A term sometimes referring to the entire body of teachings of a Manifestation and sometimes designating the process by which He receives and spontaneously transmits the Word of God to man.

Riḍván: "Paradise." A name given to two gardens visited by Bahá'u'lláh. The first was the garden outside Baghdád where Bahá'u'lláh revealed to His followers in 1863 that He was the Promised One foretold by the Báb; the second is the garden outside 'Akká which He frequently visited during the last period of His life. The term also designates the most important festival of the Bahá'í calendar, the commemoration of the twelve days in 1863 when Bahá'u'lláh announced His station.

Seal: An engraved stone or other material used to impress or stamp a device as a proof of authenticity. The seals of Bahá'u'lláh contained various quotations from His writings; the engraving was sometimes imprinted in wax, otherwise on His tablets to authenticate them. Some of His seals may have been mounted on rings.

Shaykh: A man of authority or wisdom, sometimes an elder or a spiritual leader.

Shaykh Aḥmad-i-Aḥsá'í: The first of two heralds of the Báb. Born in 1753, he spent the last forty years of his life teaching the imminent advent of the Qá'im and died in 1826. In the story, he appears to Ali in a dream to assist the boy in his quest for fulfillment.

Shaykh Sulṭán: An Arab Bábí related by marriage to Bahá'u'lláh's family, he journeyed to Sulaymáníyyih to beg Bahá'u'lláh to return to Baghdád.

Shaykh Ṭabarsí: See Fort Shaykh Ṭabarsí.

Shí'ih: One of the two main Muslim sects, and the most prominent in 'Írán. Its members believe that the successorship in Islám rightfully belonged to Muḥammad's cousin 'Alí and his descendants.

Shoghi Effendi: 'Abdu'l-Bahá's eldest grandson, whom He appointed as Guardian of the Bahá'í Faith in His Will and Testament. (See "Guardianship.") He was born in 1897 and served as the Guardian from his appointment in 1921 until his death in 1957.

Shrine: The tomb of a figure of importance in a religion, or sometimes a place made holy by its association with events from religious history.

Síyáh-Chál: "The Black Pit," an underground prison where, in August 1852, Bahá'u'lláh was taken and put in chains with about 150 others whom He described as "thieves, assassins and highwaymen." It was here, during His four-month imprisonment, that He received the first intimations of His mission.

Siyyid: A title designating a descendant of the Prophet Muḥammad.

Siyyid Káẓim-i-Rashtí: With Shaykh Aḥmad, he was one of the two heralds of the Báb. It was from him that Mullá Ḥusayn received his inspiration to go in search of the Qá'im.

Siyyid Muḥammad of Iṣfahán: The instigator of Mírzá Yaḥyá's opposition to Bahá'u'lláh. He had become jealous of Bahá'u'lláh earlier in Karbilá and continually used Mírzá Yaḥyá to undermine Bahá'u'lláh's authority and to disrupt the Bahá'í Faith in general. He is designated the Antichrist of the Bahá'í Revelation.

Ṣúfí: A term denoting the mystics of Islám who practice a mystical approach to spiritual development. In general, its adherents believe in an ascetic life in which one attains enlightenment without the need of Prophets or religious institutions.

Sulaymáníyyih: A town in northeast 'Iráq, in and near which Bahá'u'lláh lived in retirement during His two-year sojourn away from Baghdád, from April 10, 1854, until March 19, 1856.

Súriy-i-Amr: "Súrih of Command," a tablet of Bahá'u'lláh that clearly affirms His station and mission as a Manifestation of God. Bahá'u'lláh commissioned Mírzá Áqá Ján to read this tablet aloud to Mírzá Yaḥyá and to demand a conclusive reply because of Mírzá Yaḥyá's continued efforts to divide the Bahá'í community in Adrianople.

Súriy-i-Múluk: "Súrih of the Kings," a work of Bahá'u'lláh revealed in Adrianople in which He announces to the rulers of the world, as well as to many others, that the Promised One of all ages has come with the remedy for the ills of humanity.

Súriy-i-Ṣabr: "Súrih of Patience," a tablet of Bahá'u'lláh revealed on the first day of Riḍván, 1863, in which He extols the sufferers of Nayríz.

Ṭabarsí: See Fort Shaykh Ṭabarsí.

Tablet: A term which translates *Lawḥ*; in English it is used generally to refer to any particular work of the sacred writings of Bahá'u'lláh, the Báb, or 'Abdu'l-Bahá.

Tablet of Aḥmad: A tablet of Bahá'u'lláh written in Adrianople and addressed to a Bahá'í who had demonstrated exemplary patience in his search for the Promised Manifestation.

Tablet of the Holy Mariner: The Lawḥ-i-Malláḥu'l-Quds, a work revealed by Bahá'u'lláh in Baghdád immediately before the news of His removal to Constantinople was received. In it He prophesies the turmoil and afflictions He will face.

Ṭáhirih: "The Pure One"; a title given by Bahá'u'lláh to the only female Letter of the Living. A figure of great importance in the Bábí Faith, Ṭáhirih was born about 1817–18 and was martyred in 1852.

Táj: A tall felt headdress adopted by Bahá'u'lláh in 1863 on the day of His departure from His house in Baghdád.

Tell al-Fakhkhár: A hill outside 'Akká from which Napoleon bombarded the walled city in his unsuccessful attempt to conquer it. In the story, the hill is one of Ali's favorite places.

Threshold: The entrance into a room. In the Shrines of Bahá'u'lláh and the Báb, a low step separates the burial chamber from the outer room. It is customary for Bahá'ís to pray at the threshold and for the custodian of the shrine to place fresh flowers on the step.

Ṭihrán: The birthplace of Bahá'u'lláh, the capital of 'Íran, and the place where Bahá'u'lláh lived, and later was imprisoned, until His exile in 1853.

Túmán: A unit of currency in 'Íran.

'Ulamá: "One who knows," one who is learned, a scholar. In English books an "s" is sometimes added for the plural form, though strictly speaking the word is already plural.

Vaḥíd: One of the most learned and influential of the Báb's followers. He was sent as an emissary of the Sháh to interrogate the Báb, but after three interviews he accepted the Bábí Faith and was later martyred at Nayríz.

Vizier: A high officer in Muslim government. In 'Íran, the grand vizier was the prime minister, the highest government authority beneath the Sháh.

Yá Ṣáḥibu'z-Zamán: "O Thou Lord of the Age!" This became the battle cry of the Bábís. During the period from 1848–1850 they had to fight repeatedly against overwhelming odds to defend themselves against the attacks of government troops bent on the complete extermination of the Bábí Faith and its adherents.

Zaynab: A heroine in the Bábí defense at Zanján who assumed the dress of a soldier and fought with great courage until she was killed.

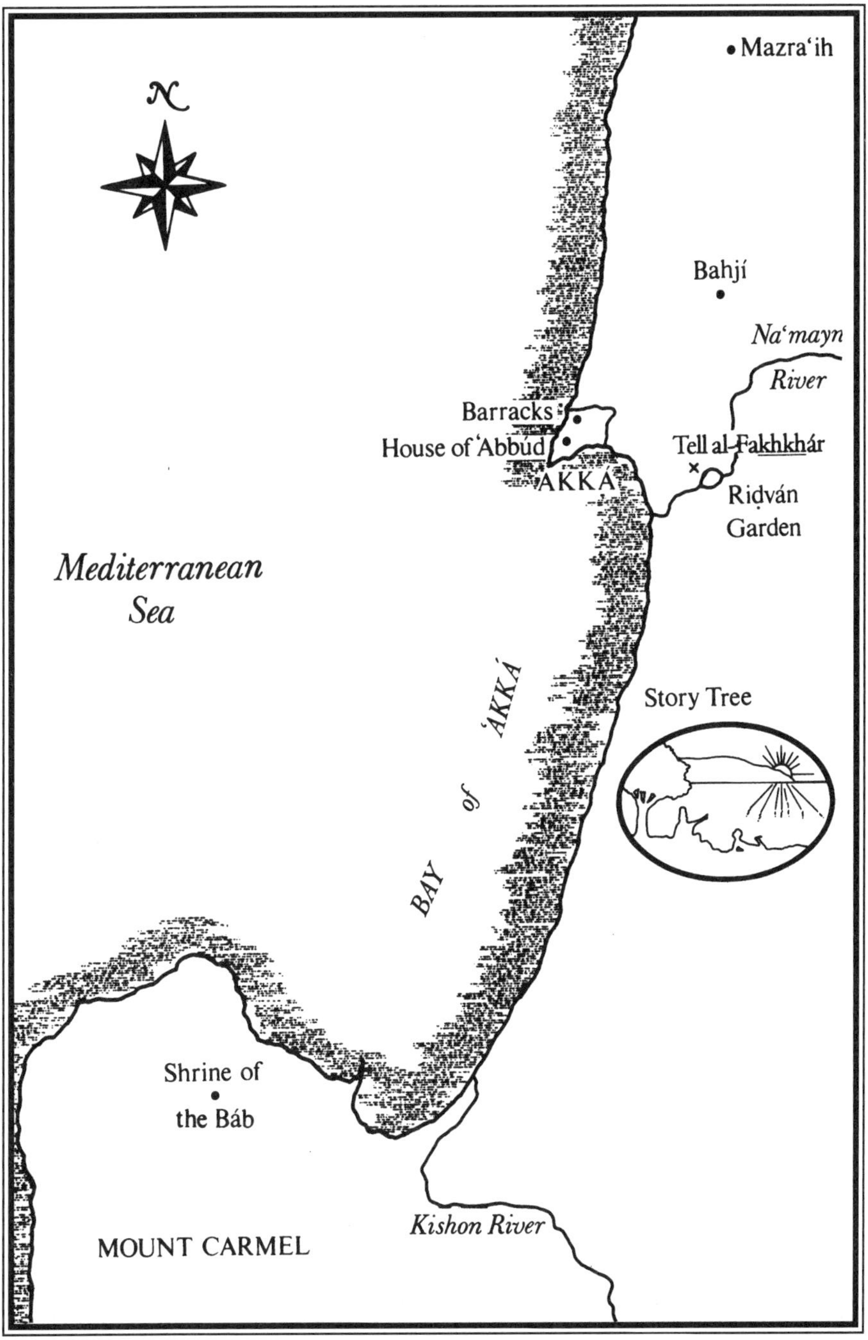
• Mazra'ih
N
Bahjí
Na'mayn River
Barracks
House of 'Abbúd
'AKKÁ
Tell al-Fakhkhár
Riḍván Garden
Mediterranean Sea
BAY of 'AKKÁ
Story Tree
Shrine of the Báb
Kishon River
MOUNT CARMEL

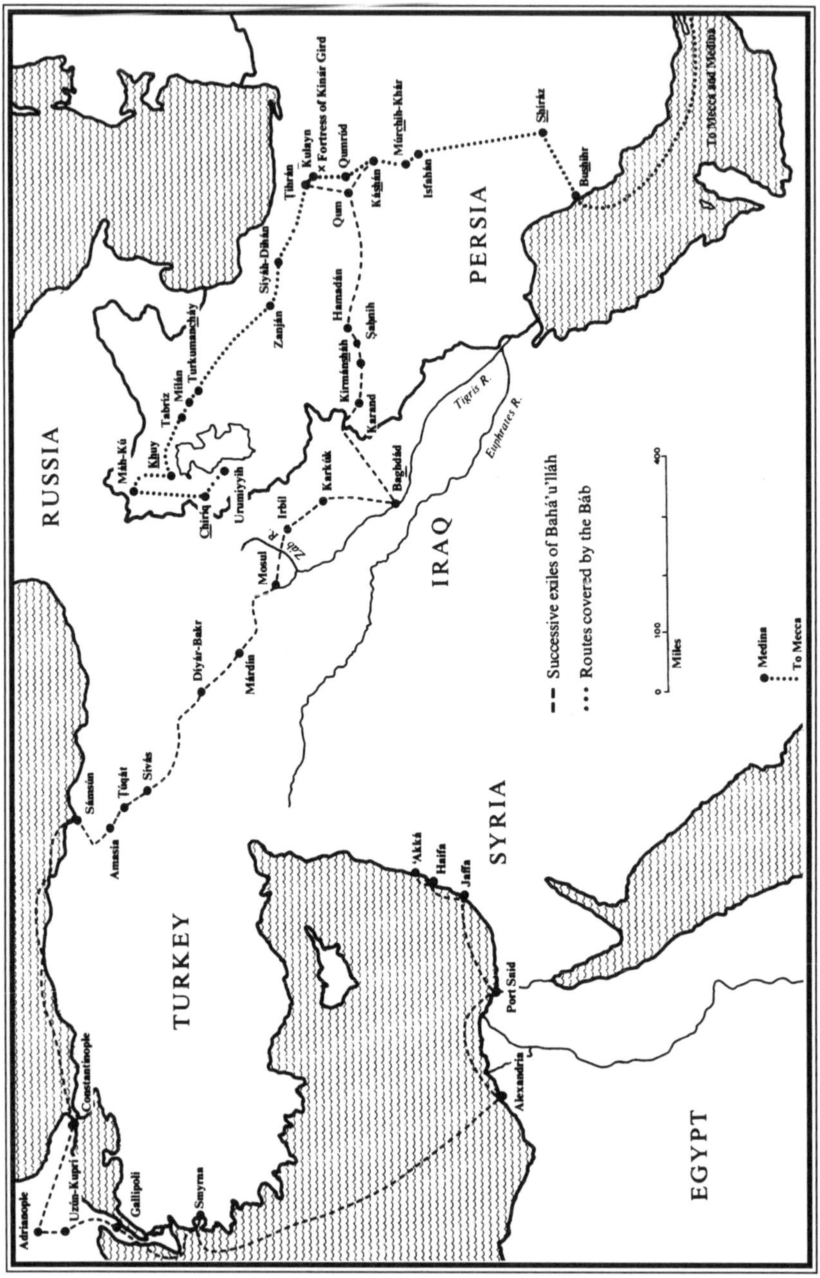
RUSSIA
TURKEY
PERSIA
IRAQ
SYRIA
EGYPT
Adrianople
Uzún-Kuprí
Constantinople
Gallipoli
Smyrna
Sámsún
Amasia
Túqát
Sivás
Diyár-Bakr
Márdín
Mosul
Zab R.
Irbil
Karkúk
Baghdád
Tigris R.
Euphrates R.
Máh-Kú
Khuy
Chihríq
Urumíyyih
Tabríz
Milán
Turkumanchây
Zanján
Siyáh-Dihán
Ṭihrán
Kulayn
× Fortress of Kinár Gird
Qumrúd
Qum
Káshán
Múrchih-Khár
Iṣfahán
Shíráz
Búshihr
Hamadán
Ṣaḥnih
Kirmánsháh
Karand
'Akká
Haifa
Jaffa
Port Said
Alexandria
To Mecca and Medina
Successive exiles of Bahá'u'lláh
Routes covered by the Báb
0
100
400
Miles
Medina
To Mecca

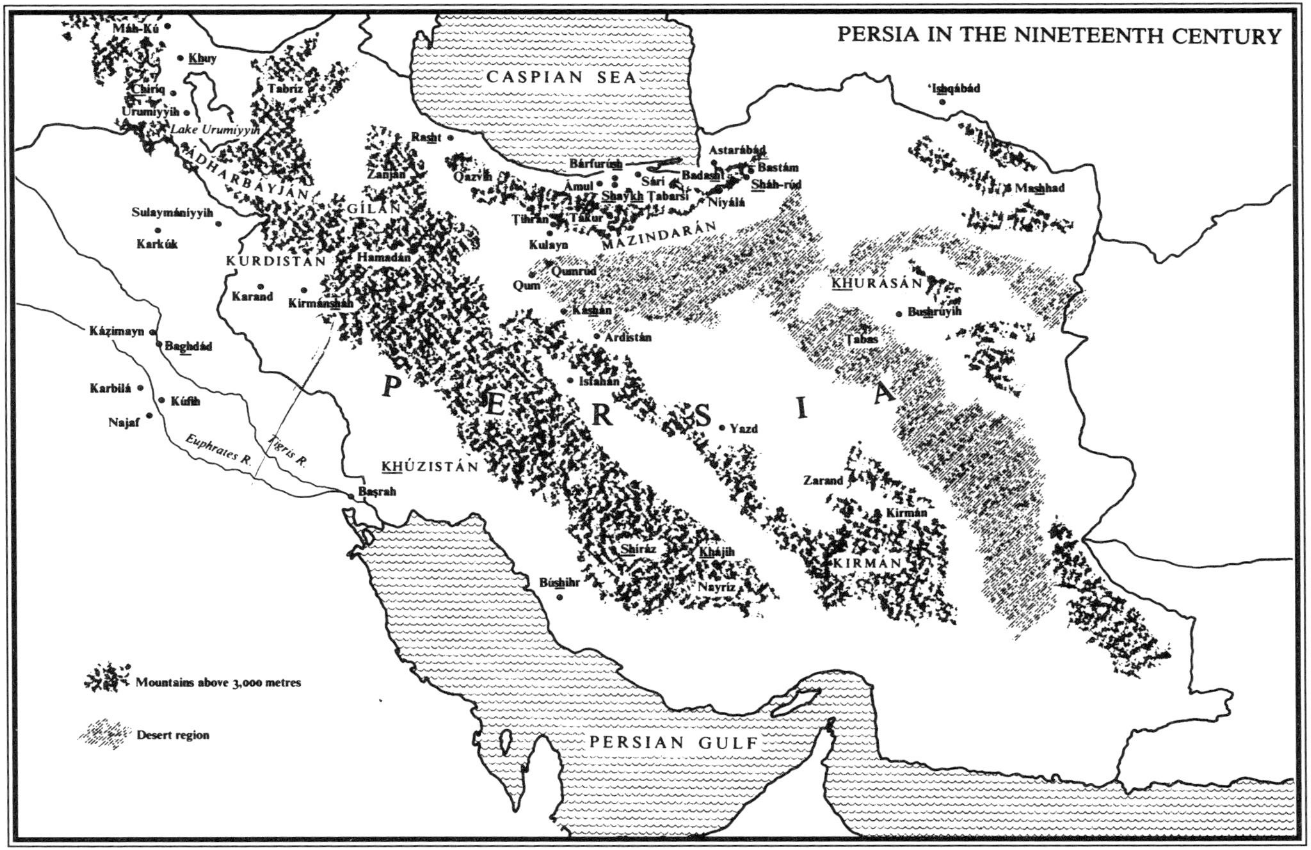

PERSIA IN THE NINETEENTH CENTURY

A Note on Sources

The author has based his story primarily upon two histories of the Bábí and Bahá'í Faiths: *The Dawn-Breakers,* by Nabíl-i-A'ẓam, and *God Passes By,* by Shoghi Effendi. Most of the references to exact quotations—which are chiefly of words spoken by Bahá'u'lláh and various other people—come from these two books. Other sources exactly quoted are *Gleanings from the Writings of Bahá'u'lláh; Memorials of the Faithful,* by 'Abdu'l-Bahá; *The Chosen Highway,* by Lady Blomfield; *Bahá'u'lláh and the New Era,* by J. E. Esslemont; *'Abdu'l-Bahá,* by H. M. Balyuzi; and *An Early Pilgrimage,* by May Maxwell. For those who wish to refer to these quotations and the episodes surrounding them, page references to these sources are listed below. A few well-known writings by Bahá'u'lláh—such as *The Seven Valleys,* the Tablet of the Holy Mariner, and the Tablet of Carmel—are identified in the story; these are readily available and need no further reference. The letter of Shoghi Effendi mentioned on p. 281 is included in the collection entitled *Bahá'í Administration.*

Page	Source
24	*Bahá'u'lláh and the New Era,* p. 24.
26–7	*Dawn-Breakers,* pp. 104–106.
28	Ibid., p. 107.
30	Ibid., pp. 107–108.
39	Ibid., p. 116.
41	Ibid., p. 118.
45	Ibid., p. 201.
47	Ibid., p. 294.
48	Ibid., p. 296.
50	The Hidden Words, Persian, no. 18.

Page	Source
59–60	*Dawn-Breakers,* pp. 324–25, 351, 326.
62–3	Ibid., pp. 330, 336.
64	Ibid., p. 341.
65–6	Ibid., p. 344–45, 349.
68	Ibid., p. 363.
70	Ibid., p. 369.
71	Ibid., p. 374.
76	Ibid., pp. 381, 70.
85–6	Ibid., pp. 507, 508.
87	Ibid., p. 514.
99–100	Ibid., p. 33.
106	Ibid., p. 632.
107	Ibid., p. 634.
109	*'Abdu'l-Bahá,* p. 11.
109 10	*Epistle to the Son of the Wolf,* p. 21.
110–11	*God Passes By,* pp. 157–58.
118–19	*Dawn-Breakers,* pp. 636, 648, 649.
122	*Selections from the Writings of the Báb,* no. 1:2:4.
128	*God Passes By,* p. 170.
130	Ibid., p. 425.
139	Kitáb-i-Íqán, ¶278; *God Passes By,* p. 185.
142	*The Chosen Highway,* pp. 55, 54.
142–43	Ibid., pp. 54.
155	*Gleanings from the Writings of Bahá'u'lláh,* no. 57.1.
158	*God Passes By,* p. 212.
174	*God Passes By,* p. 231; *Bahá'í Prayers,* p. 327.
189	*The Chosen Highway,* p. 59.
194	*God Passes By,* p. 258.
196	Ibid., p.163.
213–14	*The Chosen Highway,* p. 65.
214	*God Passes By,* p. 295.
219	Ibid., p. 297.
220	Ibid., p. 291.

Page	Source
226–27	Ibid., p. 298.
230	Ibid., p. 301.
232	*The Chosen Highway,* p. 88.
234	Kitáb-i-Aqdas, ¶121.
235	*Bahá'u'lláh and the New Era,* p. 36.
254	*God Passes By,* p. 108.
255	*The Revelation of Bahá'u'lláh,* vol. 4, p. 30.
269–70	*Tablets of Bahá'u'lláh,* pp. 3, 4;
270	*The Chosen Highway,* p. 105.
271	*God Passes By,* p. 351.
281	*Will and Testament of 'Abdu'l-Bahá,* p. 18; *Bahá'í Administration,* p. 69.
289	*Gleanings from the Writings of Bahá'u'lláh,* no. 157.1.

Bibliography

Works of Bahá'u'lláh

Epistle to the Son of the Wolf. New ed. Translated by Shoghi Effendi. 1st ps ed. Wilmette, IL: Bahá'í Publishing Trust, 1988.

Gleanings from the Writings of Bahá'u'lláh. Translated by Shoghi Effendi. Wilmette, IL: Bahá'í Publishing, 2005.

The Hidden Words. Translated by Shoghi Effendi. Wilmette, IL: Bahá'í Publishing, 2002.

The Kitáb-i-Aqdas: The Most Holy Book. 1st ps ed. Wilmette, IL: Bahá'í Publishing Trust, 1993.

The Kitáb-i-Íqán: The Book of Certitude. Translated by Shoghi Effendi. Wilmette, IL: Bahá'í Publishing, 2003.

The Seven Valleys and the Four Valleys. New ed. Translated by Ali-Kuli Khan and Marzieh Gail. Wilmette, IL: Bahá'í Publishing Trust, 1991.

Tablets of Bahá'u'lláh revealed after the Kitáb-i-Aqdas. Compiled by the Research Department of the Universal House of Justice. Translated by Habib Taherzadeh et al. Wilmette, IL: Bahá'í Publishing Trust, 1988.

Works of the Báb

Selections from the Writings of the Báb. Compiled by the Research Department of the Universal House of Justice. Translated by Habib Taherzadeh et al. Wilmette, IL: Bahá'í Publishing Trust, 2006.

Works of 'Abdu'l-Bahá

Memorials of the Faithful. Wilmette, IL: Bahá'í Publishing Trust, 1997.

Will and Testament of 'Abdu'l-Bahá. Wilmette, IL: Bahá'í Publishing Trust, 2013.

Works of Shoghi Effendi

Bahá'í Administration: Selected Messages, 1922–1932. 7th ed. Wilmette, IL: Bahá'í Publishing Trust, 1974.

God Passes By. New ed. Wilmette, IL: Bahá'í Publishing Trust, 2010.

Compilations

Bahá'í Prayers: A Selection of Prayers Revealed by Bahá'u'lláh, the Báb, and 'Abdu'l-Bahá. Wilmette, IL: Bahá'í Publishing Trust, 2008.

Other Works

Balyuzi, H. M. *'Abdu'l-Bahá: The Centre of the Covenant of Bahá'u'lláh.* London: George Ronald, 1971.

Blomfield, Lady (Sitárih Khánum). *The Chosen Highway.* Wilmette, IL: Bahá'í Publishing Trust, n.d.; repr. 1975.

Esslemont, J. E. *Bahá'u'lláh and the New Era.* Wilmette, IL: Bahá'í Publishing Trust, 2006.

Maxwell, May. *An Early Pilgrimage.* 2d rev. ed. London: George Ronald, 1969.

Nábil-i-A'ẓam [Muḥammad-i-Zarandí]. *The Dawn-Breakers: Nabíl's Narrative of the Early Days of the Bahá'í Revelation.* Translated and edited by Shoghi Effendi. Wilmette, IL: Bahá'í Publishing Trust, 1932.

Bahá'í PUBLISHING AND THE BAHÁ'Í FAITH

Bahá'í Publishing produces books based on the teachings of the Bahá'í Faith. Founded over 160 years ago, the Bahá'í Faith has spread to some 235 nations and territories and is now accepted by more than five million people. The word "Bahá'í" means "follower of Bahá'u'lláh." Bahá'u'lláh, the founder of the Bahá'í Faith, asserted that He is the Messenger of God for all of humanity in this day. The cornerstone of His teachings is the establishment of the spiritual unity of humankind, which will be achieved by personal transformation and the application of clearly identified spiritual principles. Bahá'ís also believe that there is but one religion and that all the Messengers of God—among them Abraham, Zoroaster, Moses, Krishna, Buddha, Jesus, and Muḥammad—have progressively revealed its nature. Together, the world's great religions are expressions of a single, unfolding divine plan. Human beings, not God's Messengers, are the source of religious divisions, prejudices, and hatreds.

The Bahá'í Faith is not a sect or denomination of another religion, nor is it a cult or a social movement. Rather, it is a globally recognized independent world religion founded on new books of scripture revealed by Bahá'u'lláh.

Bahá'í Publishing is an imprint of the National Spiritual Assembly of the Bahá'ís of the United States.

OTHER BOOKS AVAILABLE FROM BAHÁ'Í PUBLISHING

JOURNEY OF SORROW, JOURNEY OF HOPE
Carol Handy
$19.00 US / $21.00 CAN
Trade Paper
ISBN 978-1-61851-067-9

A powerful story of sorrow, love, and faith, and of finding the strength and will to survive and overcome hardship.

Journey of Sorrow, Journey of Hope tells the story of Shirin, a woman living in Persia in the mid-1800s, a time of great religious fervor. When the government burns her home because of her association with the Bahá'í Faith, a religion considered to be a heresy by the Persian government, she is forced to leave her native land and seek protection in Russia, where she falls in love and learns about the Founder of the Bahá'í Faith, Bahá'u'lláh. When she must leave Russia to settle in France, she has learned much about the new Faith, as well as discovered the strength within herself to survive and overcome hardship.

CALL TO THE NATIONS

EXTRACTS FROM THE WRITINGS OF SHOGHI EFFENDI
Shoghi Effendi
$15.00 US / $17.00 CAN
Hardcover
ISBN 978-1-61851-066-2

A collection of extracts from the letters of Shoghi Effendi, the great-grandson of the Prophet and Founder of the Bahá'í Faith, who served as the Guardian of the Faith from 1921 until his passing in 1957.

Call to the Nations is a collection of extracts from a fascinating series of letters penned by Shoghi Effendi, the Guardian of the Bahá'í Faith, to the Bahá'ís of the world. For thirty-six years (1921–1957), from the age of twenty-four, Shoghi Effendi served as the head of the Bahá'í Faith, directing the affairs of its worldwide community and giving practical expression to its ideals. His insightful letters offer a glimpse of the scope of the Bahá'í Faith and provide context for its ultimate mission of the unification of mankind. The book is divided into five chapters organized around the following themes: Humanity's Ordeal, The Oneness of Mankind, A Pattern for Future Society, World Commonwealth, and The Destiny of Mankind.

SELECTIONS FROM THE WRITINGS OF 'ABDU'L-BAHÁ
'Abdu'l-Bahá
$23.00 US / $25.00 CAN
Hardcover
ISBN 978-1-61851-065-5

A timeless collection of writings, containing spiritual and practical guidance for all aspects of life.

Selections from the Writings of 'Abdu'l-Bahá is a compilation of correspondence and other written works of one of the central figures of the Bahá'í Faith. The book covers a wide range of topics including physical and spiritual health, death and the afterlife, the reality of man, the oneness of mankind, and the elimination of prejudice. 'Abdu'l-Bahá was the eldest son and appointed successor of Bahá'u'lláh, the Prophet and Founder of the Bahá'í Faith, and is considered by Bahá'ís to be the authorized interpreter and the perfect exemplar of the Faith's teachings. The wisdom imparted in this volume of his writings remains as timeless and relevant today as when it was first committed to paper.

PEARLS OF WISDOM
Illustrated and Compiled by Constanze von Kitzing
$12.00 US / $14.00 CAN
Paper Over Board
ISBN 978-1-61851-069-3

A beautiful, full-color, illustrated children's book containing simple yet profound passages from the writings of the Bahá'í Faith arranged around themes of spiritual significance.

Pearls of Wisdom is a beautifully illustrated book of passages from the Bahá'í writings presented in a manner that will appeal to children of all ages. Arranged around themes such as God, the soul, prayer, friendship, and love, all passages are accompanied by vibrant full-page color illustrations by award-winning illustrator Constanze von Kitzing, whose work strikes the perfect balance between playful and reverent. *Pearls of Wisdom* is an ideal book for the whole family to enjoy together, and it is hoped that it will lead to rewarding discussions about important spiritual topics in the home.